Force of Eagles

Richard Herman Jnr

CORONET BOOKS
Hodder and Stoughton

First published in the USA by Donald I. Fine, Inc. and in Canada
by General Publishing Company

First published in Great Britain in 1990
by Hodder and Stoughton Ltd
a division of Hodder Headline PLC

New English Library Edition 1991

Coronet edition 1994

Herman, Richard
Force of Eagles
I. Title
813.54[F]

ISBN 0 340 62492 2

Printed and bound in Great Britain by
Clays Ltd, St Ives plc

Hodder and Stoughton
A division of Hodder Headline PLC
338 Euston Road
London NW1 3BH

About the author

Richard Herman Jnr. retired from the US Air Force in 1983 with the rank of Major after serving for twenty-one years. He has flown over 200 combat missions himself and was stationed in Vietnam, West Germany and Great Britain. He has flown the F-4 and C-130 and received five medals, including the Bronze Star. He and his English-born wife now live in Fair Oaks, California.

DEDICATION

For the MIAs, the men who went missing in action in Southeast Asia, and whose only homecoming is in the memories and love of those they left behind.

ACKNOWLEDGMENTS

Many thanks are always due to those who help a writer and I am no exception. I am indebted to: Lt. Col. Dave "Bull" Baker who made me regret ever retiring and leaving the world of tactical flying and who makes me wish I was with him in F-15Es; Lt. Col. (Ret.) Mel Marvel for making AC-130 gunships come alive; Majors "Butch" Young and Keith Elliott for showing me what a wondrous old jet the F-111 is; S/Sgt. John Geerlings who was willing to spend hours talking to a complete stranger about parachutes and saved me from a tactical blunder; and S/Sgt. Al Altro, a Ranger in every sense of the word.

Among the many who gave of their time are: Maj. John Lerned, Maj. Myke Gable, and M/Sgt. Erich Zeisler of the 431TES; and Sgt. Greg Tolley and the men and women of the U.S. Army Sacramento East Recruiting Co. And thanks to Dennis LaClair for the never-ending use of his reference library.

Finally, I wish to give special thanks to my agent George Wieser and to Donald I. Fine, an editor and publisher of the old school.

PROLOGUE

Sergeant Javad Khalian, a Revolutionary Guard commando, kept watching his target, trying to convince himself that he had found the foreigner. He had almost missed the man at first—he did not match the description passed out by the Guards. But as he watched, he became more certain that it was the young American the Council of Guardians was so eagerly seeking. The ten thousand dollars in gold the mullahs were now offering as a reward was ample proof of their eagerness.

Yet he had to be sure, for it meant much to him, maybe even command of a company or battalion in the Revolutionary Guards. Command meant power and prestige and with that, dominance over his so-called equals. Khalian thought of the fools he had to serve with in the Guards—idiots who needed the type of leadership he could give them. But he wasn't about to be the scorn of many jokes by bringing in the wrong man—again.

The fading light made it difficult to follow the man through the crowded market of Khorramabad, a small town nestled in a pass by the Zagros mountains of western Iran. Khalian paused by a stall the vendor was closing in preparation for evening prayers that would start in a few minutes. He studied his quarry, struck by the man's appearance, so much like his own. No wonder he had been so difficult to find and capture.

The young Iranian's ego swelled as he thought about his future. He almost strutted as he followed the American, not wanting to lose sight of him. Still, he had his doubts. Too many suspects had been brought in, only to be released or executed after their identity was established. It did not bother Khalian that innocent men had been hanged in public, left to squirm at the end of a rope or piano wire as they choked to death. He agreed that the executions were necessary if the integrity of the Guards was to be maintained before the public. Khalian cursed the whisper of doubt that kept him from acting—the suspect did move and act like an Iranian. But there was still something wrong, he couldn't quite pinpoint . . . the way he moved? . . . gestures . . .?

Khalian hurried after him, not wanting to lose his prey in the thinning crowd. He did not see him stop to talk to a fruit seller and almost ran into him. To keep from arousing the man's suspicions, Khalian walked on past. He quickly blended into the crowd and doubled back, wanting to talk to the vendor.

"The one who just bought some fruit, old man. Tell me, was he a foreigner?"

"No." The old man's answer was abrupt, bordering on the edge of hostility. He did not want to talk to the young sergeant with his swagger and bravado that carried none of the politeness and dignity that Allah demanded of the faithful.

Khalian's ego would not tolerate even the suggestion of an insult. "And tell me, you heap of pig shit, how do you know this?" He made a menacing gesture with his AK-47.

"He spoke and acted as one of the faithful," the old man said, letting the obvious comparison sink in.

The young Revolutionary Guard wanted to shoot the vendor on the spot, punish him for his insolence, but the noise would only make the American bolt for cover. If he was the American . . . He would settle with the old fool later, after he had caught the foreigner. His confidence rose as he caught sight of the doomed fugitive, thirty meters away, eating at another stall. He swung his assault rifle down on its sling, letting it hang from his shoulder. By grasping the pistol grip, he let the crowd see him prepare for action. He strode after the American, ready to capture his prize, every inch a soldier of Allah, still not positive that he had the right man but now ready to act, tired of his caution.

Ten meters short of the stall where the American had been eating Khalian lost sight of him. Where had he gone? Then he saw the narrow alley and felt a surge of disappointment that the American had chosen to run for cover, away from an appreciative audience that would have remarked on his bravery and skill in capturing the most wanted man in Iran.

Seeing no one in the alley, he started to run, afraid that he was losing the foreigner. He skidded around a blind corner, seeing nothing in the fading light. The last thing he remembered was a searing line of pain circling his throat, cutting off his scream.

The man twisted the wire garrote, cutting deep into Khalian's throat. At the same time he guided the twitching body into a soundless slump, making a heap in the shadows. Moving quickly but with no appearance of being rushed, he untwisted the wire from around the Iranian's neck and wiped it clean on the dead man's shirt. A quick search turned out the man's identification papers and money. He arranged the body to look as if he were napping, taking care to hide the AK-47 under the body.

Carefully, he inspected himself, taking time to be sure that no blood had gotten on his clothes. He found two small spots near his left knee. By rubbing in dirt and then scrapping it off with a small but very sharp knife he removed the two spots. Checking to make sure that he was still alone, he walked around the corner into better light. Again he inspected himself for blood. Then he thumbed through the commando's identification papers, satisfied that they fit him much better than his current set. He walked back to the body and placed his old papers and some of the money in the left-hand pocket of the commando's shirt, carefully buttoning the flap.

He reached into the shadows and retrieved the shoulder bag he had hidden two hours before. He rummaged in a side pocket and pulled out a note pad and pen. He quickly scribbled a note in Farsi, the Iranian language, "For dishonoring my sister, my family, and spreading corruption on earth." Then he pried open the corpse's mouth and shoved the note between its teeth, mumbling in English as he worked, "They won't have any trouble believing that, you bastard."

Aware that he was talking to himself in English, he switched to Farsi. "That could be a fatal mistake." He had been alone too long and was talking to himself out of loneliness. "God, you were thick," he continued in Farsi, "I thought you'd never take the bait, using my left hand when only you were watching. For a moment, you had me worried." He chided himself for taking so many chances in order to get the Iranian's attention and then leading him to the killing ground he had selected. All very necessary he decided, pulling a large plastic bag out of his bag that he had purchased days before in another town.

With some trouble, he shoved the body into the plastic bag, satisfied that he had made a good choice in luring the young commando after him. He tied the bag shut with an overhand knot and carried the body to a hole he had scooped out in a pile of garbage when he hid his shoulder bag. Quickly, he collapsed the hole over the body, calculating that Islamic prohibitions against handling unclean waste might keep the corpse from being discovered until it was well decomposed. Then they would have only his old papers to rely on, and perhaps the note would satisfy the authorities. He hoped, but he doubted it. He shouldered his bag, picked up the AK-47 and walked back to the alley. At least he had bought some time.

A sudden tiredness overcame him as he walked away from the marketplace. Switching from the near-perfect Farsi he had been speaking, he spoke two words in faultless Arabic, "Insh' Allah." Then muttering in English, "as God wills." Especially for what happens to a loose cannon in Iran, by necessity undirected and uncontrolled.

CHAPTER 1

D MINUS 34

CENTRAL ARIZONA

The two compass-gray F-15 Eagles punched out of the top of the broken cloud deck scudding over the Arizona desert. The flight lead's voice came over the UHF radio, "Fence check."

His wingman, Colonel Rupert Stansell, did not acknowledge the call as his fingers flicked the switches that would arm the fighter for combat. Without looking, his left hand flashed over the IFF, Identification Friend or Foe, panel just behind the throttles, touching the toggle switches that would turn the four modes on the radar transponder to standby and deny an enemy the capability of interrogating the F-15's radar beacon. Automatically, he reached forward with his left hand and moved the Master Arm switch up on the armament control panel. "IFF standby. Master Arm on," he told the instructor pilot riding in the back seat of his D model Eagle. Stansell had simulated the exact actions he would have taken if they had just penetrated into hostile territory.

"Contact, bogies, on the nose at fifty-five miles," the flight lead, Snake Houserman, radioed. Stansell suppressed a grunt and pressed the center button on the left throttle in an upward motion, increasing the range of his radar display to eighty miles. Two blips flashed on the Vertical Situation Display, the VSD, at fifty miles. He had made a basic mistake—it was hard to see targets at fifty miles using a forty-mile scope.

1

"Rog," Stansell replied, "contact bogies." The radar contacts were their "adversaries," two other F-15s from Luke AFB. The colonel was vaguely aware that he was breathing very rapidly.

"Just do it as briefed, sir," Captain Greg Donaldson, the instructor pilot in his back seat pit, cautioned. Donaldson was worried about the colonel. He hadn't been doing well in Air Combat Tactics.

"Toro, Lobo One and Two entering air-to-air now, North Point, ready." Snake Houserman called over the UHF radio, checking them into the area on the flight frequency. Snake was Lobo One and Stansell was Lobo Two. They were flying straight and level at 500 knots Calibrated Air Speed. Snake was at 15,000 feet and Stansell at 19,000.

Snake was a very young captain who was showing promise of being an outstanding fighter jock. Stansell was envious of the young man's potential, already more than anything he had.

The bogies checked in, "Lobo, Toro One and Two entering air-to-air now, South Point, ready."

"Roger, Toro," Snake answered, "fight's on, tape's on." Stansell tried to control his rate of breathing, knowing he could hyperventilate. They still had over two minutes before they came together in the merge, lots of time. His fingers played the piccolo, those series of switches and buttons on the throttles and stick that gave the pilot control of everything he needed in combat. He blipped the range button down, decreasing his radar range to forty miles. He moved the Target Designation Control switch on the left throttle and drove the acquisition bars on the Vertical Situation Display over the left target. He mashed the TDC button and immediately released it. The radar system did as it was commanded and locked on.

"Too early, Colonel," Donaldson told him. Stansell grunted, conceding the instructor pilot was right. In combat the radar-warning gear in the enemy's cockpit would be screaming "lock on" at the pilot, giving him ample time to react and avoid a head-on medium-range missile shot. Stansell broke the lock on, losing the capability for the launch of an AIM-7M Sparrow missile. "Sort the formation and don't take your final lock until the range is about fifteen nautical miles," Donaldson said.

Stansell waited, working to control his breathing for the seventy seconds it took for the range to decrease from thirty-five to fifteen miles. He selected a twenty-nautical-mile scope and drove the acquisition bars with the TDC to the left target and mashed it. But this time the radar wouldn't lock on and stayed in the scan mode. Either the system was malfunctioning or Toro was jamming him.

"Go for a Fox Two," Donaldson commanded, hoping the AIM-9L Sidewinder could acquire a heat signature off the approaching F-15's intakes for a short-range, front-aspect missile shot.

The colonel broke his attempted lock and used his left thumb to toggle the weapon switch on the side of the right throttle to the middle detent, calling up the Sidewinders. The characteristic growl of the Sidewinder filled their earphones, masking all other communications. Stansell had made another mistake. He reached for the volume control knob and turned the tone down just as he visually acquired the on-coming F-15s. Once a visual contact was established, they were free to maneuver and engage the bogies in a turning engagement.

"Tally two, left ten o'clock, seven miles, slightly high!" Snake radioed. At least his eyeballs were no better than Stansell's.

At the same time, another voice broke into the radio transmission. "Toro One. Fox One on the west F-15 at nineteen thousand." The interceptor symbol on Stansell's Tactical Electronic Warfare System scope was flashing at him, warning him that the pilot in the approaching F-15, Toro One, had just taken a simulated AIM-7M shot at him. How had he missed the audio warning on his own TEWS? The Sidewinder's growl must've overridden it. Another mistake. In action a Sparrow with a sixty-six pound high explosive warhead would've been streaking toward Stansell. The smoke trail that "The Great White Hope" left behind it would get any pilot's attention and force a violent evasive maneuver, anything to break the radar lock-on guiding the Sparrow.

Almost immediately, the same cool voice announced, "Toro One, Fox Two on the west F-15 at nineteen thousand." Now Stansell had a Sparrow and a Sidewinder coming at him.

"Break right!" Donaldson shouted. "Honor the goddamn threat, Colonel!"

Stansell didn't hesitate and for the first time, he reacted quickly. Burying his right foot in the rudder pedal, he pushed the stick forward and to the right, starting a Split-S maneuver toward the ground and reversing course. "Put your nose on him, colonel. You're solving the goddamn problem for him," Donaldson bellowed, the strain of grunting against the six Gs they were pulling laboring his voice. Stansell pulled the nose of the F-15 up and reversed course to meet his pursuer head-on, but he was too heavy-handed and snatched over eight Gs on the F-15, causing the Over Load Warning System to activate. He was so engrossed that he did not hear the double rate beeper and then the computer-activated female voice saying, "Over-G, Over-G, Over-G," to warn him of the excessive forces he was loading on the jet.

Stansell grunted hard to fight the Gs, exactly the way most people fight constipation. While not very elegant, it did work. Stansell could feel a granddaddy slip out, making its presence known in the cockpit.

It was too much for Donaldson. He keyed his mike and transmitted for the other aircraft to hear. "Lobo Two, knock it off, knock it off," while he toggled his oxygen regulator to one hundred percent oxygen, cutting off all cockpit air to his mask. The four Eagles immediately flew wings level and checked in with their call signs. "God, Colonel," Donaldson muttered over the intercom. "You over-G'd the jet with that last maneuver. Call an over-G and head for home."

Stansell keyed the radio, "Lobo Two, RTB at this time. One hundred and six percent overload. Level two on the wings—8.2 Gs."

"Rog, Two." It was Snake's voice. "Land from a straight-in approach."

The short colonel scanned his instruments and wings. "Roger."

"I'll give you a battle damage check," Snake told him, slipping his aircraft under Stansell's for a visual check. "You look OK. Recover single ship. See you in debrief." Snake peeled off and headed back for the center of the area to set up the next engagement with the other element of two aircraft.

"He's going to have some fun now," Donaldson said. "Two-vee-one is Snake's idea of an interesting fight." The "vee" was shorthand for "versus" and two against one would tax every skill Houserman possessed. The captain knew the other three pilots would go to the backup mission of low level intercepts they had briefed in case Stansell aborted. They would drag the fight down to five hundred feet—exactly as in combat—into the environment where they excelled and none of their potential opponents ever trained in peacetime, making the first few days of any war that involved F-15s something of a turkey shoot until the opposition got the message. But at the moment neither Stansell, Snake or Donaldson knew how close one of them was to having a chance to show just how good the F-15s were.

Stansell relaxed into his seat, drenched with sweat from the aborted engagement. He lifted the green tinted visor of his helmet and rubbed the sweat from around his eyes with the back of his glove. His right ear itched, demanding a scratching. The colonel fought the urge. After all, it wasn't there. I've heard of that reaction he thought, but never believed it until now.

The recovery into Luke AFB was uneventful, and Donaldson relaxed as he evaluated the way Stansell flew the graceful fighter down final. The colonel wired the airspeed at 145 knots and the Angle of Attack at twenty-one units. It was a smooth and relaxed approach and the colonel's voice and breathing were as normal as an airline pilot's. "A wonderful thing, the CAS. It made anyone look good," Stansell observed, more to himself than Donaldson. The Control Augmentation System sensed pitch, yaw and roll rates; AOA, lateral and vertical acceleration. It then automatically adjusted the electrical inputs into the control surfaces commanded by the pilot, relieving him of the constant task of trimming for changes in control surface pressure when the aircraft's speed or G forces changed. Stansell squeaked the landing.

Captain Donaldson wasn't flying with just any other newly-minted colonel who had grown rusty after serving time in some desk job in the Pentagon that guaranteed promotion. He was flying with Rupert Stansell, a former F-15 squadron commander, a blooded pilot with one MiG to his credit, and one of the three men lucky enough to have escaped from Ras Assanya on the Persian Gulf after it was captured. Donaldson couldn't figure out what was wrong with the colonel.

While Stansell debriefed Maintenance on the over-G, Donaldson headed for the personal equipment section of his squadron, the 555th Tactical Fighter Training Squadron, the Triple Nickel. He stripped off his G-suit before retrieving a wedding band and an Air Force Academy class ring from his locker shelf. Stansell, he thought, being an old boy from the Academy ain't going to get you through this refresher course if you don't have a clue. He decided it was time to talk to his squadron commander.

Donaldson stood at the open door of Lieutenant Colonel "Buzz" Rutherford's office, waiting for his squadron commander to motion him in. The tall and lanky black L.C. waved him into a seat the moment he saw the captain. Rutherford continued to talk on the phone pulling faces to express what he thought of the caller's message. Finally he hung up. "Same old bull," he said. "Public Relations has another request to interview the only black squadron commander in TAC. Interviews aren't my job." He fixed on Donaldson. "You look like you've got a problem. Stansell?"

"Yeah, he didn't have a clue today. Little, almost no situational awareness. He was flying around out there with a great big question mark over his cockpit."

Rutherford waited, not about to say a thing until Donaldson laid it all out for him.

"Over-G when he reversed—8.2—dumb. We had to make an early return."

"Wasn't today his first two-vee-two ride?" Rutherford asked. "That's an important phase of training."

"True. But he was doing the same thing when he was flying one-vee-one. Something's blocking him, getting in the way. He can fly the jet as good as anyone, but when the fight starts to develop, he becomes mechanical and rigid. It's like he's considering each move. Nothing's natural, nothing flows. For a moment there I thought he might hyperventilate he was breathing so hard. I get the feeling I'm in the cockpit with a second lieutenant on his first ACM ride. You wouldn't believe he's downed a MiG and has over a thousand hours in the bird."

"He was my first flight commander," Rutherford said. "He was a good stick . . . he was a lieutenant when he caught the tail end of Vietnam. In fact, he flew combat with the Triple Nickel out of Udorn in Thailand. Flew F-4s then. The squadron was *the* MiG killer in those days and got over forty MiGs."

"He's changed, sir."

Rutherford reached into his memory, tapping his experience, education and training to figure out what ailed Stansell. His ability to solve problems was one of the things that had earned him the command of the Triple Nickel. That, plus the fact that he could fly the Eagle like a demon and the men trusted him. "Right now he's too deliberate, cautious, but it shouldn't be a big problem to overcome. Probably tied in to that business in the Persian Gulf when the base at Ras Assanya was overrun, his C.O. caught it and he just got out thanks to a couple of sergeants. Yeah, I think the key is in what happened to him at Ras Assanya, must've been pretty traumatic for him . . . keep working with him, schedule me in the same flight when he flies tomorrow."

"Thanks, appreciate the help," Donaldson said as he stood up. He knew from past experience that Rutherford would take an active role with Stansell's training and start taking the heat if the colonel couldn't hack the program. It was one of the things he liked about the L.C.

Rutherford tapped his desk with a pencil after the captain had left, considering what to do. The Air Force system identified men who had been through the crucible of combat and when they performed as well as Stansell had, they were given the inside track for command. But if the colonel could not put the traumatic effect of his last experience behind him and do the job demanded, he would be put out to pasture in some meaningless slot, passed over for promotion and retired at his present rank. Rutherford did not like what he had to do if Stansell couldn't cut it.

The debrief of the flight went as Stansell expected, and Donaldson came right to the point. "Colonel, let's talk about what went wrong now and not in front of the rest of the flight. You started the engagement with your radar at forty miles range, not eighty. Then you were going to take your final lock-on too soon, giving your opposition plenty of time to react. When I told you to break you started a Split-S toward the ground, but I didn't think you'd continue it until your tail was pointed at the threat. You should've reversed back into the fight when your nose was about ninety degrees to the threat. When you did come back, you over-G'd the bird. You missed the voice warning, sir. Not good."

The instructor pilot was using two foot sticks with F-15 models on the end to demonstrate how Stansell should have maneuvered. Then he moved to the white board on the wall of the small briefing room and used four different colors of magic markers to diagram how he would've engaged the two F-15s. Finally he ran the video tape that had recorded the flight through the Head Up Display.

Stansell sat quietly, making notes, accepting what the captain had to say, and only nodded his head when Donaldson had finished. Get it together, he raged at himself. What's wrong? This course should be a piece of cake.

The other three members of the flight came into the squadron for their debrief. Snake was loudly telling anyone who would listen how he had "knocked their dicks in the dirt." Again, the colonel sat quietly through the debrief, thinking how much Snake was like himself when he was younger.

When the debrief was over he escaped from the squadron and headed for the condominium he was renting from a friend.

Barbara Lyon, the condo's owner, was holding court by the swimming pool. Two younger men were stretched out on the deck chairs beside her, both intent on acing the other out in a bid for her attention, favors. Stansell couldn't blame them. Barbara was on the spectacular side and the string bikini she was wearing would cause traffic accidents.

"Rupe," she called, twisting around on the deck chair and leaning forward. Stansell wondered if the rumors about her being a Las Vegas showgirl before she married and later divorced an Air Force major were true. He paused and walked toward her, deciding that even in her mid-thirties she had the body and looks many twenty-year-old girls would kill for. "I need to check your security system, we had a false alarm today," she said, tugging the top back into place. Barefoot she was two inches taller than he was. The two younger men decided Stansell wasn't in the game.

He followed her up the stairs, startled at how the beige color of the bikini blended with her tan, making her look almost naked from the back. God, she does make it hard for the troops.

Barbara turned in time to catch his half grin. She gave her long ash blonde hair a toss, a gesture she had practiced in front of a mirror, sure it would add to the effect she wanted to have on the colonel. Actually she found herself attracted to Stansell and his rather quiet ways. The difference in their heights didn't bother her— she knew that it didn't make a difference in bed. She liked his well-conditioned body and pleasant looks. And if he would let his dark hair with the few strands of gray at the temples grow long on the sides . . . She stepped aside to let him unlock the door to his condo, deliberately brushing his arm.

"Let me deactivate the alarm," she said. "What's the code?" Stansell told her the four digits that worked the alarm. She carefully punched in the numbers and watched the digital display flash from "secure" to "ready to arm." Her lips made a slight pout as she studied the box and shifted her weight onto her right leg. She recycled the alarm, fingers playing with the knot on the left side of her bikini, snapping it against her hip. "The problem's not here. Must be the main box. I'll get the repairman to check it." She knew there was nothing wrong with the alarm.

Stansell nodded. Barbara decided she was going to have to be more obvious. Some men just didn't pay attention. "It's hot today, you wouldn't have anything cool to drink?"

"Iced tea? Beer?"

"Iced tea would be fine." She leaned over the kitchen's bar while he got the tea for her and a beer for himself. She had noticed the framed photograph of two small girls and a startlingly beautiful woman on the fireplace mantle. "Is that your wife?"

"Was. Divorced. Three months ago."

It fell into place for Barbara. She had seen the same pattern before and knew there might be a future for her with Stansell.

He handed her the iced tea.

"Don't those flight suits get awfully hot during the summer?" She reached out and drew a finger across his chest, touching the Nomex flight suit, stopping at the zipper. "All those zippers, and I do like the patch." She ran a finger over the Triple Nickel's squadron patch on his right shoulder.

She waited. If Stansell didn't take the opening it would be plan B-time.

"I only wear it while I'm here. You can have it when I leave."

"I've got to go. Thanks for the drink." She set the half-empty glass down, smiled at him and turned to leave. "Oh, could I interest you in dinner some evening? I do have some old friends in the Air Force. We might have some mutual acquaintances."

"Thanks, I'd like that."

She smiled at him again and left, running plan B over in her head.

Alone, Stansell took his beer and sat down on the couch, wondering what the hell was wrong with him. Once, he would've been over Barbara like white on rice. Now—nothing. He didn't want to get involved? Old hat but maybe true. He pulled the Mission Data Card out of the flight suit's leg pocket and reread the notes he had made during the debrief. Donaldson was right. He was flying like a newbee right out of basic fighter maneuvers. What was the problem? He knew how to fly the jet but was letting the damn past get in his way. Concentrate on flying, the program, quit the damn looking at ghosts, wondering about failing, feeling guilty about surviving when all those people died and now some were POWs.

Shake it off and get with it, he told himself as he went into the bathroom, peeled off the sweat-stained flight suit and stepped into the shower. The water felt good against his skin. He heard a knock at the door but ignored it. Since he had come back from the Persian Gulf, he seemed to linger a lot in showers.

"I came back for the rest of the tea," Barbara called from the kitchen.

"Help yourself."

The door of the shower swung open and Barbara stepped in. "That feels good." She gave a wiggle and her bikini bottom fell to the floor. "Untie me, please." She turned her back to him and held her long hair up, showing Stansell the knot that barely held her top in place. "God, it's hot today."

He pulled the knot free and she shrugged off the top.

"Here, let me wash your back." She faced him and reached around, scrubbing his back. "You must pay more attention." She laughed, rubbing against him.

Nothing happened.

"Oh well, never mind, I did want to talk to you about dinner. Tomorrow night okay?" She scooped up her bikini and stepped out of the shower, not bothering to dry off. "Seven o'clock," she told him, and walked out of the bathroom.

A moment later he heard her close the front door. He shut off the water, toweled down, rubbed his hair dry and stared into the water-streaked mirror, not wanting to see too clear an image of himself. For a moment it could have been his old wing commander at Ras Assanya staring back at him. "Muddy" Waters ... damn you, Muddy. How to live up to you? To your sacrifice and the way the Wing felt about you? And then: oh, come off it, colonel, this is bull. So you have doubts you can be the man the late Muddy Waters was. Remember what he had done, what you learned from him about the human side of the Air Force and just do what Rupe Stansell can do and not what Waters would have done if he'd lived. Easier thought than done, but he was getting there, and actually felt much better.

He wiped the steam from the mirror and studied his reflection, then slowly turned his face to the left and ran his hand along the right side of his head, brushing his hair back, trying to cover the scar where his right ear used to be.

CHAPTER 2

D MINUS 33

THE WHITE HOUSE

Michael Cagliari leaned against the back wall of the East Room of the White House, content to stay behind the cameras during the Friday afternoon press conference. As the President's National Security Advisor, he preferred it that way and worked hard to maintain a low profile.

The dean of the press corps, Peter Whiteside from the Affiliated Broadcasting System, sat quietly in the first row, waiting. Whiteside's dislike of the President was well-known.

"Jean," the President pointed to the back row at the stylishly dressed older lady from Savannah, Georgia, starting the press conference.

Predictable, Cagliari thought, he likes Jean Ramsey.

"Mr. President, there's a growing concern about the buy-out of many U.S. corporations by foreign interests. Many are fearful that the wealth producing capability of our country is falling under the control of overseas investors. How do you intend to address this problem?"

The President was well-prepared for this and subsequent questions, and then he recognized Peter Whiteside with a "Pete." It had been decided to avoid recognizing Peter Whiteside and only allow him the privilege reserved to the dean of the press corps of ending the press conference with the traditional, "Thank you, Mr. President." The Chief must be feeling very confident, the National Security Advisor thought. The microphone boom was carried down front and put in front of the reporter. "Mr. President, during your election campaign you said, and I quote, 'I will never trade arms or money for hostages nor will I engage in negotiations that could bring discredit on the United States.' Reliable sources report that your representative is sitting at a negotiations table right now in Geneva bargaining for the release of the two hundred and eighty hostages captured by the Iranians after our defeat in the Persian Gulf. Can you tell us if progress has been made in these negotiations, and I have a follow-up."

"Pete, that sounded more like a political statement, but I'll answer it. First, the Iranians are holding two hundred and eighty-two prisoners of war. They are not hostages. And yes, I am pursuing negotiations at Geneva for their release. We have reached a critical juncture, and to discuss negotiations in public could well compromise the progress we've made."

"Mr. President, this is not my follow up, but is it true that Secretary of State Cyrus Piccard is the negotiator?" Whiteside's heavy eyebrows seemed to knit together.

"I have nothing more for you on that."

Whiteside shouted his last question, interrupting the next reporter, loud enough for the boom mike to pick up. "Sir, are you trying to outbid a Libyan offer to buy the hostages from Iran for a million dollars each?"

The President fixed Whiteside with an icy stare. "Pete, you need to check your sources."

"End it," Cagliari growled into the small microphone attached to his lapel that linked him to the press secretary. Where the hell does Whiteside get his information? It was partly true. The Secretary of State was trying to convince the Iranians to reject the Libyan offer relayed through a third party. Well, at least the President had sidestepped the question.

The man holding the boom mike made sure he understood his directions from the press secretary, walked back to Jean Ramsey and spoke to her as he held the mike up to her. "Thank you, Mr. President," she said in a loud voice, ending the press conference.

Whiteside literally spun around, angry-faced, while the President waved at the reporters and retreated up the red carpet of the main hallway. Cagliari made his way through a crush of reporters and slipped through the door leading to the Green Room. He hurried after the President.

The President's chief of staff, Andy Wollard, was waiting for him in the hall outside the Oval Office. "The Chief is pissed," he said, announcing the obvious.

Cagliari followed him into the Oval Office, where the President was sitting at his desk.

"Sit down, Mike, get comfortable. This is going to be a long one." His voice was flat.

"That was a bad question from Whiteside," Cagliari said quickly.

"There're no bad questions, only bad answers. Besides, it's true, the Libyans are trying to buy the POWs. We needed secrecy and time to bring the Iranians around. I'd say we've lost both of those now."

Cagliari braced himself as his Chief lit a cigar; a habit he had forsworn months ago. He puffed once and stubbed it out.

"Filthy habit," he said. "Andy,"—he gestured at his chief of staff—"get the Secretary of Defense, the Director of Central Intelligence and the Chairman of the Joint Chiefs in here. Now." The intense precision of his voice propelled Andy Wollard out of the office.

"Mike, if the negotiations fail, and now it seems they will, I want the POWs rescued."

CHAPTER 3

D MINUS 32

THE PENTAGON

General Lawrence Cunningham's driver drove directly from the general's residence to the River Entrance of the Pentagon—the Joint Chiefs of Staff entrance. The driver had timed the Saturday morning traffic, and Cunningham had plenty of time to walk the thirty yards through the almost deserted corridor to reach the command section in E-ring. He wasn't worried about being late to the hastily called meeting—there would have to be an all-out emergency for it to start without him. He didn't look at the portraits of former chairmen of the JCS that lined the wall. It was a group he would never join.

His aide, Colonel Richard Stevens, was waiting for him outside the Tank, the conference room where the Joint Chiefs met. The Tank was opposite room 3E880, the Secretary of Defense's office. Stevens had just come from the Joint Special Operations Agency around the corner in Corridor Eight. The close proximity of Special Ops to the command section signified its importance. Stevens held the door of the conference room open for the general. "The meeting has been changed to the Command Center and delayed until 8:30," Stevens said. "I was just told. We need a secure place to talk."

They entered the large room. A conference table surrounded by soft leather chairs filled the center. The general sat down in the one reserved for him—the Air Force Chief of Staff. Since the room was vacant, Stevens sat in the chair next to him. Normally he would have taken one of the office chairs that lined the wall.

"Sir, I talked to General Mado in Special Ops. The President has ordered a task force to rescue the POWs if negotiations fail."

The general focused on the opposite wall, absorbing the news. The POWs were etched in Cunningham's conscience. They were, after all, his people, left behind when the 45th Tactical Fighter Wing had been extracted out of its base at Ras Assanya on the Persian Gulf.

The President had ordered the Air Force to deploy the 45th into the Gulf to support the United Arab Command in an attempt to block an invasion of Kuwait and Saudi Arabia through Iraq by the latest revolutionary group running Iran. And the 45th had done its job. The situation was stabilizing when Mid-East politics raised its head and a face-saving gesture was needed to induce the Iranians to the negotiating table. What looked like a symbolic attack on Ras Assanya to prove the Iranians were still a force to be reckoned with turned into a full scale battle. The base was in danger of being overrun before the U.S. Navy could get its ships back into the Gulf. The wing commander of the 45th, Colonel Anthony ("Muddy") Waters, had thrown his F-4s at an oncoming Iranian invasion fleet crossing the Gulf and fought a rear-guard action while he evacuated his wing out of Ras Assanya.

But the cost had been high. Over three hundred men and women had been killed, another five hundred wounded and sixty-seven F-4s destroyed. Waters had been killed before he could save the people he could not get out in time.

It was left to Lieutenant Colonel Rupert Stansell to surrender Ras Assanya and march three hundred men and one woman into a POW cage. Only two men had avoided capture, dragging Stansell with them, and seventeen had died in captivity.

Cunningham wanted revenge, and his people back.

"Get Mado in here." Major General Simon Mado was the ranking Air Force member of the Joint Special Operations Agency, the JSOA, which fell under the command of Army General Charles J. Leachmeyer. Mado was the youngest major general in the Air Force, earning his second star for his forty-third birthday. He was also a Rhodes scholar and B-52 pilot. To the people who worked for him, he was a fast-burner who used people for fuel.

"It may be a few minutes. The JSOA is bouncing off the walls. They're getting ready for the 8:30 meeting."

Cunningham shot a look at his aide.

"I'll get him, sir."

Two minutes later Simon Mado was sitting in the same seat Stevens had vacated. The two-star general looked like a recruiting poster; tall, well-built, square-jawed, blond hair, stern blue eyes. The works. He came to the point. "General Leachmeyer says the President will be at the meeting and is rehearsing a briefing on the JSOA's plan for rescuing the POWs."

Cunningham jammed his ever-present cigar into his mouth. "The President is coming here? Unusual. What's in the plan for the Air Force?"

"Very little, sir, only rear echelon support. It's going to be an all-Army show with Black Hawk helicopters and Delta Force."

"Dammit, those are *my* people over there. Get the word to Leachmeyer that I want in on the action."

"Sir, JSOA does have another plan for using Air Force C-130s but it's rough and undeveloped—"

"I want it presented to the President with Leachmeyer's plan."

"I'll see what I can do." Mado said, rising from his chair.

At 8:30 the President walked into the National Military Command Center in the Pentagon and took a place on the command mezzanine at the back. Normally he would have sat in the Command and Authority Room, the glass-enclosed room to the right. He was flanked by Robert "Bobby" Burke, Director of Central Intelligence, and Michael Cagliari, the National Security Advisor. He looked at the Chairman of the Joint Chiefs, Admiral Terrence Scovill. "Let's see what you've got, Terry."

"Mr. President, I'm going to turn this over to General Leachmeyer, head of JSOA."

The President nodded. The Joint Special Operations Agency had been created to unify the response of the elite units of the U.S. armed forces—the units that would carry out any rescue operation.

Leachmeyer mounted the low stage at the head of the room and stood in front of the huge computer-generated situation maps. The center map displayed a portion of the Middle East centered on Kermanshah, a small city in western Iran. "Sir, I'd like to start out with a look at our latest intelligence and then show you the two plans we're working on. General Mado will cover the intelligence situation and present our first plan."

The President sank back into his chair. It was going to be a standard military dog-and-pony show. He endured it because it seemed to work and besides, Leachmeyer was one of his poker-playing buddies.

Mado took the stage and glanced at Cunningham, his way of saying he had done his best. He used an electric pointer to draw a circle around the center of the screen. "Intelligence confirms that the POWs are located in a prison on the outskirts of Kermanshah." He pointed to the city in the Zagros mountains of western Iran located about halfway between the Persian Gulf and the capital of Tehran.

"How good is this information, general?" Admiral Scovill asked.

"Solid as we can get." Mado flicked the button of the remote control in the handle of the pointer. An enhanced infrared high-resolution photo flashed on the screen. "This was taken Thursday night by a Stealth reconnaissance flight. The POWs were lined up in ranks during the night." Mado pointed to the assembled ranks of men standing in the courtyard of a large prison-like compound. "We suspect they were made to stand outside as a form of punishment. We were able to get a head count—281. Two independent operatives confirm the number and report cases of brutal treatment."

The President was leaning forward. "And how reliable are the operatives?"

"Very," Bobby Burke, the DCI, said. "They're both our people. There's one POW unaccounted for—Captain Mary Lynn Hauser."

"How are you going to get them out?" The President was looking at Mado.

"Our first plan stresses speed and surprise," Mado said. "We launch C-130s out of Turkey and ingress through the tri-border region of Turkey, Iran and Iraq." His pointer traced the route. "We paradrop Delta Force into the compound and at this airfield." He pointed to an unused airstrip three miles northeast of the compound. "Delta Force frees the POWs and secures the airfield. The C-130s land and we transport the POWs to the waiting aircraft."

Cunningham split his attention, listening to Mado go over the details of the plan and concentrating on the President's reaction. The man wasn't telegraphing a thing. Frustrated, Cunningham looked around the room for other reactions. Michael Cagliari and Admiral Scovill were just listening attentively. But then, Mado was probably the best briefer and public speaker in the Pentagon. The DCI, Bobby Burke, twiddled a pen and fidgeted in his chair. What an incompetent asshole, Cunningham thought. He couldn't stand the man and didn't trust him. Leachmeyer was smiling at the army colonel who would present the second plan. Charlie knows something, Cunningham decided.

"Any questions, sir?" Mado said, finishing.

The President shook his head. "But don't go away, Simon. Okay, Charlie, who's next?"

"Sir, I'd like to introduce Colonel Sam Johnson, commander of Delta Force," Leachmeyer said.

"Another golden mouth?"

"Hell no, Mr. President." Leachmeyer smiled. "Few people can pitch like Simon. I just thought you'd rather hear the second plan from the man who will actually have to go in and do it."

Cunningham's jaw tightened—Charlie Leachmeyer was scoring points for his plan.

The burly colonel who stood up was six feet tall, moved with an agile grace. His massive hands made the pointer he picked up look somehow inadequate. Visibly corded muscles ran down his thick neck.

Cunningham hoped the man would be a cretin, hard lines and no brains. He was disappointed. The colonel's briefing was as short and cogent as Mado's. Johnson's army plan was simple: a massive helicopter assault mounted out of Iraq. The timing, tactics, communications and logistics were well thought out. There was little for the Air Force and nothing for the Navy—an Army show. Cunningham had to allow that the plan had merit, but also a flaw.

"Well, gentlemen," the President said when the colonel had finished, "I'm encouraged." He turned to his National Security Advisor. "What do you think, Mike?"

"Either one could work," Mike Cagliari said. "I do see drawbacks to both, though. For example, the first one needs support inside Iran to provide vehicles for moving the POWs to the C-130s—"

"Bobby"—the President turned to his Director of Central Intelligence—"do you have operatives inside Iran who can do that?"

The DCI stopped fidgeting and calmed down. "We have operatives inside Iran, and yes, they can do that. But"—he stared straight at the President—"that type of action qualifies as a covert operation and we can only do that with the approval of the Congressional intelligence committees. Politics, as you know, sir, is alive and well in those committees. Since the Senate committee is controlled by the other party, that almost guarantees a leak to the press. I'm not willing to put my operatives at risk."

Only the Army colonel did not know the name of the Senator's aide who would leak the operation to the press.

"Mr. President," Mado said, "as an option, we can fly in our own vehicles and destroy them when we pull out. It's not difficult with the C-130s."

Cunningham gave Mado an appreciative look, he was thinking on his feet.

"Why did you make that an option?" Cagliari asked.

"Three reasons, Mr. Cagliari. First, surprise. The trucks or buses would be in place when we get the POWs out and they just drive off. Second, speed. With our own vehicles we'd have to make three, maybe four round trips. With transportation supplied it's a one-way trip—once. Third, efficiency. It reduces the number of aircraft we'd need."

"Okay, Mike," the President asked, "what's the matter with the second plan?"

"It's a big operation using a fleet of helicopters. And we have to launch out of Iraq. I don't like doing business with the Iraqis and it's almost sure to be compromised. It's too big a force to hide while we position."

"Sir"—it was Colonel Johnson—"we can launch from another country. But that means we'll have to refuel. The Air Force can fly in or airdrop fuel bladders at a remote site."

Cunningham was warming up to this army colonel. "This is beginning to sound like Eagle Claw," he grumbled, loud enough for everyone to hear. He meant the attempt in 1980 to rescue the American hostages out of the U.S. embassy in Tehran had failed because of helicopters. Three had mechanical problems and one had crashed when it moved into position to refuel.

"Anything else?" the President asked.

Cagliari huddled with the President, talking rapidly in a low voice. The President listened, nodded, leaned back in his chair. When his decision was made, his orders tended to erupt like a machine gun. "We go with the second plan using Delta Force and helicopters. But launch out of Turkey or Kuwait. Be ready for an execute order in thirty days. There's a real possibility for a compromise and it seems logical that the opposition will be watching Delta Force, expecting them to mount a rescue mission. This is the type of operation they were created for. So I want the Air Force to provide a cover for Delta Force and the helicopters."

The President pointed his pen at Cunningham. "Put a task force together using C-130s like the first plan calls for. Don't tell anyone they're a decoy for the real thing, make it credible. If the opposition doesn't cotton to what you're doing and take the bait, we'll oblige and leak it to them.

"But"—he pointed at Burke, the DCI—"you had damn well better *control* the leak and clear it with me. That's it." And the President rose and was out of there.

Cunningham put a cigar in his mouth, the muscles in his jaw working. He would not light it until he was in the sanctity of his own office. "Mado, come with me."

"I wanted more of that mission, Mado." Cunningham was pacing his office. "Now we're a goddamn Quaker cannon sitting on the sidelines with our thumbs up our ass. During WW II Patton was tapped to be one for the invasion of Normandy. It almost drove him crazy playing the decoy. I don't like it any more than he did. But . . . I'm going to provide the best damn cover operation ever created and I want you to honcho it—be the joint task force commander."

"Sir, I'd rather stay where the action is in JSOA and work with Delta Force."

"You're my expert for special ops and while you may be assigned to the JSOA under Leachmeyer, you're still, I believe, in the Air Force."

Mado nodded, pretending to go with rank. Actually he saw Cunningham as a Neanderthal blocking progress, one of the old guard that would keep the Air Force out of the twenty-first century, gung-ho to fight World War II all over again but not remotely prepared for the modern world—a world of neatly integrated commands that General Leachmeyer was going to make happen. "I'd be less than honest if I didn't tell you my preferences, sir. But I'll give you a fake task force that will water their eyeballs. But even though the Air Force puts a Quaker cannon together, since it has to do with special ops, command will still fall under the JSOA."

"Mado, I *know* that. Just remember those are my Air Force people over there." As he talked, a plan was taking shape in Cunningham's mind—the President wanted a cover operation, but he was going to create a force in being—a group so good that they would have to be considered for the actual mission. But it would take the right people and some intricate maneuvering to make it happen . . . "You're going to need a mission commander, someone with believability," he said.

Mado did not hesitate. "Colonel Rupert Stansell."

"Why him?"

"High visibility, and he's an obvious choice. He's the only colonel you've got with combat experience in the Middle East. That gives him a feel for operations that can make the difference. He's good and won't underestimate the competition. We're not taking on a bunch of incompetent ragheads. And, general, he's motivated. Revenge is a lovely thing when you want results. He'll make it look real. Also, he's known to the opposition, which might get them looking at him."

"Get him here. Today."

PHOENIX, ARIZONA

The security policeman rapped again on the door of Stansell's condo—much louder the second time. When no one answered, he thought for a moment and headed for the manager's apartment. He had seen the sign when he entered the complex. He rang the doorbell beneath the discreet sign that announced the manager lived there. The door cracked open and Barbara stuck her head and a bare shoulder around the edge.

"Ma'am, I'm Sergeant Wayne Jenkins from Luke. I'm looking for Colonel Rupert Stansell. He's not at home and I was wondering if you might know where he is."

"I can take a message and see that he gets it," Barbara said.

"Ma'am, this is very important, we've got a message from the Pentagon and if we can't find him really quick we'll have to get the police involved."

"Wait a minute, maybe I can get him." She pushed the door closed, not latching it.

The sergeant gave the door a test shove, cracking it open about six inches. He glanced into the apartment just in time to see Barbara's bare backside disappear into a bedroom. "Looks like a full-service condominium," he muttered.

Barbara sat on the edge of the bed, looking at the sleeping man. She pulled the sheet down and studied his body—a smile appeared on her lips. "You had me worried last night, Colonel," she whispered. "Turned out all you needed were the right strokes in the right places."

She drew her legs up and leaned over him, resting on her left arm. Lightly, she traced a line from his forehead down his nose, across his lips and down his neck. Her tongue flicked and moistened her lips as she continued the line down his stomach. She repeated the trip.

As her fingers touched his lips he grabbed her wrist and held her hand. "There now, you awake?"

He groaned.

"Not too loud, lover. There's a security cop come a-callin' from the base. Says he's got a message from the Pentagon."

Stansell rolled out of bed and pulled his shorts on, hurrying to the door. Barbara followed him into the hall and leaned against the wall, not caring if the security cop saw her naked.

Jenkins stared a moment, then came to the point. "We got a telephone call from the Chief of Staff, sir. You've got to be at the Pentagon today. There's an F-15 waiting on the ramp. Grab your flight suit and dress in the car, sir."

Stansell bolted back into the bedroom, leaving the door wide open. Barbara didn't move. He scooped up his clothes and ran for his apartment. Jenkins reached in and reluctantly closed the door. By the time the sergeant reached his patrol car, Stansell was ready, in flight suit and carrying his flying boots and shaving kit. In the car Jenkins twisted the key and hit the siren switch at the same time. "Duty can be a terrible burden," he told the colonel, somehow maintaining a straight face.

The sergeant drove directly to the ramp, up to a two-place F-15D. Buzz Rutherford was sitting in the back seat. Jenkins dropped Stansell off and headed back for the condominium, for what he suspected would be a warm reception. Rank might have its privileges, but when rank was away . . .

"It's preflighted and ready to go," Rutherford said. "We're filed and the tower is holding the Active open for us. You want the stick?" He knew the answer. He had flown with Stansell the day before and had seen a marked improvement in Stansell's confidence and the way he was fighting the bird in air-combat tactics. Even Snake Houserman had commented on it.

Stansell's G-suit and parachute harness were hanging on a missile rail under the left wing. He zipped on his go-faster-chaps, buckled the harness into place and clambered up the boarding ladder. His helmet was on the right canopy rail waiting for him, its oxygen hose and comm cord connected. The cockpit was ready for him. All the switches were set and the straps laid neatly open. "This must be a big deal," he told Rutherford.

"The wing commander thinks so. He took the call. Came right from Cunningham's office. I was working in the squadron and got tapped for the flight. Got to bring the jet back today."

Stansell hit the jet fuel starter, cranked the right engine as he finished strapping in. Four minutes later they were airborne.

"I filed us for .95 mach," Rutherford told him. "Should rendezvous with a tanker over St. Louis for an inflight refueling. Otherwise we land and refuel at Scott."

"How in the hell did you get a KC-135 laid on so fast?"

"What Cunningham wants, Cunningham gets."

THE PENTAGON

The waiting staff car at Andrews AFB had driven Stansell directly from the F-15 to the Pentagon's River Entrance. Another sergeant was waiting and escorted him to Mado's office.

"Rupe, good to see you again." Mado stood, extended his hand, studied Stansell and decided that he looked healthy enough after his ordeal at the hands of the Iranians. "God, I keep hoping you'll grow up someday." It was a standing joke between the two men left over from when they had been assigned to the Pentagon as majors. Mado had stayed when Stansell returned to operations and flying the F-15.

"Hell, General, I'm five inches taller than Napoleon," Stansell said. Mado towered over the five foot seven colonel and did a quick assessment of Stansell as they talked. He had to make a decision—could Stansell take the stress that would build as they went through the drill? Stansell's hazel eyes were clear and he did look fit and trim. No nervous ticks or mannerisms to indicate instability. The colonel wore a regulation haircut and did not brush his sideburns over his ears in an attempt to hide his missing ear. He looked his age, forty-two, but not worn or haggard.

"How's Linda and the girls?" Mado asked.

"They're fine. We've separated, the divorce was final three months ago."

"Sorry to hear that. How's the refresher course going?"

"I've had problems in ACT. I was screwing up by the numbers and didn't figure out what the problem was until last Thursday. To put it simply, lack of confidence. My flight yesterday was much better. I'll be okay now."

Mado nodded. Stansell's blunt revelation of his marital difficulties and the problems he was having becoming current in the F-15 were good signs that he had it together. And it tracked with what Buzz

Rutherford had told him over the phone. Stansell would do. He should be credible for the cover operation.

"General, what the hell is this all about?"

"How would you like a chance to do something about the POWs?"

Stansell sucked his breath in. Mado wouldn't tell him any more until he bought in, committed to what was going down. The possibilities raced through his mind. It could be anything from a simple intelligence gathering exercise or operation to . . . His mind faltered at that end of the scale. Were the heavies making contingency plans? Or better yet, was the President thinking of going after the POWs? Rescuing them? For a moment, Stansell did not realize he had stood up. This was his chance to make it all right.

"Yes, sir, I want part of that. I'll do *whatever* . . ."

"Okay, we're going to see Cunningham. He wants to lay it out for you. This is a big one."

They had to wait in Cunningham's outer office. At first it amused Stansell that Cunningham would keep a two-star general like Mado cooling his heels, then it started to worry him. Cunningham had earned the nickname "Sundown" from his habit of relieving officers on the spot and ordering them to be cleared out of the Pentagon by sundown. Thule, Greenland, was considered a good follow-on assignment for those unfortunates.

What went on behind Sundown's exterior was a mystery, except to a very few who knew him well. And to those he was a man who not only gave a damn, he couldn't stand bureaucrats, assholes and anybody who gave less than everything they had—plus.

"The General must be busy," Stansell ventured, surprised that Mado seemed unconcerned by the delay.

"That's the way he works," Mado said, closed his eyes and leaned back.

Mado had called it right. Cunningham had used most of the morning and early afternoon framing his own version of the plan and what he would have to do. He had filled two sheets of a yellow legal pad with notes. A special fire was burning in him—he wanted the Air Force to rescue the POWs. He had to prove, to himself above all the rest, that he did take care of his people. So it had to be his show. Finally he called his aide to show Mado and Stansell in.

The general motioned the two men to seats while he lit the cigar he had been rolling in his mouth and paced the floor. It was the first time Stansell had met Cunningham and was surprised that the man was so short. The general's silver gray hair, portly build and pale complexion seemed not to go with the nervous energy that obviously drove him.

"Stansell, the President has ordered us to rescue the POWs." Cunningham paused to watch the colonel's reaction—a sharp nod and compressed lips.

"You're here because General Mado thinks you can help us do that. General Mado is the joint task force commander and you're his mission commander. Your job is to work out a detailed operations plan and put the task force together. You pick the training site and work out of there. Mado will stay here, line up the resources you need, run interference and fight off the sharks. Quite a few generals and colonels will want a piece of the action. They'll go into a feeding frenzy if they think it's good for a promotion.

"The President has approved our basic plan. Mado will fill you in later. But you need some guidelines to work with for your ops plan. First, keep the mission simple as you can. Second, expect to take losses—try to come up with a good estimate. Third, you need good intelligence. We'll put you in contact with the CIA and open up the DIA for you. Fourth, you'll get the best people and resources we've got. If what we send you isn't working out, make it Mado's problem. But keep working with what you've got. My aide, Dick Stevens, will get you set up. I'd suggest you start by paying a visit to Brigadier General Eichler." The general punched his intercom. "Dick, take care of Stansell. Put him in contact with Eichler and Camm at CIA . . . Colonel"—Cunningham stopped Stansell before he cleared the door—"you were the last person to see Muddy Waters alive. Pay your respects to Mrs. Waters, she lives near Eichler. And get the hell out of that green bag. People around here get upset when they see a flight suit. It reminds them of what their job is."

I hope he can do it, Cunningham thought after Stansell had closed the door.

Stevens took Stansell into his office and placed a series of calls, getting him a room in the VOQ at Bolling AFB and a car. "A car should be waiting for you at the mall entrance. How'd it go with the general?"

"Well, he didn't match his reputation. I expected fire and horns."

"That part of him tends to surface in public. And it's usually for a reason." Stevens changed the subject. "I'd suggest you get changed. If you need clothes, try this place." Stevens handed him a business card. "Your contact at CIA is Allen Camm, Deputy Director for Intelligence. I'll set up a meeting for Monday morning. Pass and ID is waiting for you and we'll cut you a restricted area badge. I'd suggest you work out of the Watch Center this weekend. There's always an analyst available. I'll clear you in."

The colonel handed Stansell a card with Brigadier General Melvin Eichler's phone number and address. "I'll let you contact 'Messy' Eichler. A real character."

"The general told me to pay my respects to Mrs. Waters when I see Eichler."

Stevens took the card back and spun his Rolladex, finding another address and phone number to write down. "Most people call Eichler 'The Brigadier.' Keep your visit short—the man's dying. Leukemia."

CHAPTER 4

D MINUS 31

THE ZAGROS MOUNTAINS, IRAN

Captain William G. Carroll, United States Air Force, shifted his weight, trying to find a comfortable position on the broken-down seat. Its padding rearranged itself and by leaning against the window the jolting, bouncing ride lost some of its harshness. He gazed out the window that was closed to keep out the dust kicked up by the front wheels of the bus as it careened down the road through the Zagros mountains of western Iran. The road and the bus were both in pitiful condition, worn out by overuse and little maintenance during the wars Iran had been fighting with its neighbors.

He caught a glimpse of his reflection in the window. It amazed him how much he looked like an Iranian and how he blended in with the people. He thanked his mother's Armenian parents for his dark complexion, brown eyes and black hair.

The heat of summer had broken but it was too early for the winter rains and snow. Carroll calculated that the road would be impassable once it started to rain. A sudden quiet followed by moans from the passengers enveloped the bus when the engine died. It was the third time that day the engine had quit. The driver guided the bus to a halt and got out to see if he could coax it back to life. Carroll decided the Iranian driver was a much better mechanic than driver.

"Will you ever get home?" the man sitting beside Carroll said.

"As Allah wills," he replied.

The man smiled, accepting Carroll as he appeared—a young veteran of the Revolutionary Guards, made wise by his experiences in battle and his belief as a Shi'ite. He is fortunate, the Iranian thought, so many of our best sacrificed. He liked and respected the sergeant who called himself Javad. He followed the other passengers out of the bus, leaving Carroll to stare out the window at the surrounding mountains.

So much like the mountains of Southern California, Carroll thought. And like Greece. He remembered the time he had landed at Athens in a C-130. It seemed so long ago.

The C-130 had landed at Athenai Airport after a five hour flight from the Persian Gulf carrying ninety men and women on their first Rest and Recuperation leave from Ras Assanya. Cheers and whistles greeted the hard squeal of the tires as they touched down. Carroll had sunk back into the webbing of the parachute jump-seat and let the tension of the past months in combat slip away. He had wanted to talk to Captain Mary Hauser, the radar controller from Ras Assanya's radar control post who was sitting next to him. He had tried during the flight but the noise on the cargo deck had reduced them to screaming at each other.

"Cheated death again." He smiled as the engines wound down, the noise dying away.

"You surprised?"

"No," he said, "I was looking for a way to open a conversation."

"Why so?"

Why so aggressive? Carroll thought. He had no big-deal ulterior motive . . . On reflection he decided that wasn't quite true, Mary intrigued him, he found her attractive. But he said, "Just being friendly, I guess."

"Oh."

Nothing to say to that but good-by. He climbed out of the Hercules and followed the passenger-services sergeant into the terminal.

Mary had watched him go, annoyed with herself for being so damn abrupt. But then . . . don't be a fool, he's probably like the others at Ras Assanya—any woman would do in a pinch, so to speak. Mary Hauser had looked at herself in mirrors for so long that all she saw was a tall gaunt figure crowned by an unruly mass of reddish brown hair.

What Bill Carroll had seen was a tall and slender body that moved with controlled grace. Unlike many of the pilots, he found her hard brand of *professional* competence easy to live with and did not feel threatened by her abilities and rank.

Mary, as penance, she told herself, had spent the next two days seeing the sights of Athens alone. A poster in a travel agency's window off Omonia Square advertising the island of Mykonos caught her eye. Suddenly she was very tired of the city. She went in, booked a room on the island and got directions to the ferry. A traffic jam had delayed her taxi the next morning and the forward gangplank was already up when she got to the ferry. She just made the second gangplank before it too was raised. After buying a ticket from the purser she found a seat on the sundeck and did her best to enjoy the seven-hour voyage. When she got off one of the small boats that served as lighters, carrying passengers and cargo from the ferry into the dock at Mykonos, she discovered the travel agency had not made her room reservation. Her search for a room had turned up nothing, and Mary was eating a late dinner, resigned to finding a table at some *taverna* until they kicked her out and then finding somewhere to hole up until she could catch the ferry back to Athens the next day.

"Enjoying Mykonos?"

She turned to see Bill Carroll. This time she smiled, relieved to see him, and told him about the lost room reservation.

"Well, don't take this all wrong." he said, "but my room has twins and you're welcome to one of them . . ."

Mary looked at the slender young captain, earnest brown eyes and all, and accepted. Next morning she woke up to find his bed empty. After a moment she saw a shadow move across the balcony at the end of the room. She kicked her long legs out of bed and padded across the room to join him at the railing, wearing only a tee shirt.

He was watching a magnificent sunrise, drinking coffee. "Something else, isn't it?" They watched the morning hues paint the village as it came to life. "I'm going over to Delos today to see the ruins. Want to come?"

A comfortable feeling had replaced earlier skepticism she had felt on the C-130, and for the next four days the relaxed charm of the island had its way with them as it forced their world to, momentarily, yield its harsh demands and allow them to play and discover each other, in the end as lovers.

The bus's engine coughed to life, bringing Carroll back to the present.

The Iranian sat down as the passengers crowded back onto the bus, chattering about getting under way again. He handed Carroll a pear. When Carroll at first refused he forced the fruit into his hand. The bus jerked into motion and Carroll ate the damn pear, an unintentional gift on his twenty-seventh birthday from a friendly Iranian, yet.

Mary, he thought, why didn't you leave when Muddy Waters ordered you out? Mary . . . now a POW . . .

WASHINGTON, D.C.

The silver blue Dodge Omni that Stevens had arranged for Colonel Stansell to drive struck him as typical of the Air Force—plain, boring and functional—nothing like the big dark blue BMW behind him. He wheeled the car through Washington's light Sunday morning traffic, heading for Interstate 95 and General Eichler's home in Fredericksburg, Virginia. And also Muddy Waters' widow. After a few miles he started to enjoy the drive and left the Interstate for old Highway One that paralleled 95. A more interesting road, he thought. Apparently the driver of the BMW felt the same way.

The trees barraged him with autumn color. What a contrast to Luke and Ras Assanya, he thought. I'm really turning into a desert rat. Ras Assanya . . . the name came back to him, wouldn't let him go. He forced himself to think about where he was going. What kind of woman would Muddy Waters have married? He ran through some possibilities but knew Waters had been too complex to pin down . . . "Muddy, I was lucky to have known you," Stansell said to the image burned in memory.

Stansell had first met the tall colonel at Ras Assanya. Waters was in command of the 45th Tactical Fighter Wing, a collection of old F-4s and young fighter jocks. Somehow, Waters had whipped them into shape and had turned the 45th into a top-notch outfit. But they had been taking heavy losses and Stansell's squadron of F-15s had been deployed to provide a combat air patrol for the 45th. Together, they had provided the key that opened the door for negotiations to stop the fighting. But the enemy wanted a price. And the price had been the 45th. Waters had a way that captivated people, and Stansell had found himself wanting to follow the man. It was a new experience for him. When the F-15s were withdrawn, Stansell had stayed behind rather than return to a new desk job at his old base. And when the Iranians sent an invasion fleet across the Persian Gulf against Ras Assanya, Stansell had watched Waters fight for his wing's survival, launching his F-4s against the oncoming ships, forcing himself to sacrifice them while he evacuated his men and women. Stansell had run the evacuation for Waters, and had been especially impressed by how reluctant the men and women of the 45th were to leave—most wanted to stay behind and fight. Waters' influence reached deep.

And then those final hours assaulted Stansell . . . images of the civil engineers and the herculean task of keeping the runway open while two C-130s dodged artillery barrages shuttling people out, the last five F-4s escaping, and Waters being killed in an artillery salvo when he tried to surrender the rear guard rather than sacrifice them. Command had fallen to Stansell, and he had been obliged to surrender the 45th. Afterward the Iranians had interrogated Stansell . . .

Waters . . . who could replace him?

The sign announcing Fredericksburg brought Stansell back. He was sweating. The quiet beauty of the town helped calm him and he understood why Eichler chose to retire here. It was easy finding the two-story white-framed house. He took a deep breath, put his memories back into their carefully guarded box and rang the doorbell. A plump, white-haired old woman answered the bell. "You must be Colonel Stansell, please come in." She led him down a hallway to a study. "The Brigadier never says much," she warned him. Her soft Southern accent, the way she was dressed and the house all made Stansell think of a more courtly, softer way of life. She ushered him into a wood paneled room. The French doors were open to the warm October morning, letting the sun shine in on Melvin "Messy" Eichler, Brigadier General USAF (Retired).

"Brigadier, Colonel Stansell is here," she announced before leaving them alone.

"The bastards don't know how to do it," Eichler said. The cancer killing him had extracted its price. The early stages of the disease and chemotherapy had wasted him. Now it was bloating him as his systems closed down. But there was nothing wrong with his voice. It still carried command.

"Pardon, sir."

"How to rescue those POWs. I'm not stupid, just dying. Cunningham wants you to figure out how to do it. Right?"

Leukemia had not defeated the searing intellect and blunt words that had made the maverick intelligence officer such a controversial figure. Eichler's career extended back to World War II and the OSS. He had been a driving force under General Curtis LeMay in the early days of the Air Force and had later become an expert in special operations. If he had been a pilot and worn wings he would have made four stars. And if he had kept his mouth shut during Vietnam. He had repeatedly told the top brass and the President how they were making a mess of it, earning his nickname "Messy." He told them how to use special operations to fight the war but no one listened and he had been retired.

"They didn't bother to ask when they tried to get the hostages out of the American embassy in Iran. 'Eagle Claw' was a fiasco. Should have hung a few of the bastards out to dry on that one. And Grenada . . . a world-class fuckup that we managed by sheer mass. We should have gone in at night, only the Rangers saved our bacon. Learn from them—" Stansell started to interrupt but Eichler waved him to silence. "Anna's not going to let me talk long, so listen. You need good intelligence. Without it, you're dead. You've got to know the rules of special operations. A special operations force does not hold ground or try to defend a place. Ignore rules like that and you'll get your ass blown off.

"Your team needs to be totally self-contained. Everyone works for you—ground, air, intel, maintenance, everyone. No split command. It's your show. And no duds, everyone pulls his own weight. Don't rely on your machines. One hundred percent backup for aircraft. Avoid helicopters if you can. For God's sake, keep it simple, make it fast." Eichler leaned back in his chair, his breathing labored, tired from talking. His eyes closed, and Stansell could see the man's body relax.

After a few minutes Stansell stood up, walked to the French doors, went into the hall, surprised to see Anna Eichler standing there leaning against a wall.

She walked him to the door. "He was wrong, you know. I would have let him talk. It's his last chance." She stopped at the door and put her hand on his cheek. "Thank you. Both our boys are dead, he's given this one to you. Please do it right."

* * *

Stansell drove through the town until he found the Waters address. This time a handsome middle-aged woman answered the door. "Mrs. Waters, I'm Colonel Rupe Stansell. I called yesterday."

"Oh, yes. Sara is expecting you." She smiled at his confusion. "I'm Martha Marshall, Sara's mother." Stansell followed her into the combination kitchen and family room. A young woman was on the floor changing a baby's diaper.

She stood and held the baby up for inspection. "Melissa, meet Colonel Rupert Stansell. He knew your father."

The colonel was obviously at a loss for words. Sara Waters was in her late twenties and beautiful. Her dark-gold hair cascaded to her shoulders and her brown eyes held a warmth and friendliness. Giving birth to Melissa had not hurt her figure. She decided to let him off the hook. "We hadn't been married too long. I met Anthony when I was in the Air Force working at the Watch Center."

Within a few minutes, Melissa was cradled on his lap and he felt comfortable with the two women. Mrs. Marshall invited him to dinner and suggested he and Sara take Melissa for a walk while she finished preparing the meal.

Sara pushed the stroller as they walked down a tree-lined street. "Please tell me about Anthony and that last day," she said. She turned to him, her eyes calm. "I've got to know. They never returned his body."

Stansell decided that Sara was asking for blunt honesty. "I don't think they will," he said. "The Iranians interrogated me for over twelve hours after I surrendered the base. They were only concerned with finding your husband. They wanted him bad. Two guards took me out to the security police bunker where he was when the last artillery barrage walked across the base. It took two direct hits. Not much left. I couldn't identify anything."

"How did it happen?"

"Artillery was chewing us up. The civil engineers worked all day to get enough runway open to launch our last F-4s. I was hoping we could get the C-130s in again and get some more of our people out. We got the F-4s launched but no luck on the C-130s. About three hundred of us were left. Mostly security police, some maintenance, wounded, and civil engineers . . . They wouldn't evac out. Even when they could. Your husband ordered an intelligence officer out, Bill Carroll—"

"I know Bill," Sara said. "He wouldn't leave."

"He didn't."

"And you didn't either."

Stansell shook his head. They walked in silence for a few moments. "Near the end he hadn't slept for two days. He was dog-tired. There was a lull in the fighting. He told me to run the show and wake him up in an hour. I let him sleep for over three hours. When I did wake him he didn't get on my case for letting him sleep so long, just asked for the current status. When I did he knew what he had to do—surrender, stop the waste. He was killed before he could do it . . .

"There was something about the man, I wanted to serve under him. I'm not easily led, certainly not given to hero worship, but I would have followed that man just about anywhere."

"I followed him too," she said.

After dinner Stansell stayed longer than he intended before heading back to Washington. He drove the Omni north, still preferring the old highway. Mado had outlined the plan after the meeting with Cunningham, and he had spent Saturday night in the Watch Center with an analyst going over intelligence from Iran. Eichler's advice kept going around in his head. Pieces were fitting together. He could make it work—

A dark blue car flashed into his rearview mirror. "Looks like the same BMW I saw driving down," he mumbled. As the BMW accelerated and overtook him Stansell glanced at the two men in the car. Both were dark-complected and wearing sunglasses. The BMW accelerated away, disappearing into the Sunday evening traffic, and Stansell found himself breathing hard. "You can't get paranoid every time you see someone that looks like an Iranian," he told himself. "And you've got to stop talking to yourself."

Stansell's pencil traced the first two letters of the BMW's license plate—AN—the only two numbers he had been able to read when it had briefly pulled abreast of his car. He crumpled the paper up and threw it in a corner, then sketched a diagram of the prison where the POWs were being held. His pencil seemed to move of its own accord, creating an oblique view of the compound, much like a pilot would see as he approached it from low level. The drawing skill that he'd always had allowed him to add surrounding vegetation and buildings, and his artist's eye had no trouble changing the vertical reconnaissance photos the Watch Center had shown him to another angle with different perspective and details.

Why does this look so familiar? he thought. He was a military history buff from way back, did this come from a book or . . . ? As though doodling, the pencil changed the flat roof on the three-story main building to a sloped roof. Something was moving deep inside his memory, emerging . . . He threw the pad to the floor beside the easy chair he was stretched out in, then got up and walked around the VOQ room, stopping at the window, staring into the night—

"My God," he whispered, "it's Amiens jail," where the Gestapo in World War II held hundreds of French Resistance fighters and the RAF raided it to help break them out . . . Was it a farfetched leap from then to now, or a possible way out for those POWs?

CHAPTER 5

D MINUS 30

THE PENTAGON

Simon Mado was standing in front of an easel in his office. Rough block letters at the top of the twenty-by-thirty-inch briefing charts on the easel spelled out "Top Secret."

"The President wants the POWs out within a month."

"A D-day within thirty days—that's going to be tough," Stansell said.

"I've worked up a milestone chart showing what's got to be done if we're going to be ready," Mado said. "It's D minus thirty today." He pointed to the chart that was numbered from thirty down to one and filled with neatly printed notes showing what had to be accomplished by each day. It was an ambitious plan. "Use this week to get an intelligence and training section together, find a training site and complete the operations plan. While you're doing that I'll line up the C-130s and the army unit that will be going in. By D minus twenty-three, next Monday, I want you in place at the training site ready to bed down the C-130s and the army and start training. By Tuesday, D minus twenty-two, have the ops plan completed. After you talk to Allen Camm at the CIA today, touch base with Air Force Special Activities Center at Fort Belvoir. I've told them you're coming."

The meeting over, Stansell left, impressed by the general's work. No wonder he's a fast-burner and made general so fast, he thought as he headed for the Pentagon's huge parking lot, hoping he could remember where he had left his car. Eventually he located it and was soon headed toward the exit that led to the George Washington Memorial Parkway and Langley, Virginia, home of the CIA. In spite of himself, he kept looking for a blue BMW in his rearview mirror.

Heavy traffic on the parkway turned the seven mile drive into a twenty minute ordeal, and a white Chevrolet sedan three cars back kept changing lanes with him. He was so intent on watching the Chevrolet that he almost rear-ended a car in front of him. A prominent sign over the parkway pointed to the CIA's exit in plenty of time for him to make the turnoff. The Chevy sped by in the inside lane. You're getting paranoid, he cautioned himself.

A bright, protypically eager-looking college girl was waiting for him at the security desk inside the main entrance. She looked all of twenty years. After signing him in, she led the way through the building, up to the third floor. Stansell noticed many of the hallways were next to the windows and that the offices were set inside, windowless.

"Worked for the company long?" he asked.

"We don't call it that. Not long. I'm Mr. Camm's gofer." She beamed at him, then ushered him into Camm's office and left.

"Well, Colonel Stansell, what can we do for the Air Force?"

The man extending his hand was clearly old school—establishment—tall and slender with a mane of carefully styled, graying hair. He wore a dark gray tailored suit and a regimental tie. His old, well-brushed shoes added to the image of understated refinement. Allen J. Camm was a member in good standing of the old Harvard-Yale-Princeton triumvirate at the CIA.

"General Cunningham suggested I contact you to open a channel for a special Air Force operation," Stansell said.

"We prefer to funnel all our information through the DIA." Camm's accent was proper Bostonian.

"We're going to need direct access, if possible. I talked to Brigadier Eichler yesterday and he stressed the need for *current* intelligence."

"Ah, the POWs, no doubt. Sorry to hear about The Brigadier, he died yesterday evening." Camm let the news sink in, gauging Stansell's reaction.

"I'm very sorry to hear that," he said, but was hardly surprised. "You're right about the POWs. General Cunningham seemed to think you're the man to see . . ."

"It will take a major policy decision to open a new channel and my office can't make that decision. I'll have to take it to the Director, and Mr. Burke has a rather full plate right now. But if you forward your request in writing I'll put it before him." Camm pressed a button on his intercom panel. He was dismissing Stansell.

"Thanks for your time, Mr. Camm. I'll get the request to you."

The self-styled gofer reappeared at the door and chatted about the changing weather as they walked back to the entrance. After saying good-by Susan Fisher walked briskly back to her office, made a phone call, picked up two files and went directly into Camm's office. In real life she was the case officer he had assigned to the POWs.

"Well?" Camm said.

"We got some good ID shots. No right ear makes him easy to pick out." The cutesy college-coed act was gone. "This is the first I've heard of the Air Force planning a rescue mission. Leachmeyer's got a well-developed plan in rehearsal right now at Fort Bragg. Looks like the services are competing with each other again. You know Cunningham."

"He's a wild card."

"We've got a team monitoring the action-arm of the Islamic Jihad. They've at least five agents operating in the U.S., and the team reported two of the Jihadis followed Stansell yesterday. Apparently, he made them. They were driving a blue BMW. Very damn obvious. We put a surveillance team on Stansell to see if the Jihadis followed up. Stansell made our people this morning."

"Is he that good? And is the Islamic Jihad onto the rescue mission?"

"We don't think so. Two other Jihadis are at Holloman Air Force Base in New Mexico. They've staked out the two sergeants who rescued Stansell, killed the guards and dragged him out of Ras Assanya when they broke out. It tracks with a report out of Beirut. The Jihad is trying to kidnap or assassinate the three men who escaped out of Ras Assanya, which would embarrass the U.S. at the Geneva negotiations."

"How did the Jihad get onto Stansell so quick?"

"One of their agents has taken over a sergeant that works in Pass and ID at the Pentagon." She handed Camm a sharp color photograph. "She's turned him every which way but loose. Sex still works. She's working two others."

Camm handed the photo back to Fisher. "Few men would stand a chance against someone like her. Okay, keep on top of the situation. When we get a request from Stansell through channels, send him a copy of everything we've given Leachmeyer and the JSOA on the POWs. Make sure he gets a copy of anything new we send to the JSOA. Give the FBI enough information on the Jihad agents so they can roll them up. For God's sake, make 'em work for it. If the Bureau finds out we're operating inside the U.S. again . . ." Camm paused, then: "See if you can turn the woman. We might be able to use her. Find out who's financing the Jihad's operation here and which embassy is providing them support. I don't like the Islamic Jihad expanding their operations into the U.S. They specialize in hostages."

Fisher was scratching a few notes. "Should we sanitize and pass on intelligence from Deep Furrow to the JSOA and Stansell?"

"No way." Camm was determined to protect Deep Furrow, the net of contacts and operatives he was developing inside Iran. "Deep Furrow would surprise too many people who don't need that kind of shock right now," he told the young woman.

Stansell was back on the Parkway heading for Fort Belvoir. His eyes kept darting to the rearview mirror, looking for a tail. You're not being paranoid, just prudent, he told himself. The traffic was lighter as he passed the Pentagon and continued south into Virginia. What a complete waste of time that was, he thought, the CIA is caught up in bureaucratic bullshit and old school ties.

A sharp MP at Fort Belvoir's main gate directed him to the northern part of the post, where an isolated compound housed the Air Force Special Activities Center. A guard at the Center escorted Stansell through the double chain-link fence.

The Special Activities Center was responsible for the management of all Air Force human intelligence activities, HUMINT, the Air Force's version of old-fashioned spying. The Center started life as the 1127th Field Activities Group, a collection of oddball con artists whose job was to get the right people to talk. When the generals couldn't stand having such a screwball outfit in the Air Force, they changed its name to the 7612th Air Intelligence Group in a try for respectability and conformity. When that didn't work they changed it to the Special Activities Center and clamped a bureaucratic umbrella over it. The building Stansell walked into looked and smelled like a military organization.

The brigadier general running the outfit was a no-nonsense type, and Stansell snapped a salute when he was shown into his office. A prominent autographed photo of Eichler on the wall caught his attention.

"Sorry to hear about The Brigadier," Stansell said.

A quizzical look on the one-star's face told him that the Center had not yet heard.

"He died Sunday evening, I'm told. Probably right after I talked to him—"

"You talked to him?"

"Yes, sir. About rescuing the POWs. He was very weak but entirely lucid."

"That would be just like Messy." The general picked up the phone and relayed the news to his executive officer. "Thanks for telling us. The Brigadier was special around here." He rolled a pencil in his fingers, studying Stansell. "What can you tell me about your conversation?"

Stansell recounted the visit and the reason behind it.

"You mentioned Simon Mado."

"He's my boss, sir. General Cunningham has made him the task force commander."

"Mado is an asshole, but a damn competent one. Well, The Brigadier was right, intelligence is the key. You're going to need all the help you can get. A beautifully planned and executed mission can go bust without up-to-date accurate intel. The Son Tay raid to free sixty-one POWs in North Vietnam in 1970 was a textbook example. Perfect, except when they got there the POWs were gone. An old-fashioned operative on the ground would have prevented that. The Center isn't allowed to run foreign operatives any more but we can do other things for you."

The general hit his intercom. "Dewa, can you please come in?" For the first time the general smiled. "Just one of our civilian intelligence specialists. Fluent in Farsi."

The woman who entered the office stood five feet three in high heels and seemed a direct descendant of the women who inspired the Rubáiyát of Omar Khayyám. Black shoulder-length hair framed her dark eyes and fair complexion. The general introduced Stansell to Dewa Rahimi.

She extended her hand. "My pleasure, Colonel. I've read about you and what happened at Ras Assanya." There was no trace of a foreign accent.

"Colonel Stansell is working on a mission to get the POWs out of

Kermanshah. I want the Center to give him all the help we can. He's going to need an operative on the ground, which we don't have. You've debriefed quite a few Iranians. Let's see if we can pull some-one out who would be willing to work for him and go back inside. I want you to be his contact with us. Give him whatever he needs."

Dewa played it with a straight face.

"Colonel, if you like, I'll detail Dewa to you on temporary duty for your intelligence section. Besides speaking Farsi, she's a com-puter whiz. But we want her back."

Stansell caught himself from expressing excessive gratitude. "Thank you, general, that would be most fine. I can't think of anything else for now. Thanks for your support. Much more, I might say, than I got from the CIA."

Rahimi spoke up as he was about to leave. "Colonel Stansell, I need your number."

Stansell stared.

"I need to know who to call so I can report to work."

The general smiled. Dewa did have that effect.

THE ZAGROS MOUNTAINS, IRAN

The blow ricocheted off Carroll's shoulder before hitting his head. But the boy had swung the rifle butt with enough force to knock him out of his seat. Carroll was vaguely aware of a woman's shrill voice—"Kill him . . ."

The driver pulled the bus to the side of the road and turned off the headlights. Carroll could hear the brakes groaning through the floor-boards. A sour smell assaulted his senses. Was it the tattered rubber floor matting? He pretended unconsciousness, trying to push away the fuzz swirling through his head. All the passengers were awake, jabbering and shouting, undecided and confused.

"Kill him." It was the same woman's voice. No one seemed to be listening to her.

"Move him," a male voice said. "He's blocking the aisle." Four hands picked him up and shoved him into a seat.

Carroll didn't move, his chin on his chest. The fuzz was shred-ding, leaving a splitting headache. He could feel the right side of his head throb. What the hell had happened? He could hear most of the passengers clambering off the bus, anxious to get away and not be involved. The padding under him shifted—he was in the same seat. The side of his head didn't feel warm or moist, apparently he wasn't bleeding. Only the woman's voice dominated the conversation around him and no one seemed to be listening to her repeated demands to kill him. There was no one in charge. He listened for traffic, tried to figure a way to escape. Now he was sure they were on a deserted part of the highway. But what had given him away? He decided to risk a groan.

"Kill him—" the woman said again—"my sons, my husband, martyred, and now this foreign devil lives, filth on the earth—"

"His name is Javad Khalian," the man who had been sharing the seat with Carroll said. "He is a sergeant in the commandos of the Revolutionary Guard. He is one of the elite."

"You believe him? He is the man the Council of Guardians is looking for . . ."

"And how many suspects have they already hung?" another voice said.

Carroll decided it was time to become a player before someone with a clue took charge. He moved and groaned again, opening his eyes. A black-shrouded figure hovered in front of him. He blinked at the woman and she jumped back. A twelve-year-old boy held his AK-47, the muzzle pointed directly at him. Was he the one who had knocked him down? "Point it at the ground," he told the boy. "Only raise it when you intend to kill in the name of Allah."

"Kill him now," the woman carried on.

The boy did as Carroll said.

"The devil speaks English in his sleep. What more proof do you need?" the woman said.

At least she had given Carroll his answer.

Slowly Carroll raised his hands, looking at the boy like they were playing a game. "My papers are in my shirt pocket." He pointed at his left pocket with his chin. The boy propped the AK-47 against a seat and reached for his pocket. "No," Carroll ordered, "you are the guard. Hold the rifle ready to use if I make a wrong move. Order someone else to search me."

The boy grabbed the rifle and pointed it at Carroll before he remembered to drop the muzzle. A man made his way through the small crowd and pushed Carroll back against the window, ripping the identification papers out of Carroll's pocket.

"Now search me," Carroll ordered. He shouldered the man back as he stood up, testing the newcomer. The man pushed back but not hard enough to make him sit down. "I said search me."

The man awkwardly patted him down. "I will be the one to pull the trigger," he told Carroll.

Carroll shrugged the man's hands off before they reached the knife taped to the inside of his calf or the coiled wire in his thigh pocket. "This is the way to search," he said, and pulled off his camouflaged shirt. He pointed to the long scar on his stomach that was a reminder of a bicycle accident in the sixth grade. "I was wounded four years ago in front of Basra." He pointed to a burn scar on his right shoulder, the result of brushing against a hot exhaust pipe when he was working under his first car. "From a phosphorus shell. Now show me your scars."

Even the woman was silent as Carroll established control.

"Enough of this, let's finish it. You have my papers. Where is the nearest unit of the Guards? Which of you is going to call Abbas Gharazi of the Saltanatabad Revolutionary Committee in Tehran? He will describe me to you."

The crowd was silent—Gharazi was well known as a dedicated butcher.

"No," Carroll said, "you do not walk away from this. You knock me to the ground"—he could see the boy wince—"and you demand my death. You say you will pull the trigger"—he stared at the man who had searched him—"and I say enough, where are the Guards headquartered around here?"

The bus driver, standing at the rear of the crowd, wanted nothing to do with this angry commando. "Sixteen kilometers behind us."

"Good. We will delay you no longer. This brave man and woman who only bear imaginary scars in their heads will take me to them." He gestured at the two. "We will walk or commandeer a passing car—"

"But he speaks English in his sleep," the woman persisted.

"I am an interpreter and I also speak Arabic and French. I must have been dreaming. In which language was I speaking?"

No one was really sure. They only knew he had been speaking a foreign language that sounded like English. The woman seemed momentarily subdued but hardly convinced.

"You,"—Carroll nodded at the boy—"must make a decision. Either give my rifle to this heap of shit"—he nodded at the man who had searched him—"or keep it. It has served me well in the holy wars against our enemies. It will serve you well. Or you can turn it in when you reach home and explain to the authorities how you got it."

The bus driver had returned to his seat and started the engine, urging them to get off his bus and let him escape this business.

"I'll need the rifle to guard him," the searcher said, reaching for the AK-47. The boy shook his head and backed up, clutching the assault rifle.

"Here, take this," another passenger said, shoving an old pistol at the man, eager to be rid of him and the commando.

"My bag," Carroll said, and reached under the seat. He threw the shoulder bag at the woman and led the way off the bus, putting his shirt back on. The woman started to protest but the other passengers shoved her out and threw her suitcase after her. The man picked up his bag and followed, hurried along by shouts.

"I will use your rifle well," the boy called from the bus.

"*Insh' Allah*," Carroll replied.

The bus driver snapped the door close as he ground away, kicking up a cloud of dust, leaving the three standing beside the road in the dark.

"Kill him now, before it is too late," the woman said. "He is trouble—"

"But what if you're right?" Carroll said. "Ten thousand dollars in gold?" Greed lit up in the man's eyes. The three sat down and waited for a car. After a few minutes Carroll stretched out, waiting for his headache to ease its pounding. He even fell asleep.

ALAMOGORDO, NEW MEXICO

"Ray, you smell." Lorrie set a mug of beer on the bar in front of the sergeant. "Don't you ever take a shower?"

"Get off my back. Take showers all the time." Staff Sergeant Raymond Byers was the only customer in Piccolo Pete's Pizza Palace in Alamogordo, New Mexico. He had worked a late shift at Holloman Air Force Base getting his F-15 ready for an early morning flight and had stopped for a beer on his way home. Byers had dogged Hydraulics until they fixed the leaking speed brake actuator to his satisfaction. As usual he had spent another half hour cleaning up their mess after the technician had signed off the maintenance forms. He kept the best jet in the wing.

Lorrie leaned across the bar and sniffed, letting him look down her blouse. "Not today, you didn't. Who knows, I might be a little interested if you didn't always smell like a grease pit." She flipped the flap of his unbuttoned shirt pocket.

"*Okay*, I'll be sure to take a shower and smell like a baby next time before I come here."

She flounced away, cleaning up the bar and getting ready to close.

Byers turned and leaned against the bar, stretching his lanky frame out. He was working on his second mug of beer. He liked watching Lorrie move.

Lorrie started turning off lights. "Finish your beer, I need a ride home."

"No shower?"

"Shut up. I'm talking about a ride."

He waited by the door while she finished locking up. They walked out to his waiting Jeep, and the girl admired the immaculate 1974 customized CJ5.

"This have a top? It's cold tonight."

Byers handed her the fatigue jacket he wore on the flight line. She zipped it up and settled into the custom seat. He helped her with the shoulder harness as she strapped in. The big V-8 engine came to life on the first blip of the starter and he wheeled out of the parking lot. After his F-15, the Jeep was the most important thing in his life.

A dark Thunderbird shot by them, its headlights off.

"Assholes," Byers said, "barely saw the son of a bitch . . ."

The Thunderbird cut hard to the left and skidded to a halt, blocking the road. Byers jammed at the brakes and dragged the Jeep to a stop. The doors of the Thunderbird swung open and two men got out.

"You dumb—" One of the men had reached inside his coat and pulled out a gun. Byers hit reverse and accelerated backward, throwing Lorrie against her shoulder harness. He jerked the wheel back and forth as two shots hit the Jeep, one ricocheting off the winch on the front bumper, the other slamming through the windshield. He spun the wheel, skidding the Jeep around.

The two men jumped into the Thunderbird and backed around, coming after the Jeep. Byers, seeing the Thunderbird turn after them, floored the accelerator and the Jeep leaped forward, the speedometer touching a hundred miles an hour. He headed south, looking for open country. They were on the outskirts of town when Byers slammed on the brakes and turned off the road, heading cross-country, fighting the wheel as they bounced into an arroyo. He drove two hundred yards down the dry stream bed and stopped.

"Stay here," he told Lorrie. "I want to get a look at those bastards." He reached under his seat and fumbled for a moment, pulling out a .357 handgun and running back down the arroyo and scrambling up the bank.

Lorrie, scared, twisted around when she heard a footfall on the bank above her head and almost screamed before Byers jumped down and hopped inside the Jeep.

"Ragheads," he muttered, starting the motor. "They're gone."

"You really know how to show a girl a good time."

CHAPTER 6

D MINUS 29

THE ZAGROS MOUNTAINS, IRAN

"A car is coming," the woman said, gathering her chador around her for warmth. Bill Carroll and the two Iranians had been waiting beside the road for hours; now it was early morning. The man stood and walked into the road to wave down the car. Carroll stood with him and unzipped his pants. As the car slowed, he urinated in full view of the headlights. The driver ignored the frantic waving of the Iranian and sped away, disgusted with the sight.

The man came back and waved his pistol at Carroll. "You insulted him, I should kill you for that—"

"If you had let me relieve myself when I asked earlier it would not've happened." Carroll ignored the man and sat back down. "I think we should start walking, it will help keep us warm. Besides, I'm tired of this."

The Iranian could not make up his mind. He wished he had ignored the incident like the other passengers on the bus, but the young man had spoken a foreign language in his sleep and there was the promise of a reward . . . still, the man did seem to be what he claimed, which meant trouble for him and the woman. He cursed his impetuous behavior, and the woman. "Yes, you are right. She will carry the bags." He waved the pistol at the woman, making her carry Carroll's bag and the two battered suitcases. "As a soldier of the Jihad you know what we do is necessary."

Covering his ass, Carroll thought, hedging his bets. "Yes. I understand your position, I will explain that your conduct was proper and that I would have done the same if I were you." Carroll could see some of the tension drain from the man.

It became colder as they trudged up a long grade. It was time to act. He couldn't afford to carry on this charade any longer. "May we stop? I need to relieve myself again, this time I need to squat."

The man agreed and told the woman to put the cases down. She crumpled to the ground, worn out. Carroll walked toward two large boulders a hundred feet away. When he was out of sight he pulled the coiled wire out of his pocket and scrambled in the dirt until he found two small stones of the right size and shape. He wrapped an end of the wire around each stone for handles and tugged the wire tight. Next he crawled to the far end of the rocks, crouched, checking to find the man standing at the place where Carroll had entered behind the boulders, looking the other way. The distance was too great to sneak up on him, so Carroll retreated into the rocks and walked noisily back toward the man, still out of sight. When he estimated he was about twenty feet away he stopped and found a shadowy niche to hide in, took off his shirt, not wanting to get blood on it, scuffled his feet and made a loud grunting sound.

"What's the problem?" The Iranian was closer than he thought.

"My ankle, it's very dark back here. Can you help me." Carroll pulled back into the shadows as he heard the man's approaching footsteps. The Iranian stopped in front of the niche. Carroll was looking at the right side of the man's head, barely three feet away.

"Where are you?"

Carroll swung the garrote over the man's head and jerked. "Here." It was too dark to see the surprise in his eyes. Carroll kicked out the back of the man's right knee and dropped him. The dying sounds were quickly muted . . . he doubted that the woman could hear them. Four spasms and he was dead.

Slowly Carroll picked his way back to the road. About thirty feet from where he left the woman he stopped and ripped apart the bandages that held the knife to his calf. Unless a searcher was very careful it could pass for a dressing. When he reached the road, the woman was gone.

Shivering from the cold, he stood looking up and down the road. The two suitcases were piled with his bag. She must have heard more than he'd thought and panicked. Which way did she run? The gun, who had it? Probably still with the man, but he didn't have time to search for it now. You were careless, he warned himself.

He walked along the side of the road, calculating the woman was tired and had run downhill. Every few hundred feet he would stop, listen, look around. A quarter of a mile later he caught the faint sour odor of the woman's chador, and then it was gone. He sat down and waited, wishing he had put his shirt back on.

A rustling behind a clump of bushes.

"Come out, old mother, we must continue with this."

A dark shadow stood and headed back up the road. The woman's steps were hesitant and unsure as she walked.

She knows, Carroll thought. Damn it. He closed the distance between them, catching up with her, holding the knife in his right hand. She did not stop or turn. He circled his left arm around her neck and pulled her back, driving the knife into her chest, into her heart.

He trudged back to the boulders, carrying her. The Jihad had another victim.

He laid the woman's body beside the man's and collapsed, shaking, but not from the cold.

NORTHERN NEVADA

"Awesome, totally AWE-some." Ambler Furry, Jack Locke's Weapon Systems Officer, couldn't shut up.

Locke was ready to tell him to go cold mike to stop the incessant chatter over the intercom but decided not to. Ambler would stop talking if things got hot. Like Furry, Locke was new to the E model of the F-15 and had only been recently assigned to Luke Air Force Base, upgrading into the Air Force's latest jet. The transition into the new bird had been easy and proved to be a diversion, letting him put the memories of combat in the Persian Gulf and his old fighter, the F-4E, behind him. He raised his seat a fraction of an inch, still looking for the best sitting position for his six-foot frame. Satisfied, he cross-checked the digital readouts on his Head-up Display and scanned the horizon.

The young captain sitting in the pit of Locke's two-place F-15E Strike Eagle was like a kid with a new toy—he couldn't get enough of the systems he had to play with. Like most wizzos, Weapon Systems Officer, Furry was fascinated by the capabilities of the Hughes-developed APG-70 radar and what it could do when used with their mouthful-named Low-Altitude Navigation and Targeting

Infrared System for Night as well as on-board computers. No wonder they shortened the system to LANTIRN.

Furry kept playing with the four video screens in front of him. The missionized cockpit had been developed using state-of-the-art electronics and presented all the information the wizzo needed. Furry controlled the left two screens with the hand-controller on the left console and the right two screens with the right-hand controller. He was uninterested in the stick in front of him and would only fly the jet reluctantly. He figured that Locke only existed to drive him around the sky so he could do his job.

The Tactical Situation Diplay, TSD, an electronic moving map that was tied in with the ring laser gyro in the inertial navigation system, scrolled on the far left MultiPurpose Color Display, the MPCD, constantly updating their position and showing them their route. The next screen in was a MultiPurpose Display without color and it was blank. Furry had selected air-to-ground radar for that screen, and as they were flying a limited electronic-emission profile, the radar was in standby. The third screen, an MPD, was programmed to show the pilot's Head-Up Display, HUD, and Furry was seeing what Locke was seeing through the wide-angle twenty-one-by-twenty-eight inch HUD. Unfortunately he did not have the holographic effect that could be projected onto the pilot's HUD. Furry had the far right MPCD slaved to the Tactical Electronic Warfare System.

"Cosmic, ab-SO-lutely cosmic," Furry mumbled to himself.

Locke agreed—the instrument panel in front of him hardly resembled a traditional cockpit. Three video screens and the Up Front Controller dominated his main panel. Actually the UFC was a computer keyboard that controlled the Strike Eagle's systems and was located directly underneath the HUD. Locke could call up the different menus with his left hand and never take his eyes off the HUD. Underneath the UFC, the Tactical Situation Display showed Locke where they were on a color display. The right MPD was tied into the Terrain Following Radar in the LANTIRN navigation pod hung underneath the right intake. His left MPD was tied into the air-to-ground radar. The only concession to tradition was in the lower left-hand corner of the instrument panel, where five small back-up gauges were nestled.

Locke squeaked the F-15 down another fifty feet and tweaked the throttles, riveting the airspeed on 480 knots groundspeed. He checked the Terrain Following Radar and decided it was being honest and the presentation jibed with the desert terrain he saw in front of them. Things happened fast below three hundred feet. Locke could have coupled the autopilot to the TFR but chose to manual Terrain Fly because he liked to hand-fly the jet. Furry was right, the fighter was sweet but its low wing loading and high gust response gave them a much harsher beating than the F-4 did at low level. Sometimes he missed the old bird.

"Turn point in thirty seconds," Furry told him. "New heading 198."

Locke waited for Furry to tell him when to start the turn. Once they overflew the next turn point, the TSD would program the command steering bar in the HUD to the next steer point. But he preferred crew coordination. Locke wanted to use the equipment, not rely on it. Combat had taught him some hard lessons about what battle damage did to the magic in black boxes.

"Turn . . . now, 198."

Locke loaded the F-15E with four-and-a-half Gs through the turn and rolled out. Furry had led the turn and they were right on track . . .

Locke and Furry were on a single-ship mission working their way south through the mountains of northern Nevada heading for Tolicha airfield, a target on one of Nellis Air Force Base's numerous bombing and gunnery ranges. Tolicha was set up to resemble an eastern European air base for U.S. aircrews to practice on during Red Flag exercises. But for the mission Locke was flying it was a friendly field and Locke was the intruder. Somewhere along the route he could expect a Combat Air Patrol of two F-15s to jump him. Their job was to find and intercept him before he reached the target; his job was to get past them and drop a bomb on the airfield.

"Okay, Amb, start looking for Snake. He'll CAP someplace around here." Locke had a healthy respect for Snake Houserman's abilities. It was going to be hard to sneak by the Snake and as long as the Eagle's pulse Doppler radar was working, Snake should be able to find them. Locke inched lower. That's not the answer, he told himself. Maybe some terrain-masking might do the trick—get some mountains between him and Snake. "Hey, Amb. I want to get out of this valley. Everyone flies down it. Reprogram the turn points so we go down the western side of Stillwater Range and over Carson Sink. We'll turn over Salt Wells and dogleg back to our original course."

Locke could hear Ambler Furry mumbling as he picked new turn points out of his Eagle Aid and punched them into his up-front controller. "Roll out on a heading of 182 on the other side of the ridge. You have steering to Salt Wells . . . now." The command steering bar on the HUD swung and the miles to go counter rolled to 78. Furry was fast, Locke thought, but not as fast as Thunder Bryant, his old backseater in F-4s.

They were still on the wrong side of the mountain range if he intended to fly over Carson Sink. "When I hop us over do a quick search for bogies," Locke said. He scrolled the TFR presentation off his left MPD and called up the air-to-air radar. The screen showed only guidelines but would come to life when the radar was turned on.

"Inverted again? Don't do this to me," Furry complained, his fingers flying over his hand controllers and UFC.

Locke turned the Eagle to the west and headed for the mountains they were paralleling. He gently stroked the throttles and the new F-100-PW-229 engines responded crisply. He lifted the jet up the slope, rolled it upside down as they created the ridge and pulled the velocity vector back down to the steering box in the HUD, keeping them at two hundred feet, their clearance-set limit. Locke, using gravity to help reduce his exposure time when they were above the mountains, didn't worry about the overload warning system talking to him about pulling excessive Gs. They were stressed for nine Gs throughout the flight regime. Now he rolled upright as they came down the western slope and turned onto their new heading.

When they crested the ridge Furry hit the EMIS LIMIT switch and brought the high volume radar to life. When Locke rolled out on the down slope, Furry hit the EMIS LIMIT switch again and returned them to silent running. During the few seconds the radar was operating it had swept the horizon for hostile aircraft and fed information into its processor. The results showed up on the screens in the cockpit—they had four aircraft in front of them and Furry had a frozen radar picture on his display.

Someone had it very right when they called the F-15E Super Eagle.

"Got the primary target on the TSD," Furry told Locke. "They're over Salt Wells. Want to look again?"

Locke glanced down at his TSD and saw a red aircraft symbol right over Salt Wells. Furry hit the EMIS LIMIT switch again, allowing the radar a single sweep before returning to silent running. The same targets reappeared on the radar scope, still over Salt Wells.

"Probably some Navy birds out of Fallon," Locke said. "Snake's a flight of two and he'd never set up a wheel to circle a target. That's dumber than dirt."

"If it's below average headwork it must be Navy," Furry agreed. "Oh, oh, just got a tickle on the TEWS, we've got an interceptor sweeping the area with a pulse Doppler. That's Snake. Looks like he's to the east of Salt Wells. We would've flown right under him on our old track."

"He'll still find us," Locke said, again lowering his altitude, searching for a way to out-fox the Snake. "Go Guard, front radio."

Without looking, Furry's right hand dropped down on his up-front controller and rotated the present channel selector on the left until G appeared, switching the UHF radio switch to GUARD, the preset emergency channel on 243.0 MHz. One of Furry's jobs in the back seat was to be an audio-commanded radio-frequency shifter.

Locke pushed the radio transmit button on the throttle quadrant forward with his left thumb. "If you Airdales over Salt Wells would like some action, come up 356.0."

Furry pushed the channel-manual button on his UFC and switched them to 356.0. Snake Houserman was on the same frequency.

Almost immediately, Pedro flight checked in on 356.0 with a flight of four.

"I think we've got ourselves four F-18 Hornets in the area," Locke said.

"Pedro flight, this is an Air Force assigned frequency," Snake radioed.

"Rog," Pedro flight lead acknowledged. "We're in a wheel, beating up the old emergency field near Salt Wells, practicing a little dive bombing. Please stand clear."

"Almost perfect," Locke told Furry, heading straight for Salt Wells. "If Snake wants us, he's going to have to go through a nest of Hornets."

"Pedro flight," Locke radioed, "this is Dobo. I'm transiting the area underneath you. Please hold your altitude until I'm clear." He could clearly see the F-18s through his HUD along with digital readouts on his own altitude and airspeed. He didn't need to look inside the cockpit.

"A radar's got us," Furry said, monitoring his TEWS. "Still east of Salt Wells. Must be Snake."

"That's fine as long as the Navy is between us and him."

"Pedro flight, please clear the area," Snake transmitted. "I intend to intercept Dobo."

Pedro lead answered, "This is our airspace and we like Dobo."

Locke flew his dark gray F-15E down the valley, heading straight for a small collection of buildings surrounded by a cyclone fence near Salt Wells. The four F-18 Hornets were breaking out of their wheel pattern and zooming toward the east.

"Pedro one and two are on the left F-15," the Navy pilot radioed. "Three and four take the right man. Both are dead meat."

"Rog, Pedro. This is Snake and Jake. Keep the flight above five hundred feet AGL and everything is copacetic."

"Screw you, flyboy. Fight's on."

"I think Snake's got his hands full," Locke told Furry. He pushed the throttles up, touching 540 knots as he headed toward Tolicha.

"We got two of 'em and scared the other two so bad even their laundress knows for sure," Snake said. Locke and Furry had met Snake and his wingman Jake in one of the 461st's briefing rooms for a debrief when they had all recovered at Luke AFB. A debrief with Snake Houserman after a flight was always a colorful affair.

"Amb, what was our bomb score on Tolicha?" Locke asked, his blue eyes serious.

"A bull."

"Who give's a rat's ass about iron bombs." Houserman grinned. "Like the sainted Baron von Richthofen said, roaming your allotted airspace and destroying other fighters is our job. Anything else is rubbish. That's the trouble with you friendly clowns," Snake said, pointing at Locke's 461st squadron patch, the black and gold of the Deadly Jesters, "you forgot what the fighter business is all about."

"You sure about that direct hit, Amb?" Locke could be like a bulldog and wanted to make his point that dropping bombs was an important part of their mission. Like Snake, he hadn't a clue, yet, that he would soon have a chance to prove it.

"Sure am. That would have been one busted air patch."

"Get a grip, Furry." Snake smiled, leaning back in his chair, banging against the wall of the small briefing room. "Wizzos ain't shit."

"We accomplished our mission, Snake," Locke said. "You can't say the same."

"What do you call two F-18s?"

Locke saw he couldn't reach the young pilot. He stood up and motioned Furry to follow him out.

"I think we lost that one," Furry said.

"Nope," Locke told him. "We got our bomb on target and that

was what we set out to do." He looked at his dejected backseater and slapped him on the back. "Hell, Amb, the air-to-air pukes make movies, us air-to-ground jocks make history. Cheer up, you don't win an engagement in the debrief. Besides, if that had been Snake's home airfield he would have had to divert somewhere else after shooting down the Hornets because we blew the hell out of it."

"One thing," Furry said, "how come you were so sure that Snake would be in a CAP near Salt Wells?"

"That collection of buildings we turned over at Salt Wells is a whorehouse, Amb. You got to know the opposition. Where else would you expect to find Snake?"

"Or the Navy," Furry added.

THE PENTAGON

"Rupe, I don't know if Cunningham will give you F-15s to CAP for the C-130s. You'll have to sell him on it."

Dewa Rahimi sat behind the computer console listening to Stansell and Mado. They were buried in a small office deep in the Pentagon's basement, hidden behind the guarded doors of the Air Force's Directorate of Operational Intelligence. She scanned the screen again and decided they needed to see the incident report from the Office of Special Investigations.

"Colonel," Rahimi said, breaking into their conversation, "I think you need to see this. There's an OSI incident report on a Sergeant Raymond Byers."

"Excuse me, sir. Byers is one of the sergeants who pulled me out of Ras Assanya." Stansell looked over Rahimi's shoulder reading the report, distracted by her perfume until he saw Byer's statement about hearing the men speaking Arabic.

"General, you had better read this."

Rahimi spun the screen to face Mado, who read it and gave a noncommittal "humm."

Stansell knew what he had to do. "If some Arabs are going after Byers, they might be after me. I think you may need a new mission commander."

Mado quickly arranged to see Cunningham. "Bring your map, Rupe. We can kill two birds while we're up there." Mado stopped when he reached the door. "You come too," he told Rahimi. "It's time you met Sundown."

Cunningham studied Stansell's map, tracing the route the colonel was proposing. He tried without success to visualize what a pilot would see on the low-level route through the mountains of western Iran. The general was angry with himself for losing the ability that fighter pilots needed to survive in combat. Running the Air Force had apparently dulled his ability to take a few clues and create a mental three-dimensional image of reality. Like flying a fast moving jet through mountains he had never seen before.

Mado, a master at judging Cunningham's reactions, had sensed from the moment he and Stansell had entered the general's office with Rahimi that it would be a rough meeting.

"Okay, Colonel, what the hell does this tell me?"

"The POW compound is 275 nautical miles from the tri-border region of Turkey, Iran and Iraq. For a slow mover like a C-130 at low level, that's about an hour's flying time—"

"Dammit, colonel, be specific."

"One hour and eight minutes from time of penetration of Iran's border to the prison at 240 knots indicated airspeed. Low-level all the way. Given the increasing capability of the Iranian air defense net that's a long time over hostile territory. That's why they need a combat air patrol for escort."

Cunningham lit a cigar and drew it to life. He liked the way Stansell refused to be intimidated.

Mado read the signs and started to relax but quickly put himself back on edge, giving the appearance of being worried. The cigar was the clue to the general's attitude, and Mado did not want Cunningham to know that someone could read him enough to anticipate his reactions.

"What type of aircraft do you want for the CAP?"

"Strike Eagles—F-15Es," Stansell said.

"You want to put at risk one of the most cosmic jets I own? Not at twenty-nine million dollars a copy."

"It's also the most versatile jet you have, general, and can do a lot more for us than fly a CAP. We're facing a lot of unknowns, and flexibility can make the difference."

"Back burner that for now. What's the other reason you're here?"

"General, we've seen an OSI incident report on Sergeant Byers," Mado told him, and summarized the report and Stansell's connection with Byers, believing that it fitted into the cover they were building for Delta Force. Cunningham's face told him nothing.

"Miss Rahimi," Cunningham said, "this is your area, how do you see it?"

Dewa Rahimi looked at Stansell. Everything the colonel said and did told her how much he wanted to be part of the rescue mission, and she wanted to help him. But the connection with Byers was too obvious . . . "It opens up the possibility of compromising the mission if they're also after Colonel Stansell," she said.

"Is there any indication Stansell's being watched?" Cunningham asked.

"None." She felt better.

Stansell volunteered no information about the tails. Or what seemed like tails.

"I'm not about to switch horses this early on," Cunningham said. He caught the look of relief on Rahimi's face, quickly followed by one of surprise. Maybe she suspected something . . . One smart female, he thought. He would have to think harder about how to distract her and the colonel before they tumbled onto the truth—which he hated and still hoped to overcome by making a diversion into the real thing . . .

Now Cunningham turned on the two men. "Not enough progress, you need more people to help get this thing moving. Get 'em. I can think of three reasons why this mission will fail—for starters, poor intelligence and piss-poor training. You've got to weld strangers from Air Force and Army into a tight team. Where the hell are you going to train so this doesn't turn into a fiasco? None of the crews you'll be using has ever been in combat. No test can predict how an individual will react the first time someone starts to hose him down. You need a training program. So what is it, and where?"

Stansell looked at Mado, who offered no support. "We'll have all that to you by this time next week, sir. But I still want F-15s for CAP."

Good answer, Cunningham thought. You'll make this into plenty more than a cover operation, or goddamn Quaker cannon . . . "I'll decide later when I see the threat estimate in your ops plan. Talk to Byers if you're worried about him, he may be involved in something else. Dismissed."

Stansell was convinced the meeting had turned into a disaster, especially with Cunningham's voice chasing them out of his office . . . "Don't screw this one up."

As they walked to Mado's office Dewa said, "Is that for real or a front he puts on as a commander?"

"Most of that was meant for me," Mado said. "I was trying to read him, watching his cigar, and he caught me out."

Stansell ignored the exchange. "Cunningham said to get help and get moving." There was an edge in his voice. "General, I know you're working eighteen hours a day bringing this on line, but I've got to start making things happen. I know who can help, and I need airlift."

KERMANSHAH, IRAN

Vahid Mokhtari, commandant of Kermanshah prison, stamped his feet on the hard dirt in front of the building that served as both administration and quarters for the guards. He could have waited in his four-room apartment in the corner of the second floor that over-looked the yard where the POWs stood punishment and he would have seen the car the moment it drove through the inner gate of the main entrance into the prison, but anticipation and impatience drove him outside. The two guards waiting on the entrance steps knew Mokhtari was not stamping his feet to keep warm in the cold night air.

The loud squeal of the outer iron-barred gate that opened into the entrance tunnel of the compound echoed through the quadrangle as it rolled back on its track. Mokhtari's lips twitched slightly as he turned and retreated up the steps.

He was ready for his next guest.

The two guards glanced at each other, relieved that Mokhtari ignored them. They walked down the steps when they heard the outer gate winch shut. The car was in the tunnel. After a few mo-ments they could see the inner gate split open and each half swing back, tripping the consent switch that activated the ramp. The tracks of the ramp had been greased earlier that day and now it moved silently, covering the deep pit in the entrance tunnel and allowing the car to drive through.

The headlights of the car swept the compound as it turned toward the waiting guards. The main building was dark except for the light in the office window at the end of each floor. Two heads appeared in the window of the top office on the third floor and watched the car drive in and swing up to the smaller administration building.

A series of tap codes began working through the walls of the main building, alerting the inmates of the car's arrival. Unseen faces crowded into every barred window that overlooked the compound while other inmates listened for any reaction from the guards. The building became eerily silent.

Colonel Clayton Leason, the senior ranking officer who commanded the POWs while they were in captivity, pulled himself out of his bunk and joined his cellmate at the window. "What do you think, Doc?"

"It's too late for normal business. Maybe a courier, or they're bringing another prisoner in." Both men stared into the night, looking for clues, gathering whatever wisps of information they could use to resist their captors.

When the car stopped beside the two waiting guards a man jumped out of the front passenger seat and jerked the rear door open, then reached in and pulled out the lone occupant. "She's yours," he said, and got back into the car. The driver mashed the accelerator and spun the car's wheels, kicking up a shower of dust as he headed for the gate, anxious to leave the prison.

The two guards grabbed the woman and hurried her up the steps. The black canvas bag over her head hid her features. Stiff from the long ride, she stumbled on the steps and fell, only her handcuffed wrists in front of her helping her break the fall. The guards pulled her to her feet and guided her into the building and to the basement office where Mokhtari was waiting.

The tap codes started again.

The woman pulled herself to attention when the guards released her. She could see light through the bottom of the bag and was aware that three other people were in the room. All men, she thought. Her latest set of jailers.

Mokhtari said nothing, using silence as his opening move. It became a waiting game. He pulled off his wristwatch and set it on the desk in front of him so he could time the interval.

The woman started an internal count—one thousand one, one thousand two, one thousand three . . .

Mokhtari understood the rationale behind the orders he had received from Tehran—humiliate her, extract all the information you can and then break her. In the end, send a shell back to the Americans.

His superiors, badly wanting vengeance, had picked the commandant of the prison as their weapon. It had infuriated them that a woman had been the commander of Caravan, the radar Ground Control Intercept site that had directed the fighters launching from Ras Assanya against them. They had monitored her voice over the radio as she set up engagement after engagement, never making an error. Finally they convinced themselves that she was using a newly developed radar system—no woman could have *that* degree of skill. They also wanted to know about the radar so as to use it as currency in negotiations with the United States or Russia.

Most of all, though, they wanted revenge.

Mokhtari had once served as a sergeant in Savak, the Shah's secret police, and had developed a reputation as their best interrogation specialist. Amnesty International had a thick dossier on him filed under "Torturers/Active." When the Shah had been overthrown in February of 1979, Mokhtari had quickly switched sides and aligned himself with the Ayatollahs, providing them with information on his former superiors.

Rather than exploit the turmoil of the revolution and seek promotion, he became an obscure, hard working jailer. He made sure to treat his charges carefully and developed a reputation as being incorruptibly honest. When the shadow of his years in Savak had faded and the revolutionary committees had decimated the ranks of professional police officers, he started to move up the ladder of promotion, never appearing to be self-seeking. He let events and the lack of competitors work to his advantage. Finally he had been appointed commandant of the prison at Kermanshah.

At thirty-nine years of age the husky, balding Mokhtari had taken over the prison and quickly established a rigid and brutal authority over the inmates and guards. During his first day as commandant he had discovered a cook was selling prison rations on the black market and had a firing squad execute the man in the compound. When the order came down to prepare the prison for the POWs from Ras Assanya he had been equally efficient in creating room. The POWs arrived to find an empty prison waiting for them.

Mokhtari was the logical choice—his own—to interrogate the woman.

For nineteen minutes she stood there, not moving.

"Remove her handcuffs," Mokhtari ordered.

So you're impatient, she thought. I thought we'd be here at least three hours before anything happened, not twenty minutes. She had the count slightly wrong.

"Strip her," Mokhtari ordered.

THE PENTAGON

The tall black captain walked briskly through the corridors of the Pentagon. He checked his watch—only slightly before five P.M. It might be an early day, his wife Francine would be delighted to see him home before seven. The assignment to ASTRA, the Air Force's elite leadership training program in the Pentagon, was demanding his full attention as well as straining his new marriage. Captain James "Thunder" Bryant had been married less than two months.

Bryant tugged at his moustache, a reflex. Who the hell was General Simon Mado? And why did he want to see Bryant ASAP? He hesitated before entering Mado's office to check his uniform. The buttons on the coat of his new Class A blue uniform were already tight. "Got to start working out and cut down on the calories," he mumbled, pushing through the door into Mado's outer office.

The secretary told him to go right in, motioned him into an open door and checked her watch. It was quitting time.

"Thunder, good to see you." Stansell stood up and stuck out his hand when Bryant entered the office.

For a moment, Bryant didn't move. His stomach tied a knot. The last time he had seen Stansell was on the ramp at Ras Assanya just after a rocket attack. "Damn, Colonel," he finally said, shaking the offered hand, a smile spreading across his face. Then he turned to the two-star general and snapped a salute. "Captain Bryant, reporting as ordered." He also took notice of a petite woman sitting quietly in the corner.

General Mado waved a salute back at him. "Relax, Captain. Make yourself comfortable." He waited while Bryant undid the buttons on his coat and sat down on a couch. The big man moved like a professional football player, impressing the general. "Don't want to use up too much of your time. ASTRA keep you hopping?"

"I'd say, sir."

"Good to hear nothing's changed." Mado smiled. "Colonel Stansell here seems to think you might want to help us on a special project. It would mean losing your ASTRA assignment and extensive travel. You'd have to leave the Pentagon, which might not help your career."

"I'd like to know more before taking a bite of that, general."

"Sorry, I can't tell you more unless you buy in."

How much more could Francine take? "Sorry, sir," Bryant said. "I'll have to pass on this one."

"It's for Waters," Stansell said.

The black man stared at the colonel, "Waters? Really? Well, in that case . . . I'm in."

The woman stood and walked out the door. She made sure the

secretary's office was empty and the outer door locked before she returned, closing the general's door after her. The three men said nothing, their eyes on her.

"Thanks, Dewa," Stansell said.

"Captain, you're looking at the team that's going to rescue the POWs, late of Ras Assanya," Mado said. "I'm the joint task force commander, Colonel Stansell is the mission commander and Dewa Rahimi is heading up our Intel section. We want you to be our mission planner and responsible for training. Dewa, bring Captain Bryant up to date."

Rahimi sat down beside Bryant and opened a folder. In quick order she handed him a series of photos and explained the situation. Finally she spread out the map that Cunningham had seen and summarized their planning. "We haven't got much time before they disperse the POWs," she said. "I calculate two months at the most before they start trading POWs as a sort of currency among the power factions in Iran—"

Mado interrupted: "Please stick to facts."

Rahimi nodded, wondering what he wanted—a photo interpreter or an analyst. She did not much like Mado and gave him low marks for his performance with Cunningham. Stansell had shown much more gumption in standing up to the crusty general. She had pegged Mado as just another of the sharks swimming in the Pentagon's tank.

"So far," Stansell said, disturbed by the general's abrupt disagreement with Dewa, "we're still in the planning stages and I'm trying to get F-15s to CAP the C-130s." He quickly told about their meeting with Cunningham.

Bryant studied the map. "Cunningham said three things screw up these types of missions?"

"He named two," Stansell said. "Poor intelligence and training."

"He didn't say what the third was," Mado added.

"Poor maintenance," Rahimi told them, hiding what she was thinking—challenge me on this one, General, and I'm gone.

Mado drummed his fingers on the desk.

"That was one of the lessons of Operation Eagle Claw," she explained, ready to go at it with the general. "When we tried to rescue the hostages out of the American Embassy in Tehran the *helicopters* weren't up to it and the mission died on a desert airstrip."

He nodded. "Agreed. We need a training site. Suggestions?"

"It's got to be desert and mountainous," Bryant said. "Nellis is our best bet. Lots of training areas and activity to hide behind." He stood up and walked to the U.S. map hanging on the wall. "Most of the area north of Las Vegas is deserted and we can avoid observation." His eyes narrowed as he visualized the terrain. "And we can blend in with Red Flag."

"Let's make it happen then," Mado said. "Relocate to Nellis as soon as you can. I'll stay here and bring the C-130s and Delta Force on line. Also, we need a code name. Suggestions?"

"Task Force Alpha," Stansell said.

"Good enough. Okay, get to work."

As they filed out of the office, Mado gestured for Stansell to come back. "Please close the door," he said when Bryant and Rahimi had left. "Colonel, I want an all-Air Force intelligence team on this one. *No civilians.*"

Meaning Dewa Rahimi, who looked good and talked smart. Stansell had already chosen up sides.

KERMANSHAH, IRAN

Mokhtari leaned back in his chair and watched the guards rip off the woman's fatigues. For him it was merely part of the routine he would use to break the woman. He saw himself as a professional.

"You look ridiculous," Mokhtari said in heavily accented, formal English. The woman was still standing at attention, wearing only her combat boots and the canvas bag over her head. He nodded at the guards, and one picked up a two-foot length of rubber hose while the other grabbed the top of the canvas bag. When Mokhtari nodded again, the coarse bag was yanked free.

The woman staggered, then came back to attention. Her eyes blinked against the harsh light, blue eyes turned crystal hard as she focused on the man sitting behind a desk in front of her.

"Don't you salute superior officers?"

"I never salute without my hat on."

A guard swung the rubber hose across her shoulder blades. She would have fallen to the floor except for the tug at her hair that pulled her upright.

Weakly, she raised her left hand in a salute. Mokhtari nodded again and the guard swung the hose, knocking her to the floor.

"Salute correctly."

Slowly she stood and saluted with her right hand. Mokhtari did not see the rigidly extended middle finger of her left hand against her left thigh.

"I am Colonel Vahid Mokhtari, the commandant of this prison. You are a prisoner under my command. You will conduct yourself accordingly." It was a rehearsed speech given many times to the other Americans in the prison. "You will answer all questions I ask."

"Mary Lynn Hauser, captain, United States Air Force, serial number five-five-two dash five—"

Mokhtari nodded and the guard swung the hose, not hard enough to knock her down.

". . . Date of birth: twenty November, nineteen-sixty."

"Do you really think you can stand on the formalities of the Geneva Convention, Miss Hauser?"

"Iran has signed the Geneva Convention and I'm a captain in the military. I assume I'm a POW and not a hostage." She could hardly believe she was standing naked in front of three men and arguing, giving a speech . . .

"If your country is stupid enough to use women in its Air Force and put them in a war, then you must expect to be treated as any other prisoner when you are captured. We do not play children's games, Captain Hauser. What were your duties as a radar controller and what type equipment did you use?"

"Mary Lynn Hauser, captain, United States . . ." She couldn't believe the frontal, unsophisticated approach of this man.

Mokhtari nodded and the guard laid the rubber hose across her back, much harder than before. She staggered and grabbed at the edge of the desk.

"You're terrorists—"

"Again."

The guard swung the hose, knocking her to the floor.

"Again."

She rolled over to take the blow on her back. The two guards pulled her to her feet. She tried to raise her right arm in a salute but the pain stopped her.

If Mokhtari had been left on his own he would have ordered the guards to drag her out and hang her from a hook in the basement ceiling with piano wire. He would have enjoyed watching her jerk and twitch as she strangled, wearing only boots and the canvas bag over her head. But his orders did not allow him that personal pleasure, and there was the matter of his past . .

"Take her to a holding cell."

One guard scooped up her clothes and the other jammed the canvas bag over her head before leading her into the hall toward the two cells in the administration building's basement. Out of sight of Mokhtari, they treated her less harshly.

"This one has courage," one of them said in Farsi.

"Don't let Mokhtari hear you say that," the other cautioned.

The cell door was open and they guided Mary Hauser to the narrow bunk and sat her down. The one carrying her clothes dropped them in her lap. "When the door opens be sure the bag is over your head," he said in English. "The first rule for prisoners is silence." They left, bolting the door behind them and turning out the light.

Mary Hauser lifted the bag off her head and threw it down. She moved her arms back and forth and reached over her shoulders, trying to massage her back. Well, she thought, at least I'm a better actor than I thought. She waited, hoping her eyes would adjust, but it was too dark to make out anything. Including the rat that scurried across her feet.

CHAPTER 7

D MINUS 28

HOLLOMAN AFB, NEW MEXICO

The FBI agent shook his head and handed Byers' written statement to the Air Force OSI agent. "He's almost illiterate," he said.

"We don't hire 'em for their literary ability," the agent replied. "He's the best crew chief in the Wing and tough as they come. I'll get his story on tape and have a stenographer transcribe it."

"Cussing and all, I suppose."

"You should read his account of how he and his partner Sergeant Timothy Wehr escaped from Ras Assanya. A masterpiece, sort of. Top kicks take notes to improve their vocabulary." The OSI agent shook his head, doubting if the FBI could appreciate the value of Staff Sergeant Raymond Alvin Byers. "I'll call him in and try to get it down this morning. The Pentagon's sending two officers out to interview him. Special project. They should be here this afternoon."

Byers pulled at the necktie of his Class A uniform, trying to get comfortable. Frustrated with the poor-fitting uniform, he stood up and unbuttoned the coat and sat back down, not caring who saw him while he waited in the Office of Special Investigations. He jumped back to his feet when the two officers walked in.

"Sarge, how are you!" Thunder Bryant stuck out his big hand.

Byers wiped his hand on his uniform but for once it was clean. "Captain Bryant, the last time I saw you, you were taxiing my jet out of the bunker at Ras Assanya. It's damn good to see you. What happened to 512? She was a good bird." He glanced then at the man who had walked in behind Bryant, and recognized him. "Colonel Stansell. Well, I'll be . . . look a hell of a lot better than last time."

Bryant said, "Five-twelve is at March Air Force Base with the National Guard. They're taking good care of her. How's your partner, Wehr?"

"Ah, you know Timmy, always screwing off. He's launching our bird today and if I don't get out of this monkey suit and get back on the line he'll screw it up for sure."

"Let's talk," Stansell said. "We heard what happened to you the other night. You sure they were Arabs?"

"I'm sure." Byers hunched forward and clasped his big hands between his knees. "Heard enough Aye-rab lingo at Ras Assanya. They was Aye-rabs." He recounted what happened the night at the pizza tavern. "Once I got my Jeep Baby Doll hid down in a gully I doubled back onto the road. Got close enough to hear 'em jabbering away and get their license number. They tried to follow Baby Doll and got stuck in the sand. Should've shot the fuckers."

"Just as well you didn't," Stansell said. "We think the FBI got them when they tried to cross the border at El Paso."

"Good deal." Byers stood up, ready to leave, anxious to get back on his jet.

"Sarge, this is important," Bryant said, "could they have been after you for a reason you haven't told anyone about?"

Byers looked at the door, wanting to leave, "Shee-it, no. Not 'less one was a jealous husband." He ran now for his Jeep, ripping off his coat and tie as he went.

"What do you think?" Stansell asked Bryant.

"Have to read the complete report. But I think we've got the meat of it."

"Not good," Stansell said. "Too many unknowns. Are they looking at me? I don't think the mission's been compromised, only a handful of people know about it. But can we take the chance?"

Bryant nodded. He realized the colonel's concern and wanted to break the connection between the rescue mission and what had happened to Byers. But Stansell knew the facts and read them the same way he did. Just like Waters, Bryant decided, you don't run away from the hard decisions.

"Okay," Stansell said, his decision made, "you go on to Nellis, I'm going to get us an Eagle driver."

LANGLEY, VIRGINIA

Allen J. Camm liked his office as Deputy Director of Intelligence for the CIA. The room was large, comfortable, well lit and tastefully furnished. Unlike his last office this one had windows. Camm had been a Baron, one of the area division chiefs buried safely inside the bureaucracy of the CIA. He had exercised almost feudal control over his division, the Middle East, and developed a reputation as a comer. Now he had reached a position that had real power—much more than he had ever imagined.

The door swung open and two men entered unannounced. The first one in held a finger to his lips and handed him a card—a routine security sweep for bugs. The second man ran a wand over the walls, looking for magnetic abnormalities. The first man then connected a delicately calibrated ohmmeter to Camm's phone console and made a dialing motion. Camm was to test the phone. Camm, who had been through the routine many times, picked up the phone and punched the button to Susan Fisher's office.

"Susan, please bring in the file you're working on, say in about five minutes." He hung up. The two men continued to sweep the office. They gave him a thumbs-up signal and left, Susan Fisher passing them as she came in.

She handed Camm the file on the Islamic Jihadi agents the FBI had arrested in El Paso.

Camm smiled at the young woman and shook his head. "My God, this reads like Keystone cops. They haven't got a clue about how to kidnap someone."

"They got their training on the streets of Beirut," Fisher said. "What works there doesn't work here. But they're tough, the FBI hasn't been able to crack them."

"Is the Bureau onto the agents here?"

"No. We've also backed off and lost contact with the Jihadis. The FBI would be upset if they discovered us working their turf. We could drop them a few more hints, claim we monitored a phone call in Beirut."

"No," Camm told her. "Make them work for it. Besides, the more I think about it, the more I want the Agency to interrogate the bastards. By the way, have we turned the woman they're using?"

"Yes. We told her she could expect a quick deportation to Iran if she didn't cooperate. Also, to get her chador cleaned. I'm not sure which did the trick."

He didn't smile. "We can use the woman to flush out the agents." A plan was taking shape. "Monitor Colonel Stansell's movements. The next time he comes to Washington have the woman tell the Jihadis. We'll pick the Jihadis up when they try to get Stansell."

Fisher nodded. "We've never dropped Stansell."

Camm was pleased with his case officer. She understood what was needed and did it. Both of them knew that if the FBI found the CIA operating inside the U.S. they would be in deep shit. The National Security Act of 1947 that established the CIA had been very specific: the CIA would have no role inside the U.S. or the power to arrest. Those two functions were the FBI's. And the FBI had a simple remedy when they found the CIA infringing on their territory—publicity—the one thing no intelligence agency could stand.

But that would be nothing compared to what Congress would do if they learned about "Deep Furrow." In the late 1970s, feeling hamstrung by Congressional oversight, the Director of the CIA had looked for ways to bypass the Congressional watchdogs, and found his solution in transferring agents from the closely watched Directorate of Operations to the Directorate of Intelligence. Agency money and personnel mushroomed in the Directorate of Intelligence, all accounted for in other departments. The DDI, the Deputy Director of Intelligence, had barely started moving into the covert operations business when the President fired the Director of the CIA, and the new head shook the headquarters building at Langley from top to bottom. Out of that Camm found himself the new Deputy Director of Intelligence.

He was delighted, especially when he found he had field operatives working in the area he had specialized in—the Middle East. When he learned that neither Congress or the new Director knew what he had, he decided to resurrect covert operations and make the CIA into the kind of organization he believed in. A good bureaucrat, he saw a chance to build an empire with himself at its head. And it was he who called his growing operation in the Middle East "Deep Furrow."

"What does Deep Furrow tell us about the Jihadis?" he now asked Fisher.

"Quite a bit. The Council of Guardians in Iran is the mover behind the Islamic Jihad. The Albanian Embassy is providing support for the Jihad's operations in the U.S. along with some help from Libya. We're trying to find the channel they use for moving people in and out of the States. We've got an operative inside the POW compound at Kermanshah, who tells us they've got a Captain Mary Hauser and are . . . interrogating her.'' She took a deep breath. ''Another operative in Tehran reports that the Council of Guardians is putting on the heat to capture Captain Carroll. So far, he's still on the loose. We've got our operatives trying to make contact and bring him out.''

''What in the hell is he doing there?'' Camm asked.

''No idea, sir.''

''We're running out of time on this one and need to fill in the gaps. Nail the two Jihadis. Turn them over to primary section. They'll talk. Terrorists are like rats, see one, and be sure there's more in the woodwork.''

She stood to leave.

''Susan, time's critical. If Defense fumbles at Kermanshah . . . I want Deep Furrow to rescue the POWs.''

And he, of course, would get the credit. Maybe even be in line for Director.

LUKE AFB, ARIZONA

''Whoever's on that baby that wants to see me must be important,'' Captain Jack Locke said to his wife. The two were standing in front of Base Operations at Luke Air Force Base watching a C-20 taxi in. The sleek military version of the Gulfstream III looked elegant in its blue-and-white paint scheme, and the two Rolls Royce Spey engines on the small executive jet were much quieter than the F-229 engines on the F-15.

Gillian, Locke's English wife, had picked him up at the squadron after a Wednesday's doctor's appointment when a sergeant had run out of the building, telling them the Command Post wanted him to meet a VIP flight that was landing in ten minutes. The inbound pilot had radioed ahead the request. Gillian had protested that she was two months pregnant, but Locke had told her, ''You're beautiful, you can charm whoever it is with your tony English accent.''

He had driven her over to Base Ops, where the C-20's engines spun down and the hatch flopped down. ''Well, I'll be . . . that's Colonel Stansell.'' Locke shook his head. ''I thought he was a first-class ass when I first met him, comparing him to Waters. Turned out to be a decent guy."

Locke saluted when the colonel was still several feet away. "Got your message, sir."

Stansell waved a salute back and the three stood together for a few moments while Locke introduced Gillian. Not the type I'd have guessed Jack to marry, Stansell thought, she's real pretty but not the flashy type our ace used to favor. I better quit trying to match up people. I'd never have put Waters with his wife Sara either . . .

"Gillian, you'll have to excuse me, but I've got to talk to your husband and I am pressed for time."

Gillian bestowed a dazzling smile on him. "I'll wait, Colonel." What else was new?

As the two officers walked along the ramp and passed the waiting C-20, Stansell was aware of the contrast between them—Locke, almost six feet tall, dark blond hair, rugged looking. His green Nomex flight suit looked like it was tailored for him, and he could model for an Air Force recruiting poster, except for the scars over his right eye and along his left jaw.

"Jack, I'm on a special project. I need your help. Can't tell you much more except that it will mean temporary duty at Nellis for a few months and it could be . . . interesting . . ."

"Ah, damnit, Colonel. Gillian's two months pregnant, I can't leave her alone—"

"Thunder's on board, he's at Nellis right now."

Locke froze. "He gave up his ASTRA assignment?"

Stansell nodded.

"It's got to be the POWs," Locke said, understanding. "Okay, okay, count me in, Colonel. I owe Waters and the 45th big time." An emotion Locke could not identify worked through him. "I know most of them." He didn't trust himself to say more.

"Thanks. I need all the help I can get."

"Then you need Chief Pullman. Best first sergeant and dog robber in the Air Force. He can cut through red tape faster than anyone. I think he holds markers on half the NCOs in the Air Force. He's really a great first shirt."

"I met him once," Stansell said, "at Ras Assanya. Where is he now?" He remembered the big chief master sergeant who had helped with the evacuation of the 45th out of Ras Assanya. It had been Pullman who had shanghaied the extra C-130 that had made the difference for so many of them, except for the unlucky POWs.

"Still at RAF Stonewood in England. Why don't you give him a call while I try to explain to Gillian what's happening."

They walked back into Base Ops. Locke found Gillian while Stansell used the AUTOVON line to England. Within minutes Stansell was back with them. "The retirement ceremony for Chief Master Sergeant Mortimer M. Pullman is Friday afternoon," he said.

"He'll cancel that if he knows. That C-20 belong to you?"

"For a while."

"Let's use it." Locke turned to Gillian. "Sorry, honey. I've got to do this."

"Not to worry, you go. I'll get us moved to Las Vegas." She touched her husband's face. "I'm really a camp follower at heart, you know that."

"Jack, you go home and pack," Stansell said. "You're going to Stonewood. I'll have the crew refuel and file a clearance for England. I need to pick up my car, I'll drive to Nellis."

"You need to touch base with my boss," Jack said.

"I'll talk to your wing commander. He's not going to like me stealing you so easy."

Locke, often a joker in the past, looked at the colonel. "Sir, this mission may be impossible, but it's my meat. Thanks."

PHOENIX, ARIZONA

Barbara Lyon decided that her exercise classes were definitely worth the effort as she bicycled home. Four times a week she pedaled to the gym three miles from her condominium in Phoenix, went through the routine, studied herself in one of the wall mirrors, then went through the process of comparing herself to the young instructors.

I've still got a few good years left, she calculated. Not bad for a thirty-seven-year-old ex— She cut the thought off and pushed her bike through the condo gate, almost running into Colonel Stansell. "Well, Rupe"—she smiled warmly—"you're back." She leaned forward over the handlebars, looking at the suitcases he was carrying. "Trying to sneak out?"

"Caught." Stansell laughed, dropping the bags. Barbara was hard to ignore, wearing tight shorts and a cut-off top. A scarf held her hair back in a loose ponytail. "I left a note under your door. Been reassigned to Nellis at Vegas." He wanted to say more of what he felt but the words weren't easy.

"Then we might see each other again. I go to Vegas quite a bit to take care of an apartment building I own there." She sat back on the bicycle seat and stretched her legs out. "I just finished a major remodeling and most of the apartments are vacant. Why don't you stay there?" She waited, hoping he would take her offer. He nodded. "Super," she said. "Can I catch a ride with you? I need to see how things are going . . ."

And to herself: You're not going to be the one that got away, Colonel Stansell.

CHAPTER 8

D MINUS 27

RAF STONEWOOD, ENGLAND

As the C-20 Gulfstream taxied into the blocks at RAF Stonewood the pilot turned around and frowned at Locke. "We've got to go into crew rest," he announced, wondering why the captain was getting such VIP treatment. "Where to next?"

"Be back here in twelve hours," Locke told him, "we're going to Nellis."

"Captain," the pilot muttered at Locke's back, "there's a shorter way to Nellis from Luke."

Locke commandeered the Follow Me truck and headed for Chief Pullman's office, passing a parade practice being held in front of the Base Operations building. "For Chief Pullman's retirement ceremony Friday morning," the driver told him.

Locke found the chief in his office in wing headquarters. Pullman didn't look surprised to see him. "Don't tell me you came over here to wish me bon voyage and good luck in my future life."

Locke shook his head. "Chief, this is important. I need your help for a few months. Will you postpone your retirement until then?"

The chief stared down his big nose at the captain. "I got me one great retirement ceremony going, complete with band and general. Now, you think I'm gonna shitcan that because you need my help?"

Locke tried to think of a way to convince Pullman without telling him about the rescue mission. "Chief, I've seen you kick the Air Force into action. I'm working on a special mission that's going to take a lot of ass-kicking to make it work and you've got the best boot around." Locke could tell the chief was not moved. "It's for Waters," he said, not wanting to say more.

"Waters is dead." But there was some pain in the chief's voice.

Jack Locke knew what it would take to convince Pullman. "Chief, I'm calling in a marker on this one. You know about markers."

"I don't owe you, Captain."

Nothing left but to tell him ... "Colonel Stansell is putting together a rescue mission to get the POWs out of Iran. That's close-hold information. You know a leak means it won't go. We haven't got much time. We need you."

Pullman sat down, a pain shooting through his stomach. "Dammit. My stomach hasn't squeaked since I decided to hang it up and retire. Now it's squeaking like hell. Captain, my markers don't go that high. Besides, you need the heavies backing you up, not me."

But he was still the first sergeant of the 45th Tactical Fighter Wing. The POWs were his men. Pullman couldn't shake off his sense of responsibility for them. He had become the wing's first shirt because he knew when to cajole, teach, bribe and kick people along. And now the captain was standing in front of him, asking that he finish his job and do what all first shirts did when they got to the bottom line—protect their people. It wasn't a debt he owed, it was an obligation he had undertaken when he started his climb through the ranks to become one of the top noncommissioned officers in the Air Force.

"Chief, I know that, and they're behind us. But you know the people, the working troops who can make things available to us. You can make that happen double-time." Locke had played his last card.

"I'm about to collect my biggest marker," Pullman said. He picked up the phone and hit the button to the wing commander's office. "Sir, I've got to talk to you. Something has come up." He walked into the hall, heading for his commander's office.

Minutes later he was back, a rueful look on his face. "The Old Man wasn't happy when I told him I wanted to postpone my retirement. He says the next ceremony will take place at the out-processing desk in base personnel. Hell, that's nothing compared to what my wife is gonna say."

THE ZAGROS MOUNTAINS, IRAN

The stream he had been following through the rugged Zagros Mountains of western Iran cascaded out of a canyon and turned southward, flowing into a long valley. Carroll could see an occasional clump of small shacks nestled along the streambed where families tried to keep a farmstead alive. He was surprised by the number of people who lived in the area, grazing mostly goats and irrigating small plots of land. It was hard to disappear.

After burying the woman and man in a shallow depression, Carroll had scrambled down a steep embankment at first light and headed cross-country until he stumbled onto the stream, which he was willing to follow until it turned south, away from where he wanted to go.

He found a spot in a clump of bushes that surrounded a small pool of water and made sure he used his right hand while he ate the last of the bread he had been rationing. It seemed like he was always hungry. He washed his shirt and pants and spread them out to dry. After shaving and washing himself, he stretched out in the warm late October sun. Trying to figure what the hell he should do.

Had the passengers on the bus or the driver reported the incident to the authorities? From the way the driver had acted and the passengers had almost thrown the man and woman off the bus, he doubted it. But it only took someone to start asking about their missing relative and that would lead to the bus. He had two, maybe three more days to find cover. Luck had to be running out. He couldn't help talking in his sleep, and being left-handed eventually would probably trip him up. Islamic cultures demanded that the right hand be used for doing "clean" things while the left be used for "unclean." One slip and he would be recognized if, say, someone caught him eating or leading with his left hand. How did he get himself into such a mess, he asked himself, a sense of total aloneness adding to his misery.

The images that drove him came back, much as they always did, were violent and crystal clear—his final hours at Ras Assanya . . . his commander Colonel Muddy Waters ordering him out and he refusing, remembering too Waters then telling him to stay with the flight surgeon and help with the wounded . . . the surrender of the base and the terrible moments when three Iranians broke into the aid station and started shooting, hitting the sergeant on the operating table while Doc Landis was working on him . . . He had shot one of the Iranians in the face and killed the other two before escaping into the night. But Doc Landis was left behind, still trying to save the wounded sergeant on the operating table. He'd made it to the beach and was in the water for over four hours. When he did reach safety he made a promise to follow the last order his commander had given him—help the wounded, the ones left behind . . .

Lying in the sun on that rock beside the quiet pool, Carroll knew he had to go on but he needed allies. He searched his memory for all he had read on Iran. His duties as an Air Force intelligence officer had given him information to draw on, but blending what he knew into action was tough. He tried to recall the intel summaries and maps he had seen about Kurdistan, the undefined area to the north about the size of Wyoming that stretched through Iraq, Turkey and Iran. Okay, he decided, he knew where he'd likely find the help he needed.

He dressed and forced himself to start walking away from Kermanshah, where the POWs were, and toward the airport at Ahwaz, a town one hundred and fifty miles to the south.

He needed to catch a flight. He needed some allies.

NELLIS AFB, NEVADA

Captain Bryant was waiting for Stansell when he came into building 201, the home of Red Flag at Nellis Air Force Base. The building was surprisingly quiet for 7:30 A.M. "Sorry, Colonel, we've got a problem I can't handle," Bryant told him, tension in his voice. "A real kludge."

"Is that ASTRA lingo?" Stansell asked, looking at the big captain.

"Yeah. Kludge means bottleneck. In this case it's one Colonel Wilford, Red Flag's commander. He's bent out of shape and is digging his heels in. Not much cooperation. He claims we're getting in the way of his mission."

"I know Wilford," Stansell said. "First name's *Tyrone*. We used to call him Tyrant Wilford. I'm gonna have to get his attention real quick."

Bryant followed Stansell to Wilford's door. "Wait out here, this may not be pretty," Stansell said, knocking on Wilford's door.

"Come," said the commander of the 4440th Tactical Fighter Training Group known as Red Flag. Wilford did not offer Stansell a seat when he entered. "Well, colonel, it seems your captain, the big black guy, wants to take over my operation. I run the biggest, the best, the most for real war game in the Air Force. Nobody comes as close to the big game as we do. Red Flag teaches our fighter jocks the pressure of war, the sensory overload, the disorientation of flying in combat. We get the tactical Air Force ready for the first ten days of combat and you're not going to get in the way of that."

"Mind if I sit down? This sounds like a pitch for a bigger budget."

Wilford pointed to a chair. "Colonel, I don't make dumb-ass jokes around here. I've got fifty-six jets with their crews landing here tomorrow for the next exercise—which starts Monday. I've also got a cryptic message from some paper-pushing flunky in the Puzzle Palace saying to support you and your Task Force Alpha. Then a captain with a sexy foreign number shows up wanting to use my facility. No way José. In case you didn't get my message, read my lips." The burly colonel leaned across his desk, his face rigid, humorless.

"Can I borrow your phone?" Without waiting for an answer Stansell dialed a number. "Dick, Rupe Stansell here. I'm having a little trouble convincing the commander of Red Flag that I need his help, can you explain it to him?" He handed the phone to Wilford. "I think you know who Dick Stevens is—Cunningham's aide."

Wilford did all the listening. Gently he replaced the phone. "Stevens asked if I knew why they call Cunningham 'Sundown'." The Air Force's chief of staff was legendary for ordering colonels to be cleared off base by sundown when their performance fell short of his standards. "He wouldn't tell me what you're doing but it seems I've two choices, help you or start packing. Colonel, it looks like I don't have a say in the matter. I've got three old forty-foot trailers in the parking lot out front you can use. But for God's sake keep what's her name—"

"Dewa Rahimi, our intelligence specialist."

Wilford stared at Stansell. "That means she'll have to use our intelligence shop in the main building. Not good. She'll drive the jocks coming in for the next exercise up the wall."

Stansell left, having heard enough from Tyrone. Bryant was waiting for him in the hall. "I think we have Colonel Wilford's attention," he said deadpan. "Let's get to work."

They found Rahimi in a large office in the back of the Intelligence section. She explained how the Air Force Special Activities Center had opened the door for her with a message. Judging by the way the men in the section danced attention around her, Stansell decided she might have had some influence on the cooperation she was getting.

"Okay, Dewa," Stansell said, closing the office door, "give me an update on the situation in Iran."

"Unchanged." She pulled a folder out of one of the office safes. "Here are current photos of the prison at Kermanshah. The last two are infrared. We're getting heat signatures from the barracks behind the rear wall that indicate they're occupied. Trouble is, we don't know by who or what. I've got a request into the DIA for info. So far, nothing. We do know that all the POWs are at Kermanshah, but we still haven't accounted for Captain William Carroll. Apparently he's running around loose in Iran. No idea at all about what he's doing."

"The political front?"

"Hold on," she said, and turned to a computer terminal beside her desk, keyed up a data bank from the Defense Intelligence Agency and the screen filled with Arabic script.

"You can read Arabic?" Bryant said.

"No. Farsi uses the Arabic alphabet. These are recent newspaper articles and verbatim TV and radio reports." She read for a few moments, then called up short intelligence summaries in English. "Captain, there are four factions trying to take control of the Council of Guardians away from the Islamic Republican Party. Whoever controls the Council of Guardians controls the POWs. As of yesterday the Islamic Republican Party was trying to align with the IPRP, that's the Islamic People's Republican Party." She shook her head, "Hey, sometimes even I get confused. Anyway, the IPRP wants half the POWs as a sign of good faith. So far the Islamic Republican Party is stalling."

"Sounds like the POWs are a hot ticket," Bryant said.

"Just like the American hostages they held in 1980," Stansell said. "How long before the POWs start getting traded off?"

"I can only guess," Rahimi told him. "It depends on how bad the Islamic Republican Party needs the support of the IPRP to keep control of the Council of Guardians. I'd say maybe six weeks at the outside."

"You can't hardly tell the players without a program," Stansell said. "Okay, we've got a lot to do, and not much time to do it in."

"Let's get with it."

CHAPTER 9

D MINUS 26

KERMANSHAH, IRAN

The guard had received fresh orders from the commandant and hurried across the dusty prison compound. He could feel Mokhtari's eyes following him—the commandant, he knew, watched all activity in front of the administration building from his corner office. The guard stomped through the entrance into the main cell block, glad now to be out of Mokhtari's sight and out of the same building. The sharp smell of bodies and dirty clothes was nothing compared to the fear Mokhtari generated. He turned to the left and walked down the iron steps to the basement, past the room where the prisoners were interrogated and to the small punishment cells.

"The commandant has ordered Leason back to his cell," the guard told the on-duty warder.

The two men unlocked the wooden door to the smallest cell, the one the POWs called the Box. It was only forty inches high, twenty-four inches wide and forty inches deep. They reached in and pulled the man out, knowing he could not move on his own after being locked up for two days in his cramped position.

Colonel Clayton Leason, over six feet tall and towering above the guards, rested his weight on their shoulders. His jaw clenched as blood flowed into his cramped legs and pain replaced numbness. The two guards let go of Leason, then caught him when his legs crumpled.

"Wait a minute," the colonel told the warder, who spoke English. "Give my damn legs a chance."

"A shower, Colonel?" the warder said. "You can wash out your clothes."

Leason looked at the man. He was being offered two unheard of luxuries. As Senior Ranking Officer among the POWs he had to be careful of everything the Iranians gave him or his men. "Nothing's free with Mokhtari," he said. "What's the price?"

The warder shook his head. They helped Leason into a shower and handed him a bar of soap. He still could not stand alone and sat on a wooden stool. The shower, though was pure heaven. The guard took his clothes after he had washed them and hung them up to dry. Leason let the warm water stream over his head as he scrubbed his graying hair. He could feel lice wash out. Briefly he thought that if Mokhtari had not ordered the shower and found out, the two Iranians would be in deep deep trouble. Forget it and be grateful for big favors . . .

The colonel looked down at his body. He had been overweight when captured, weighing over 260 pounds. At Ras Assanya the flight surgeon had been on his case about losing weight, but his duties as the Deputy for Maintenance with the 45th seemed to interfere with any serious dieting and exercise. Now the same flight surgeon, Lieutenant Colonel Jeff Landis, was saying that his roll of fat was helping him survive. Leason was down to 180 pounds but the flight surgeon was emaciated, and only Leason's sharing of his meager rations was keeping the doctor going. Something had to be done. Maybe the guards were the answer.

"I owe you," he told the guards when he dressed. His clothes were still wet but he could dry them off in the cell he shared with Doc Landis. "Do you know why Mokhtari threw me in the Box?"

The warder translated for the guard, who shook his head no.

"Besides asking for more rations, I told Mokhtari that he had better think about his future. We'll be released eventually or rescued. Think about it. When an American tank drives through that wall, you'll want a friend. I told Mokhtari that if he treats us right we will be fair when we report our treatment. Sooner or later, it will happen."

Leason let his words sink in. "I also told him to stop interrogating Captain Hauser. We know she's here and what you're doing to her."

NELLIS AFB, NEVADA

The sleek blue-and-white Gulfstream III arriving from RAF Stone-wood taxied into the blocks in front of Bas Ops and shut down. The door flopped down, and Locke and Pullman clambered down the steps and walked toward the two waiting men. Locke tried to keep his face impassive but broke into a grin when he shook hands with his old buddy Thunder Bryant and then Stansell.

"How's Gillian?" Bryant asked.

"Two months preggers," Jack said, trying to affect an English accent. "She should be here in a few days. And Francine?"

"She's with her mother in Wilmington." Bryant shook his head. "The Air Force is pretty rough on her."

Stansell and Pullman were following them and overheard Bryant's remark. It was a familiar story in the Air Force—failing marriages. They looked at each other, both thinking the same thing; would Bryant's personal problems interfere with the mission that needed total commitment.

"That's going to be home." Stansell pointed out the three trailers in front of building 201 as they drove into the parking lot. Pullman got out of the car and walked through the trailers. "I've seen better chicken coops," the chief said. "We're talking shacks here, Colonel, shacks. No electricity, no furniture, nothing. When did you say they got to be ready?"

"Monday."

"You expect me to get them ready over the weekend? You're going to need some miracles around here, Colonel."

Miracles better be our stock-in-trade, Stansell thought.

REZAIYEH, IRAN

The gate guard turned his back to the wind and tried to hunch down lower beneath his collar as the small Fokker F-27 transport plane taxied up to the fence and cut its two turboprop engines. The passenger door swung open and people started to clamber down the steps, most of them wrapped up against the wind blowing off nearby Lake Urmia. October nights in the mountains of northwest Iran were very cold at forty-two hundred feet.

The passengers ignored the guard and hurried toward the bus waiting to drive them into the town of Rezaiyeh three miles to the south. The guard waved new passengers through, angry because his replacement had not shown up. When the last of the passengers had boarded the airplane for the flight to Bandar Abbas he banged the gate closed and ran for the bus, not wanting to spend the night at the airport or walk into town.

The guard sat down now in the only empty seat next to a soldier. The two glanced at each other, acknowledging their mutual profession. "The driver is a pig," the guard said. "I was lucky he didn't leave without me."

Bill Carroll unwrapped the scarf around his head. He did not want to get into a conversation but the guard might become suspicious if he ignored him. "It used to be different," Carroll said. "Not too long ago they would have asked you when you wanted to leave and waited for you."

The guard sighed. "Things change. Even here." They rode in silence for a few moments, then: "Are you from Rezaiyeh?"

"No, passing through on business. An uncle lives nearby and this is a chance to visit him."

The guard looked hard at Carroll. He wanted to be sure he did not sit next to a Kurd. He had killed enough of them, too many of these traitorous tribesmen lived around Rezaiyeh. Satisfied that Carroll did not look like a Kurd, he relaxed. "What is your business here?"

Carroll turned and stared at the guard. "I'm here because the Council of Guardians sent me. What is your name?"

The guard wanted nothing to do with the Council of Guardians. "I'm just a guard—"

"Yes, I understand," Carroll said, facing the window.

"I can find you a room for the night . . ."

"It is late. Thank you. What is your superior's name? I'm not after loyal soldiers like yourself, only incompetent leaders." Carroll was getting into it.

Here was the guard's chance to even matters with his sergeant. But then he thought about it, better not get involved. "Sergeant Afrakhteh . . . but he is honest and hard working."

"Good. Do not mention that I am here. It would make my work much more difficult and that would not be wise."

"Yes, of course." Anyone from the Council of Guardians was dangerous.

Carroll stared into the night. How much longer can I bluff like this? My luck can't last, I've got to find help and get to Kermanshah.

CHAPTER 10

D MINUS 25

KERMANSHAH, IRAN

Vahid Mokhtari was pleased with himself. The visit by the commanding general of the Peoples' Soldiers of Islam was going well. The PSI was the military arm of the communist Tudeh Party and had recently been integrated into the Iranian armed forces, reviving and strengthening the Iranians with a massive infusion of Soviet arms, aircraft and supplies. The general had insisted on walking by himself, hobbling along on crutches, still not used to the loss of his right leg. His one eye blazed when he looked at the Americans, and he constantly adjusted the black eyepatch over his empty eye socket.

"Their commander, a Colonel Waters, led his Phantoms in an attack on my headquarters," he told Mokhtari. "His bombs did this to me. I killed him."

Mokhtari had escorted the old man through the main building, explaining the smell. "The Americans are willing to live in this filth. They will not wash or care for themselves."

He did not mention his rigidly enforced rule of not allowing the prisoners to bathe or wash their clothes. Eventually, filth and bad diet would have their effect, exactly as he planned. Then Colonel Leason would do as he was ordered or watch his men die like vermin. Mokhtari found the thought of Leason collaborating against the men he claimed to command very satisfying.

Mokhtari concluded the tour by escorting the general into the small interrogation room in the basement of the administration building. "I am personally questioning the controller from the radar site at Ras Assanya who directed aircraft against your pilots. We are extracting information about the secret equipment she was using. Would you care to observe an interview?"

The general nodded and sat down.

A guard positioned a chair in the middle of the room facing a metal desk and left. Mokhtari leaned against the front edge of the desk and folded his arms. The door swung open and two guards shoved Mary Hauser into the room, her wrists manacled and the canvas bag over her head. One grabbed her arm and wrenched her around, forcing her into the chair.

"Remove the bag and handcuffs," Mokhtari ordered, then spoke in English. "*Captain*, we have been through this before. Salute your superior officers." The general did not speak English and an aide interpreted for him.

"Permission to speak, Commandant?" She was playing the game, studying the old man sitting slightly to her left. Somehow he reminded her of a peregrine falcon.

"Granted."

"Military protocol says that I must be standing in order to salute. Permission to stand?"

Mokhtari nodded. She stood, saluted. "Captain Mary Lynn Hauser reporting as ordered, *sir*."

The general's one eye dissected her.

Mokhtari nodded at the guard standing behind Hauser, who took hold of her shoulders and pushed her back into the chair.

"Tell us about the equipment you were using at your radar post. Don't make me repeat myself."

Mary Hauser steeled herself. The interrogation sessions followed a set pattern, beatings came next. Mokhtari used such anticipation as a way to break her. "I've explained it before, there was nothing special or new, it was a standard radar, the same type we used in Vietnam . . ."

Actually she had been using the latest model of the AN/TPS 59, a state of the art 3-D air surveillance phased array radar. By using high-speed computers it could handle five hundred targets on every ten second scan of its rotating planar array antenna—a powerful and sophisticated command-and-control radar system.

Before she had abandoned the radar post perched on a low hill nine miles inland from the base at Ras Assanya her crew had blown the site apart with high-explosive charges, and she had poked through the wreckage to insure nothing important could be recognized or salvaged.

Mokhtari nodded at the same guard who slapped her with his left hand, the force of the blow twisting her face to the left.

"Again."

The guard slapped her the second time.

"Again."

The general leaned forward. "We are not fools. Our technicians did not find a parabolic radar antenna in the wreckage." The aide translated the general's words into English for Hauser. At least it gave her a bit of time to think.

"Permission to speak?"

"Again," Mokhtari snapped. The guard hit her, harder, matching the blow to the volume of Mokhtari's voice.

She fell to the floor, exaggerating the effect of the blow, staggering part-way back into the chair but fell again to the floor, willing herself to control the pain.

The guard picked her up and dropped her into the chair. She rested her elbows on her knees and dropped her head, not wanting the men to see her face. "I'm sorry, sir, but I'm telling you the truth. I was using the radar out of the old SAGE system we had in Vietnam. That's semi-automatic ground environment. I did not have the command-guidance computer that interfaced the system with airborne aircraft—"

"Why not," the general asked after his aide had translated.

"Too old, too unreliable. We rely on airborne equipment now. I don't know anything about that."

"You're lying."

She looked up, forcing tears. The men would expect her to cry at this point. "Sir, I'm not lying." The pleading in her voice sounded about right. "Must I lie to answer your questions? I'm only a woman." And she knew her last four words were a mistake the moment she said them.

The general was silent, sensing that the woman was holding her own, trying to manipulate the interrogation. "She's a lying bitch. Work on her."

Mokhtari was pleased to oblige. "Strip her."

"*Not again*, Commandant," she said, standing up. This always came after the beatings. The fear of being raped while in captivity had eaten at her resistance, wearing her down. She fought it by telling herself that rape was another form of torture and that the anticipation of torture was as destructive as the physical pain and degradation. It didn't really work. She was scared to death.

One of the guards reached for her shirt and pulled it off her. The rough hands of the two guards stripped her other clothes away. Finally she stood there wearing only her boots.

"Proceed." Mokhtari pointed at one of the guards.

"She's unclean," he protested, staring at her blood-stained legs.

She could feel the heavy silence come down on the men. Islamic prohibitions, it seemed, were protecting her. Then it came to her . . . act ashamed . . . exploit their deep-seated beliefs about women. She hung her head and strangled a sob, just loud enough for the men to hear.

"Remove her," Mokhtari ordered.

The two guards rushed Hauser to her cell, and one threw her clothes on the floor at her feet.

You won't win the next one, she told herself, breathing deeply.

TOURS, FRANCE

The Saturday night reception for the pilots assembled for Sunday's air show had reached the dying stage. The generals had all left with great amounts of rigorous French protocol and most of the civilian high rollers had departed. The F-111 pilot, Lieutenant Colonel Garret "Torch" Doucette, wandered into the bar, finding it more to his liking than the formality of the main ballroom in the French officers' club. He found his Weapon Systems Officer, Captain Ramon Contreraz, sitting at the bar, the coat buttons of his Class A Blues undone and tie pulled loose, having a beer. They were the only Americans at the air show.

"Beats the hell out of that pissy champagne they've been serving in there," Contreraz told him, motioning to the seat beside him.

Torch Doucette heaved his bulk onto the stool. Middle age had not been kind to him and his waistline was expanding as rapidly as his hairline retreated. Contreraz had been paired with Doucette in F-111s long enough to know that the flabby image was misleading, the pilot had the personality and muscles of a bulldozer. "Well," the lieutenant colonel said, "how do you like French air shows?"

"Boring," Contreraz told him. The two officers had flown an F-111F from their base in England, RAF Lakenheath, into the air base outside Tours for an air show being staged by the French Air Force. They were not part of the demonstration-flying, their jet lined up only for static display. "How'd we luck into this, anyway?" the captain asked.

"My good looks and your Latin charm," Doucette told him. "Be nice to the natives."

Contreraz grunted into his beer. "I'm here 'cause you're here, and you're here 'cause you speak frog and have a froggy last name." The WSO looked around the room, focusing on a pretty brunette who had come in with a group of French pilots they had met earlier. "Ah, *la belle demoiselles*."

Doucette shook his head. Contreraz was slightly drunk. "It's *les belles*, pronounced *lay*, not *la*."

"Right on—lay." Contreraz stood and buttoned his coat, still looking at the girl. He checked himself in the mirror behind the bar, straightening his tie. He was just over six feet, and the way he moved reminded Doucette of a matador. Being dark-complected, slender, muscular and good-looking added to the image.

"Remember Franco-American relations," Doucette said, deciding the captain was about to notch up another conquest.

"That's what I've got in mind."

Doucette watched him approach the French pilots before turning back to the bar. The boy's a credit to the image, he thought. He swirled his beer and stared into the glass, thinking about hanging it all up and retiring. The Air Force had turned into a drag, he needed to escape the humdrum routine he'd slipped into. He was amazed that he'd been promoted to lieutenant colonel, had no hope of a higher promotion. Still, civilian life held little more prospects than some paper-pushing desk job at a headquarters. He was definitely getting antsy. All right, he'd hang tough for a while longer—as long as he was still assigned to the cockpit. Who knew, maybe something would come along, like the Libyan raid in '86—

Loud voices from the other end of the bar. "No good relations there," he said to himself, and headed for the group, intending to take his WSO back to their rooms before things boiled over.

"Ah, Colonel," one of the French pilots said when Doucette reached Contreraz, "your navigator is a fraud. He passed himself off as a fighter pilot and then tells us he flies, what do you call it, the Aardvark? Not a fighter at all, nothing like our Mirages." A chorus of rude remarks about the F-111 broke out among the pilots.

"Tell Qaddafi that," Doucette said. He couldn't tell them that he and Contreraz had led the attack on Libya in April of '86 and they were the crew that had walked a stick of five-hundred-pounders across a Libyan air base.

"But you missed him," the pilot replied. More rude comments from the pilots.

"How did we know it was the camel's turn to be on top?" Doucette shot back. "Got the camel, though. Qadaffi's been heartbroken ever since."

"Is it true," the same pilot said, "that flying the F-111 is like beating off—it's fun while you do it but you're ashamed afterward?"

"Old, old joke, my friend," Doucette said as he took Contreraz by the arm and hauled him out of the bar.

"Sorry, Ramon. That was getting out of hand."

Yes, he thought, he definitely needed some real action.

CHAPTER 11

D MINUS 24

NELLIS AFB, NEVADA

Chief Master Sergeant Mortimer M. Pullman had made the coffee and was waiting for the officers in Rahimi's office Sunday morning. He had been up most of the night and pleased with himself—the trailers were ready.

After a second walk-through Friday he had trashed any idea of renovation. Instead he had grabbed a base telephone directory and run through names looking for anyone he might know. A familiar name surfaced in the Directorate of Resource Management, a sergeant he had saved from a dead-end assignment when he was working in the NCO-assignments section at headquarters. He called the sergeant and collected on the favor. Late Saturday night three trailers complete with office equipment and air conditioners were delivered to building 201's parking lot and the three old ones hauled away.

Dewa Rahimi arrived with a carton of donuts and pastries. "Nice trailers, Chief," she said, working to keep a straight face. She understood that the chief had been out dog-robbing.

Pullman shrugged and sank back in a chair, watching her go to work. He liked the graceful way she moved, and wished he had a daughter like her. "What's the Colonel got planned for today?"

"We're putting the mission together." She opened the safes and pulled out maps and photos, tacking them up on the walls.

Jack Locke and Thunder Bryant came in, followed by Stansell who looked to Rahimi. "Have at it."

"Okay. Here's the nut we have to crack," she began, pointing at a large mosaic photograph—"the prison at Kermanshah. It's located on the southern edge of town next to some old Persian army barracks. The barracks appear to be mostly deserted. All of the POWs, 282 of them, are inside the prison compound. Their exact locations in the buildings are unknown." She pointed to a large three-story flat-topped building inside the walls of the prison. "I suspect they're all in the main cell block. The smaller building in the front corner is the administration building and guards' quarters. There's only one entrance," and she pointed to a thirty-foot-long above-ground tunnel with a dome-shaped roof. It looked like a concrete quonset hut stuck against the outside center of the northwest wall. "There are heavy gates at each end. It's probably booby-trapped inside. Obviously you can't go in through there. These little black circles peppered over the compound are telephone poles the Iranians have planted to discourage helicopter assaults."

"Could they be setting us up? We try a rescue mission and they bushwhack us?"

"Possible, Colonel," Rahimi said. "They would make political hay out of a failed rescue mission, just like Operation Eagle Claw in 1980 in Tehran. And the more casualties the better."

"The Army's got to get into the prison fast," Stansell said. "Dewa, you got anything on the prison walls?"

She flipped through her notes. "The DIA sent us some stereoscopic coverage that's less than a week old. Here we are . . . eighteen feet high, five feet wide at the base tapering to three feet at the top. Reinforced concrete. The guard towers at each corner have unrestricted fields of fire." She paused. "Colonel, I don't think you can go over the walls. And I found more telephone poles in the compound than are on the mosaic." She gestured to the photos on the wall. "They've also jerryrigged steel towers on top of the buildings. A helicopter or parachute assault into the prison looks suicidal."

Stansell sat back in his chair, closing his eyes, recalling the previous Sunday night when he had sat alone in his VOQ room in Washington. Had it only been a week? . . . and he thought again of February 1944, the Gestapo holding those French Resistance fighters in Amiens jail, the Maquis getting word that the Gestapo was getting ready to execute most of them. There was no way they could take the prison so they asked the RAF to bomb it, making a jail break possible. The RAF sent fighter bombers against it, and over 250 prisoners escaped . . . He told some of this to the chief and Rahimi.

"So what are you saying, Colonel?" the chief asked. "We bomb the prison and maybe kill the people we're trying to save?"

"No. We bomb the *walls* and blow holes in 'em and put a couple of five-hundred pound Snakeyes into the guards' building. While the dust is settling the rescue team parachutes in, lands outside the walls and goes through the holes we've made."

"Colonel," Pullman said, "who the hell can do that type of precision bombing?"

"F-111s or F-15Es," Locke said.

Pullman looked at him. "Could be . . . well, I'm going to build a mock-up of the prison—"

"Chief," Dewa cut in, "you haven't got *time* to build a full-scale mock-up."

Pullman turned and walked out the door. He loved a challenge. And without it this rescue wouldn't ever come off.

TOURS, FRANCE

By noon the ramp at the air base was packed with French kids who had discovered Doucette and were crowding around him under a wing of the F-111. Contreraz had a seemingly endless supply of F-111 shoulder patches that he passed out to teenagers. Doucette noticed the brunette from the bar was acting as an impromptu translator and constantly whispering in the WSO's ear. Neither of the Americans were surprised when the French Mirage pilot appeared in his flight suit to reclaim the girl.

"So like the Americans," the Frenchman said, glancing at the F-111 and then at Doucette. "Bigger, not better. Can this really fly or does it just sit on the ground looking like an old overfed anteater?"

"It flies," Doucette said, the combat juices rising, the boredom he'd been feeling at the bar the night before vanishing.

Contreraz's attention shifted away from the girl when he heard the hard tone in his pilot's voice. "Sorry, love," he told her, "got to go. Torch is about ready to engage." He was too late. Doucette had already agreed to do a low level, high-speed flyby at the end of the show when they launched for Lakenheath.

"Torch, don't do this," Contreraz told him. The two were a strange combination. On the ground Contreraz was the wild man and Doucette was all sobriety and responsibility. In the air the roles reversed. The WSO was the hard-nosed professional and Doucette became an animal. Only his flying skill and Contreraz's constant restraint kept him out of serious trouble and still flying.

"One pass, haul ass." Doucette's motto on a mission. Knocking out enemy targets with his bombs was what he was about, and even a practice run turned him on. But the real thing was where it really was. Still, until a hostile target and a real enemy were in his sights—and it wouldn't be long—he'd settle for the Frenchman who had insulted his jet.

The WSO groaned, doubting the French knew how low and fast Doucette could take the F-111. "Don't jump us when we do it, okay? Single ship only."

"*Mais oui.*" The pilot smiled, fully intending to intercept them with his Mirage when they flew down the runway.

Doucette reverted to his normal routine and spent the afternoon entertaining children while Contreraz and the girl slipped away for a long lunch. When the WSO returned, Doucette had zipped his G-suit on and was pacing. "Time to go. Flight plan's filed and our clearance is on request."

"I don't want to do this," Contreraz grumbled as he strapped in. He could see a sleek delta-winged Mirage 2000 taking off. Fifteen minutes later they were airborne.

Doucette lifted the jet off and raised the gear and flaps, cleaning it up and turning the ugly duckling into a graceful swan. He claimed that the old saying about aircraft applied to the F-111—if it looks good, it is good. And in flight, the F-111 looked good. The pilot headed to the east, sightseeing while Contreraz studied his map and punched a short route into the computer for the run that would guide them around any obstacle, towns or villages. When they were ready Doucette dropped down to the deck, swept the wings back with the variable sweep handle to twenty-six degrees, set the Terrain Following Radar to four hundred feet, engaged the autopilot and headed for the field. "Relax," the pilot said, "he won't find us down here in the weeds."

"Wish I was sure of that," Contreraz said.

Fifteen miles out from the airfield Doucette called the tower for permission to fly down the runway. He pushed the throttles up when the tower cleared them in and rooted the indicated airspeed meter on .95 mach—610 knots and swept the wings back to fifty-four degrees. Both men kept twisting in their seats, looking for the

Mirage. "He'll be there," Doucette said. "Wants to impress the home-town crowd." He milked the F-111 down to 200 feet as they crossed the perimeter fence around the air base. "Got him," Doucette shouted. "Left eight o'clock high. Coming to our six."

At mid-field the pilot reefed the plane into a sixty-five degree climb, his eyes locked on the Mirage that was converting to their six o'clock position. Doucette shoved the throttles full forward into the fifth and final stage of afterburner. The 25,000 pounds of thrust being generated by each Pratt and Whitney TF30-P-100 turbofan engine pushed them through the sound barrier. Now he switched hands on the stick, his right hand reaching forward for the fuel dump switch on the center panel between them. He flipped the red guard covering the switch to open . . .

"No," Contreraz shouted. Too late. Doucette hit the switch and JP-4 pumped out the fuel-dump mast located under the tail of the F-111 between the burner cans of the two jet engines. The plumb of the afterburners lit the raw fuel streaming out of the dump mast and a torch, four hundred feet long, flashed out from under their tail toward the Mirage. From his side of the cockpit Contreraz could see the Mirage fly through the long plume reaching out behind them as the French pilot pulled off and away.

"Shit oh dear! He was too close. I think you french-fried him."

"One does hope."

THE MOUNTAINS OF KURDISTAN, IRAQ

Bill Carroll had been watching the mountain trail since early morning, not sure which side of the border he was on, Iraq or Iran. The trail he was watching showed signs of heavy use, by the Kurdish tribesmen who moved at will across the border, he hoped. The fierce tribesmen had been fighting Iraq for generations, trying to carve out an independent homeland. The Kurds might be able to help him—if he could just make contact with their leaders.

Occasionally the three-and-a-half-million Kurds living in Iran would press for more independence and the Iranian government would execute a few of its own Kurds and take reprisals. When relations between the two countries were strained, Iran would encourage the Iraqi Kurds by increasing the flow of arms and supplies across the border. The Kurds were a people caught between two unfriendly governments.

After arriving in Rezaiyeh Carroll had tried to make contact with the Kurdish Democratic Party but the town-dwelling Kurds he had approached were too wary of strangers. Afraid to delay longer, he had caught a bus and headed south into the vague area called Kurdistan. He needed to find a Kurdish village where a single stranger would not be feared. Forty miles south of Rezaiyeh he had gotten off the bus and hitched a ride on a truck headed southwest toward the Iraqi border. The truck driver had warned him about a large army garrison at the village of Khaneh four miles from the border. He had jumped off the truck before they ran into a roadblock and headed into the mountains.

Movement down the trail now caught his attention and he pulled back into the bushes. He could make out four soldiers moving single-file toward him. They moved quietly, maintaining fifty-foot intervals, scanning the brush and trail for any signs of a booby trap. Just below him the squad leader spoke in Arabic, telling them to find hiding places along the trail.

Carroll studied their uniforms and weapons—Iraqi soldiers. The leader had picked the same place to hide along the trail for the same reasons he had: good concealment and a clear view of the trail. Carroll settled down to wait out the soldiers . . .

It was dusk when Carroll heard the slow hoofbeats and squeaking harness of a pack train, but he did not move, afraid the soldiers might see him. The way they had disappeared into the brush and remained concealed warned Carroll that they were professionals. The few minutes that passed before the pack train came into view stretched into hours.

Through the brush and rocks Carroll could make out a young man on foot leading four heavily laden donkeys. He sucked in his breath and held it when the man stopped his donkeys short of the waiting ambush. He looked around, satisfied with the spot, and propped his assault rifle against a tree. He produced a small submachine gun, an Uzi, from under his baggy coat and hung it from a branch. Carefully he then unpacked the animals, talking to them in a low voice, checking for sores as he stroked them.

The man's moustache, wide sash around his waist and baggy trousers drawn at the ankle, identified him as a Kurd, and Carroll could make out a dagger and pistol stuck in his sash. Like most Kurds he was a walking armory. When the donkeys had been watered and fed, the Kurd settled to his knees, and in the failing light tended to his evening prayers, the low rhythmic chant of the Shahada reaching the soldiers. "*Allah-u Akbar, Allah-u Akbar,*" God is most great, God is most great. Carroll could see the words capture the praying man, embracing, reassuring him.

A shadow moved behind the Kurd. Carroll tensed, waited, his eyes searching for the other three soldiers. The Iraqi soldier now stood behind the Kurd, and drove the muzzle of his rifle into the base of the Kurd's skull, knocking him spread-eagled to the ground. He grabbed the Kurd's wrist and jerked the prostrate man's arm up and forward. Carroll could hear a laugh from one of the hidden soldiers below him when the attacker kicked the Kurd in the armpit. Another kick turned the Kurd over, followed by the Iraqi stomping on the man's chest.

Now the other three men emerged from hiding. "Miteif," one called to another, "there's nothing left."

"He is not dead," another said.

The men gathered around the prostrate body. One bent down and bound the Kurd's wrists and ankles with white nylon-reinforced plastic shackles. Two others dragged him to a tree and propped him against it while another built a small fire. Then the four men settled around the fire and prepared their dinner, content with their work.

Carroll moved out of his hiding place and worked his way toward the fire, a cold anger inside him. He crouched in the shadows, twenty yards from the fire. He did not have to wait long. Soon one of the men stood and walked into the darkness, answering a call of nature. Carroll moved silently toward the man, his knife in his left hand. He could just make out the vague image of the soldier urinating against a rock. He worked closer and stood beside a tree, blending into the dark.

The man turned and stumbled toward the fire, zipping his pants up, walking straight toward Carroll, not seeing him. Carroll's left hand shot straight forward out of the shadows, jabbing the knife into the Iraqi's throat while his right hand grabbed the soldier's hair. Carroll pulled the knife across his throat, cutting the right carotid artery, dropped the man to the ground by his hair, allowing him to bleed to death.

He moved toward the tree where the Kurd had hung the Uzi.

The odds were now acceptable.

The donkeys brayed and pounded the ground when they caught the scent of blood. The three men were looking at the donkeys when Carroll lifted the small Uzi off the branch and crouched behind the tree. Miteif pulled two steel rods out of his pack, banged them together and turned his attention to the fire. "This will pass the time tonight," he said, shoving the ends of the rods into the hot coals of the fire.

"What will you burn off first," one of the Iraqis said, "his moustache?"

"Why not? The Kurds are proud of their ability to sprout hair under their noses. Then his manhood?"

"Do Kurds have any?"

The men were laughing when Carroll shot them, then quickly checked each body. Miteif groaned and looked at Carroll when he bent over him. Without hesitating he held the Uzi's muzzle against Miteif's head and pulled the trigger and two bullets ripped into the back of his skull.

Carroll now hurried over to the Kurd. Remarkably, the man was still alive and conscious. The Iraqis had pulled the white plastic straps tight around his wrists, cutting deep into the skin and cutting off the flow of blood and both hands were swollen. Carefully, Carroll sliced through the straps.

"You're in bad shape, friend. I've got to get you home."

Carroll had, he decided, made the contact he needed if he was going to get the Kurds to help him with the POWs at Kermanshah.

CHAPTER 12

D MINUS 23

NELLIS AFB, NEVADA

The major in charge of the Red Flag exercise starting that morning was at work before 0600 in building 201 putting finishing touches on the scenario. The sign on his desk identified him as The Warlord.

He looked up at the sound of heels coming down the hall. His administration clerk, a young buck sergeant, positioned himself so he could see whoever walked pass the open office door so early in the morning. Both men then watched Dewa Rahimi walk by carrying a box of . . . donuts? She was wearing a western shirt, jeans and cowboy boots. Her dark hair was held back by a red bandana. The sergeant stuck his head around the door and his eyes followed her down the hall. "Have mercy," he intoned . . .

Stansell smiled at Rahimi when she came into the Intelligence section. He had been at work for over an hour reviewing message traffic. "Gone western?"

"Why not? This is Vegas. Besides, I love horses, ride a lot."

"We had horses when I was a kid growing up in Colorado," he told her. "My two younger sisters, everyone in the family rode."

"Maybe we can go riding sometime?" It was an opening she had been looking for. When they were in Washington, she had only seen the colonel as a professional colleague. But now she found that she looked forward to seeing him.

"Some interesting message traffic came in over the wires last night," he told her. "Rangers out of Fort Benning have been picked for the mission. Four platoons from two companies of the Third Batallion, 75th Infantry. I was expecting Delta Force . . ."

"So was I," she said, trying to hide sudden doubts. Mado had implied that Task Force Alpha was going to be a composite of Delta Force and Combat Talon MC-130Es from the 1st Special Operations Wing. They were the elite units, ruthlessly trained for tough missions. Stansell's job was to marry the two units for a raid on the prison. Something was wrong.

"I don't know much about the Rangers," she told him, deciding not to surface her doubts. She recalled the meeting with Cunningham and how she felt when it looked like Stansell might be replaced as mission commander. She had thought she saw a possibility for compromise. No one liked the bearer of bad news, especially when based mostly on suspicions.

"We'll find out." Stansell too was obviously concerned. "There's another message about movement reported near Kermanshah."

She picked up the stack of messages and sat down at her desk. The important one was on top and Stansell had highlighted the second paragraph in yellow. She turned her computer on and called up one of the Defense Intelligence Agency's data banks she could access. Her computer was linked by a telephone circuit to one of the DIA's computers buried in the Pentagon's basement. The two computers talked to each other in code, encoding and decoding any signal that went over the telephone circuit. Recently the security of the computer system had been questioned by the chairman of the Senate Select Committee on Intelligence, and the National Security Agency's watchdog group had been turned loose and were tapping the DIA's communications net.

On this Monday morning the watchdog COMSEC monitors picked up Rahimi's traffic and the intercepted signals were fed into one of the giant Cray computers the NSA used for breaking codes. After two minutes, the computer selected a subroutine and answered a series of questions. The computer anticipated breaking the code in fourteen months. The system was secure.

Rahimi's worry intensified as she jotted coordinates and numbers down off the computer. "Damn," she said, and walked up to the big map of western Iran she had tacked to the wall. "An armored regiment is moving into garrison near Shahabad." She drew a circle around a town forty-two miles southeast of Kermanshah. "They're centered on the highway airstrip south of town."

"Why there? Any clear connection with the POWs at Kermanshah?"

"It's right on the old silk route between Tehran and Baghdad. The mountains channel any invasion force coming out of Iraq toward Kermamshah and Tehran down that valley. It's a good blocking position. *And* a threat against a rescue attempt."

"Do you have an OB?"

"So far only the reported ten tanks—Soviet T-72s—in the message. There's bound to be more—antiaircraft artillery, surface-to-air missiles, armored troop carriers . . ."

Locke and Bryant came in then, and Locke immediately spotted the wall map. "Why the circle at Shahabad?"

Rahimi was explaining when Chief Pullman arrived. "Colonel, the commander is up the wall about the C-130s coming in today. Claims he doesn't have room to park eight of 'em on the ramp. Wants to see you ASAP."

Stansell shook his head. "I was expecting twelve. Dewa, work with Jack and Thunder and try to get a handle on what this does to us. The chief and I will try to calm the heavies."

Locke pulled a chair up in front of the map and listened to the last of Rahimi's information, and Bryant then motioned her to follow him outside when she had finished. "Let him mull it over for a while. I saw him do this at Ras Assanya. He'll come up with something, it's his strong suit." They walked back into the office.

"Got me an idea," Jack said.

Dewa looked at Bryant.

"What do you calculate for total time on the ground at Kermanshah?"

"With transportation in place to move the POWs, less than ninety minutes from the first bomb. Longer, maybe three hours if we fly in our own transport from shuttle," she said.

Locke studied the map. "If we surprise them, that armored regiment can't react and move the forty-two miles to Kermanshah in ninety minutes. Don't know about the three hours. We can slow 'em down by taking out this bridge." He pointed to a highway bridge half way between Shahabad and Kermanshah.

Dewa couldn't hide the worry she felt, at the same time realizing how attached she felt to these men. Men she hardly knew.

* * *

Pullman drove Stansell to the headquarters building of the Tactical Fighter Weapons Center. "Which commander were you talking about?" he asked.

"Major General John O'Brian, head honcho of the Tactical Fighter Weapons Center," Pullman told him.

The two were escorted directly into the general's office. The wing commander of the 57th Fighter Weapons Wing and his Deputy for Operations were with O'Brian. "Well, Colonel Stansell," the general said, "seems you're staking quite a claim to my base. Eight C-130s and their support take up a hell of a lot of space. My working troops here tell me we're full up with our own jets and the ones here for Red Flag. Now tell me what the hell is going on or kindly get off my base."

Stansell hesitated. Why hadn't Mado told O'Brian? "Sir, I'd be glad to explain, in private. We're working on a need-to-know basis here."

"They've seen the message from Mado asking us to support Task Force Alpha," the general said, gesturing at the two seated men.

"Sorry, sir, this is close-hold information—"

"Wait outside," O'Brian told the men. "Stansell, this had better be good."

The chief closed the door behind the departing officers. "General O'Brian, we're here to put together a team to rescue the POWs out of Iran."

The general sucked in his breath. "You're part of JSOA? Why didn't someone tell me that?"

"We're forming as a separate unit. We'll be chopped to JSOA's command later."

"Now I'm not so impressed." The hard look on O'Brian's face made his feelings clear.

Stansell thought, he's really going to be skeptical when he hears about the Army. "General O'Brian, I was planning on setting up a forward operation location on one of the dry lake beds you own. The Army contingent, most of our people, and the C-130s would operate out of there. We'd use Nellis primarily for support."

Pullman's back stiffened when he heard what Stansell was proposing, knowing who would have to get it organized.

O'Brian's fingers drummed his desk. "When?"

"Tomorrow latest."

The general walked over to a wall map of the Tactical Fighter Weapons Center. Nellis was a large Air Force Base, and when the bombing ranges and the Military Operating Areas were tacked on, the general controlled a piece of southern Nevada about the size of Switzerland. "I'm putting you at Delamar Lake. We renamed it Texas Lake for Red Flag. It's a dry lake bed seventy-four miles to the north we use for C-130 operations. You should pass for a routine exercise. I'll run cover for you but I'll have to tell the Office of Special Investigations to be on the lookout for anyone interested in what you're doing . . . When does Delta Force get here?"

Gawdamn, Pullman thought, the gray-haired fox doesn't miss much.

"We're getting Rangers and I plan to bring them tomorrow, no later than Wednesday."

"Stansell, when you decide where to build a mock-up of your target let me know. You'll need camouflage netting to hide it from the satellite the Russians monitor us with. And Mort, next time you want trailers ask." The general drilled an astonished Pullman with his hard blue eyes. "I do talk to my troops. Now get the hell out of here. Your C-130s are landing in thirty minutes."

As they retreated from the general's office Stansell said, "Chief, why didn't you tell me you knew him?"

"It didn't seem important . . . I got his ass out of a crack when he was a second lieutenant. He was responsible for a big supply kit during a deployment exercise and some expensive tools were stolen. I found them." Pullman wanted to change the subject before Stansell asked more questions. Actually, the chief had had to beat an airman almost senseless before he learned where the tools had been hidden. "What are you going to do with the 130s?"

"Find out how good they are and have them haul some valuable cargo."

Lieutenant Colonel Paul "Duck"—what else?—Mallard followed the other four members of his C-130 crew into Red Flag's auditorium. He had been there during Red Flag 85-1—the first exercise of 1985. Something's strange, he thought. Normally a unit knew months in advance if it was going to be part of Red Flag. He looked around the large room, walls covered with plaques, flags and mementoes of past Red Flag exercises. He found the other seven aircraft commanders, each surrounded by his own crew. All of his forty crew members were there.

Mallard sat down next to his navigator, Captain Percy Dunkin.

The tall skinny navigator was already asleep, probably still hung-over, Mallard figured.

"Room, ten-hut." Pullman's voice rang out from the back as Stansell walked down the aisle. Everyone but Dunkin jumped to attention. Mallard didn't bother to disturb him.

Stansell proceeded to tell Mallard and his men that he needed volunteers for a tough, hazardous operation. It would include risky low-level flying, paradrops and short field landings. There might be casualties. Mallard spoke for his 463rd Wing. They were all in.

"Good. Welcome to Task Force Alpha. We start now. You're going to launch out of here in one hour and fly a first-look low-level route to a dry lake. You've got to hit your Time Over Target plus or minus a minute, paradrop a dummy load on the panels that will be staked out there and do an assault landing on the lake bed. After you've landed you'll be launched on your second mission. Captain Jack Locke will brief you on the route and target."

Mallard's copilot, First Lieutenant Don Larson, was staring at Locke. He almost twisted his head off when he made the connection and turned to look at the departing Stansell. "Colonel Mallard, I'll bet my sweet black ass this is a biggy. Stansell is the guy that escaped out of Ras Assanya and Locke was the 45th's Top Gun. We're playing big leagues."

"And you just may be lucky enough to get your 'sweet black ass' shot off," Mallard said straight-faced, and punched on Dunkin until he woke up.

Forty-five minutes later Mallard's loadmaster was signaling him to crank the C-130's number-three engine. Dunkin was hunched over the navigator's table still working on his map. I've got the world's tallest troll for a navigator, Mallard thought. Not only is he an alcoholic, he walks around like the hunchback of Notre Dame. He also reminded himself that Captain Percy "Drunkin" Dunkin was also just about the best lead navigator in the Air Force.

Chief Pullman had a UH-1F helicopter, the venerable Huey, waiting on the ramp when Locke was finished with the C-130 crews. The captain was surprised when Pullman told him it was there to fly them to Texas Lake. "Don't ask, Captain. How else you expect to get there before the Herky Birds and stake out the drop panels?" The chief threw a bundled-up parachute canopy and a bag of steel pins into the Huey and clambered on board. "Come on, we got work to do."

As the helicopter lifted off and headed for Texas Lake seventy-four miles north of Nellis, Pullman unfolded a 1:50,000 scale map and pointed to a spot on the dry lake. He had to shout to be heard over the noise. "This is where Captain Bryant wants us to stake out the panels. He said to cut the parachute up and make a big cross." When they reached Texas Lake the pilot sat the Huey down near the spot Pullman had marked on the map. Locke tapped the pilot on the shoulder and pointed to the southern end of the lake.

"What the hell?" Pullman yelled.

"Stansell said to throw them a curve," Locke shouted at him as the Huey lifted off. "He was expecting C-130s from the First Special Ops Wing. He's really pissed."

Dunkin was standing behind the copilot's seat, clutching a map in one hand and steadying himself with the other. He had a death grip on the left side of Larson's seat. Two stop watches were dangling from his neck, bouncing up and down from the light turbulence, and his battered yellow baseball cap was on backward. He claimed it was lucky.

"Where the hell is the lake?" Mallard shouted over the intercom.

"Over the next ridge. Trust me," Dunkin answered. "We're on time." They were the first in the string of C-130s flying five minutes in-trail. "After you pop over the ridge in front of us level off at sixty-two twenty. That will give us thirteen hundred fifty feet above the ground just like a troop drop," Dunkin said. "The panels will be on the nose. Loadmaster, six minute warning."

"Rog. Six minute check complete." Master Sergeant Glen Moore had the door over the C-130's ramp raised and a 150-pound canister of concrete with a T-10 parachute ready. He would lower the ramp to a level position after they popped.

Dunkin grabbed the back of the copilot's seat with both hands as the ridge line filled their windscreen. "Pop . . . now."

Mallard ballooned the Hercules over the ridge, trading off his airspeed for altitude and slowing from 240 to 130 knots.

When he could see the lake Dunkin shouted, "Those bastards got the panels at the wrong end of the lake. Abort the drop, circle south for another run."

"Rog," Moore said, "aborting the drop." Nothing ever seemed to upset the old sergeant.

Dunkin reached back to his station and rotated his intercom switch to UHF radio. He looked over the dry lake bed as Mallard turned away, then hit his transmit button. "Ruff flight, Ruff One-One aborting first drop. The panels are at the south end of the lake. New UTMs are"—he paused while he picked off the coordinates from his map—"8150–3080. Use the western edge of the lake for a timing point." He paused before he rattled off another eight-digit set of coordinates. "Duck, reverse course and fall in behind tail-end Charlie. We drop last."

"Hell, Dunk, we ought'a abort the whole shoot'n match and land," Mallard said, thinking about their time over target and hitting the target.

"No," the navigator told him. "All they got to do is slip south on the last leg and recompute a new elapsed time from the timing point to green light for the drop. They'll only lose a few seconds so they'll be okay on their TOTs. Everything else is the same. We'll drop last." He reached into his navigation bag and pulled out the gadget he had made for emergencies like this one . . .

Locke was standing beside the helicopter monitoring the C-130 frequency on the Huey's radio. He watched the first Hercules turn away and head back to the west. "Looks like an abort for number one," he told the chief.

Another C-130 popped over the low ridge in front of them like some pterodactyl rising from its desert nest with the sun at its back. It leveled off at its drop altitude and flew straight for the panels. A small bundle dropped off the ramp under its tail and arched behind the C-130, the parachute streaming out and snapping open when it reached the end of its static line. The canister swung back and forth until it bounced on the hard crust of the lake bed. "Looks short about seventy yards," Pullman said. "That's good for a free drop."

One after another the C-130s popped over the ridge to drop their loads. Locke listened on the radio as each crew fed information back to the trailing birds about the winds. Most of the drops were inside a hundred yards. Finally the lead ship reappeared, popping over the ridge slightly north of the others. "He's off course and too low," Locke said, expecting the big cargo plane to slip south. Instead it headed straight for the helicopter. The load dropped off the back and the parachute blossomed out.

The helicopter pilot shouted, "It's gonna hit us," and the three men scattered away. The concrete-filled canister swung once before it bounced twenty feet short of the helicopter, and the parachute canopy collapsed over the rotor blades.

"They blew the hell out of that drop," Locke said.

Pullman shook his head. "Someone up there was sending us a message, Captain. They may not be what the colonel was expecting, but these guys are good."

The first C-130 to drop was circling to land on the dry bed and came down a short final, nose high in the air. The pilot slammed the big bird down onto the hardpan of the dry lake and reversed props, sending a dust storm in advance—a giant announcing its arrival with a roar and gust of breath.

"You want me to marshal them into parking?" the helicopter pilot asked.

"Nope," Locke said, "let's see how they handle it."

The C-130 completed its landing roll-out and turned toward the helicopter. The pilot played a tune on the engines, varying the prop pitch by jockeying the throttles. The bird stopped, the crew-entrance door flopped down, and a green-suited crew member with shoulder-length hair climbed down the three steps built into the door. The door snapped closed, and the woman directed the pilot into a parking position next to the helicopter, signaling the pilot to set the brakes and cut the engines.

The pilot climbed down the steps and walked toward them. "Looks like your women did the first drop," Pullman said.

The C-130 pilot, a captain, was a woman slightly taller than Locke. Her nametag announced she was Lydia Kowalski. "Dirty pool, Captain, moving the panels like that. Any more nasties up your sleeve?"

Locke shrugged. "Just routine cargo hauling. We're sending most of you to Elgin Air Force Base to pick up a Harvest Eagle kit—want you back tomorrow. Then you'll all be going to Fort Benning to bring some army troops and their equipment in Wednesday."

"What's a Harvest Eagle kit?" Kowalski asked.

"A whole tent city," Pullman told her. "We're goin' to be camping here for a while." He didn't add that she and the others would appreciate their time here once they got to Iran . . .

After turning the C-130 crews over to Locke and explaining to Bryant what he wanted done, Stansell headed for Rahimi's office, his mouth set. He had to work his way through the crowd of Red Flag players jamming the corridors of Building 201.

"Yo, Colonel," a familiar voice called from one of the briefing rooms. It was Snake Houserman from Luke. "Didn't know you were here." Snake stuck his skinny face around the door. His features alternated between elfish and demonic depending on the situation.

"Not a player, Snake. I'm a coordinator."

"Oh, no," he laughed, the elf emerging, "another Warlord." He disappeared back into the briefing room.

The sign on the door to the Intelligence section said, "Open" but the combination on the four-key cipher-lock had been changed. Stansell buzzed for admittance and Dewa unlocked the door. She was alone in the office. "Wild bunch, colonel. I had to change the combination to get a little work done. You know a Captain Houserman? He doesn't waste any time."

"I'll put some salt on his tail if he's bothering you."

"I can handle him. How'd the briefing go?"

"I'm worried." He poured coffee and followed Dewa into her office. She sat at one end of the Air Force issue couch. He sat at the other end and told her about the meeting with General O'Brian and the C-130 crews.

"It doesn't make sense," he said, "we should be working with Delta Force and Combat Talon C-130s from the 1st Special Operations Wing."

"Why Combat Talon C-130s?"

"They train for deep-penetration missions like this one. Their aircraft are specially configured. They've got terrain-following radars, upgraded inertial navigation systems and computers for precision navigation and airdrops, not to mention more powerful engines, armor plating, jamming capability . . ."

Dewa went over to her desk while Stansell stared at the floor, annoyed and frustrated. She sat and faced her computer, fingers moving over the keyboard. "Let's see if I can find out what the 1st Special Ops Wing is doing with its aircraft," she said as she called up the data banks she could access. "Nothing, so far." She sat back. "I don't have access to aircraft movement. What command does the First belong to and where's it based?"

"Military Airlift Command, 23rd Air Force, out of Hurlburt Field," he told her.

Again her fingers went over the keyboard. "Bingo. I'm talking to the Resource Management computer at Hurlburt through MAC's logistic supply computer. Bureaucracies are wonderful things. They like to keep track of *everything*. Let's see how Hurlburt's Resource Management office is reporting their aircraft." She studied the screen. "What does UE stand for?"

"Unit Equipment, how many aircraft an outfit owns."

"Colonel, Hurlburt's computer is reporting all but two of the First's C-130s on station. I'd say that they're all home."

"They should be *here*. We're not getting the support we were promised . . ."

Dewa heard the frustration in his voice. He badly wants to be part of this, she thought, not wanting to tell him what she saw. She was a trained analyst, and evaluated *all* the evidence, friendly and hostile, good and bad, on *both* sides of the fence. And she had drawn the only logical conclusion, which she was obliged to report to Stansell, an engaging pattern that was sure to add pain to his frustration. "Rupe"—she tried to make her voice sympathetic—"deception is part of what we do . . . it seems you're not going to rescue the POW's."

Stansell stared at her.

"Task Force Alpha is a decoy operation," she told him. "A cover for the real mission. We get to play Quaker cannon."

Like hell, he thought. Cunningham might seem to be playing along, but Stansell didn't believe he'd let his Alpha go down the drain.

KERMANSHAH, IRAN

Mary Hauser sat in the cracked bathtub scrubbing her hair, hoping the soap they gave her was strong enough to kill the lice. She couldn't quite believe it, she had not been interrogated since the general had left, the food was improving and now this—a bath. Either they're getting ready to release us—possible?—or an important visitor is coming for an inspection, she decided. She sank down into the tepid water and let it wash over her. As she reached for the ragged towel the guard had left her when he took her clothes the door swung open and Mokhtari stood there, holding a dark blanket. Two guards were behind him.

"Put this on. Now." It was not a blanket but a chador, the shroud-like robe all Iranian women wore.

She stood, drying herself. They'd seen her like this before, she reminded herself, trying not to be upset by what the chador meant—a symbol of subservience. Part of the technique, don't read too much into it. "I want my uniform back," she said, slipping the chador over her head and letting the rough cloth fall over her body.

"The hood," Mokhtari ordered.

She raised the hood and covered her head, and the two guards stepped around the commandant and took hold of her, dragging her out of the bathroom and down the stairs toward her cell. Mokhtari, leading the way, turned into the interrogation room short of her cell. The guards followed, dragging-carrying her. Mokhtari turned, sat behind the desk. One of the guards grabbed the chador and jerked it off.

Mokhtari ignored her, looked into a corner of the room. She followed his eyes, to a man standing in the corner. A dirt-stained shirt barely covered his barrel chest and potbelly. He had massive arms, and fists that slowly clenched and unclenched as he watched her. His pants were unbuttoned. He was barefoot.

"One of my former prisoners," Mokhtari told her. "He has learned to do what I tell him." He then spoke to the man in Farsi, after which the man exposed himself, and as Mokhtari watched, reached out and grabbed Mary Hauser, pushed her against the desk and proceeded to perform as ordered.

CHAPTER 13

D MINUS 22

NORTHEASTERN IRAQ

Bill Carroll led the pack train into the mountain camp of the Pesh Merga, careful to keep his hands in the open. He glanced at a woman huddled against the wall of a hut, her face covered with sores.

"That's what an Iraqi gas attack does," Mustapha Sindi said in Kirmanji, the Kurdish dialect. "She's one of the fortunate ones." Sindi was riding the lead donkey, still not able to walk very far before his strength gave out, thanks to the severe beating the Iraqi soldiers had given him.

Carroll had asked Sindi only to use his native language so he could learn to talk with the Kurds. With Carroll's knack with languages, similarities between Kirmanji, Farsi and Arabic were enough to allow him to pick up quickly the rudiments of the Kurdish tongue.

"Do you have a doctor here?" Carroll asked Sindi, "you need attention." He had come to like the man, who talked nonstop and never complained.

"My cousin Zakia. She is the only female doctor in Kurdistan." Sindi explained everything to Carroll, a sign that he trusted the American. "She was here when I left but she often goes with the soldiers on raids."

The makeshift village served as a base camp for the Pesh Merga, the Kurdish patriots fighting for their own homeland inside Iraq. The camp was filled with women and children, refugees from the repeated attacks the Iraqi army had carried out against the Kurds, their own people. There were only a few old men in the camp, and Carroll did not see a single young one.

"Over there." Sindi pointed to a mud-brick hut. A woman in her mid-thirties appeared in the doorway, leaned against the doorjamb and crossed her arms, face expressionless, waiting for them. She wore camouflaged fatigue trousers and boots, tee shirt stretched across her breasts, and her dark hair was pulled back into a tight bun at the nape of her neck. As they approached, Carroll thought he could see a resemblance between Mustapha Sindi and the woman.

"Zakia," Sindi sighed as Carroll helped him off the donkey.

The woman appraised Carroll, then turned to Sindi. "Wait here," she ordered, taking her younger cousin inside.

Carroll tethered the donkeys and sat down, his back against the wall, and soon dozed off in the warm sun.

A toe of a boot prodded him awake. Zakia was standing over him. "Mustapha has told me how you saved him." Her voice had a kind of lyrical undertone. "I thank you." She was not smiling. "My cousin trusts you, but then he is very young and foolish. It is dangerous to trust strangers in this country."

Carroll searched for the right words in Kirmanji. "If you give me a chance I will prove myself." He tried to choose his words carefully, not wanting to be misunderstood. "I rescued Mustapha because I was trying to make contact with the Pesh Merga."

"Why?"

Might as well level with her. "I'm trying to help the POWs the Iranians are holding at Kermanshah, and I need help. Yours."

"An American needs our help?" She turned and walked back into the hut.

"Give me a chance."

She looked back at him. "It's not me you have to convince. It is Mulla Haqui. And he hates all foreigners—especially Americans." She disappeared then into the hut.

KERMANSHAH, IRAN

Colonel Clayton Leason was looking out the cell window, counting the guards in the watch towers. The distance was too great to see their faces so he would try to identify them, individually, by their actions and habits. He had instructed all the POWs to gather information on the guards—their routines, habits, what they liked . . . It all would be passed on to his escape committee. He had established a series of cutouts in the prison, isolating the escape committee and shielding it from compromise. Even if Mokhtari were to break him he could never tell who was working on escapes or what their plans were. "Doc, why did you join the Air Force?"

"I guess I was bored with my practice," flight surgeon Lieutenant Colonel Jeff Landis told him. "You get tired of looking down throats, treating colds, flu, and an occasional case of the clap." Leason nodded. The Doc's sense of humor was coming back—a sign he was recovering from his last brutal going over by two guards.

"One of my patients was a master sergeant assigned to the local recruiting office," Doc was saying. "He did a sales number on me. Anyway, the middle age blahs were getting to me and the thought of being a flight surgeon in the Air Force and zooming around in the back seat of a fighter became more exciting with each case of whooping cough that came through the door. So I signed up for a two-year tour."

"No one can blame you for having regrets," Leason said, "not after this . . ."

"Hey, I've loved the Air Force, flying in the back seat of an F-4 . . . And I've met some of the best people I've known."

Both men became silent when they heard a cough followed by two rapid coughs—the signal that a message was being passed. Each pressed an ear to the wall and listened to the faint tap code working its way down the cells.

"It's about Espinoza," Leason said.

Doc motioned him to be silent. "Sounds like pneumonia. Clay, if I can get to him I might be able to save him, at least ease his suffering."

"I'll try to work on Mokhtari, but don't expect anything." Leason passed command to Landis. "You've got it until I get back."

"My turn," Landis said. "Let me see him."

"Doc, he's brutal."

"I'm no good sitting in this cell. I'll try to cut a deal with him, I'll treat the guards if he'll let me treat our men."

"That might qualify as collaboration—"

"Collaboration is not what I have in mind. I'll try to open up a channel to the outside, another source of information. You can't keep taking all the risks and you're in no better shape than I am.

And it's not collaboration when I trade off my services for the sake of your men."

"Can you take three or four days in the Box?"

"One way to find out."

Mary Hauser huddled in the corner of her cell, clasping her knees, occasionally rocking back and forth. She unfolded and sat on the edge of her bunk when she heard the dull thumps made by a sand-filled rubber hose impacting against a body coming from the interrogation room. She pressed an ear against the door and listened. She could hear the rage in Mokhtari's voice as it echoed down the hall. They had not closed the door. "Prisoners do not talk to each other, silence is the first rule—"

"I'm a doctor, Commandant."

She heard sharper, more distinct thuds. They were using their fists.

"Who told you the prisoner was dying of pneumonia?" Mokhtari's voice.

"Amnesty International."

It was Doc Landis' voice. Good lord, Amnesty International. Did he think Mokhtari gave a damn about that?

The beating finally stopped and she could hear voices muttering in Farsi. The words were too low and indistinct for her to recognize any familiar word but she thought she could make out an under-current. Footsteps came down the hall. The door to the cell next to hers creaked open and she heard the guards drop somebody, prob-ably Doc, on the floor. The footsteps retreated down the hall.

For three hours Hauser listened at the wall, occasionally hearing a gasp for air. Then a faint tapping started. It was the same code she had been taught in survival school at Fairchild AFB in Washington. It took her several moments to recall the pattern. Fear and a rush of nausea swept over her when she deciphered the first four letters—W-H-O-R. Whore—Mokhtari was still at work. Then the fifth letter came through—U. W-H-O-R-U. It didn't make sense. "Oh . . . Who are you?"

R U O K, she tapped back, testing the sender and identifying herself.

BRKN RIBS LANDIS.

HAUSER, she tapped.

Another message started. HOWS THE FOOD

It *was* Doc Landis, not a trap set by Mokhtari.

They tapped messages back and forth until they heard footsteps in the hall. The door swung open and the warder handed her a plastic bowl and spoon. Hauser looked at him, not believing what she saw. The bowl was full, and the indecipherable stuff in it was topped by a large chunk of bread. The man's face was impassive as he reached and turned the light on, breaking the perpetual darkness she lived in. When the door banged closed she had to force herself to eat slowly, not wolf the food down.

And a new feeling came to her . . . a dangerous one, she knew, but she would allow it. For the first time since she could remember, she thought she might actually make it.

DULLES INTERNATIONAL AIRPORT, VIRGINIA

"Nasir, there," Hasan Zaidan said, pointing Stansell out as he broke free of the knot of people coming down the passenger ramp at Dulles International Airport. The phone call alerting the two agents of the Islamic Jihad had been vague about the colonel's movements, and the caller only knew that Stansell was expected to fly into Dulles from Las Vegas that day.

Nasir Askari removed his sunglasses, calculating his next move. He had been right to insist they watch the flights arriving from St. Louis and Chicago, the two most common connections with Las Vegas. His partner Hasan Zaidan had wanted to leave immediately, not patient enough to wait and see if Stansell would appear. Nasir doubted if Hasan could understand, much less appreciate, the demands their controller at the Albanian Embassy was making on the Islamic Jihad. They had to take their objective quickly or the funds that kept them alive would disappear. He envied Hasan's simple approach to problems—all action, no thought.

Stansell headed for the car rentals, deciding that would be the quickest way to get to the Pentagon twenty-five miles east. He glanced at his watch, nine o'clock traffic on a Tuesday morning shouldn't be too bad. He was determined to confront Mado and if need be, Cunningham about Task Force Alpha. He felt he had been used and anger churned inside as he thought about the sacrifices Thunder, Jack, and Pullman had made to join him.

He shifted his carry-on bag to his right shoulder and pushed his way through the thinning crowd. The complete ops plan was in the bag, sealed in a large envelope.

"Rupe."

Stansell paused when he heard his nickname. Maybe someone had been sent to pick him up. He didn't see a familiar face or an Air Force uniform. He hiked the bag's strap up on his shoulder and walked quickly away. A vice-like hand grabbed his left arm just above the elbow.

"Keep walking," a heavily accented voice said on his left.

He glanced quickly to the left, saw Hasan's face. The Arab was three inches taller than Stansell and outweighed him by fifty pounds. His grip bore down on Stansell's left arm, sending the first tingles of blood starvation down the colonel's forearm. Hasan's left hand brushed against his unbuttoned coat, moving it aside, letting Stansell glimpse a small Beretta clipped to his belt.

"Don't be stupid," Nasir's voice on his right warned. "We need to talk." Two other men were now walking straight toward them.

Stansell raged at himself, nailed in my own front yard by four terrorists? Memories of his captivity at Ras Assanya flashed through him, and without thinking he threw his right shoulder into Nasir, then spun toward Hasan, kicking at his knees. He felt a satisfying crunch, slipped the strap of the bag off his shoulder, grabbed it with both hands and swung it as hard as he could in the general direction of Hasan's head. A direct hit.

He almost lost his balance and fell as he jerked around to face Nasir, whose arm bounced off his head—Stansell's height, or lack of it, had worked to his advantage. Now he barreled into Nasir, throwing him into three white-turbaned Sikhs. Nasir reached into his coat for his revolver, but before he could pull the gun free a gunshot echoed through the concourse. For a moment, silence. In that frozen moment Stansell saw one of the two men that had been walking toward him in a shooter's crouch, hands extended straight out in front of him holding a gun. He was vaguely aware of Hasan, a Beretta in hand, crumpling to the floor, and as he did, squeezing the trigger. A last shot in more ways than one for the dying man.

People, panicked by the gunshots, screamed and ran for safety. And Stansell, still holding onto his bag, moved quickly behind the Sikhs and disappeared into the crowd before the other two men could reach him.

Susan Fisher had been waiting in the basement of the warehouse the CIA used for one of its cover operations. The elevator doors opened. Allen Camm was alone, and his confident look reassured her that she had done the right thing. She had never "neutralized" a foreign agent before.

"Where are they?" Camm asked.

She pointed to an office and held the door open for him. The man who had shot Hasan was pacing the floor. His partner was sprawled out in a chair, relaxed and at ease.

"Tell me about it."

"We made the two Jihadis at Dulles," the pacing man told Camm, voice under tight control, trying not to reveal the stress working through him. It was his first time. "Carl"—he nodded at his seated partner—"saw them first as they nabbed Stansell. That guy is tough—broke free and clobbered one with his bag. The Arab pulled a gun, and that's when I took him out. A clean shot. Stansell disappeared into the crowd. You can imagine the confusion." He took a deep breath. "We grabbed the other Jihad and brought him here. It was easy in that mess."

"What about the one you dropped?"

"We left him," Carl said. "He was dead. Murphy's a good shot."

"Anyone follow you?"

"Please, Mr. Camm," Carl said. "It was clean."

Murphy was still pacing. "It's okay," Camm reassured him. "You did exactly right. Get your report to Miss Fisher."

"Where's the Jihad?" Camm asked her when the two agents had left.

"In primary, want to see him?" Camm nodded and followed her out of the office and down a well-lit hall that reminded one of a hospital corridor. She stopped in front of a steel door and buzzed. They both looked up at the TV camera above the door, waiting to be recognized. The door clicked open. Inside, two white-smocked technicians were sitting at desks watching a TV monitor. "What's his status?" Fisher asked.

One of the technicians said, "He isn't talking, yet."

"Nothing at all?" Camm asked.

"Only what we already know. His name is Nasir Askari, twenty-eight. Born in Tripoli, Lebanon." He glanced at the elapsed-time master-clock on the wall. "He should be spilling his guts within sixty-eight hours. I've never seen anyone last more than seventy-two before they go crazy." He pointed at the TV screen.

Camm pulled a chair up and sat down, studying the screen. "Is the audio up?"

The technician nodded. "Got to be if we're to pick up the clues in time. Once they break, we get 'em out fast."

The infrared image on the TV screen was amazingly sharp, letting them see the man clearly in the darkened cell. Nasir Askari was lying on the floor, naked. The padding on the floor partially enveloped him, yielding to his movements. His arms and legs were bound together with wide soft straps, holding him in a fetal position. The straps would stretch and contract with his movements, always holding him secure.

"Why the mouthpiece?" Fisher asked.

"It keeps him from chewing on his tongue or cheeks," the technician told her. "We try to shut off all tactile, auditory and visual stimuli." He smiled at her. "Sometime when you haven't anything to do, come on down and we'll put you in there for a few minutes. You can't believe how quiet and *dark* it is in there. After a while they'll do almost anything to create a tactile sensation. That's why we restrain them."

"How long has he been in there?"

The technician glanced at the master clock. "Three hours, sixteen minutes. We've had some telling everything they know by now."

"What if someone lies just to get out?"

"We always put them back in for a few minutes until the story is the same." He paused, studying the screen. "This one is going to go for a while. We may have to increase his dosage. We heighten the effect of sensory deprivation by using a new drug, Dicayocaine-Neural-Propoxylase, DNP for short. It reduces the sensitivity of the nerve endings in the skin."

"What happens if they don't break?"

"It happened once. Subject flipped out."

"What did you do then?"

"What we had to do. Look, Miss Fisher, we're not here to torture people. We're after clean, accurate information. That's our job and we do it."

The brigadier general commanding the Air Force's Office of Special Investigation headquartered at Bolling Air Force Base in Washington fidgeted in his chair. He found the waiting difficult and wondered why the shortish colonel with no right ear was taking so much of General Cunningham's time. Still, when the Air Force's chief of staff beckoned and called, he waited. He ran the colonel through his mental bank of pictures, trying to place a name with the face. Finally the general's aide ushered him into the inner sanctum of Cunningham's office.

"Sit down, Hoskins." Cunningham pointed at a chair. "I've got a problem. Colonel Rupert Stansell here has got his ass in a crack. Apparently four terrorists tried to kidnap him this morning at Dulles International. It's complicated because I've got him on a special mission."

"I haven't heard a thing about Dulles—yet," Hoskins said. "Why would terrorists be after Colonel Stansell?" The stony look on Cunningham's face warned him. The general obviously thought he should know who Stansell was.

"We think they were from the Islamic Jihad." Cunningham was rolling an unlit cigar in his fingers and staring at Hoskins—two danger signals. Hoskins had not heard about the Islamic Jihad, and it was his job to know about threats against Air Force personnel and investigate them. He played for time. "I'll have my people check it out—"

"Are you going to staff this one to death, Hoskins?"

The very newly appointed brigadier didn't kid himself—he was in trouble. Cunningham wanted action. "Sir, I don't know enough at this point—"

"At this point, Hoskins, I don't know if you're naturally stupid or have worked to get that way. The *trouble* is that one of the terrorists was shot. Colonel Stansell got away and hasn't talked to the police."

"No problem sitting on it then," Hoskins said, trying to recover.

"Dammit, general, you're my chief investigative officer and you're telling me not to report the involvement of an Air Force officer in a shooting to the civilian authorities?"

"Excuse me, sir," Hoskins said, determined to go down fighting, "you haven't told me what Colonel Stansell's special mission is. If it's too important for me to know about it, I can only assume you want it protected at all costs."

Cunningham sat back in his chair and reevaluated the man in front of him.

I just might survive this, Hoskins thought. "I was not suggesting we cover up Colonel Stansell's involvement," he continued, pressing his advantage, "but control it. I'll use my contacts to explain what went down and that we are protecting him because of the terrorist threat. I'll use up a lot of my markers with the law in Virginia, but I believe I can keep Colonel Stansell out of it that way."

"Do it."

Hoskins threw a salute at the general and disappeared out the door.

"He should be all right," Cunningham said. "Only been on the job a week." He paused, carefully picking his words, deciding how much he was going to have to tell Stansell.

But Stansell was ahead of him. He handed Cunningham the completed ops plan. "General Mado is out of town today. Sir, why didn't you tell me that Task Force Alpha was a cover for the real mission? Didn't you trust me? I wanted that mission, sure, but more than anything else I want those people out. General, I'll do anything to make that happen." A fire of disappointment was building in him but what he told Cunningham was still the truth. He badly wanted, though, at least to be part of the rescue, to finish what he had started when he had led a squadron of F-15s into Ras Assanya to fly Combat Air Patrol for the 45th, Muddy Waters' wing. Waters had taught him what it meant to lead in combat, and now he felt he had to finish it—to bring the last of the wing out. Well, if it wasn't going to be him he would still do everything he could to help.

Cunningham noted the passion in Stansell's voice, rare around the Pentagon, where the officers were mostly chasing promotions and covering themselves with the protective coloration of the Air Force's bureaucracy. The fire in Stansell had nothing to do with personal advancement—he was committed to a mission.

Cunningham put down his cigar in the large ashtray on his right, leaned across the desk, clasping his hands, his carefully cultivated facade of command shredding in front of the colonel. Even his voice changed. "Rupe, I feel like you, those are my people and I'm the one that put them in harm's way. Yes, as of now you're a cover for the main effort. But there are serious flaws in that mission. It amounts to a major invasion and requires the cooperation of Kuwait and Iraq. Under the circumstances, not the best of plans, and to tell you the truth, I can't buy into it.

"So . . . I want *you* to make Task Force Alpha *more* than a cover operation. Make it a *creditable alternative* for the President to consider seriously." Stansell started to protest that he couldn't do that with what he was being given, but Cunningham held up his hand. "You've got to do it with what you've got because right now you do not look like a rescue force. That's *your* cover. Why do you think I sent you Rangers? Or a C-130 crewed by women? They know about our restrictions on using women in combat . . . This is ironic, but I believe glasnost is a factor. It has made it easier for the Russians to spy on us, and my guess is that they'll be watching Delta Force. Let's use that."

"General, are you saying the Soviets will tell the Iranians?"

"I am. A warning from them that might cause the rescue attempt to fail would help solidify their position with the Iranians. They'd figure it that way. Rupe, I want you to go back to Nellis and get your team ready. Bury them in the desert, no security leaks. Act exactly like a warlord out there and you'll be seen as part of Red Flag. If anyone is still looking at you, the fact that we haven't replaced you after the attempted kidnap can mean only one thing—what you're doing has nothing to do with the POWs or the Persian Gulf.

"Make it happen while I play bureaucratic games over this. Also make sure I know everything you're telling Mado." Cunningham punched his aide's button on his intercom. "Dick, have Andrews lay on a C-20 for Colonel Stansell. I want him back at Nellis today." He sat back in his chair. "Rupe, don't tell Mado what I said about being a creditable alternative to Delta Force. He's the best planner I've got for special operations, but—" He cut it off. Stansell didn't need to know about the bureaucratic maneuverings Mado was involved in, how he was working to advance his career by using his connections with Leachmeyer and the Joint Special Operations Agency . . . "Now get going."

Cunningham's aide Dick Stevens was waiting in the outer office while a secretary placed a call to Andrews AFB to arrange for the flight to Nellis. Stevens smiled and shook his head at the look on Stansell's face. He had seen it before. Stansell had learned one of the best-kept secrets in the Air Force—the rough, profane, nail-eating Cunningham was a carefully forged mask.

CHAPTER 14

D MINUS 21

NORTHEASTERN IRAQ

"Come," Zakia said, pointing out the door of her small infirmary. Carroll followed her into the bright morning sunlight, blinking his eyes. Two battered Land Rovers stood in front of a nearby mud hut and a small group of armed men were clustered around the door. Zakia shouldered her way through the men but two of them grabbed Carroll and searched him. They found the garrote wire in his thigh pocket but missed the small knife under the bandage taped to his calf. While they examined the wire he pulled his pants cuff up and ripped off the bandage, handing them the knife.

Zakia had been watching them search Carroll, and now grabbed him by the arm and shoved him into the hut. It probably saved his life.

A wizened man of indeterminate age sat by the only table in the room and motioned to the chair opposite him. "Mustapha tells me you saved him from the Iraqis," Mulla Haqui began in English. "I am grateful but I find it hard to believe what Zakia tells me—that you seek help from the Pesh Merga."

Carroll chose his words carefully, using phrases in Kirmanji when he could. He decided to tell the truth. "I am trying to reach Kermanshah in Iran and establish contact with the American prisoners of war being held there. I want to rescue some of them if possible but I need help. I was hoping you could put me in contact with your people in Kermanshah. I know many Kurds live there and have been treated badly by the Ayatollahs . . ."

"My concern is with the Iraqis, not the Ayatollahs in Iran," Haqui told him. "The Americans have done little to help our struggle. The Israelis have been much more helpful. For saving Mustapha's life I will help you reach Turkey. Nothing else."

Carroll stared at the floor. "I thank you. But I must go back to Iran." He raised his head and looked directly at the leader of the Pesh Merga. The old man could have been easily lampooned by a political cartoonist with his carefully wrapped turban and huge mustache. But in person he had an aura of implacable will. Haqui had led the Iraqi Kurds in their struggle for an independent homeland for more than a generation, and recognized something of himself now in Carroll—a strong, uncompromising dedication. It was the stuff that won revolutions, and too valuable to waste.

"Prove yourself to the Pesh Merga and I will help you." He nodded at Zakia, who motioned him out the door.

Haqui's bodyguards were silent as he left the hut. One of them handed Zakia the knife and wire. "Now how in the hell can I prove myself to Haqui," he mumbled under his breath.

"By hurting the Iraqis," Zakia said. "Talk to Mustapha."

RAF LAKENHEATH, ENGLAND

The lieutenant backed the alert truck into the reserved spot in front of wing headquarters and let out the two men. The young officer stayed in the truck, telling Doucette that he was close enough to Colonel Billy Joe Barker and would have the motor cranked if the alert horn went off and they had to scramble for the waiting jets on the alert pad.

"What the the hell does Barker want?" Captain Ramon Contreraz muttered as he followed his pilot, Torch Doucette, down the hall toward the Deputy for Operations offices. The captain had figured the week they were spending on alert because of the "incident" at the French air show was only a warm-up for what the DO was really going to do to them. "I didn't think he'd be dumping on us this soon," he told Doucette.

Doucette tried to reassure his WSO. "He can't do too much more to us." Barker had thrown them onto alert as punishment after having confronted them Monday morning with the bad local publicity about their hotshoting against the French Mirage in their F-111. But now he was worried as he lumbered into Barker's outer office. Lieutenant Colonel Mark Von Drexler, the Assistant Deputy for Operations, had gone into Barker's inner office ahead of them.

"How do I get out of this chickenshit outfit?" Contreraz moaned. Von Drexler was the wing's golden boy, the officer singled out for early promotion, the fast-burner. And he looked it. Handsome and articulate, some had figured he should have gone into the movies. Doucette wished he had, seeing as how he couldn't fly the F-111 worth squat-all.

"Aah, he only looks good in the showers," Doucette said.

"I beg your pardon?" the prim Englishwoman who served as Barker's secretary asked.

"It's about—"

"Yes, I get the point." She buzzed Barker and told him the aircrew was there.

Doucette and Contreraz stood in front of Barker's desk. They did not expect to be offered seats. "The wing has been tasked to send three of our jets to Red Flag for a special exercise," Barker said. "Volunteers only. I can understand why they want F models with Pave Tack and came to the 48th. The message also asks for crews who were on the Libyan raid in April of '86. Obviously they want someone with combat experience. It bothers me that you two are the only Libyan raiders left in the 48th, the rest have rotated back to the States—"

"We'll take it," Doucette said.

"To avoid a repeat of what happened in France, Colonel Von Drexler is going to lead the contingent. He'll take two of our aircraft to Nellis. You two will leave today for McClellan AFB and pick up an aircraft that has just come out of maintenance. The 431st Test and Eval Squadron out there says it's tweaked and ready to go. Be at Nellis Monday morning. That's *all*."

The two saluted and left. "See, I told you not to worry," Doucette told a skeptical Contreraz.

THE PENTAGON

Damn, he's good, Cunningham thought as he listened to the commander of Delta Force, Colonel Sam Johnson, outline the planned rescue for the group gathered around the table. Where in the hell did Leachmeyer find him? I'd trade Mado for him in a heartbeat, the man's a natural leader. Well, he did have Stansell . . .

The group gathered around the table deep in the bowels of the Pentagon were there at the direction of the President and comprised one of the most important working committees ever assembled in the name of Intelligence. And they had one objective—to insure that the best intelligence the U.S. had was at the disposal of the rescue force going after the POWs. Cunningham listened as the chief of the National Reconnaissance Office announced he had repositioned a Keyhole satellite to pass over the compound at Kermanshah every eight hours. The Deputy Director of the CIA assured them that the barracks behind the prison were only occupied by a few families seeking shelter from the coming winter and were not a consideration. The select group then spent more than thirty minutes discussing the armored regiment moving into position at Shahabad, forty-two miles southwest of the prison compound.

And Cunningham saw the plan start to come apart. The Army was going to insert a blocking force at the highway bridge halfway to Kermanshah to destroy the bridge and delay any relief column that tried to move down the road. Near the end of the meeting Cunningham asked the deputy director of the CIA if they could get operatives into the area to support the rescue team or at least to determine how fast the armored regiment could react to the American raid. The man seemed flustered until Camm came to his rescue. "General Cunningham, the president has been very specific in our marching orders. We are to provide you with everything we've got that can help. But we cannot get operationally involved without the knowledge of the congressional select committees on intelligence. And the President doesn't want to take that step at this point." Camm's boss shot him a grateful look. Camm had decided that he would only relay sanitized intelligence from Deep Furrow to the military and to hold back from involving the CIA, until Susan Fisher came up with a plan for the CIA to rescue the POWs.

Cunningham was disgusted. Any help from the CIA for the ground support the Air Force's plan called for was down the drain. The general chalked it all up to bureaucratic politics.

As the group broke up, Cunningham cornered Camm and the Deputy Director for the CIA. "I think you should explore ways to get a player in place at Kermanshah to help Delta Force. If nothing else he can relay last minute intelligence and arrange an overland escape route if things go to hell in a handbasket."

"General," Camm answered, "we're doing exactly what the President has directed—"

"But you can offer him valid alternatives to consider."

Stony silence from the two men. The disgust that had been eating at Cunningham broke through. It was time, he decided, to send them a message. "If I find out that you two *gentlemen* haven't done everything you can to help, I'll personally fly the B-52 that'll bomb your goddamn temple at Langley back to the Stone Age. Count on it, assholes." He left then without waiting for an outraged reaction.

A phone call had alerted Cunningham's aide that the general was upset, and Stevens was waiting in his office. "Dick," Cunningham said, not sounding the least angry, "please ask Colonel Ben Yuriden to see me soonest."

Yuriden was the Israeli air attaché.

NELLIS AFB, NEVADA

Stansell was waiting with Pullman for the C-130 carrying the first of the Rangers to taxi into the blocks. The battalion's commander, a burly army officer, led his staff off the Hercules, marched up to Stansell and snapped a salute. "Lieutenant Colonel Leland Gregory." Stansell studied the man in front of him as he returned the salute. Neatly tailored fatigues hid most of his expanding waistline, his round face seemed to glow. His big hand engulfed Stansell's when they shook—the reason for Gregory's moniker, "Ham."

Gregory then introduced his headquarters staff—two company commanders and his Command Sergeant Major, Victor Kamigami. Stansell was stunned by the size of Kamigami, a huge Japanese-Hawaiian whose proportions approached those of a sumo wrestler.

Pullman shepherded the group to their headquarters in the three trailers he had commandeered, and Gregory and his group were quickly settled in and at work. "We've got two companies one hour behind us," Gregory said. "Where do we bivouac?" Pullman explained how they were going to establish their training camp at Texas Lake and that the tents and equipment had been brought in the day before.

"Sir, I'll take care of that," Kamigami said. His voice was startlingly soft, incongruous with his size. Pullman arranged for a helicopter to fly Kamigami and the two company commanders to the dry lake to set up the camp, and at the last minute decided to go with them.

Stansell stopped by the trailers an hour later. "Colonel, we appreciate the trailers," Gregory said. "The VOQ is full and we're booked in at a motel downtown. We should have some rental cars for transportation here late today. Looking good."

But it was all too routine for Stansell. "Colonel Gregory, I think we need to talk—inside." He pointed to building 201. "Bring your key men." Gregory motioned for his S-2, the staff's intelligence officer, and S-3, his operations officer, to follow them into the Intelligence vault, where Dewa spent her days. Bryant closed the door as they found seats.

"Our code name here is Task Force Alpha," Stansell began. "I assume you know why you're here and are all volunteers."

Gregory nodded. "General Leachmeyer said Task Force Alpha is a training program for large-scale integrated rescue missions. We don't need to ask for volunteers. This is what we're all about."

Stansell swallowed back a rising sense of frustration. "There's more to it than routine training. We could"—will be, he wanted to say—"be called on for the real thing."

The Army officers exchanged glances. The S-3, the tall major in charge of operations, shook his head. "Don't bet on it, Colonel. Delta Force at Fort Bragg specializes in this type of operation. We always suck hind tit to them. And to the First Battalion, and to the Second . . ."

Stansell ignored it. "We're on a tight schedule here. Colonel Gregory, you're the ground commander. Your objectives are to assault a prison, free the prisoners held there, secure an airfield and get your Rangers and the prisoners to the airfield."

"Right," Gregory boomed, gung ho to be a field commander.

Stansell's annoyance wouldn't go away. He warned himself that he was getting hyper and had better wait and see how the Rangers performed before making a judgment. For the next two hours he watched as the men went over the mission, and Gregory said he would organize a composite rescue team to storm the prison and free the prisoners.

"We've got a dozen men who've been through the Special Ops School at Fort Bragg," his operations officer said. "They can blow those doors open in a minute. We organize Lieutenant Jamison's platoon into a composite rescue team—call it Romeo Team, 'Romeo' for 'rescue.' "

"We need someone with more experience than a first lieutenant to head the team," Gregory said. "Captain Trimler will have to be in command, Jamison his exec."

Stansell started to feel a little better.

Pullman stuck his head in the door and motioned for Stansell to join him outside. "Damndest thing you've ever seen, Colonel. This Kamagami has got the camp almost up. When a platoon gets finished he's having them do calisthenics, the old daily dozen, and finishes them off with a two-mile run."

"Quite a top kick?"

"Colonel, he hardly says a word. Doesn't need to." Pullman then handed Stansell a message. "From General Mado. We're getting three F-111s in Monday, and Sundown has approved your request for F-15s. We get one E model out of Luke and eight C models for escort. You get to choose the units and the pilots. Looking pretty good, Colonel."

Stansell had to agree, but then why was his right ear demanding a scratching?

THE WHITE HOUSE

Admiral Scovill nodded at the naval officer sitting in an armchair outside the Oval Office reading a book. Scovill nodded in approval when he saw it was Hawking's *A Brief History of Time*. The "football," the soft leather bag carrying the nuclear launch codes, was in the chair beside him and the wrist chain was long enough for him to get comfortable. A boring job, following the President around with nothing to do. But the military aides who rotated the duty did not complain—after all, it was a path to promotion, and when you thought about it, you could say you had the whole world in your hand.

Andy Wollard, the President's Chief of Staff, ushered the Chairman of the Joint Chiefs into the office. Scovill was surprised to see Cyrus Piccard, Secretary of State, sitting on one of the couches next to the Secretary of Defense. Piccard had been at Geneva conducting the failing negotiations with the Iranians for the release of the POWs. The meeting late in the evening and the sudden appearance of Piccard could only mean one thing—something had gone very very wrong.

"Please sit down," the President said. Scovill sat next to Mike Cagliari, the National Security Advisor, directly across from Bobby Burke, the Director of Central Intelligence. Wollard found a chair in a corner and would take voluminous notes. "Okay, Cy, lay it all out for us."

"The talks are stalled. Hell, they've all but collapsed. The Libyans keep upping the bid for the hostages and I think the Iranians expect us to match it. It's been coming apart ever since that press conference when Whiteside told the world what the Libyans were doing."

"You're not talking directly to the Libyans?" the President said quickly.

"Of course not, it's all coming through a third party."

"Who?"

"The Russians. Who else? The Libyans have the bid up to a million and a half dollars for each POW. The only good news is that the Iranians aren't biting. At least not yet."

"Any ideas why?"

"Internal politics, sir." This from Burke, the Director of the CIA. "The Islamic Republican Party is trying to align with the IPRP to keep control of the Council of Guardians. But the IPRP wants half of the POWs as a sort of collateral. An Iranian show of good faith."

"So it's a rescue or nothing," the President said. Determination had replaced long-felt frustration. "Terry, when will Delta Force be ready to go?"

"Fifteen to eighteen days," Scovill answered.

"Why so long?"

"Mr. President," the Secretary of Defense put in, "that's not a long time to get a mission like this ready. And there are problems. First, the Iranians are moving an armored regiment into place forty-two miles from the POWs. We've got to find a way to block them. Second, Soviet agents have been sighted around Fort Bragg, where Delta Force is training."

"What the hell is going on?" The President was looking at Burke. "I thought the Air Force was going to run cover for them?"

"It's *glasnost*, Mr. President," Burke told him, tight-lipped. "We have to reciprocate as things loosen up in the Soviet Union and our people are allowed to move around inside Russia. All of which gives the Soviets more freedom to move around over here. While we're getting dividends in other areas, we're paying for it by allowing them increased freedom of movement. Those agents are pros and they know where to look. They haven't bitten on the Air Force cover and probably see it as a Red Flag exercise. We're fairly certain they don't know what Delta is preparing for but they're curious. If the FBI rolls the agents up, the Russians will get even more interested."

"Can we use the Air Force and Rangers at Nellis?"

"Doubtful, sir," Scovill said. "They're really a second team."

"Okay, continue. Don't leak anything as we originally planned. I want a tight security lid on this whole operation. Find a way to sneak Delta Force into position and keep the Air Force and Rangers at it. Cy, get back to Geneva and stall. If you have to, make it look like I'm seriously considering outbidding the Libyans. It will help give the Iranians a reason to keep the POWs together. Gentlemen, we're fast running out of time on this one."

CHAPTER 15

D MINUS 20

KERMANSHAH, IRAN

Mokhtari stomped up the steps to the third floor, two guards behind him. He wanted the POWs to hear his hard leather heels ringing, to let the fear of anticipation work for him. He moved down the wide corridor, stopping occasionally and having the guards throw open one of the twenty-six cell doors so he could see inside. He could have slipped the small shutter back that covered the barred window set into each door but that would have been too quiet. He wanted them to think he was picking someone at random.

"No, not that one," he shouted in English, slamming a door shut. The tension and fear could be felt as he worked his way down the cell block. When Mokhtari tired of the game, he pointed to a cell. The guards threw the cell door back. The four men in the cell were sitting at attention on the edge of their bunks, as Mokhtari dictated they must be during the day. The two men on the top bunks were lucky because they did not have to keep their bare feet on the cold cement floor. To be caught talking to each other or not sitting at attention was worth a stay in the Box or a beating.

"Him." Mokhtari pointed at Master Sergeant John Nesbit. The guards wrenched him to his feet. One hit him in the stomach. Then they dragged him out of the cell and down the stairs to the basement.

The men appointed as lookouts were already on the floor of their cells, peering through the gaps under their doors, monitoring the movement of the guards. Feet were off the floor and blankets unfolded as the men sought warmth. A warning tap by a lookout would send the entire floor back into position as Mokhtari's regulations dictated. It was a carefully rehearsed routine and most of the men could fold a blanket quicker than a guard could unlock a door.

By the time Mokhtari had Nesbit in the basement a message was on its way to Leason's cell. "What the hell . . ." Leason mumbled to himself as the tap code came through. His cellmate, Doc Landis, was still locked up in the administration building in the cell next to Mary Hauser. The reports reaching the colonel indicated the doc was okay but that Hauser had been raped.

Nesbit was a command post controller and an expert on communications equipment, codes and procedures. Mokhtari would either break the sergeant and make him talk or kill him. Leason considered if there would be a vital compromise of U.S. security if Nesbit told what he knew. "Vital, but not fatal," he decided. He wanted to keep Nesbit alive, but he needed a way to pass that message to the sergeant. He tapped out a code asking for a volunteer to go into the box. Maybe one volunteer could do it if the guards threw the man into the right box—the one with a water pipe running up the back wall that made for an effective transmission line into the prison.

Within minutes he had his reply when he heard a voice shouting for the "muthafuckin' guard." It was Macon Jefferson, the skinny black kid from Cleveland who had pretzellike qualities and a street-bred contempt for authority.

"Jefferson, I'll make it right when we get out of here," Leason promised himself.

The guards quickly threw Jefferson headfirst into the Box. He held his body rigid, making them think it was a tight fit. Finally they got his feet in and slammed the door. His head was resting against the water pipe, and within minutes his two-word message, IN OK, had been relayed to Leason. Jefferson drew his legs up and started to squirm, twisting around. When he had his head against the door he felt for the nail that covered the peephole that had been bored out by previous occupants of the Box. Finally he had the nail out and a view of the basement.

The guards, he saw, had Nesbit sitting on the floor, legs straight out in front of him, ankles bound together, his hands behind his back. Jefferson could see the legs of a third man—Mokhtari, judging by the highly polished brown boots. For a few moments Jefferson could not tell what the guard at Nesbit's back was doing. Actually the guard was retying the rope around the sergeant's wrists. He took another length of rope and looped it around Nesbit's elbows, then pulled the rope, drawing Nesbit's elbows together behind his back. When the sergeant screamed the guard pulled the rope again, drawing Nesbit's elbows closer together. And the sergeant screamed again.

"You have lied," Mokharti said. "You were a command post controller at Ras Assanya, not a security policeman." The guard worked the rope, drawing Nesbit's elbows still closer. "I guarantee you will tell us what we want but only after you've been punished for your lying." The commandant then left the basement, leaving the guards to their work.

One guard held Nesbit's head down while the other cinched the rope up, working it until the elbows were almost touching. Then he tied the rope off, making sure the knot would not slip. The other guard let go of the sergeant's head and threw a rope over a hook in the ceiling. They tied one end of the rope to Nesbit's wrists and pulled on the other end, lifting his arms up behind him, his screams ricocheting off the walls, filling the room with his pain. Jefferson saw Nesbit's shoulders dislocate. When Nesbit's buttocks were barely touching the floor, they tied the rope to a ring in the wall and walked out, leaving the sergeant sitting on the floor in his agony.

Jefferson fought to control his urge to beat against the door. Instead he threw himself against the walls of the box, twisting and turning around. He laid his check against the pipe and tapped out what he had seen, all the while listening to Nesbit, whose sounds had been reduced to a whimper.

TEXAS LAKE, NEVADA

"I hear you've never been on a drop before, Colonel?" Dunkin said, leading Stansell, Locke and Bryant around the C-130s as the Rangers marshaled for the airdrop. "You oughtta' go along and watch them go out the back. Quite a show. We'll drop a stick of twenty on each pass—ten out'a each door—then come around and drop the second stick."

"You going to come as close as you did last time?" Locke said, thinking about the dummy load Dunkin had almost dropped on the helicopter.

"Naw, I only do that with canister drops. Never for the real thing."

"How's this drop shaping up?" Stansell asked.

"No problems. Looks like it's gonna be a Hollywood jump." No combat equipment, he meant.

Stansell scanned the ramp, annoyed he hadn't noted it sooner . . . The Rangers were going about the loading routine with measured precision, but he didn't see a single Ranger waddling around with a rucksack slung in front under his reserve chute, bouncing against his knees as he walked, or a weapons case strapped to his side. "They're only wearing K-Pots," he said, referring to the Kevlar helmet the Army used. He looked for the battalion C.O., Lieutenant Colonel Ham Gregory. "We're not on a picnic here."

"Too late to do anything about it now," Dunkin said, checking his watch. "We crank engines in nine minutes."

Stansell headed for the flight deck of Dunkin's Hercules, his right ear itching for real.

THE PENTAGON

Now it was coming together, Cunningham could feel it. Hoskins, the brigadier general running the OSI, had just left after assuring him that no foreign agents were watching Task Force Alpha at Nellis. Mado had taken Stansell's operations plan and added to it, working in an AWACS for command and control, and had a bureaucratic polish on it, thereby providing Stansell with what he needed to create an alternate for Delta Force. Cunningham had told Mado to give the ops plan a name—OPORD WARLORD—Operation Order WARLORD. Let everyone think we're playing some goddamn shogunate epic out at Red Flag, Cunningham thought. It all added to Stansell's cover as a Red Flag warlord.

The intercom buzzed and Cunningham's secretary told him that Colonel Ben Yuriden, the Israeli air attaché, had arrived. Cunningham had first met Yuriden when the Israelis were getting their F-16s. Even then the general could sense the commitment in the man, and Yuriden had proved it in the raid on the Iraqi nuclear reactor near Baghdad in June of 1981, as well as in the air battles over the Beka'a Valley in Lebanon in '82 where the Israeli Air Force had downed over thirty MiGs, without a single loss. Cunningham made a mental promise to ask someday if there was any truth to the rumor that after the F-16 raid on the PLOs' headquarters in Tunisia, the PLO had directly threatened Yuriden's family. According to the legend that surrounded Yuriden, his reply had been to fly a lone F-16 against the group that had issued the threat and put a single bomb in the backyard of the PLO commander—when no one was home. The PLO got the message about Israeli intelligence, bombing accuracy—and Ben Yuriden.

"Ben, thanks for coming." Cunningham stuck his hand out, welcoming the middle-aged man that entered his office. Average looking in the extreme, only his intense brown eyes marked him.

"General, why do I think you're calling in . . . what do your people say? . . . a marker?" Yuriden had a knack for cutting to the quick.

So did Cunningham. "I need a favor—a very unofficial one. It's something I'll probably never be able to repay." The colonel said nothing, gave no indication. Cunningham thought, I'd hate to play poker with you. "One of my officers is loose in Iran and I need to get a message to him. Can your people do that for me?" Cunningham calculated that WARLORD'S best chance for success hinged on having trucks or buses in position to move the POWs to the airfield. Task Force Alpha could do everything else, even fly in their own transportation, but vehicles in place were their best option. The CIA had told him they wouldn't do it, so maybe Bill Carroll could, providing he could contact him.

"Captain William Carroll," Yuriden said. "He's not in Iran right now but, I hear, with the Kurds in Iraq—Jalali tribe. Yes, we can do that. Perhaps we can do something else to help?"

Cunningham kept a straight face. An opportunity he hadn't counted on had just presented itself . . . The Israelis had the best secret intelligence service in the Middle East, and he had just been offered their help. He knew that making an unauthorized contact with the Mossad could stir up a hornet's nest, but he'd take the chance. "I need about ten trucks or buses—"

"At Kermanshah."

Cunningham's mouth almost dropped open. Although he trusted Yuriden, he did not want to tell him why he wanted the vehicles. Did Yuriden understand all that? The position he was in? Were the Israelis onto Task Force Alpha?

"No doubt for Delta Force," Yuriden added, also with a straight face. It was a game of poker between two allies who liked and trusted each other, but neither could ever turn over all his cards.

Cunningham said nothing, relieved that Task Force Alpha was still apparently secure, even from Yuriden.

Smart for a *goy*, Yuriden thought, understanding the delicate position Cunningham was in. "Why don't you have Carroll work with the Kurds to get the vehicles you need? There are many Kurds around Kermanshah. They only need some money."

"Then you'll play postman for me and deliver a message to Carroll?"

Yuriden nodded, calculating how Israel could use the rescue operation to its advantage and weaken its Arab enemies.

After the colonel had left, Cunningham asked for OPORD WARLORD to be brought in from the safe. He thumbed through the plan, mentally checking off what had been accomplished so far. He briefly wondered if he was making a mistake by not telling Mado what he was setting up. No, he decided, better Mado think Alpha was still a cover operation. He leaned back in his chair and folded his hands over his rotund stomach, thinking about his next move. His eyes snapped open when Stevens knocked at the door, waiting to be acknowledged before entering.

"Dick," Cunningham said, "tell General Leachmeyer that I'll be glad to send him some AC-130 gunships to support Delta—if he wants them. And send one out to Nellis for WARLORD. Also have Operations coordinate with the Turks and move up our annual air defense exercise with them two weeks, and use AWACs and EC-130s this time." The "exercise" would be a good cover for the rescue activity . . . Am I getting too involved with nuts and bolts again? he wondered briefly. Trying to do too much myself on this one? I've got a bagful of two- and three-star generals . . .

Stevens turned to leave. He had not taken a single note. Sundown Cunningham didn't favor note-takers, just doers.

CHAPTER 16

D MINUS 19

NELLIS AFB, NEVADA

Red Flag's building was deserted except for Dewa's back office in the Intelligence section. The sergeant responsible for locking up had checked the building and asked Stansell if he would be sure the front door was secure when he left. Stansell watched the sergeant disappear out the door, anxious to get to the NCO Club for a Friday night.

The colonel kept working on the sketch he was making of the prison at Kermanshah. By recapturing it on paper he committed every detail to memory. When he had finished he compared his sketch with polaroid pictures Pullman had taken of the mock-up in Tikaboo Valley that was nearing completion.

As he relaxed in his chair his pencil, seeming to move of its own accord, sketched a three-quarters profile of his oldest daughter Lisa. He let the pencil move, drawing in the face of his youngest daughter, Marilee, alongside Lisa. "I miss you," remembering . . .

He snapped the pencil in two and threw the pieces in a waste basket.

The phone rang, breaking the hold that loneliness and a sense of loss had on his life. "Yeah?" It was the night manager at the officers' club telling him that one of his men was turning into an ugly drunk and asking if he could handle it before they had to call the security police. Stansell slammed the phone down and hurried out of the building.

The casual bar in the officers' club was alive with fighter jocks in for the Red Flag exercise telling their latest war story earned over the Nevada desert. The night manager pointed to a corner table occupied by one Captain James "Thunder" Bryant. An empty space surrounded him, a safe zone. "He's drunk on his ass," the night manager told Stansell. "The bartender refused to serve him so he just helped himself. One of his buddies tried talking to him. Didn't do any good. That's when I called you."

Stansell bought a drink at the bar before he pushed his way through the crowd and sat at Bryant's table. "Get lost, Colonel."

"When you tell me what's got a hold of you."

Bryant focused a cold stare on the short colonel that sent a warning signal—he was on the edge of violence. Stansell sipped at his drink and waited. Bryant fumbled in his jacket pocket, pulled out a crumpled folded envelope and threw it across the table. "Read it."

The return address was a law firm in Wilmington, Delaware. Stansell smoothed the envelope flat, not opening it. "I got one just like it," he said, "when my wife gave me the boot."

"So that makes us buddies?"

"No, it only means I've been where you are." He stood up. "Get it together and stop feeling sorry for yourself. Come talk when you're sober."

"That's easy for you to say now—"

"You think so? Twenty minutes ago I was drawing pictures of my girls. I don't get to see 'em growing up."

"So what the hell do I do right now?"

"You hurt, you take it, and you work like hell not to hurt anyone else."

CHAPTER 17

D MINUS 18

NORTHEASTERN IRAQ

The old Kurd squatted outside Zakia's infirmary, sketching the floor plan of the Iraqi army headquarters in the dust with a short stick. He was, Carroll was certain, key to the support needed from Mulla Haqui.

After talking to Haqui, Carroll had gone through the camp asking if anyone had a relative or friend that worked in Irbil, the town where a rifle division of the Iraqi army was headquartered, and found a young woman who told him about an old uncle who collected trash in the city. With Zakia's help he and the woman found the only available telephone twelve miles away and she contacted the relative in Irbil.

The second day after the phone call the old man appeared in camp, dog-tired but anxious to tell his fellow tribesmen what he knew. When he had finished he rested back on his haunches, pleased he could help his people and that someone had had enough sense finally to ask him.

Carroll told them they needed to attack the Iraqi headquarters, and to do that, they would give the Iraqi "a real target to chase and bad information. What kind of information do the Iraqis trust?"

"What they see," one of the men said. "And what they torture out of Kurds."

"Have the Iraqis captured a Pesh Merga lately?" Carroll asked.

"Four days ago," Mustapha told him. "Rashid Shaban. He will die before he tells them anything—"

"Would you like to free Rashid? It will be difficult and the Iraqis will take reprisals." The burst of words, shouting, and animated gestures that erupted around him confused Carroll until he sorted out what they were saying. They weren't arguing if they should do it, just how and when. Quietly he sketched his plan in dirt, interrupting occasionally to ask for specific information. One by one they stopped talking and turned their attention to the rough map he was creating. "Old uncle," he asked the trash collector from Irbil, "can you get a message to Rashid?" The old man spat a glob into the dirt. Loud and clear, Carroll thought, suppressing a smile.

LAS VEGAS, NEVADA

"Okay, Colonel, what's eating you?" Dewa sat down at her desk in building 201, then saw the sketch he had made of his daughters and regretted her question.

Stansell shook his head. "Sorry, forget it . . . but," he said, looking at Chief Pullman and Bryant and Locke, "I don't like what I'm seeing, I didn't like the Hollywood jump on Thursday or what I hear went on at the Red Stallion last night, the Rangers brawling in a parking lot . . . We've got to build a fire under our people, weld them together into a tight team, make them want to commit to what we're doing."

"Why don't you tell them we're here to rescue the POWs?" Locke asked.

Dewa ruffled through a stack of messages on her desk, avoiding eye contact with Stansell. Would he tell them the truth? If not, she would still do her job, but as for the future . . .

The burden of command was on Stansell. It was a tricky thing, telling them the official mission of Alpha was a cover for the real operations, and at the same time letting them in on Cunningham's intent that it be a lot more . . .

"We were created to be a cover for Delta Force. Officially, as of now, they're tasked for the rescue mission."

Dewa turned to look at him, her eyes bright.

"Shee-it," Pullman muttered, thinking about the day Locke had appeared at Stonewood.

"This *cover* cost me my marriage," Bryant said, looking at Stansell, then relented. It wasn't Stansell who'd ripped apart his marriage.

Locke shook his head. "You knew all along—"

"No, I found out last Monday when Dewa put the pieces together. I had it out with Cunningham Tuesday, and he told me there's plenty more to it. Sure, we *started* life as a cover operation—"

"A goddamn Quaker cannon," Pullman broke in.

"Chief, *listen* for a moment," Stansell said. "The invasion of Normandy worked in 1944 because the Germans were looking at Patton, who was a *decoy* for the main force. Deception is part of what we do," echoing Dewa earlier. "*But* there is one big difference between Task Force Alpha and Patton. His army only existed on paper and in fake message traffic. We're alive and for *real*."

"Big deal," Pullman said.

"It is a very big deal, chief," Stansell said. "If we're good enough, Cunningham is going to make the brass look at us and think twice about who they send in after the POWs. And you're the people who can make that happen. But you've got to *work* to make this thing happen."

"You going to tell the troops all this?" Bryant asked.

"If I have to, but I'd rather not. Could compromise the whole deal."

"It could happen," Dewa said. "Foreign agents have been reported monitoring Delta Force. The OSI says we're still clean—"

"You mean Delta Force might be compromised?" Locke could see what that would mean . . . "Okay, I'm still in."

"Shee-it," from Pullman, who also understood the possibles. "What's another couple of weeks?"

Bryant said nothing. He didn't have to.

And for the first time since Ras Assanya Stansell felt he was acting without looking over his shoulder for the approval of a tall, shadowy image named Waters.

"We start building fires today. Thunder, you start living with the C-130s. Get with Colonel Mallard and that lunatic navigator . . ."

"Drunkin Dunkin," Bryant said.

"Yeah. And work out a series of low levels that train for penetration of Iranian airspace. You're going to have to look at the Iranian's radar coverage. Find gaps. Jack, the F-111s and F-15s belong to you," he told Locke. "I don't care where the F-15s come from but get us the best people you can and get them ready. Chief, you and me are going to work on the army starting today. How's the mock-up coming?"

"I got the front wall, four guard towers and a cell block in Tikaboo Valley almost finished. The valley is oriented like the one in Kermanshah and pretty isolated—next to Dreamland, so nobody goes around there."

"Dreamland?" Dewa asked.

"Yeah, the Air Force's never-never land. Do a lot of top-secret stuff out there. No one gets near the place. We sorta fall under its umbrella. Until the mock-up is finished I found an old confinement facility at Indian River Auxiliary field the Rangers can practice on. There are twelve cells in an old World War II barracks they can blow the hell out of."

INDIAN RIVER AUXILIARY AIR FIELD, NEVADA

The lone Hercules threaded the gap through the Spotted Range seven nautical miles northwest of the field, lined up on the axis of the southeast runway, popped to twelve hundred and fifty feet above the field's elevation and slowed to one hundred and thirty knots.

"Captain Kowalski," Pullman said. "We only needed one C-130 and she won the toss."

"She's looking good from here," Stansell said.

The first stick of twenty jumpers streamed out of the C-130's jump doors, ten to a side at one-second intervals. The drop broke off and the Hercules circled for a second run in, dropping the second stick of five. Even at over a thousand feet the men on the ground could tell the last jumper was Victor Kamigami, the battalion's Command Sergeant Major. The first man on the ground was Robert Trimler, the young athletic captain that Gregory had picked to lead the rescue team. His second in command, First Lieutenant George Jamison, a tough black man two years out of West Point, joined him and the two reported in. "First Platoon, Alpha Company, sir," Trimler said. "We're your Romeo Team." No salute—they were in a combat mode.

"Glad to see you've got all your combat equipment this time, captain," Stansell said. "No more Hollywood jumps. Where's Colonel Gregory?"

"Downtown bailing some of our men out of jail. Had some trouble at a bar last night."

"Captain, didn't the training schedule get posted yesterday?"

"Only for Romeo Team, sir. Colonel Gregory gave the rest of the men Saturday and Sunday off. First weekend in Vegas."

Kamigami came lumbering up in full battle gear, an impressive sight. "Sergeant Major," Stansell said, nodding to him. "Okay, Captain Trimler, supposedly your team is made up of experts in jail breaking—"

"The best we've got."

"Good. Chief Pullman will show you what you're up against." He pointed at the barracks. "From now on, Romeo Team is locked in concrete, no personnel changes."

"Sir, that decision really belongs to Colonel Gregory," Trimler said.

"I'll talk to him later."

Kamigami gave a sharp nod and walked toward the barracks, wanting to inspect the cells. One of the squad leaders, Sergeant Andy Baulck, had overheard them talking and muttered, "Fuckin' earless wonder," loud enough for the CSM to hear. Kamigami pointed at the man, shutting off any further comments.

CHAPTER 18

D MINUS 17

NELLIS AFB, NEVADA

"Thunder babes, what's the distance from the front wall to the main cell block?" Locke asked.

Bryant searched through a stack of photos and diagrams on the table for the one he wanted. "Just over a hundred feet. Make it a hundred and ten, maybe a hundred and fifteen."

"Problems," Locke said. "Too big a bang with a GBU-15. We need something smaller than a two-thousand-pounder to blow holes in the walls. Otherwise we'll blow out every window in the facing-side of the cell block and flying debris might puncture its walls." Locke was working on a computer, running a weaponeering program. The GBU-15, the guided-bomb unit, with its combination infrared and TV seeker head, was the most accurate launch-and-leave bomb they had. Unfortunately it was mated with a Mark 84, a two-thousand-pound high-explosive bomb. Stansell and Bryant gathered around Locke, looking over his shoulder.

Bryant butted Locke out of his chair and ran the program calling up a laser-guided version of the Mark 82 five-hundred-pound bomb. "That'll do the trick," Locke said. "Only, the F-111s will have to hang around and lase the target or we've got to get someone on the ground to mark the wall with a ground-laser designator."

"Okay," Stansell said, making a note to relay the information to

143

both Mado and Cunningham that they would have to use GBU-12s and needed a ground team to spot each DMPI, desired-mean-point of impact. "Start training with five-hundred pounders, I'll take care of the rest."

Two hours later Dewa came in from church, a black lace shawl around her shoulders. For a moment Stansell found himself staring at her, caught by her quiet beauty. She brought him out of it with: "Colonel Gregory has got his officers together in their trailer. I think he's reading them the riot act about Saturday morning."

"He wants to be a Patton," Locke said.

"Yeah, he does," Stansell said, picking up the phone. "Take a break, people." He dialed the number and asked for Gregory to come see him. The group filed out as Gregory walked in.

"I think Ham Gregory is going to learn something about Colonel Stansell and what's underneath that quiet exterior," Dewa told Bryant as she closed the door behind her . . .

"Colonel Stansell," Gregory began, "let me assure you what happened Saturday morning at the Red Stallion has been taken care of."

"I hope so." Stansell's voice was cold. "It set our progress back. I had work for you Saturday morning."

"Yes, about the airdrop without my approval and freezing Romeo Team—"

"Have you seen the cells they practiced on?"

"No, but that's beside the point. You tell me that I'm the ground commander for this exercise and then bypass me on Saturday and order Trimler's Romeo Team on an airdrop. The army doesn't work that way."

"Colonel, you weren't here when I needed you."

"It could have waited."

"Colonel, you can't be that fucking stupid." Stansell's voice was calm, almost friendly. He leaned forward. "We are running out of time on this. Think back, remember I told you the very first day that we might be tasked for the real thing?" Gregory nodded. "You should have keyed on that. Obviously I've got to get someone that understands the name of the game. I'll ask General Leachmeyer to replace you—"

"Colonel, for God's sake, that'll be the end of me. Just for an exercise?"

"Still haven't got the picture. This is *not* an exercise."

"I didn't understand that . . . I do now . . ."

Stansell sank back in his chair, satisfied that he had been right about him, and for the next few minutes he filled in Gregory on the entire situation.

"Colonel Stansell, I missed Vietnam and Grenada. This may be my only chance to lead men into combat. I can't tell you how much I want that. Hell, I don't give a damn about making full colonel and ending up assigned to the Pentagon. Okay, I'm not a brain and need things spelled out. But dammit I can fight and I can lead men. I want that chance, and I'll do it your way."

"You got it," Stansell said.

"Would you mind coming with me?" Gregory stood up, waiting for Stansell. They walked together to the trailers, and it was a different man that called his officers together.

"Starting now," he told them, "we start training for a mission that is going to be real rough. We're dealing with a lot of unknowns now but, just but, we might get a Go order. If we do we will be ready. I hope you're reading me on this because the mission objective is close-hold for security reasons. Romeo Team will train for storming the prison and lead the way in. Bravo Company, you'll train for holding the airfield and road security. Then we cross train. Check out of the motel. We move to Texas Lake in two hours."

Stansell walked back to building 201, satisfied he had made the right decision and realizing that he had made a mistake by not confiding in Gregory from day one. Locke was waiting for him. "Colonel, I've picked four F-15 drivers from Luke and four from Holloman for Task Force Alpha. You know one of 'em—Snake Houserman. They're all here for Red Flag and can move over to us. Looks real natural. We'll be using their F-15s. Tomorrow I want to pick up the E model and my wizzo, Ambler Furry, from Luke. The F-111 crews are due in and we got two Libyan raiders." The captain was obviously excited. "Oh," Locke added, "we also got an AC-130 gunship coming in. With the radios its got on board we can use that puppy for a command-and-control platform. Colonel, this is coming together, I think we're going to make it happen . . ."

CHAPTER 19

D MINUS 16

KERMANSHAH, IRAN

Jefferson recognized the footsteps before the guard came into his narrow view. The man's routine never varied—come down the stairs early in the morning, always alone, enter the room, listen to be sure no one was moving around above him; set the bowl down and loosen the rope that held up Nesbit's arms; lower his hands a fraction of an inch. The sergeant had his full weight on the floor, his wrists at least two inches lower. The guard would massage Nesbit's legs and give him a drink, then spoon some of the watery slop into his mouth. When the guard was finished with Nesbit he would unlock the Box and help Jefferson out, supporting him until some circulation came back to his legs, helping him walk to the grimy toilet in the corner, then hand him the bowl and let him finish what he had not fed to Nesbit. Finally he would motion to the Box, and Jefferson understood that their benefactor had done all he could for them and would crawl back in.

This morning, though, the guard broke the routine, he drew a stool up beside Nesbit and motioned Jefferson to sit there while he ate. The guard walked over to the stairs and sat down.

"Colonel Leason says to start talking," Jefferson said, barely audible. "Spill what you've got to but get off the goddamn ropes."

The sound of quick hard footsteps echoing on the stairs jerked the guard to his feet. Panic lit his eyes. Jefferson set the bowl down and scurried for the Box. The guard was right behind him, locking the door. Jefferson glued his eye to the peephole, taking in the scene.

Mokhtari was in the room. He walked over and examined Nesbit's bonds, looked directly at Jefferson's box. Could Mokhtari know he had been out of the Box? The guard was standing at attention looking straight ahead. Mokhtari walked over to him, drew out his pistol, jammed the muzzle into the guard's mouth and pulled the trigger. The gunshot reverberated through the building. Mokhtari pointed the gun at the back of Nesbit's head, changed his mind, swung and pumped four shots into Jefferson's box.

Holstering his pistol, he walked over to the wall and grabbed the rope that lifted Nesbit's arms. As he yanked on it Nesbit's screams split the air. Mokhtari untied the rope and pulled, lifting Nesbit into the air. Every prisoner and guard in the building heard Nesbit's cry, until he slipped into unconsciousness.

Silence was a punctuation mark before the echo of Mokhtari's heels as he climbed the stairs.

Mary Hauser lay on the cold floor, an ear pressed to the crack under her cell door. Doc Landis had sent her a message that they would try talking under the door, and they had discovered that in the early morning hours, when the guard was asleep and snoring, they could whisper back and forth, their words scurrying over the hard cold floor seeming to carry strength.

Doc Landis was saying, "The guards have sodomized eight men in the cell block. It's a sort of degradation, a way to destroy our will to resist. They increase their own feeling of impatience when they degrade us. And it's torture, doubly effective when it's part of a routine. Anticipation becomes a working fear, as you well know . . ."

" . . . Doc, were you one of the eight?"

A pause. "Yes."

"I shouldn't have asked."

"Talking helps me too."

"He's . . ." She forced herself to talk, she wanted to help him, and herself, by sharing. "He's done it to me three times. Questions, beatings, strip and . . . and him . . ."

They stopped talking when they heard shouting upstairs. Their guard woke up and went to the stairs and spoke to someone above him. They could hear him climb the steps. "It's Mokhtari," Mary whispered, translating for the doctor, "I got the words 'shooting a prisoner.' "

"I heard the word 'guard,' " Landis said. "It sounds like Mokhtari went on a rampage."

Neither gave words to the new terrors that started to work at them.

LANGLEY, VIRGINIA

The report detailed how Nasir Askari broke after seventy-three hours and twenty-two minutes in Primary, a new record. The technicians were changing shifts Friday evening and almost missed the first clues of rapid, agitated movements followed by muffled groans. By Monday morning the report was complete, much of the data correlated and verified, and on Allen Camm's desk.

"Susan," Camm said, "top drawer. I'm surprised at the number of Islamic Jihad over here. They really have a grip on what the Joint Special Operations Agency has been doing."

"Well, we've put a dent in their organization. They have it right about the JSOA, though—terrorists should worry about them. Maybe we can change that and make them worry about us too." Camm said nothing. "We're expecting the Islamic Republican Party to give the IPRP some of the POWs in exchange for their support on the Council of Guardians. We're moving Deep Furrow into place to rescue the POWs that are exchanged."

"How?" Camm asked.

"They'll be moved by an airliner. We plan to hijack the plane in transit and kidnap the POWs. It will look like a splinter group of the Islamic Republican Party did it as a protest against giving the POWs away."

"How many POWs will be exchanged?"

"Probably about half, we figure."

"Good. Real good. Keep on it," Camm told her. He was feeling better and better about his prospects.

NELLIS AFB, NEVADA

The Huey hovered beside the approach end of the runway until the tower gave it clearance to taxi to the ramp. It flew a few feet above the ground until it was near building 201, then settled to earth. Stansell and Chief Pullman jumped down and ran out from under the rotating blades, their heads ducked. They were just back from an early Monday morning inspection of Texas Lake and headed for Stansell's office.

"How is it going at the lake?" Bryant asked when they entered the trailer.

"Lots of action out there," Stansell deadpanned, "someone seems to have stirred the pot."

Bryant could sense the new upbeat in Stansell. "The F-111 crews are here and waiting in Intel."

Stansell headed for Intel, but the surge of confidence that had been building burst like a popped balloon when he walked into Dewa's office . . . "It's been a long time, Mark," he said, shaking Lieutenant Colonel Mark Von Drexler's hand. He had met V.D. when they were cadets at the Air Force Academy and had learned to dislike the man for the way he used and manipulated other people to get a leg up. A real operator and angle man. Trouble . . .

THE PENTAGON

It was a casual meeting, an Army four-star general running into an Air Force two-star that worked for him. "Simon," Army General Charles Leachmeyer said, "haven't seen you around lately. Drop in and talk when you get a chance." Both men knew it was more than polite chatter. Simon Mado followed Leachmeyer into his office and closed the door behind them.

"Dammit, Mado, there're at least four Russian agents moving around Fort Bragg watching Delta Force. I thought the idea was to get them looking at your troops at Nellis."

"They haven't bit on Task Force Alpha. Stansell's got them buried out of sight in the desert."

"I thought we were going to do a controlled leak to keep that from happening."

"You know the President ruled that out."

"Look, Simon, I've pushed your career. I was the one that got you assigned to the JSOA and made sure you got the right visibility. How often does an Air Force officer pick up a sponsor from the Army who plays poker with the President of the United States? Now repay the goddamn favor and get behind Delta Force. They're the experts at rescue missions. They're my experts, and they better be yours."

Mado felt shaken when he retreated from Leachmeyer's office.

What the hell did Leachmeyer expect him to do? He slammed through the set of doors that led to his own office, stopped at a major's desk. "Hal, remember that message you sent out a few days ago ordering GBU-15s shipped to Turkey for exercise WARLORD?" The major nodded and braced himself—he had seen Mado in one of these moods before. "Stop action on that and ship twelve GBU-12s instead."

"What priority you want me to give this, sir? I've got seven other projects in the mill that all needed to be done yesterday—"

"Major, what in the hell do you think you get paid for?"

"Well, make up your mind what you want," the major mumbled at Mado's retreating back. He marked his notepad to get the message out. "Looks like a low priority to me." He decided it would be easiest just to let the order for shipping the two-thousand-pound GBU-15s stand and he'd get a message out ordering the twelve five-hundred-pound GBU-12s shipped when he had a breather. He wasn't about to get bent out of shape over some goddamn exercise and a pissed-off general who went up and down in his moods with the weather.

CHAPTER 20

D MINUS 15

KERMANSHAH, IRAN

Any movement was intense pain for Nesbit, even blinking his eyes. He could hear the guards working as they pried Jefferson's body out of the Box. Mokhtari had ordered the two bodies—Jefferson's and the guard's—be left in the basement, and rigor mortis had set in after a few hours. All the guards had to parade through the basement, witnesses to the punishment for disobeying the commandant's orders while Nesbit hung on the ropes.

"Sergeant Nesbit," Mokhtari said, standing behind him, "I'm tiring of this. We end it now or you will join them." He drew out his pistol and pulled the slide back, let it snap closed, chambered a round. The metallic crack filled the room.

The sergeant took to heart Jefferson's last words, a message the man had died for. Still, he hated to seem to be giving in . . . "I was a command post controller, in charge of the command-and-control equipment that linked us with higher headquarters . . ."

Mokhtari keyed a cassette recorder as the sergeant talked. When he was satisfied the sergeant was finished he turned off the tape recorder and motioned for a guard to jerk on the rope that suspended Nesbit from the ceiling. "We will continue tomorrow," he said, leaving Nesbit withering in pain. He went directly to the basement in the administration building and ordered his interrogation team to gather for instructions. Hauser would also be talking today, he was confident, and his nightly report to the Council of Guardians would be most complete.

NELLIS AFB, NEVADA

"Colonel, I just don't know . . ." Duck Mallard kept looking at the captain standing in front of them. Rather than discuss the matter in front of the young officer, Stansell asked him to wait outside. The captain saluted and left the trailer.

"All right, what's bothering you, Duck?" Stansell asked.

"I know we can use an AC-130, Colonel. A gunship like that gives us awesome firepower . . . But that's the Beezer, Hal Beasely."

"Is he a good pilot?"

"The best, a natural. I knew him as a lieutenant before he went to gunships. He was infamous then, still is . . ."

"So what's his problem?"

"He's a skirt-chaser, a womanizer of the first order. Hell, he'd screw a snake. In fact he'd screw a woodpile if he thought a snake was in it. And drink? Only Drunkin' Dunkin can match him."

"Then why keep Dunkin on your crew?"

"Best nav in the Air Force."

"Okay, Beasely is a great pilot. We keep him. I plan to use his AC-130 as an airborne command-and-control platform and put General Mado and Thunder on board." Mallard shook his head at this. "Is that a problem?" Stansell asked.

"Colonel, I'm just trying to give you the whole picture. The Beezer has absolutely no respect for what they call duly constituted authority." Stansell didn't blink. "Oh, hell, let's keep him, he's the most likable S.O.B. you'll ever meet. He'll fit right into this collection of misfits."

CHAPTER 21

D MINUS 14

KERMANSHAH, IRAN

Doc Landis could hear the guard snoring. Old habits had reestablished themselves and the guard had slipped into a light sleep in the early morning hours. "Mary, talk to me," he whispered under the door, his cheek against the damp concrete. Somewhere in the dark he heard the scurry of a rat. "Mary?"

"I need help, doc." The words were faint. "It was awful, the worst it's been . . . I'm still bleeding. Oh God, they even had a VCR, filmed it. Made me watch it. I don't know how much longer . . ."

"Mary, how much have you told him?"

"Nothing. Yet."

"Start talking some next time. Don't let them get to the beating stage. Feed them a little at a time. Try to trade a few words for some relief. See if they'll let me treat you."

"But—"

"No buts. Do it."

NELLIS AFB, NEVADA

Crew Chief Staff Sergeant Raymond Byers jerked the chocks from around the main gear, freeing his jet for flight. He motioned the pilot to taxi forward and stop. He darted under the wings and ran his hands over the tires, making sure they were clean and uncut. His knowing eyes swept over his F-15, giving it one last check. Baby was ready. He ran out front, to the pilot's left, gave him a thumbs-up, and with a backward wave motioned for him to taxi out into the stream of aircraft moving down the taxipath.

Grudgingly he admitted that the jet of his old partner, Tim Wehr, looked as good as his, and Timmy had launched his F-15 just as quick. They had had the two best jets in the wing at Holloman. "Yo, Timmy," he called across the ramp, "looking good. Our drivers will beat the shit out of those assholes from Luke."

Timmy joined him as they walked in. "Did you see Cap'n Locke? He was in that E model that taxied out. What d'you think Stansell will say when he sees us here?"

"Who gives a rat's ass?"

Locke watched the four F-15s from Luke fly a low level combat air patrol for the string of C-130s working their way along a low-level route through the heart of central Nevada. His WSO, Ambler Furry, kept up a running commentary from the pit, the backseat of the Eagle.

"The C-130s are right on course," Furry told him. "The lead C-130 looks like he's flying a precision approach the way he keeps on track."

"That's Drunkin Dunkin on Mallard's crew. He's the navigator I told you about." Locke was trailing behind the package, evaluating the F-15s and C-130s on their first integrated flight. He kept watching for the flight of four Holloman F-15s that were supposed to intercept them somewhere en route to the target.

"I got 'em on the TEWs," Furry said. "Nine o'clock on us."

Locke pointed the nose of his jet toward the threat. His APG-70 radar system found the four Holloman Eagles on the first sweep. The radio came alive with chatter as Snake Houserman called his F-15s onto the Holloman birds. The four Eagles surged up and away from the C-130s, leaving them naked.

Locke was raging. "Snake knows better. The LOCAP was supposed to maintain radio silence and stay with the C-130s until Holloman found them and got a visual. Holloman was briefed to act like Iranians and not use their look-down capability to find us at low level."

"Yeah," Furry said, "well, Holloman sure forgot about that. The

49th was using everything they had to find us. Look at that, they're really mixing it up now." Furry watched the eight F-15s come together in the merge.

"We'll stay with the C-130s," Locke said.

The range controller in the mobile trailer that served as the range-control tower keyed his mike, "Cleared in hot," he radioed, trying to get a visual on the F-111 that was running in on the tank hulk that was serving as a target.

"There," Stansell said, pointing to the south. He could see the F-111 hugging the desert floor through the large window of the glass cupola on top of the trailer. "You can see the shock wave," he said. A visible wave of air was rolling behind the F-111, kicking up a shower of dust and dirt.

"You're in the green," the range controller radioed. The F-111 pulled up in a forty-five-degree climb over five miles short of the target, loading the aircraft with four Gs in two seconds. It was a perfect toss.

"Bomb gone." It was Torch Doucette's voice.

"No laser guidance on this pass," the range controller said. "Strictly a radar and computer delivery. The APQ-146 radar in the F-111F is cosmic, the wizzo shouldn't have any trouble breaking out the target we're using today."

"They can tell the difference between that tank and the building next to it?" Stansell asked, impressed.

"Yeah. He drives the cursor's over the target, activates the system and the Weapons/Nav Computer and INS do the rest. The inertial nav system feeds winds, groundspeed, drift into the computer as they pull up. The computer knows the ballistics of the weapon they're using, takes G forces into account and computes a release point thirty-two times a second. When it gets a solution it automatically releases the bomb." The bomb was still in flight while the range controller talked and tracked the arcing bomb with his binoculars.

A puff of smoke enveloped the tank. "Bull!" the controller radioed.

"Why use laser guidance when they've got accuracy like that?" Stansell asked.

"Gives 'em more flexibility and precision refinement on the target. Also allows the pilot more slop on delivery. When you're coming in just below the mach and Charlie is throwing everything he's got at you, you can't always do a perfect toss like you just saw. Might want to do a laydown, and for sure you're jinking like hell. For sure . . ." The controller stared over the desert, remembering a run he had made over Libya in 1986 . . .

The next F-111 checked in. It was Von Drexler. Stansell listened to the radio traffic as the F-111 ran in and pulled up in a toss maneuver. "He's steeper than Doucette," the colonel said.

"Sure is." The controller was shaking his head. "V.D.'s honking back too hard on the stick—too aggressive and he's way outside the max release range of the weapon. Way too steep. No way the computer can reach a solution. He'll go through dry."

"Off dry," Von Drexler radioed, "system malfunction."

"Malfunction, my ass," the controller said. "He hasn't changed since I was in the 48th. No hands."

"I'm not surprised," Stansell said, wondering what excuse Von Drexler would be using in the mission debrief.

"He's probably giving his wizzo hell right now," the controller said. "He don't give a rat's ass about droppin' bombs where they belong—just wants to play it safe and look good."

CHAPTER 22

D MINUS 13

IRBIL, IRAQ

The convoy moving out of the Iraqi Army headquarters picked up speed as it cleared the edge of town and headed toward the first low ridge of hills four miles to the northeast. Bill Carroll sat in the rear of the dilapidated truck the Kurds had loaded with two goats and vegetables to take to the marketplace in Irbil and counted the vehicles as they roared past. His truck had been forced to pull to the side of the road by the lead armored personnel carrier, a Soviet-built BTR-60. Five more of the eight-wheeled ten-ton APCs passed, the last one swinging its 14.5 mm and 7.62 mm turret-mounted machine guns on them.

"I count six APCs in the lead," Mustapha Sindi said.

"Figure fourteen troops inside each one," Carroll said. He was worried about the attack he had planned and organized for the Kurds—suspicion that the Kurds might blame him for a defeat would not go away. "That's a good armored car, you've got to be careful around them." Mustapha only shrugged. Like all Kurds, the Pesh Merga tended to forget heavy odds against them in battle.

The two men counted twenty-four ZIL-157 trucks, each packed with troops. "About twenty to twenty-five to a truck," Mustapha observed. "Good trucks, we could use some of them." Two more BTR-60s passed, one a command vehicle. Another twelve trucks passed, heavily loaded with supplies. Four BTR-60s brought up the rear.

"They separate their supplies and personnel," Carroll said. "We need to change our tactics. It's not enough, the Iraqis have got to commit more troops before we attack." He dug a small Israeli-made field radio out of a sack of vegetables and started to transmit. Mustapha pounded on the roof of the cab and told the driver to go on into Irbil.

Ghalib al-Otaybi sat in the commander's seat of the command BTR-60 monitoring the radios, the noise of the two GAZ-49B engines muffled by his headset. The freshly promoted *muqaddam*, Iraqi equivalent of lieutenant colonel, was leading his first operation as a newly appointed battalion commander. Both rank and command came from family connections and friends who had insured his combat experience in the Iran-Iraq war had been limited to the safety of a rear-echelon headquarters.

Now he noted the traffic on the road heading for the marketplace in Irbil, if anything lighter than normal, and by the time his convoy entered the first low range of hills the traffic had all but disappeared. The next seven miles leading to a small village nestled at the base of a steep escarpment were covered on time, and Otaybi saw nothing that indicated the Kurds were active in the region. Their intelligence was wrong and the prisoner had lied. He would settle up *that* when they returned. He keyed the radio, ordering the convoy to close up when the lead BTR reported the village in sight.

Ahead of him, unseen, over three hundred Kurds were running to new positions after receiving Carroll's latest radio message.

Otaybi's rear guard had cleared the village when the convoy came under attack. "Small arms fire," the lead gunner reported, closing his hatch and crawling into the turret. A hail of 7.62mm bullets rained down on the aluminum skin of the BTR ricocheting harmlessly into the air. The gunner swept the hillside with a burst of heavy machine gun fire as the driver accelerated down the road. Three BTRs followed him while the last two halted, stopping the unarmored trucks behind them, ready to act as a shield. Men poured out of the trucks, searching for cover.

The last armored car was less than a hundred yards beyond the village when a turbaned boy of sixteen popped up from behind a rock with a dark green tube—a U.S.-made, Israeli-supplied light antitank weapon. The small rocket with a shaped charged warhead streaked toward the BTR less than forty yards away. The Iraqis never saw the boy or the shot that penetrated the aluminum armor and gunner. Now the boy ran for cover while two more LAWs riddled the BTR. The last hit blew askew the two wheels that steered in tandem on the left side, and the momentum of the BTR slued it to the left, blocking the road . . .

From the safety of his armored car in the middle of the convoy, Otaybi ordered his dismounted troops to sweep the area to the rear and the village, to shoot any Kurd on sight, armed or unarmed, woman or child.

The soldiers sweeping the village reported no activity or Kurds, and the village was known to be friendly. A hit-and-run attack, nothing to stop him, the battalion commander decided. Otaybi had convinced himself that the Kurds were not as brave, or as suicidal, as the Afghanis and too weak and disorganized to put up any resistance in force. He radioed for two of the BTRs surging ahead to return to the convoy and for the other two to scout the road. Most of the men clambered back into the trucks while a detail zippered the dead BTR gunner into a body bag and the three wounded men were treated and taken to the village. None was seriously hurt, and Otaybi radioed the division headquarters in Irbil to send an ambulance. A BTR pushed its destroyed mate to the side of the road and the convoy resumed its chase . . .

The Kurds who had attacked the rear of the convoy could still see the dust of the disappearing trucks when they approached the destroyed BTR and started packing it with high explosive charges. The smell of blood was still fresh inside the armored car. Only when they were finished did they send a message to Carroll that the road could be sealed off . . .

The two BTRs scouting ahead reached a bridge twelve miles down the road thirty-three minutes later, radioed their position and were told to secure the bridge and wait for the convoy. The lead armored car did not cross the bridge but waded the river and climbed the far bank to reach the other end. The three Kurdish patrols watching the bridge from different vantage points each sent a runner to the rear.

When the convoy reached the bridge Otaybi sent a demolition team to inspect it. They reported finding two satchel charges wired to the girders of the central span, noted the fuses were wired to a small transmitter, and withdrew. Otaybi sent them right back to disarm the charges. Two hours later the team exploded the satchels in the river gorge a half mile downstream, and Otaybi felt the area secure enough to crawl out of his BTR as he sent his trucks across the bridge.

The high-pitched shrill of incoming mortars shattered his confidence. Explosions echoed down the river gorge, adding to the confusion and making it impossible for Otaybi's commands to be heard. He leaped into the BTR and slammed the hatch shut, locking his driver out, as the bridge disappeared in a geyser of smoke and sounds. The Iraqi demolition team had missed the two-hundred-pound charge the Kurds had buried at the base of the far pylon. The attack ended as quickly as it had started, and Otaybi could only stare at the ruins of the bridge, with most of his troops on the far side of the six lead BTRs.

He grabbed the radio's mike and ordered his men and BTRs to ford the river and reform on his side, abandoning the trucks. A BTR leading the return nosed over the embankment and presented the tail of its boat-shaped hull to the sky. An 84mm Carl Gustav anti-tank missile streaked from the hillside and punched a hole in the engine compartment. Otaybi saw a tail of flame erupt from the disabled BTR before he heard the muffled explosion and saw the two hatches flop open and men spill out. A fresh hailstorm of small-arms fire and mortar rounds swept over his Iraqi troops, driving them for cover. The battalion commander cursed in frustration when he saw the two-man team that had fired the Carl Gustav scamper over the top of the ridge to safety.

Suddenly, it was quiet again. Then a series of explosions from the rear of the convoy resonated through the river valley and the leading shock wave rocked the command BTR. Panicked, Otaybi yelled into the mike, trying to reestablish contact with his rear guard. Nothing. He cracked his forward hatch and ordered the driver to send a squad to check on the rear of the convoy. No answer. Fear was his only companion as he jabbed at the radio, sending a plea for help to Irbil.

Zakia Sindi was hidden inside a house next to the army compound in Irbil, scanning Iraqi tactical frequencies. The sweep on her monitoring equipment locked on to Otaybi's channel and she relayed his distress call to Carroll. "Now we have to see how they react here," he told her. "Unless they send a relief force the attack is off and we can withdraw." But he wished he could *know* something for sure. Alone and guessing . . .

NELLIS AFB, NEVADA

The soft, rhythmic buzz of the plotter filled the corner of the room. Dewa and Bryant moved aside, letting Stansell watch the computer-generated map printout. "Where did you get that program?" Stansell asked.

"Courtesy of the Defense Mapping Agency," Bryant told him, "and a little wheelin' dealin' by Mizz Rahimi here."

Stansell watched them plot a route from Turkey into Iran that twisted and turned through the rugged Zagros mountains. "The radar site at Maragheh is our biggest problem," Bryant said. "Got to work around it." Then he turned his attention to a 1:250,000 scale map of Nevada, finding equivalent routes to train on. Everything Stansell had seen indicated the C-130 crews could hack the mission and what Bryant was laying out was within their abilities if the weather cooperated.

Jack Locke stuck his head in the door. "Sir, need to talk to you." Stansell motioned him in.

"I can't get the F-15 drivers to stick to the scenario. They're more interested in going head-to-head with each other than escorting C-130s."

"Fangs starting to hang out?"

"Yeah. They know the LOCAP is supposed to stick with the C-130s until the bad guys get a visual. I've briefed the HICAP flight that they can only use vectors from Blackjack, the Range Control Center—just like the Iranian defense net—to find the intruders. But they seem to forget that and use everything they've got to find each other. Snake left the C-130s uncovered yesterday when the HICAP was still beyond visual range. Not good."

"Any ideas?"

"Other than telling them what we're really doing here, Colonel? No."

"Can't do that. All we need is some idle chatter at the bar. Keep at 'em and I'll work on it—"

They were interrupted by Bryant. "Message from Texas Lake, sir. Seems there was a fight between a couple of Rangers and C-130 loadmasters. Colonel Gregory would appreciate your presence."

TEXAS LAKE, NEVADA

Kamigami was waiting with a jeep and driver for Stansell when the helicopter landed at Texas Lake. He waited until Stansell was in the passenger's seat, then vaulted into the back seat with an ease that belied his bulk, which tilted the jeep down on his side as the driver headed for the battalion's headquarters tent.

Four men were standing at attention against the back wall when Stansell entered. A livid Duck Mallard was with Ham Gregory. Gregory told Stansell about the fight between two Romeo Team Rangers and the two C-130 loadmasters in front of the mess tent. "If you want, I'll build a gallows right now," Gregory said.

A soft voice came from behind them. "If you will, sir, let me handle it." It was Victor Kamigami.

"You've got it, Sergeant Major," Gregory said.

Kamigami pointed to the entrance. "Baulck, Wade. Out." The two Rangers double-timed outside.

Mallard turned to the two loadmasters. "What in the hell were you thinking of?"

"Sir, one of those pukes said that I had to be a certifiable cock-sucker to fly with a crew of two-bit whores and —"

"Petrovich, I don't give a damn what they said. I've a mind to turn you two over to the CSM here . . ."

"I can solve this problem, sir," Kamigami reminded him.

"You've got 'em."

Again, Kamigami pointed to outside. "Wait," was all he said. The two men repeated the performance of the Rangers.

"I think they'd rather of had the gallows," Stansell said. "How deep does this go?"

"This is the second flare-up we've had," Mallard said. "Too much tension, no sense of team effort."

"Now, how in the hell do we cure all that?" Stansell asked. Without blowing security? he silently added.

"Football," Kamigami said, leaving the tent. "Survivors winners."

IRBIL, IRAQ

The commander of the motor-rifle division slammed the phone down. What did those idiots in Baghdad expect? He had a division in name only and the forces in garrison at Irbil amounted to little more than a half-strength regiment. They withdraw battalion after battalion to reinforce the border with Iran, and now they expect him to respond like a Soviet motor-rifle division, the model the Iraqis had patterned their army after. If it had been anyone other than that fool Otaybi, the politicos, the asses that Hussein and the ruling council chose to make generals, would have ignored the ambush and let the trapped battalion fight its way out. Now he had to mount a major rescue effort. And all because of the precious Otaybi family.

Still, it wasn't worth his life to let Ghalib al-Otaybi be captured by the Kurds.

Mustapha Sindi pointed at the shadow moving along the outer wall of the compound that housed the divisional headquarters in Irbil. The last of the relief column had left twenty minutes earlier and the evening twilight was rapidly fading into darkness. The audacity of the Kurds had worried Bill Carroll at first, they seemed totally unconcerned with the risks they were taking and moved casually into place right under the Iraqi guards. He relaxed when he saw how easily they disappeared into the deepening shadows, and his fingers relaxed their stranglehold on the two-foot-length of pipe he was carrying.

The shadowy image moved on. "They're all in place," Mustapha Sindi told Carroll, fingering the transmitter that would trigger the series of C4 plastic high-explosive charges placed around the wall. If they all worked, numerous sections of the wall would be breached at the same time. Now they had to wait . . .

Twenty-three miles to the northeast, the last of the Iraqi relief column was through the small village and passing the destroyed BTR. The Kurd left behind in the village to detonate the explosives timed it well. He hit the switch on his remote actuator and the booby-trapped BTR erupted, taking out the Iraqis in the rear of the relief column . . .

The dull boom echoed across the valley, reaching Irbil. "It begins," Sindi said. The light banter typical of the young Kurd was gone. Now he was a serious guerrilla.

They heard Zakia's voice in the next room talking on the radio. She came to the doorway. "They never suspected the armored car, didn't even check it," she reported. "Two trucks and the last armored car were destroyed, the road is cratered. The relief column is trapped on the other side of the village."

"Tell our man to get the hell out of there," Carroll said. He was expecting the Iraqi soldiers to sweep through the village and kill many of the inhabitants—most of them loyal Iraqis. "Have them hit the battalion at the bridge one more time. I want that Iraqi yelling for help when we work the headquarters over. Then everyone withdraws together." Zakia went back to the radio to relay his instructions. "Mustapha—now."

Sindi keyed the transmitter, and a series of explosions marched around the walls of the headquarters, sending smoke and debris into the air. Without waiting, Carroll and Sindi charged into the smoke along with ninety other Kurds. Sindi tripped over rubble in the smoke and went sprawling—he was not fully recovered from the beating by the Iraqi soldiers but had insisted on going on the raid. Carroll picked him up by the back of his shirt and they covered together the few short steps to the wall. The C4 charge had knocked an eight-foot gap in the wall, and they ran through followed by four others.

Inside the compound they sprinted for the low building on their left, taking sporadic gunfire from the three-story building directly in front of them. The four Kurds following them headed for that building while Carroll and Sindi crossed the open ground leading to the low building. The bark of a machine gun from the rear of the compound was their first warning that the defenders were reacting and in force.

A sharp explosion ended that threat.

Carroll plastered himself to the building's wall next to a window. At a nod from Sindi he jammed one end of the pipe he was carrying through the glass and raked it around the inner edges of the window frame, clearing away the glass. Sindi shoved the muzzle of his Uzi through the opening and swept the room with a short burst. A guard in the hall had heard the sound of the breaking glass and had come into the room, meeting Sindi's gunfire. Sindi leaped through the window. Carroll right behind him stepped over the guard's body, following Sindi into the cell block.

A long row of heavy steel doors stretched down the hall—all closed and locked. Carroll searched the dead guard's pockets for a key. Nothing. Sindi was running down the hall, yelling at the door of each cell, trying to find out which cells were occupied by Kurds. They only had ribbon charges to blow open two doors. But they wanted to unlock them if possible—the concussion would probably break the eardrums of the prisoner inside.

Carroll headed for the guard room. So far the old man's diagram of the cell block had been accurate, and according to it two guards should be on duty. One was still unaccounted for. Carroll kicked the door open and crouched. Nothing. He moved through and saw a dim figure huddled in a corner. He fired a short burst, fingered the light switch by the door . . . and saw what he had done. A young boy in uniform, maybe sixteen years old, lay dead on the floor. A large key ring with one key was on the floor beside him. Carroll shook his head, scooped it up and ran into the hall, trying not to think about teenagers who hid in corners frightened and confused . . .

Sindi was attaching a ribbon charge to a cell's door when Carroll jammed the key into the lock and twisted. Inside was Rashid Shaban, unable to walk, the soles of his feet burned with an electric engraving tool. Carroll picked him up in a fireman's carry and started up the hall while Sindi unlocked the cells. Shaban was the only Kurd being held, but Carroll had told Sindi to let as many prisoners as possible out, adding to the confusion bound to follow the attack.

Outside, the fighting had stopped and only the Kurds whom Carroll had detailed to hide explosive charges with delayed-action fuses were still in the compound. They were nine minutes into the attack and running out of time. Two men grabbed Shaban and carried him to the same dilapidated truck that had carried them into town. But instead of produce the truck was now overflowing with men and weapons. Carroll motioned to Zakia, raising his right hand to his lips. She pulled a police whistle out of a pocket and blew one long blast followed by two short toots. She paused and repeated the signal. Men came running out of the compound, some disappearing into the darkness, others piling into waiting cars and trucks. All had captured weapons and ammo cases.

The last two men out were carrying a wounded comrade and rushed up to Zakia as the truck's starter motor ground, the engine finally coughing to life. Damn it, Carroll thought, the driver should have never turned it off. Zakia examined the Kurd lying on the ground while the wounded man spoke to her. She nodded and reached into a pouch on her belt, shaking free a syringe in a black plastic tube. The man spoke again and she gave him a swift injection in his left arm. He pushed his right hand into his coat and rolled over onto his stomach. She stood and ran for the cab of the truck, jumping in and telling the driver to move, and they drove out of the square, leaving the wounded man in the dust behind them.

"Dammit," Carroll shouted, jumping from the truck, running for the man.

The truck skidded to a halt and Zakia jumped out. "No!" she shouted at his back. "He's dead."

Carroll hesitated, then ran back to the truck, the men pulling him into the back as they accelerated away.

"He's booby-trapped," a voice said. "If you had moved him, a grenade would have blown your head off."

Carroll did not look at Zakia as he reminded himself that these people had been fighting for their existence long before the brave American came aboard. Their whole nation was a POW.

CHAPTER 23

D MINUS 12

NELLIS AFB, NEVADA

"Was this ever meant as an exercise?" the leader of the Romeo Team, Captain Trimler asked. He was pacing the floor in Dewa's office, obviously upset after spending an hour going over Romeo Team's objective—taking a prison that held a large number of hostages. He had seen through to the truth.

"Nope," Stansell told him. "Good chance we might do it."

"It won't work," the captain said, studying the model of the prison. "On any airdrop we're at most risk when we land. We need an objective rally point to form up, break out our weapons, get organized . . . takes time. Here"—he pointed at the model—"we've got maybe a minute to be inside, knocking the defenders down after the F-111s blow the walls. Any longer than that and they'll have time to react. Probably start killing the hostages. To get inside fast we've got to be on the ground, locked and loaded, ready to go through that wall before the dust of the last bomb settles."

"Colonel Gregory has seen this," Dewa said. "Why didn't he say something?"

Trimler only shook his head.

Stansell knew the reason. Gregory was too gung ho—show him what to do and get out of the way. It was Gregory's chance, his only chance, to lead a daring history-making operation, and after his shaky start with Stansell he wanted to leave no doubts about who should be the ground commander. Brigadier General "Messy" Eichler's words about finding an expert on special operations and listening to him came back. Stansell hoped it wasn't too late. What else had Eichler said that he had forgotten? . . . "Get Locke and Bryant in here," Stansell ordered. "Time for a head-knocking session. Captain Trimler, you're going to be my Siamese twin for the next couple of days."

NORTHEASTERN IRAQ

Mulla Haqui was pleased. The wizened man who led the Pesh Merga kept walking around the fourteen ZIL-157 trucks they had taken, waving his arms and talking. A tired Bill Carroll sat on the tailgate of a truck—everyone seemed to talk nonstop at the same time—and watched the Kurds sort and stack the supplies, weapons and ammunition they had captured from the Iraqis.

One of Haqui's bodyguards came over and said the old man wanted to speak to him. The guards surrounding Haqui split apart, letting Carroll approach, still carefully watching him. "Undamaged," Haqui said, sweeping the trucks with his hand. "We are moving tonight, these trucks will help. The village must be empty by morning. The Iraqis will search for us with aircraft but we will hide in Iran." Haqui moved closer and slapped Carroll on the shoulder, "You have helped us." Carroll was aware of the guard standing close behind him but didn't see the knife only inches away from his right kidney. When Haqui moved back, the guard relaxed.

"And the way the Iraqis reacted after we attacked the relief column . . . smart, how did you know they would destroy their own village in retaliation?"

"*Insh' Allah,*" Carroll said, hoping he had it right.

Haqui looked at him. "Are you . . . ?"

Carroll shook his head. "I'm of a different faith, the people of the Book." The tone of Carroll's voice carried conviction, but doubt lingered in the old man.

"The prisoner," he abruptly ordered. Two guards disappeared into a mud hut and dragged out Ghalib al-Otaybi. "We will leave him behind," Haqui said. The Iraqi lieutenant colonel was the same age as Carroll, twenty-seven.

Haqui stared at Carroll, eyes unblinking. "Kill him." Otaybi's knees buckled. The two men at his side jerked the Iraqi to his feet and stood back. The constant talking that marked Kurdish tribal life was silenced. It was Carroll's final testing.

Hesitation was out of the question, Carroll knew. He walked straight toward Otaybi, then walked past. Otaybi turned his head, looking at the American. A guard slapped him—making him look straight ahead. In one swift move Carroll drew his pistol, thumbed the safety off, cocked the hammer, turned and fired one shot into the back of Otaybi's head.

A guard spat. "You were too merciful. He would have tortured you like Shaban before he killed you."

"He"—Carroll pointed his toe at Otaybi—"is not my teacher." He walked off quickly then, not wanting the Kurds to see him shaking.

Zakia found him huddled against the back wall of a hut, shivering. She sat down next to him, put her arm around his neck and drew his head onto her shoulder.

"A foolish greedy man on a bus"—Carroll voice was shaky—"a bitter woman who lost her family in a war and only lived with hate, a teenage boy wearing a uniform because he found a job guarding prisoners, and now . . . damn it, I'm not a murderer . . ."

"Shush, we are all soldiers here. Old and young, woman and child. We do things no civilized human being should have to live with. I killed that man we left behind in the square when I could not save him." She pulled Carroll's head against her breasts.

After a while she stood and led him to her bed. A sharing of renewal they both needed.

NELLIS AFB, LAS VEGAS

A message arrived. "That's all we need," Stansell grumbled after he read it. "General Mado gets here late this evening. Cunningham has ordered him to move out here with us. I want to have an answer before we tell him about getting the Rangers in place ahead of the F-111's attack on the prison. Chief, you're going to have to find him an office and we've got to keep him busy until we get this hashed out. Stansell's gut warned him to handle the general with care . . . he just didn't fully trust the man who was the Joint Task Force Commander. Was it because of the last meeting he had with Cunningham?

"We've got the football game tomorrow," Pullman said.

"Need more than that."

"Barbara Lyon," Dewa said. "Our apartment owner likes playing the officer's lady. I'll talk to her and see if she'll plan a dinner party for Saturday night."

"Still leaves Sunday. We need time to get this change sorted out."

"If I know Barbara," Dewa said, "Sunday will take care of itself." Which takes care of two problems, she thought. We need to keep Mado preoccupied, and *I* need to get hot lips away from you, Colonel.

Dewa Rahimi had decided to start her own operation for this lonely man she had decided was worth fighting for.

CHAPTER 24

D MINUS 11

TEXAS LAKE, NEVADA

General Mado looked irritated as he watched the teams lining up for the kickoff on the makeshift field Pullman had chalked out on the hard desert pan of Texas Lake. "The Rangers outweigh us and we sure don't need anyone hurt right now. And who in *hell* decided to let women play?"

"That's Captain Kowalski, a C-130 pilot," Stansell told him uneasily. "It's flag football, sir. No tackling, and they can't leave their feet to block. May get a few bruises but no one is going to get hurt."

Mado looked skeptical.

The whistle sounded and the Army kicked off. Lieutenant Don Larson, Duck Mallard's co-pilot, caught the ball just short of the ten-yard line and started up-field. He fell in behind Torch Doucette, who cleared a path of would-be tacklers trying to snatch one of the two-foot streamers snapped to each side of Larson's belt, thereby signifying a tackle. They made it to their own forty-five.

"The black kid can run," Gregory told Kamigami on the sidelines. "Let's see how they pass."

Lydia Kowalski came out of the huddle first and took her position at right end. "I heard you think I go cheap," she said to the Ranger opposite her.

Andy Baulck came out of his stance on the snap, blocking her

171

back. Kowalski managed to sidestep him and ran her pattern down field, Baulck chasing her. Larson had moved through the line on a hand-off from the Air Force's quarterback Hal Beasely and was headed for the goal line. After a speedy corporal had grabbed Larson's flag and the referee blew his whistle ending the play, Baulck still threw a block at Kowalski's back, sending her sprawling.

"Clip," Kamigami said from the sidelines.

On the next play Kowalski seemed to ignore Baulck as she took her stance. A large woman, well-built, on the snap from center she threw her weight forward, blocked hard and straightened Baulck up. She then stepped into him, and kneed him in the groin, smiling innocently as she did so. Something more unpleasant might have been joined except that Kamigami hurried into the game and pointed at Baulck, who got the message.

With Kamigami anchoring his side of the line now, the Air Force drive stalled. He punched holes almost at will through the Air Force's line and let tacklers pour through, nailing the Beezer before he could pass to Larson. The first quarter ended scoreless as Doucette was carried off the field after trying to block Kamigami. Stansell had made Thunder Bryant the coach for the Air Force, since he had been a starting guard at UCLA before dropping football and turning to academics. "You coach and I'll play opposite Kamigami," Bryant said, handing his clipboard to Duck Mallard.

Now the Army was marching on the Air Force's goal line. At the snap Bryant and Kamigami blocked each other. Even without helmets and pads, everyone on the field heard it—two bulls colliding on a dry desert lake bed. On the next play Petrovich, Kowalski's loadmaster who had fought with the Rangers, got between them and was carried off the field unconscious.

At half-time the game was still scoreless but the Army was wearing Air Force down. Mallard told Kowalski she was out of the game and received no argument. Bryant lay on the ground, trying not to moan out load. At the kickoff it was Army's game, but Bryant and Kamigami still kept at it.

Baulck, also out of the game, carried two beers over to the Air Force side of the field and sat down beside Kowalski, offering her one as he did. She took it and popped the cap. "Hey," he said, "I'm sorry for what I said and . . . did out there." She looked at him, taking a sip. "I got a big mouth . . . well, hell, I'd fly on your plane anywhere."

"Thanks, I appreciate that." She pulled at the beer and gestured at the field. "Do we have to do that again?"

"No way," Baulck laughed, and went after two more beers.

The game ended Army thirteen, Air Force zero. Kamigami and Bryant walked over to the beer, Kamigami handing Bryant one. "Captain, I'm hurting," he said, loud enough for everyone around to hear. It was one of the few times the battalion saw their Command Sergeant Major allow a smile. Bryant, however, wasn't fooled . . . just grateful to have gotten out of it alive.

LAS VEGAS, NEVADA

General Mado was in an expansive mood. The meal had been fine, and if the coq au vin was any indication, Barbara Lyon was a considerable cook. Mado sipped at his wine, admiring the women. Dewa Rahimi seemed to shimmer in her simple black dress, and Barbara . . . he'd never met anyone like her.

The general's restless mind also poked and stirred through impressions from earlier in the day. What he had seen before the football game indicated that Stansell was making Task Force Alpha a *reality*. The beer bust after the game was proof that morale was now high and Alpha was a close-knit team. Leachmeyer wouldn't much like hearing any of that. And then a thought snapped into place, developed and complete, like so much of what he did: He could use Rahimi to scatter a hint of suspicion. Hadn't he told Stansell to get rid of her? And she *was* a civilian of Iranian descent— a built-in potential compromise of Task Force Alpha . . .

But play this one carefully, he warned himself. Cunningham was definitely watching him. Well, if anyone asked why Stansell had kept her on, he would just point out the obvious—they were attracted to each other. Even Barbara had mentioned it to him. Barbara, definite possibilities there—but not for the little colonel.

"Wine in the spa?" Barbara was asking.

His pleasure was interrupted by Gillian Locke coming through the gate, bundled against the cool night air, her pregnancy barely showing. "Jack just called," she said. "He's still at the office and was wondering if Dewa was available. He said something about needing her magic fingers on the computer."

"Duty calls," Dewa sighed but welcomed the chance to leave Barbara and Mado alone. "Colonel, I hate to ask, but my car is acting up . . ." There was nothing wrong with her car.

"Sure," Stansell said, "I'll drive."

"And I'll get another bottle of wine," Barbara said, leaving with Stansell and Dewa. The wait before she came back seemed endless for Mado. Finally she came through the gate, locking it behind her. Mado had trouble controlling his breathing when she reappeared in a robe and promptly shed it.

"The only way to use a spa," she announced, and stepped into the hot water. "Strip, general, and join me. I love massages," she said, as he joined her. "Most of all, I love to give them . . ."

NELLIS AFB, NEVADA

Dewa gasped when she saw her office. Jack had tacked a new map to the wall and the floor was littered with books and crumpled paper. Cabinet drawers were pulled out and her Top Secret safe was wide open, obviously riffled through at will. She took her responsibility for safeguarding classified information very seriously. Trimler was asleep on the couch, and Jack looked haggard and needed a shave. The two had been cooped up in the office since Friday night.

"I think we got it," Jack mumbled, heading for the coffee pot. "Bob"—he gestured at the sleeping Trimler—"says his people need to be inserted before the attack. We plan to parachute them in early—"

"Mado considered that when he originally laid the plan out," Stansell interrupted. "He tossed it because a paradrop is too easily observed and would warn the Iranians and blow the whole operation. We need another way to get them in."

"Not if we do it right. Bob tells me the Rangers train using MT-1X parachutes. That's the rectangular mattresslike chute that's really a non-rigid airfoil. Colonel, the chute has a forward speed of twenty-five miles an hour and if we drop them high enough with a good tail wind, they can stay airborne for an hour and cover some territory. If we drop 'em at night, nobody will see them and people make piss-poor radar returns."

"Okay, so we drop them far away from the prison. But how do we get them inside Iranian airspace at altitude and undetected in the first place?"

"We piggyback on an airliner."

"You've lost me."

"Easier to show you. Dewa, we've got all the Iranian airways plotted on that chart. Can you tap some data-base that give us their domestic flight schedules? We need a flight that takes off out of

Rezaiyeh at night—" he tapped the airport that Carroll had landed at seventeen days before—"and heads south or southeast."

Dewa went to work and twenty minutes later had the information they wanted. "There's an F-27 that takes off for Bandar Abbas in the late evening out of Rezaiyeh every Monday, Wednesday and Saturday."

"Okay. We intercept that F-27 when it climbs out of Rezaiyeh and piggyback on him. When we're about here"—Jack pointed to a spot on the airway between Rezaiyeh and Bandar Abbas—"our team bails out. A C-130 will have no trouble matching the speed and altitude of an F-27 and then we drop off when the F-27 descends to land and low level it out of Iran. No way the Iranian radar net will be able to break us out from the airliner."

He measured distances off the map. "Except the closest that airway comes to Kermanshah is seventy-six nautical miles to the northeast." He woke Trimler. "Bob, take a look at this."

The sleepy captain studied the map for a moment. "All you need is a fifty-knot wind out of the northeast." He went back to sleep.

"Jack, the prevailing winds at altitude over Iran this time of year are mostly out of the west," Stansell said. "Dewa, can you access the computer at the National Center for Atmospheric Research?"

"Where's it located and what kind of computer?"

"On a mesa overlooking Boulder. They've got a Cray."

She shot him a look. "The general I work for at the Special Activities Center is going to have fits when he gets the bill for this. I mean, someone has to pay for all this computer time, and I'm using the Center's user code. Do you have any idea what it costs to use a Cray for one second? Never mind, don't ask.

"Okay, I'm in," she said, "I'm talking to an IBM that talks to the Cray. What do you need?"

"The NCAR models weather patterns, and their predictions are remarkably accurate, especially within twenty-four hours. See what winds they're predicting over Iran at the five hundred millibar level, that's roughly eighteen thousand feet, for, say, ten days from now."

Dewa's fingers played over the keyboard. Then they waited. Less than a minute later a map flashed on her screen. Stansell and Locke looked over her shoulders. A high-pressure area was predicted to move over the eastern Mediterranean and the jet stream would bend south over Iran. A steep pressure gradient was predicted to build with it and cause a strong flow of winds out of the north for about seventy-two hours.

"Close enough" Jack said. "Print that puppy out. Northerly winds put us in the ball park."

"Okay, now how do we get our plane hooked up with the Iran airliner?" Stansell said.

"Hold on," Dewa said. "I saw some message traffic the other day about a joint Turkish-American air-defense exercise starting next week using AWACS and EC-130s." Her fingers flew over the keyboard. "I'm going to talk to someone in the Watch Center in the Pentagon." Five minutes later she had an answer. "Cunningham moved a scheduled exercise up two weeks and it kicks off Monday. They'll be operating in the tri-border area of Turkey, *Iran* and Iraq."

"That cagey son of a bitch," Stansell said.

"You figure he did that deliberately?" Dewa asked, and saw the answer vivid and clear on Stansell's face.

CHAPTER 25

D MINUS 10

KERMANSHAH, IRAN

Mary Hauser was standing in front of Mokhtari's desk, focusing on him. He was not looking at her but toward the corner of the room, behind her. Her eyes followed his gaze and she could feel the bile in her stomach rise. The man was sitting in the corner, clothes in a pile at his feet, staring at the floor. He did not look up when he heard her gasp.

The commandant asked his first question, the start of the routine she knew too well—questions, beatings, strippings... "What equipment did you use at Ras Assanya to kill our pilots?"

For a moment her spirit blazed and she almost said, The equipment that killed your pilots were the checklists they used to preflight their own aircraft. That gave them the confidence to think they were ready for a fight ... She knew the consequences of saying that was sitting there in the corner ... "I used an AN slash TPS dash fifty-nine system—"

Mokhtari held up his hand, fumbled with a cassette recorder on his desk trying to get it to work. As a guard came over and tried to make the recorder work, Mary used the time to think. She had to follow Doc Landis' advice—try to make them want to keep her alive ... Again her stubborn spirit flared—I will not sacrifice myself and all I believe in to this creature ...

The commandant gave a jerk of his head and Mary started to talk. "Is it on? The dash fifty-nine system . . . Are you sure it's working?" She gasped for air. "It's a D-band radar we use for air surveillance. It uses a phased-array antenna, not the normal parabolic style. I found that confusing because the old-style antenna on the AN slash FPS dash eight radar system gave a much more reliable return . . ." She couldn't stop herself, she was going to feed them misinformation she hoped they couldn't verify. Now she started to give out a story about how she had pointed this out to her superiors and had been chastised for not being able to use the equipment they had trained her to use. As a punishment she had been sent to Ras Assanya—

A guard rushed into the room, stopping Mary's flow of words. "Commandant, the general is here."

Mokhtari was on his feet. "Why wasn't I told he was coming?" Panic worked at the edges of his mind. Mary caught enough of the conversation to understand that the general who commanded the People's Soldiers of Islam had returned to the prison, the same general who had lost his eye and leg in an attack led by Muddy Waters of the 45th Tactical Fighter Wing.

LAS VEGAS, NEVADA

Sunday morning traffic was almost non-existent as Stansell drove back to Barbara's apartment. "How's Jack doing?" he said in a low voice.

Dewa twisted around in the front seat and looked at the pilot. "Sleeping like a baby."

"He deserves it." They waited for a red light to change. "He just may have saved the mission, but we still have a gap to plug . . . Cunningham needs to know . . ."

"Transportation on the ground," Dewa said, filling in his thought. He could only look at her, surprised at how easily she matched his thinking . . . "The light, Colonel. It's green."

They drove in silence, then: "Colonel?" It was Jack's voice from the rear. "I'd like to spend a little time with Gillian and fly over to March Air Force Base near Riverside tomorrow. Be a good chance to show Thunder what the Strike Eagle can do."

"What you got in mind?"

"I've got to get the attention of the F-15 jocks and need the help of the National Guard. If I read the situation right I've got about a week to teach them that when you're on the bad guy's turf the rules change. They've got to do it our way."

"Have at it, I've got to move on your changes in the plan. I'll tell Mado and get the word to Cunningham. I'll have to go to Fort Fumble to get his blessing . . . be back by Wednesday."

Stansell parked the car and watched Jack disappear in the direction of his apartment, where Gillian waited. He walked softly with Dewa toward her apartment, not wanting to end the moment. They climbed the outside stairs to the second floor, paused, leaning over the railing, still talking when Barbara came out of her apartment below them, complete—or incomplete—with tight jeans and a short denim jacket open in the front, revealing a clinging tee shirt. Mado walked out behind her. The click of Barbara's heels echoed through the courtyard as they disappeared out the front gate, never seeing the two watching them.

"I think the general will be busy today," Dewa said, straight-faced. "Would you like some breakfast?"

She unlocked the door, knowing they would be back at work in a few hours. But for a few minutes . . .

KERMANSHAH, IRAN

Mokhtari nervously looked over the quadrangle as the general's car drove through the inner gate of the entrance tunnel. There must not be any room for criticism. The dusty gray Mercedes halted at the base of the steps and a colonel from the second car in line ran up to the right passenger door, snapped it open. Mokhtari could see a frail shadow sitting in the back seat. "Come," the colonel said, gesturing at the door. Mokhtari ran down the steps, then was halted as he started to climb into the rear seat. He stood at attention.

"We are pleased with your reports," the general said. "You have shown progress since my last visit."

"Thank you, your excellency. Sergeant Nesbit is a good source of information. Even the woman is now cooperating and will soon be dry as a witch's tit. They will both die . . . of pneumonia . . . when I am finished."

"No, we will need them shortly."

"They are to be returned to the Americans?"

"Don't be stupid. We will give half of them to our weak-willed brothers who demand to share power with us. Of course, you will select which prisoners to send."

"Yes, I understand. One of the prisoners is a doctor. Shall I allow him to treat them?"

"No. But I want no more deaths for now. The old barracks behind the prison . . . I need them."

"Of course, sir. There are some Kurdish squatters living in there now but they will be removed today."

"Within this hour, my men must move under cover immediately." The car door slammed shut and the rear wheels of the Mercedes spun in the dust as it turned toward the gate.

Mokhtari barked orders to the captain of the guards to clear the old barracks immediately. "How many men does the general have waiting?"

"There are eight trucks outside," the captain told him, "and a tank carrier. When I approached the trucks I was ordered away."

"What type of tank is on the carrier?"

"It was covered with a canvas tarp, commandant. It looked like a small tank, perhaps a PT-76. But there was no cannon. It might be a Shilka."

Mokhtari shrugged and returned to his office, not caring about Shilkas. He slammed the door behind him, frustrated that Mary Hauser would live a while longer.

The key turning in the lock was enough warning. Mary had the bag over her head when the door swung open. She suspected the guards knew she only put the bag on when they opened the door. Why else would they fumble at the lock for so long and keep the light on? She could see a pair of boots from under the bottom of the bag. "Here," a familiar voice said, and a bundle of clothes dropped at her feet. "Wear these under your chador." The door clanged shut and the key scratched in the lock. Mary jerked the bag off and picked up the bundle. It was her uniform and it had been *laundered*.

DO WE HAVE A FRIEND, she tapped on the wall.

THINK SO, Doc Landis replied.

CHAPTER 26

D MINUS 9

MARAGHEH, IRAN

The antenna of the search radar swept the horizon with its relentless beat. The winds blew constantly at the radar site, gusting past thirty knots, and because the site's elevation was 7,000 feet, located near the top of the mountain overlooking the town of Maragheh, it was always a cold wind. The Americans had built the site for the Iranians in the late 1970s when the Shah was still in power, and its location 2,600 feet above the valley floor gave it an excellent search capability.

Inside the module at the base of the antenna the four operators were warm enough, but less than vigilant. Since the end of the Iran-Iraq war there seemed little need for manning the search radar, and all were looking forward to shift-change in six hours.

The operator on the main scope was reading a newspaper and at first missed the weak strobing. Only on the eighth sweep of the antenna did he lower the newspaper and see the streaks of light that indicated a jammer was transmitting. He dropped the paper in a drawer and keyed his boom mike with a foot pedal, calling his superior in the control center at Maragheh ten miles away. "Sir, I have jamming activity." As expected, there was no answer. The operator spun the cursor ringing the scope and read the bearing to the jamming while he measured off the distance. "In Turkey," he muttered to himself. Again, he tried to contact his superior. This time a voice answered and the operator updated the officer at Maragheh. "I have light to moderate jamming bearing two-eight-zero degrees at ninety-six nautical miles. This is in Turkey, twelve miles from our border." He keyed the button that allowed him to interrogate the IFF Mode One of U.S. and NATO military aircraft. The screen lit up with six responses. "I also have six Mode One responses squawking two-one," he said.

"Do you have skin-paints only?"

"Searching now." The operator twisted the receiver-gain knob, sending more high-frequency radio energy into the atmosphere. The returns on his scope blossomed, making him blink. Again he keyed the IFF, correlating the skin paints with the IFF squawks for both Mode One and Three. "All are squawking correct codes, sir. No unidentified skin paints."

"Read the bulletins I sent you," the officer said impatiently. "That is an announced joint Turkish-American Air Defense exercise. They are using AWACS and EC-130s operating out of Incirlik. Four of the aircraft you are monitoring will break off and head west in a few minutes. They are interceptors under the control of the AWACS. You should monitor in-flight refuelings and more interceptors from time to time. The exercise will last three weeks. Only report unusual activity, as I directed in my last bulletin."

Eleven minutes later the radar operator tracked four targets as they broke out of the race-track pattern they had established and headed to the west. Impressed with his superior's foreknowledge, the radar operator turned the receiver-gain down to a lower setting, reducing the glare of the scope, and pulled out his newspaper.

Sundown Cunningham had opened the curtain on operation WARLORD.

NELLIS AFB, NEVADA

The summons from Major General O'Brian, commander of the Tactical Fighter Weapons Center, came at 0902 hours Monday morning. By 0909, Stansell was standing in his office, surprised to see Captain Hal Beasely there. Before he had a chance to find out why the Beezer had been called in, O'Brian was talking. "Interesting reports from the gunnery range," he said, adjusting his glasses, reading from a report. "Seems like your Captain Beasely here has put in some impressive performances with his AC-130. The range control officer says he can fire that 105 cannon of his at four or five rounds a minute. Highly accurate. Never seen a rate of fire like that from a gunship." He looked over his glasses at Beasely. Stansell was puzzled. He was sure they were being called on the carpet, but why?

"Too bad the captain doesn't believe in safe sex," the general continued, his voice changing tone, threatening.

"Excuse me, sir," Stansell said. "I wasn't aware of any problem—"

"Colonel Stansell," O'Brian interrupted, "your captain here and his crew threw one hell of a wingding in the BOQ Saturday night, or more accurately, Sunday morning. They imported some hookers from downtown ... one they call Thunder Thighs." The general stood up. "You'll not turn my BOQ into a whorehouse. Do I make myself clear? Beasely, get the hell out of here while I chew on your boss."

The Beezer saluted and left.

"Colonel," O'Brian said, sitting back down, "control your people. I was talking to General Cunningham over the weekend and I realize you need that gunship and Beasely is, without a doubt, the best man in the business. But don't let it happen again." He nodded, indicating he was finished. Stansell saluted and turned to go. "Colonel, why in the hell did Thunder Thighs tell Beezer to grease his ears?"

Stansell beat a retreat. The general was, in some ways, an innocent.

Beasely was waiting outside. "You stepped in it this time," Stansell told him. "Time for a little growing up. Come with me."

An hour later they were in a helicopter circling the mock-up Chief Pullman had built in Tikaboo Valley. Stansell stuffed a photo of the prison he had taken from Dewa's office into the captain's hand. "Look familiar?" he yelled over the noise. Beasely studied the photo and the mock-up. "You know who's in there for real?" Stansell jabbed at the photo. Beasely jerked his head yes. "That's your next practice target," the colonel shouted, pointing at the mock-up.

Back on the ground at Nellis, Beasely was much subdued, no more jokes. "Excuse me, Colonel Stansell," he finally managed, "can I tell my crew what you've just shown me?" Stansell shook his head. "Don't worry, sir, you can trust me. My act's together now and you've got the best damn gunship crew in the Air Force. Fucking count on it. Sir."

KERMANSHAH, IRAN

The screams from the Box in the basement reached up the stairs into the three stories of the prison. The guards shut the heavy steel doors that opened onto each floor, but the screams still traveled down the wide corridors. It was a primeval shriek coming from the depths of a madness that tore apart the veil of sanity and let all who heard it know the reality of total despair.

Four guards rushed to the basement and crowded around the Box. "How long has he been in there?"

"Four days."

The guards braced themselves as one unlocked the door and lifted the latch. The door banged open and the American tech sergeant exploded into the room. He grabbed at the guard's leg and clung with a death grip. The guards struggled to break his hold, and when one's arm came too close to the prisoner's head he bit into the Iranian's forearm, shook his head like an animal, refusing to let go.

The two other guards methodically beat the prisoner into unconsciousness with their truncheons. The American, they decided, had gone crazy.

A fifth guard came down the stairs and took in the scene, sick from what he saw. He swore that his CIA contact would know about it within the hour.

Less than twenty-four hours later, the guard's information had worked its way through the Deep Furrow network and reached Allen Camm's desk.

CHAPTER 27

D MINUS 8

LANGLEY, VIRGINIA

Allen Camm needed to talk to Susan Fisher, his case officer for the American POWs. He suspected the POWs would be the subject of the unscheduled meeting that Director Burke had called for later that morning. He buzzed his secretary, telling her to send in Fisher.

"Anything new on the POWs?" he asked her.

She handed him a thick folder. "One of our Deep Furrow agents reported last night that a POW—no name—went crazy yesterday and that a high-ranking general from the Peoples' Soldiers of Islam visited the prison Sunday. Apparently men or supplies are moving into the deserted barracks outside the walls. We don't know which or how much yet."

"The status of our plan for getting the POWs out?"

"Our operative in Tehran reports that the deal between the Islamic Republican Party and the IPRP is about signed and sealed. Half of the POWs will be flown to the IPRP's headquarters in Tehran." A satisfied look came over Fisher's face. "Three of our Deep Furrow agents are scheduled to fly as guards on the airliner that will move the POWs. They're going to hijack the plane and take it to Algeria. Our agents are in position on the ground there. It's going to look like a splinter group of the Islamic Republican Party did it."

"Half is better than nothing," Camm said, "especially after a fumbled rescue attempt by Defense. Our stock with the President should go sky-high when we salvage something out of the shambles. The public and Congress will be more than happy to settle for half a loaf. But not before then . . . Is Delta Force ready?"

"Yes, sir, but they've been compromised. A sergeant . . . went home on emergency leave, got drunk and started bragging in a bar—"

"Our *source*?"

"The woman Jihad agent we turned. After interrogating Askari, he's the Jihad who tried to kidnap Stansell, we put her onto the Albanian diplomat who was Askari's contact. Seems he's horny and likes to impress her."

The cracking of the Islamic Jihad ring was paying results. "What about the Air Force's Task Force Alpha?"

"They're still clean, although who knows what they're doing out there in the desert . . . Mr. Camm, we have not disseminated the intelligence on the compromise of Delta Force or the current status of the POWs."

Camm leaned back in his chair, thinking about his next move. He considered himself a loyal, dedicated person who put the interests of his country above all else. He also believed the long-term interests of the United States would be better served by a strong and effective CIA capable of carrying out covert operations free of what he considered partisan political interference. If Deep Furrow could rescue half of the POWs and convince the President that unrestricted covert operations should be run by loyal and dedicated professionals like himself, well, he would have made a giant stride toward reaching that overarching goal. If pressed on the matter, he would agree that ends-justify-the-means was a hard necessity in hard-ball, head-on-head intelligence . . .

"The President has got to be told about the compromise of Delta Force. Sanitize our source so I can tell Mr. Burke without revealing how we learned about it. Maybe an intercepted phone call between the Albanians and Iranians." Should he also pass on what had been learned from Deep Furrow about the POWs? "The other information from Kermanshah . . . is it one source only?" Fisher nodded. "We'd better not pass that along then until we can confirm it." He wanted no questions raised that might lead to his Deep Furrow operations.

That, after all, was his future.

TEXAS LAKE, NEVADA

Command Sergeant Major Victor Kamigami was puzzled when he heard that Romeo Team was switching to MT-1X parachutes. He wanted to know why the change in plans. His curiosity got the better of him when he heard they were going to be using oxygen. That had to mean a high-altitude drop. He decided to get involved when a Ranger from Romeo Team bragged that they would be using high-altitude opening techniques. Rather than sound out his officers—Gregory could be evasive at times—he had done what any CSM would do . . . he had gone to another E-9. In this case, Chief Pullman.

The anger Kamigami felt when Pullman had fitted all the pieces together for him never surfaced. Just what the hell were they trying to do without telling him! Pullman had sensed the CSM's anger, knowing how he would feel in the same position. "Sorry," he had told Kamigami, "I thought your officers briefed you. Otherwise I would've back-doored 'em and filled you in."

"I'm going along," Kamigami had said. "Can I borrow your jeep?" It was a long conversation for the CSM. Pullman drove the CSM over to the C-130s in time for the final phase of mounting a high-altitude-high-opening airdrop using the MT-1X.

Trimler found a spot near Kamigami's jeep to watch the jump-master organize the stick. Kamigami walked over to a trailer to pick out a parachute.

"I guess he wants to go along," Pullman said.

Trimler gave Pullman a sideways glance. "He teaches five-hundred-pound gorillas how to go where they want."

After being rigged the CSM got in line for a safety inspection. The men in front suddenly fell out because they were not satisfied with some minor detail, and Kamigami moved quickly to the head of the line. The jumpmaster gave him a thorough inspection, starting at his helmet and finishing with the rucksack's lowering line.

"Who's the Romeo Team navigator?" Kamigami asked. The jumpmaster pointed to Baulck, who was talking to Drunkin' Dunkin, the C-130 navigator, explaining the KNS-81 tacan set that was strapped to his parachute harness. Kamigami nodded approval. Baulck would be the first man out and use the small olive-drab box to home on a portable tacan station set up on the drop zone.

Again he scanned the operation. Everything was going smoothly and according to procedures. But it was too much the routine drill

of an exercise, lacked the fire and urgency he had experienced when
Urgent Fury, the airdrop on Grenada, had been mounted in October
of '83. He needed to change that.

"*Move,*" he barked.

THE PENTAGON

"I feel like the tits on a boar hog," Stansell mumbled. Captain Don
Williamson chose to ignore that and go about his duties at the
Watch Center. The colonel had been hanging around the back offices since late Monday, monitoring the situation in Iran and waiting for a call from Cunningham's office. Actually, the captain liked
the short colonel and his dry sense of humor.

"Colonel," Williamson said, "I've got some interesting traffic out
of Tehran. The IRP, Islamic Republican Party, is getting cozy with
the IPRP. Seems they're getting ready to swap some POWs around."
He handed Stansell the printout of an intercepted message from the
headquarters of the IPRP in Tehran. It set bells ringing.

"Don, can you get a secure line to Nellis? I need to talk to my
people out there." Twelve minutes later Jack Locke's scratchy voice
came over the secure telephone in the battle cab overlooking the
main floor of the Watch Center.

"Jack, I need to talk to Dewa."

"Take a few minutes, sir. I'm in the command center at Nellis.
Hold on." Locke was quickly back on the line. "She'll be here in a
few minutes. Colonel, I want the F-15s to escort a string of C-130s
along a low-level route and go right under a HICAP of F-4s. But the
weather has to cooperate and I need a cloud deck between the F-4s
and F-15s. The ROE are that the F-4s can engage anytime they get
a visual contact on the F-15s or C-130s. But the F-15s can only
engage when they're jumped. The F-4s will operate under the same
type of control the Iranians use."

"What's the purpose, Jack?"

"I'm betting the F-15s can sneak the C-130s right under the F-4
CAP undetected but that their fangs will hang out and they'll zoom
up through the cloud deck to engage the F-4s leaving the C-130s
unprotected. Then I'll jump the C-130s with an F-4. I'll record it on
the VCR through the HUD. That ought to get the attention of the
Eagle drivers."

Stansell hesitated. What Locke was proposing was aggressive and
maybe dangerous. He knew from personal experience that so-called

Dissimilar Air Combat Tactics was a dicey thing with built-in hazards. He wanted to think about it, but he was running out of time and delaying a decision was not good for morale—he had to trust his people.

"Considering the Iranians fly F-4s, sounds like a good idea. If you can make it work, do it."

"Thanks, and here's Dewa."

"Dewa, I've seen a message here that suggests the POWs may be traded off . . ."

"I've seen the same intercept. Rupe, it won't be long"—the scrambler could not hide the concern in her voice—"I'd say in the next three or four days."

"Any back-up for that estimate?"

"No, but it's not just intuition, either. I mean, there's a rhythm to the way the Iranians work. It's sort of a cultural thing. It's going to happen very soon, and if we don't hurry the well is going to dry up before we get there."

"Okay, I'll start pressing harder from this end. How's Mado doing? Staying out of people's hair?"

"I always thought it was a joke about having a well-laid look. The general's got it. We don't see much of him."

"Sounds encouraging, I'll be talking to you."

When the call from Cunningham's office came five hours later at 8:30 P.M. Stansell hurried out of the basement and up the long corridors to E ring, to the offices of the Air Force Chief of Staff. He found Cunningham sipping a cup of tea. Somehow an incongruous brew for Sundown. "Sorry for the delay, Rupe. I've been putting out a forest fire today—some congressmen haven't got a clue. Okay, Dick tells me you've got a major change to WARLORD."

Cunningham was relaxed and alert. The hard-driving profane front was gone, a sign that Stansell had been accepted by the general into his command inner circle. Stansell outlined the changes Locke and Trimler were proposing, plus Dewa's concern about the POWs being traded off within the next few days.

"You trust her judgment?" Stansell nodded. "Anyone else agree with her?"

"An analyst in the Watch Center, Captain Don Williamson."

"I know Williamson." The general noted the surprised look on Stansell's face. "One of my jobs is to identify promising officers and see that they get the right sponsorship. This Air Force is full of people like Simon Mado—competent as hell, in many cases the work they do is absolutely indispensable. The way he's arranged to get Task Force Alpha into Turkey is brilliant. But his kind still tends to be more concerned with developing a political base for promotion and bureaucratic games than the mission."

"And General Mado has chosen the JSOA as his political base," Stansell observed.

"Exactly. Rupe, I'm tired of seeing rational, well-balanced colonels go off the track the moment they pin on stars. It tells me we're promoting the wrong people. I remember an old saw about the best colonels never get promoted. I want to change that. That's why I look for people like Williamson. But for now, Mado is the best man I've got for the job. Like I said, he's done good on this end. He may be a bureaucratic animal but he's qualified for command and deserves his chance."

The general did not mention that having Mado as the joint task force commander was also a bureaucratic gambit that accomplished two things: it appeased Leachmeyer while it gave him access and some control over Task Force Alpha. Cunningham also had to play bureaucratic chess, and Simon Mado was one of his pieces. Stansell knew the general made sense, but he wished Mado had seen combat and been shot at for real.

"Enough of all that," Cunningham went on, "let's take a hard look at where we're at."

An hour later Cunningham jabbed at a button on his intercom, summoning his aide. "Dick, we need to set up a meeting with the President tomorrow. The subject is the POWs. Get Mado here tonight and contact Ben Yuriden. Tell him it's urgent I see him ASAP."

The general spun his chair and looked out a window. "We're done playing games. I want the POWS out and I don't give a damn who does it. But Task Force Alpha is now going to be a real option for the President to consider."

CHAPTER 28

D MINUS 7

SAQQEZ, IRAN

The children scampered around Carroll as he walked around inside the walled compound on the outskirts of Saqqez. The ZIL-157 trucks were parked haphazardly in the yard, mostly against the back wall, and no one had made many attempts to organize the Kurds. The women had carved out whatever space they needed, cooking fires had been started, and a semblance of Kurdish tribal life magically mushroomed in the large one-storied structure that served as a garage, warehouse and parking lot.

Carroll estimated that about half of the group had been dropped off in villages and farms once they had crossed the border into Iran. Mustapha said they would stay in Saqqez until it was safe to return to Iraq and then would pick up their people and arms caches on the way back. The Kurds were casual when it came to doing the impossible—like sneaking across the border by driving the trucks at night through what looked like an impassable mountain river gorge. Of course, they did everything with endless chatter. Carroll liked the Kurds.

But Zakia . . . she seemed to possess an independence and special position that was outside the flow of normal tribal life. Maybe it was because she was a doctor. Carroll wandered over to the room she had appropriated for a temporary infirmary and her quarters and found her bandaging the hand of a man he had never seen before. No reason to be suspicious, she had, after all, treated many Kurds along the way, but this man seemed to be in a hurry to leave once she had finished and did not join with the men in any conversation.

Carroll looked around the room, the largest in the compound. A charcoal fire was burning in the corner fireplace. "They treat you special," he said.

She ignored the remark. "Stay if you're hungry. Food is on the way." A few minutes later a woman brought in two sticks of shish kebab and some of the pizzalike, thin round bread that he loved when it was freshly baked. He pulled the meat off the skewer and folded it up in the bread. Zakia did the same and they ate in silence. "Bill, please come and see me later this evening when things have quieted down. . . ."

The compound was mostly settled in for the night when he returned to her infirmary and found Zakia sitting on a rug, her back against a chest in front of the slowly dying fire. She had brushed out her hair, the glow of the fire catching the highlights when she turned toward him. She patted the spot beside her, sharing a blanket.

"You're not one of them," Carroll said.

"Why do you say that?"

"The women are open and friendly but still very much a part of the family. If you were Mustapha's cousin or a member of the tribe we would never be left alone together."

"It took you long enough to figure that out. You are very slow at times."

"Zakia, about that night . . ."

"I know," she said in English, surprising him. "It was a moment. We both had a need. I doubt it will happen again." The fire flared, catching their attention . . . "Bill Carroll, what are you doing here?"

"It's a long story . . ." He stared into the fire. How could he tell her about the mix of emotions that lay behind any answer? Would she understand what drove him on? Who would believe that a sense of duty and commitment could blend with a hunger for revenge, and love, too.

"My commander at Ras Assanya, Colonel Waters, ordered me out during the evacuation . . ." Slowly he then told her about what happened at Ras Assanya. "When I finally got to safety, I followed the last order Waters had given me. I was going to do my damndest to help the POWs . . ."

"What could one person do?"

Carroll shrugged. "My job was intelligence. I saw the way my Wing was hung out to dry as a political pawn and didn't like it." He choked down the bitter taste. "If I can do anything it will be something. Besides, some of the POWs are good friends—Doc Landis . . ."

"And the woman."

Carroll could only look at her in surprise.

"You talk in your sleep . . . Never mind, I have a message for you from your government—"

"Big deal."

"Please listen. There *is* something you can do. They want to rescue the POWs and they need trucks or buses waiting outside the prison at Kermanshah for transport. The Kurds will help—you helped them—and I can get you money, gold . . ."

"The Kurds will get into more trouble with the Iranians—"

"You haven't heard. The Kurds have more motive than their debt to you. The prison commandant wanted to clear out the old barracks behind the walls. There were five Kurdish families living there. They were poor and looking for a place to stay during the winter. The guards lined them up and shot them—men, women and children. Mulla Haqui will help. He understands revenge."

"So do I," he told himself. "We have the trucks," Carroll said. "How did you get the message?"

"The man you saw earlier this evening—he is my contact. You'll see him again."

"Zakia, who do you work for?"

She shook her head, turned over, and went to sleep.

THE WHITE HOUSE

"Mike, why am I worried?" The President was walking down the steps to the Situation Room in the basement of the White House. Michael Cagliari, his National Security Advisor, and Andy Wollard, his chief of staff, trailed behind him.

"The situation is unstable," Cagliari said. "Sometimes you have to read between the lines of the PDB. But it's there." He made a mental note to get on Bobby Burke's case about the President's Daily Brief that was supposed to summarize the best intelligence available. The beautifully printed document was only seen by four people and was beginning to read like standard bureaucratic cover-your-ass stuff.

A Marine guard held the door open for the President as he approached, and they could hear the shuffling of people standing up now inside the small wood-paneled room. The guard shut the door behind them. The President glanced at Admiral Scovill, chairman of the JCS, as he sat down and looked around the room. He saw a man he did not recognize sitting behind Bobby Burke, the CIA Director, and Charlie Leachmeyer. There was also a colonel sitting next to Simon Mado he had never met—but he knew a good deal about Rupert Stansell. "Well, Terry, what do you have for us this late in the afternoon?"

Scovill knew how the President worked. "Sir, I'd like to introduce Allen Camm, the CIA's DDI." The President nodded. He would never forget the new face or name, a valuable trait that always astounded his aides.

"And Colonel Stansell," the President added, "glad we've had a chance to meet finally."

"Mr. President," Scovill said, returning to business, "we're going to need a Go order on the POWs."

"Lay the situation out."

"Yes, sir, that's why Mr. Camm is here." Camm stood and moved to an easel near the President. He set a stack of twenty-by-thirty-inch briefing charts on the easel, each labeled with distinctive block letters at the top and bottom announcing that what was on the charts was TOP SECRET. Camm ran through the charts, filling the assembled in on the current situation, carefully avoiding anything that might lead to a question that would reveal the existence of Deep Furrow. He was saving his bombshell for last.

"Finally, sir," Camm said, "an agent reported yesterday that the Albanian Embassy in Tehran informed the Iranian government that Delta Force was preparing a mission to rescue the POWs and would mount the operation out of Iraq." Susan Fisher had worked out a logical explanation for the CIA learning about the Albanian-Islamic Jihad connection without revealing how the CIA had learned about it.

"How in hell did the Albanians get involved in all this?"

"Our information indicates that the Albanian Embassy in Washington has been supporting the Islamic Jihad's operations in the United States," Camm said as he flipped to the last chart, "and the Jihad is reporting through the Albanians. Of course the domestic side of this is in the jurisdiction of the FBI, and I don't believe the Bureau has cracked the Jihad's operations yet. So, bottom line, we don't know how the Jihad learned about Delta Force." Camm was scoring bureaucratic points by pinging the FBI and covering his own sources.

The last of Camm's charts was a map with the launch base and Kermanshah highlighted. "Since my office is not privy to the current plans to rescue the POWs, we cannot evaluate the accuracy of the warning passed to the Iranians. But they *have* been warned and we are monitoring their reaction."

Camm scanned the men's faces in the stunned silence that hung in the room. Burke gave him a slight nod of approval.

"How many sources confirm what you've told us?" Leachmeyer asked. "The information the Albanians passed is our original plan. We now launch out of Saudi Arabia and refuel in Turkey on the way out."

"Only the one agent in Tehran," Camm said. "But this agent has a proven track record." It was necessary to claim a CIA agent in Tehran had discovered that Delta Force had been compromised. Director Burke would be most unhappy if he suspected Camm was running a counterespionage operation *inside* the U.S.

"Ironic," the President said. "We originally set up a cover for Delta Force to prevent this from happening. Now our first team is compromised while—what are you calling the cover operation?—is secure."

"Task Force Alpha, sir." This from Mado. "And we can't be totally sure we are free from compromise."

Cunningham snapped an iron will over his reactions, insuring his face revealed nothing. That bastard Mado. He watched Leachmeyer for his reaction. The relief on Charlie's face was obvious. No wonder the President likes playing poker with you, he thought. "Mr. President," Cunningham said, "my Office of Special Investigations is watching over Task Force Alpha. So far, sir, they have reported nothing."

The President pulled a cigar out of his shirt pocket. "CIA?"

"We have nothing to indicate a compromise of Task Force Alpha," Camm said. For once being totally honest.

"Simon," the President said, "I appreciate that you are the commander in the field and see things we don't. You qualified your statement about Alpha not being compromised. Why?" He lit the cigar. No one else in the room would smoke.

"Sir, our intelligence specialist is an Iranian-American. She is fluent in Farsi and an accomplished analyst. But lately I've had doubts I can't pinpoint. I consider that at least a warning not to be ignored—"

"Mr. President," Stansell put in, "the analyst's name is Dewa Rahimi. She has been thoroughly checked out and worked for the Air Force Special Activities Center. She was born and raised in the U.S. and has never even been to Iran. Her family there has been nearly wiped out by the Ayatollahs. I've never had any doubts about her . . ."

"Gentlemen," the President said, his voice a flat monotone as he stubbed out the cigar, cutting off further discussion, *"get your act together.* Is Delta Force ready?"

"Yes, sir," Leachmeyer said.

"And Task Force Alpha?"

"We're very close," Cunningham said. "The Rangers are ready. We're arranging ground transportation for the POWs and getting a portable tacan beacon in place—"

"Who's providing your ground support inside Iran?" Burke asked.

"We have established contact with Captain William Carroll. He's with the Pesh Merga, the Kurdish liberation movement," Cunningham said quickly.

"How did you find him?"—Burke was astonished—"establish contact?"

"Through the Israelis." Cunningham stared at Burke. "We were the only ones to ask them for information," he said, adding a mental "you asshole."

"Gentlemen"—the President leaned forward, hands clasped together on the table in front of him—"does the word fubar mean anything to you? I'll help you—fucked up beyond all recognition. Why do I get the feeling that word is becoming operative here? It means neither operation is secure, neither is compromised. I want the POWs *rescued.* " He turned to Leachmeyer. "Charlie, move Delta out, since it's ready. Hide them, move them around, get them into place unobserved . . . General Cunningham, I want Task Force Alpha brought on line as fast as possible so it is a viable option. Tell me the moment they're ready. Everyone—*no more leaks.* I don't care if you have to lock up every swingin'—" he caught himself—"that knows about this."

* * *

"Dammit, Mado. What in the hell were you thinking of in there?" Mado and Stansell were standing in front of Cunningham's desk, and the general's cigar was smoking. "The only reason we're still in business is because Stansell here managed to spread a little dust over your gut feelings. Is your head up your ass and locked?"

"You want me to lie to the President?" Mado shot back.

"No. But I don't want unsubstantiated doubts surfaced either." At any other time he would have fired Mado on the spot. But time did not permit him that luxury now. "We hash out our doubts and differences in here—among ourselves. We present a united front to the President. He's got enough on his mind without having to referee our differences. That's my job. Stansell, get the hell back to Nellis. Mado, I want you here." The two men left.

Cunningham's aide appeared at the door. "Meeting with the Joint Chiefs in five minutes, General. In the tank."

"Dick, keep an eye on Mado. I don't trust that son of a bitch."

NELLIS AFB, NEVADA

The six men sat in the small briefing room in Red Flag's building watching the TV. Torch Doucette hit the rewind button when the VCR tape was finished. "Let's look at it again," he told the other five F-111 crew members. Doucette's WSO, Ramon Contreraz, wanted to escape from the room. He had caught the embarrassment of Von Drexler's WSO when they ran the Audio Visual Tracking Record of Von Drexler's last mission. The other F-111 crew tried to fade into the woodwork.

Doucette started the tape and let it run a few moments before he hit the pause button. "Right here, Colonel," he told Von Drexler, "when the two F-16s jumped you and came to your six o'clock, you should have milked it a little lower and simulated pickling off a single high-drag bomb."

"And what good would that have done?" Von Drexler rasped. "We're supposed to put those bombs on a target."

"In the real world," Doucette told him, "it would explode behind you. Because it's retarded you would escape the frag pattern but the bandits might fly right through it—nailing 'em. If nothing else, it does tend to break the bad guy's concentration when he's rooting around in the rocks working on a low-level intercept and a bomb explodes in his face."

Von Drexler shook his head. "Too much seat of the pants . . ."

Contreraz could hear the patronizing tone in Doucette's voice. It was going to be a classic face-off between the best pilot in an Air Force wing who only knew how to fly the jet and the worst pilot who only knew how to get promoted.

The tape was rolling again. "You flew down this canyon at almost eight hundred feet," Doucette said. The sarcasm in his voice left no doubt about what he thought of flying that high above the ground.

"I don't trust the TFR in 399," Von Drexler tried. The other pilot stifled his reply in time. He had flown the same aircraft, tail number 399, the day before and the APQ-146 Terrain Following Radar had worked perfectly.

"Colonel Von Drexler," Doucette said, sweetness dripping from every word, "the terrain-following radar is our *raison d'etre*. Either use the damn feature or get used to hand flying the jet down in the rocks."

"If I experience a malfunction at the altitude you're suggesting I won't have time to take corrective action—"

"Then it's not your day. Flying low and TFing is what we get paid for."

"Too many birds migrate through here this time of year," Von Drexler complained. "I don't need a damn bird strike."

"The birds have all been briefed to break down when they see an F-111," Doucette said with a straight face but also reminding the lieutenant colonel that the natural tendency of *any* bird was to drop downward. "You pull up, that's your part of the contract with birds."

The wall of the prison mock-up that Chief Pullman had built in the desert appeared on the TV screen. "You had an early acquisition of the target because of your altitude. In the real world, you wouldn't get a video through the Pave Tack until you're inside six miles . . ."

"Damnit, Doucette, quit talking about the real world. This is the real world—"

"Then after you tossed the bomb and pulled off to downwind, you broke off too fast. The bomb's time of flight is approximately thirty seconds and you've got to gauge your turnaway so your wizzo can lase the target during the last eight or ten seconds. Also, you need to do your own bomb-damage assessment to see if you need to reattack."

"I was simulating a high-threat environment—"

"That's what we've got electronic countermeasures for," Von

Drexler's WSO said, "to take care of those threats." He felt he had to speak up. "Colonel, you're job is to drive the truck, mine is to deliver the mail. We've got to stick around the target long enough for me to do that."

"I think that about says it all," Doucette said.

CHAPTER 29

D MINUS 6

THE PENTAGON

The section of E Ring near the Secretary of Defense's office was a highly restricted and well-guarded stretch of corridor. Cunningham normally barreled through the security post expecting the guards to recognize him and not challenge him. But on this day a new corporal was on duty, a nineteen-year-old who did not recognize the Air Force Chief of Staff. "Sir, may I please see your restricted area badge?"

Cunningham looked at him. "Your name?"

"Corporal Thomas Naylor, sir."

"First day on the job, Naylor?"

"Yes, sir."

"Son, there are a few of us you're supposed to recognize on sight. I'm one of that crowd." He glanced down the hall, making sure no one other than his aide could hear. "I'm supposed to do animal acts on troops who screwed up." He produced his badge for inspection.

"Thank you, sir," Naylor said, passing Cunningham through.

"Dick, am I getting soft in my old age?"

"Probably." Stevens had given his total loyalty to Cunningham when he discovered the general's ego had not swelled with self-importance when he pinned stars on his shoulders. It was a rare condition in E Ring. Stevens held the door open to the tank, the conference room where the Joint Chiefs had at each other. The general gave a grump, snapping his mask into place as he entered.

Admiral Scovill entered the room behind him and took his place at the head of the table. "Charlie, Lawrence," he nodded at Leachmeyer and Cunningham. "The President wants a daily update on the status of the POWs and how we're progressing. I don't want a repeat of yesterday so I'll be doing the briefing. We'll meet here before I go across the river. So, what do I tell him today?"

"We're moving Delta Force to Howard Air Force Base in the Canal Zone tonight," Leachmeyer said. "We'll keep Delta there for a week and make it look like they're exercising with Southern Command. We'll have the sixty helicopters in place next week and move Delta once more before we position them in Saudi Arabia. We'll be ready for a Go in ten to fourteen days."

"Sixty helicopters, Charlie?" Scovill looked worried. "That's one hell of an insertion."

"We need that many to transport the POWs and position a blocking force in case that armored regiment forty miles southwest of Kermanshah responds and moves on us."

"It will look like an invasion," Cunningham said. "Quantity, not quality—"

"Quantity has a quality all its own," Leachmeyer shot back. "We're ready to go."

"And compromised in two weeks."

"When will Task Force Alpha be ready?" Scovill asked.

"Ground transportation should be available Saturday. We still need to get a portable tacan station in place near Kermanshah for our paratroops to home on. That should happen Sunday. We're having a final mission rehearsal the same day."

"You're relying on the Israelis and betting on the come," Leachmeyer grumbled. "You're not close to being ready, and the President ought to be told that."

"Deal with facts," Cunningham said.

"I am."

Cunningham chewed on that. Why is he so confident? Who's he been talking to? Mado? "Well," he finally said, "who was it that said a good plan violently executed now is better than a perfect plan next week."

"Patton," Leachmeyer said.

"Right. And I think the President ought to be told *that*. Task Force Alpha will be ready to go after Sunday."

SAQQEZ, IRAN

The garage-warehouse compound was a noisy place as the Kurds loaded the trucks. The Iraqi insignias and sand-colored paint had been artfully painted over and the ZIL-157 trucks already had that dilapidated look characteristic of the overworked vehicles driven by farmers in the Middle East.

"Where to now?" Carroll asked Mustapha.

"Kermanshah." A hard look spread across the young Kurd's face. "To repay some outstanding debts."

"Where's Zakia?"

"She left earlier to arrange for another place like this on the north side of Kermanshah. She will be waiting." A truck cranked to life and moved through the yard and rumbled into the wide passage leading through the building. Two boys swung open the big double-doors leading to the outside and the truck disappeared down the road. "We move separately this time and mostly at night. It's about two-hundred-eighty kilometers. We should all be there Saturday night." Carroll thought that it seemed a long time to cover a hundred and seventy miles and said so. "It would arouse suspicion if we all arrived on Friday," Mustapha told him. "You know how the mullahs are about the sabbath. Besides, it will give them a chance to visit relatives along the way."

Carroll shook his head at the "arrangements," shrugged and looked for a truck to hitch a ride. Go with the flow, he told himself. Besides, how else?

CHAPTER 30

✈
 ✈
  ✈

D MINUS 5

MARCH AFB, CALIFORNIA

Jack Locke walked around the F-4E, wanting to stroke it, pat it, talk to it. It was an old friend. He ran his hand around the gunport under the long nose as memories of the time he had shot down a Libyan MiG in this very aircraft, tail number 512, came rushing back. He continued the preflight, breaking into a smile when he saw the red star painted on the left intake ramp signifying this jet had downed an enemy aircraft. "Damn, would Byers like to see you . . ."

The 163rd National Guard maintenance crews had labored hard over the Phantom, returning it to almost new condition. None of its battle scars from Ras Assanya were visible, and it glistened in the early morning sunlight in its new-found glory—an old veteran ready to fight again. "Damn, damn," was all that Jack would let himself say, not wanting to reveal what he really felt to Thunder Bryant, who was crawling into the rear cockpit.

Both men were discovering a new emotion along with their sense of déjà vu. The machine was so much a part of them that it seemed to have a life, a magic of its own. It could offer them their past accomplishments all over again. Other veterans from other wars had experienced the same emotion when they saw an old ship or air-plane they had taken into combat. Now their turn.

"I can't beam you up," Thunder told him. "You still got to climb up the side and strap it on." He was anxious to follow the other twelve F-4s that were starting their engines. "Got to hit the tanker if we're going to jump the C-130s." Locke climbed up the boarding ladder and sank into the cockpit. It was a homecoming, a reunion.

THE PENTAGON

"The President was impressed with the points you made about Task Force Alpha," Admiral Scovill was saying to Cunningham. "He still has some doubts, wants to observe Sunday's exercise in person."

"That's a bit unusual . . ."

"He's going to address a convention in Las Vegas Saturday night so it fits into his schedule," Scovill said. "There's another problem. Camm reported that our loyal allies, the Panamanians, told the Cubans that Delta Force was down there. The CIA made two Cubans watching Delta. Not good."

Yes and no, Cunningham could not help thinking.

NELLIS AFB, NEVADA

Staff Sergeant Raymond Byers was waiting by his F-15 when the crew van arrived. He cracked a half-smile when Stansell clambered down the steps. "Mornin', Colonel."

"Byers, what the hell are you doing here?"

"Takin' care of my jet, Colonel. Timmy's here too. He's got an Eagle all his own now. 'Course ain't as good as mine."

Stansell shook his head and did a quick preflight of Byers' F-15. As expected, the aircraft was immaculately prepared and despite his misgivings about the appearance of the sergeant, he had to admit that few jets received the loving care this one did. He clambered up the boarding ladder, ran the before-entering-cockpit checks and settled into the seat. He continued to run through checklist items before he started engines. He did it all from memory, not needing the checklist he carried in the leg pocket of his G-suit. He shoved a VCR tape into its slot. Everything he heard or said and all that he saw through the HUD would be recorded.

A few minutes later the four escort F-15s led by Snake Houserman taxied past. He waited until they reached the hammerhead at the end of the runway before he started engines. He was going along as a chase plane to observe the flight. His right ear had been demanding a scratch all morning. "Stop that," he commanded. "Missing ears don't itch."

"Got the C-130s and F-15s on the VSD," Stansell said, talking for the VCR to record. "They're at my twelve o'clock, twenty-two miles, in the weeds, below a cloud deck. The cloud deck is broken to overcast at five thousand. I'm at twelve thou. The four 130s are on their low-level route, two miles in trail. Good station keeping, right on course. They're maintaining radio silence. Good. Two F-15s are running a racetrack pattern in front, the other two are behind the package, doing the same and varying their airspeed."

Stansell's radio crackled as the F-4s from March checked in with Blackjack, the Range Control Center. Blackjack gave the F-4s vectors and headings, establishing a search pattern above the cloud deck, much as Iranian ground controllers would do. Stansell turned lazily away from the four C-130s, not wanting his position to give the F-4s any clues about the whereabouts of the intruders on the deck. "The 163rd is established in a HICAP," he recorded. "No contact on Joker"—Locke's call sign. He was flying single-ship as a wild card and would jump the C-130s if the F-15s left them uncovered and if, a big if, he could find them on the deck underneath the cloud deck.

"The package should be underneath the HICAP in about ten minutes." The colonel had constructed a mental map and constantly updated the position of the players. Only Locke was unaccounted for. He maneuvered in a race-track pattern, sweeping the area with his radar, trying to find Locke. "No contact on Joker. He must be using terrain-masking to avoid detection." Stansell kept up a running commentary for the recorder that he would use in debrief.

"Gambler flight"—the UHF frequency for the F-15s on the deck came alive—"twelve bogies two o'clock at forty-five miles." It was Snake Houserman's voice. "Split—now."

"Gambler lead is positioning for an engagement, moving between the threat and the C-130s," Stansell observed. "Good defensive move in case they get jumped. Damn it, they're not staying with the 130s." Stansell's radar followed the F-15s as they moved away from the C-130s and each pair fanned out in an arm of a wide pincher movement heading toward the orbiting F-4s. "They're taking the bait and going to engage the HICAP." Stansell continued talking into the recorder, detailing how Gambler flight was violating the Rules of Engagement that only allowed for the F-15s to engage when they were jumped by bandits. "Make the F-4s find you," he raged.

He pointed his nose toward the developing engagement in time to see the four F-15s punch through the cloud deck. He followed Snake in a frequency change when he called the F-15s to the same channel the F-4s were on, and the radio burst into a wild buzzsaw of sound.

"Fox One on the southbound F-4 at eighteen thousand." Snake's voice.

"Lobo flight, two bandits at four o'clock, low, eight miles, on us. Just coming out of the clouds. What happened to the goddamn ROE? Brewer flight, go to second CAP." The Phantom flight-lead was still a disciplined professional and sent four of his birds out of the engagement to another CAP point to continue the search for the C-130s.

"Skid! Break right." From an F-4

"He's on me! Boomer come back left." Another F-4 in trouble. "Where'd he go?"

"Smoky, he's coming to your six." A F-15 was warning his wing-man.

Stansell's lips compressed into a tight line as the four F-15s engaged the eight remaining F-4s. He headed after the C-130s and switched radio frequencies.

"Okay," he recorded, "C-130s at two o'clock, nineteen miles. Still on course. No Joker. Dropping through the cloud deck now." Stansell's Tactical Electronic Warfare System buzzed at him. "Got an interceptor searching in the area. Bingo, cloud bases at forty-five hundred feet and got a bogey on the VSD. Bogey converting onto the C-130s. The bogey must be Joker." He checked that the VCR was recording everything he saw through the HUD.

The four C-130s were working their way down-track, heading for the prison mock-up, still on time. "Tallyho," Stansell muttered when he saw them. "Got a visual on Joker." He watched Locke slash down onto the lead C-130, maneuvering into position for a rear-aspect missile shot.

"Puff One-One, you've got a bandit at your seven o'clock," the pilot in the second C-130 radioed, warning the lead aircraft. "On you."

"Rog," Duck Mallard's voice answered. "Check turns only. Don't do anything stupid. Seven minutes out."

Stansell watched the lead C-130 make a level twenty-degree turn to the left before returning to track. The move created a small problem for Locke before he took his missile shot. He broke the attack off before he crossed between the lead and following C-130 or broke the mandatory five hundred feet altitude separation the ROE required.

Locke then repositioned for a sequential attack, staying below the cloud deck. He rolled onto his back and pulled his nose toward the ground and swooped down onto tail-end Charlie, dropping his F-4 like a giant bird of prey. Another voice came over the radio. "Puff One-Four, the bandit's on you."

"Roger." Stansell could hear the strain in the pilot's voice. The big cargo plane jerked to the left, lowered it's nose and continued a hard downward turn.

"Puff One-Four is trying to generate an overshoot by turning into Joker," Stansell recorded. Then, "Puff One-Four," he yelled over the radio, "pull *up!*"

But it was too late. The left wing of the C-130 caught the ground and the cargo plane cartwheeled into a fireball. Dense black smoke pillared into the sky, a dark beacon marking the funeral pyre of Puff One-Four.

"Hey, Byers," Timmy Wehr yelled across the ramp, "it's our old bird—512." The two crew chiefs ran toward the spot on the ramp where the sergeant from transient maintenance was standing, waiting to park the F-4.

"Look at her," Byers shouted as the engines spun down. "She's beautiful." They watched the canopies open and the pilot rip his helmet off. He threw it over the side, letting it bounce on the hard concrete, shattering its visor. "It's Locke and Bryant," Byers said in amazement. They could sense that something was terribly wrong as the two men dismounted. Locke ignored his helmet lying on the ramp and stomped toward building 201, Bryant following close behind.

Wehr's voice was a whisper. "Geez, Locke was crying . . ."

THE PENTAGON

Cunningham's aide, Dick Stevens, took the phone call. He knew better than to hesitate and walked directly into the general's office. "General, Task Force Alpha just lost a C-130. All five crew members killed."

Cunningham spun in his chair, his back to the three generals in his office. Finally he turned back to Stevens. "Get Mado. We're going to Nellis."

NELLIS AFB, NEVADA

Dewa saw the light in the trailer that served as Stansell's and Pullman's office when she pulled into the parking lot in front of building 201. Stansell's car was out front. You're hard to find, she said to herself. She walked into the rear office and headed for the coffeepot, ignoring him. It was almost midnight, she was tired, needed a jolt of caffeine. She took a mug and waited for Stansell to start talking.

All night if we have to, Colonel, she thought.

"My fault," he muttered, "all my damn fault."

"Really," she said, her voice neutral. "You should tell Jack. He thinks it's all his fault. Gillian is barely coping with him."

"It was my decision to fly that exercise. I was pushing too hard trying to get us ready, and I killed five of my own people. Cunningham's going to be here in the morning, the President wants to watch our final exercise Sunday, Byers and Wehr show up with the Holloman jets . . . Some fucking wonderful commander I am."

Dewa wanted to shout at him to stop feeling sorry for himself. "At least I wouldn't worry about the two sergeants being here," she said quietly. "Holloman is here for a Red Flag exercise and crew chiefs come with their aircraft. And the President was scheduled for a speech in Vegas three months ago."

"Dewa, I killed five of my own people . . ."

"That isn't what I heard."

"Watch." He turned the TV on and hit the play button of the VCR. "This is a copy from the flight. The Accident Board has the original. Pullman back-doored a copy of my own tape."

Dewa watched the accident unfold on the screen. At one point she glanced down at the counter, noting the spot on the tape she wanted to replay. The horror of the C-130 pitching into the ground and disappearing in an eruption of smoke and flames stunned her. "Oh, my God . . . No wonder you and Jack . . ."

The tape ran out and stopped. She rewound it to the particular place she wanted now and sat down on the couch next to him. "Tell me about Byers and Wehr . . . how they pulled you out of Ras Assanya."

"Why? What the hell does that have to do with this?"

"Please. Just tell me." She had to break through the image of the dying C-130 that held him, that would not let him escape.

Slowly Stansell related how the Iranians had interrogated him after he had surrendered the base. "After about twelve hours they had worked me over good, kept asking me what happened to Waters. Nothing I said seemed to satisfy them. Two of 'em took me out to the bunker where he was killed. It was dark and I couldn't identify anything. That made them even more angry. One of them kept screaming death to America, death to this, death to that. I was getting pretty sick of it so I shouted 'Death to Khomeini.' I figured the old bastard was dead so what harm would it do?"

"A bad mistake, Rupe." Dewa wanted to touch his hand. "That curse doesn't mean anything to us, but to an Iranian . . ."

"Yeah. They went crazy. One threw me down and sat on my chest, the other grabbed a bayonet and started to saw on my right ear. I was bleeding and screaming like a stuck pig. Anyway, Byers and Wehr were hiding in a shelled-out bunker about thirty feet away, no one else around. They came and beat hell out of the two guys doing the number on my ear, then dragged me to a boat we'd used for laying mines around the base, and Byers managed to sneak us out, heading up north instead of south. It worked."

"Why did they take such a big chance to save you?" Dewa had read the debrief of Byers and Wehr and knew the answer.

"I asked Byers the same question. He mumbled something about it seemed like the right thing to do at the time. Real original."

"Listen carefully now." She started the tape. They stood in front of the TV and watched the scene play out again.

Mallard's voice could barely be heard as Locke's F-4 surged into the picture and the Hercules turned twenty degrees to the left. "Rog. Check turns only. Don't do anything stupid. Seven minutes out." Dewa stopped the tape.

"Did Mallard do the right thing?" Stansell nodded yes. "And Jack?" Again, Stansell nodded, this time understanding the point. Puff One-Four had crashed because the pilot, under the pressure of the moment, had made a bad decision and did the wrong thing. It was simple enough to understand, but until Dewa had led him to the truth through his own emotional wreckage, he had not seen it.

"Rupe, you've got to put this, like some other things, behind you and do what seems the right thing at the time. No guarantees in this business. We get rewards later, we pay the consequences now." She forced a smile. "End of lecture, Colonel." And tried not to look at the scar where his ear used to be.

CHAPTER 31

D MINUS 4

NELLIS AFB, NEVADA

Stansell stood outside the door leading into the main briefing room in building 201, fists clenched. Dewa was sitting in the front row against the wall with Locke and Bryant, and Stansell kept glancing at her back. Task Force Alpha entered in groups, finding seats in clumps, sitting in silence. The C-130 crews came in first, led by Duck Mallard and his ungainly navigator Drunkin Dunkin. They were followed by Gregory and his officers and platoon sergeants. Then the three F-111 crews straggled in and found seats away from Von Drexler. Finally, the F-15 pilots came in and sat near the C-130 crews. Stansell nodded at Pullman, who was standing with Kamigami just inside the door. "Let's do it."

"Room, ten-hut."

Everyone stood as Stansell marched down the aisle and climbed the steps to the stage. "Seats, please." He waited while they shuffled back into their seats. For an instant he stopped breathing when the rear doors opened and Cunningham and Mado slipped into the room. Pullman was about to call the room to attention again but Cunningham cut him off with a short chopping motion as he sat down in a seat at the rear, across the aisle from Pullman and Kamigami.

"Yesterday we took our first loss," Stansell began. The lights went dim and a slide of the burning wreckage of the C-130 flashed on the left-hand screen. "We need to know what went wrong so we can continue and not repeat our mistakes . . . This happened because we were not acting as a team and not doing what we trained to do. The F-15s were suckered into leaving the C-130s unprotected, allowing a lone F-4 to jump the 130s. Listen to this." He played the tape, letting them hear his comments and the radio transmissions of Snake and the pilot who was leading the F-4s before he hit the pause button. "The F-4 lead's concern about the ROE marks him as a disciplined pro." He restarted the VCR. Most of the audience could not clearly see the TV screen but they could all hear the audio. Stansell stopped the tape right after Mallard's comments about not doing anything stupid and replayed it.

"Puff One-Four crashed because the pilot tried to take evasive maneuvers too low to the ground. The Accident Board will probably find pilot error the primary cause, but this is not any one person's fault. The blame belongs to a lot of us, and it starts with me." Heavy silence in the auditorium.

Snake Houserman was slumped in his seat and refused to look at the screen. "All for a damn training exercise," he said in a voice loud enough to carry over the silence.

Cunningham heard Snake's comment and stood up, pointing at Pullman. He only said one word.

"Now."

Most of the room heard it and turned to its source. The general had filled that simple single word with the presence of command. Pullman and Kamigami shot to their feet and Pullman bellowed for the room to come to attention.

All but Snake Houserman snapped to their feet. He slumped lower in his seat, still stung by Stansell's words. "Stand up, asshole," Lydia Kowalski said. He stood while Cunningham took the stage.

"This is *not* routine training," he began, keeping them at attention. "Task Force Alpha was created at the direction of the President as part of the effort to rescue the POWs being held in Iran. Originally your purpose was to serve as a cover operation for the actual rescue team. But events have a way of taking unpredictable turns—you are now being considered by the President to mount the rescue. You are scheduled for an *exercise* tomorrow. The President will be here to watch you and find out for himself if you are, as someone has told him, the second team. Or"—again he packed a single word with special resources—"if you are the team that will get the execute order."

He turned to Stansell. "Colonel, if Task Force Alpha is going to rescue the POWs, it's got to be perfect tomorrow. And no security leaks." He left the stage, walked up the aisle and exited the room.

"I want it," Kamigami said in his soft voice.

"We'll go with the original plan and drop the Rangers in right after the F-111s hit the walls," Mado said. Stansell didn't move from the large-scale wall map in Dewa's office. "It's more spectacular and will impress the President," he added.

"That's just an option now," Stansell argued. "The Rangers have got to be on the ground and in place if they're to exploit the confusion right after the bombs knock holes in the walls."

Mado walked over to the colonel and stood beside him. "You may be right, but we both know we're obliged to make this look extra good for the boss—ring the bells, all the good stuff, if he's going to take up *our* option."

"Leachmeyer's going to be here," Stansell reminded him. "He'll spot what's wrong and tell the President. The Rangers have got to be on the ground *early*."

Mado, a busy thinker, was turning over *his* options. If the rumors were true, the President was going to cut through the Pentagon with a meat ax, reforming DOD around unified commands. And Leachmeyer was considered one of the architects of the unified command system. So Leachmeyer and his interests counted if he was ever to make four stars. But what if the status quo held? Then he'd need to rely on Cunningham's support for future promotion. He was a man in the middle, so he'd play both ends against the middle. Work hard on Task Force Alpha, make it and himself look good, but also keep kicking up a little dust of doubt along the way for Leachmeyer.

He slapped Stansell on the shoulder. "Do it my way, Rupe. It'll work."

Dewa, feeling sick, glanced at her watch and stood up. "Excuse me, I'll be right back." Minutes later she was, listening to the two discuss the final arrangements for Sunday's exercise.

Chief Pullman knocked on the door and stuck his big head in. "General Mado, there's a phone call for you. A Barbara Lyon."

"I'll take it in private," Mado said. Dewa followed Stansell out, leaving the general alone.

"That's a dinner invitation for tonight," she told Stansell. "Should keep him occupied for a while—"

"Dewa . . . did you—?"

Mado came out of the office. "It's looking good. The President will be in place at eight-thirty tomorrow morning. I'll be here at five o'clock. Make it all happen, Rupe." He grabbed up his hat and moved double-time out of the office.

"Well," Dewa said, "there goes a man in a hurry. We've got decisions to make. I think you should run the exercise exactly as called for in OPORD WARLORD." She waited expectantly. Rupert Stansell, she thought, you are so damn straight, even naïve about some things. Maybe that's why I go for you. Now if I can just wake you up . . .

"Right." He picked up the phone, calling the trailers. "Thunder, we start the clock for the exercise tonight. H-hour is twenty-three hundred local time. As planned all the way. No options." Stansell dropped the phone into its cradle. By H plus ten, ten hours into the operation, at nine o'clock Sunday morning, the Rangers would be in place and the F-111s would be knocking holes in the "prison's" walls. With the President watching.

Stansell picked up the phone again. "Gillian? Jack there? Good. Tell him to have his body out here by four tomorrow morning."

He frankly envied Jack, having a wife like Gillian—right there when he needed her most.

CHAPTER 32

D MINUS 3

KERMANSHAH, IRAN

Mokhtari stood back while the guard unlocked the first door in the main cell block. A powerful odor assaulted him; it was worse on the third floor. He told the waiting doctor to examine the prisoners.

The Iranian doctor reached into his bag, took out a face mask and adjusted it in place before he entered the cell. In a few minutes he was out and reporting to the commandant that all three were very sick. "That one"—he pointed to the master sergeant trying to sit at attention as the rules required—"is near death. Unless he receives medical attention within the week he'll die."

"Then we'll send him to the IPRP," Mokhtari said, remembering the hawk-eyed general's instructions. "His number?"

"One-eighty-nine," the guard said.

"Mark it," Mokhtari ordered. The guard banged the cell door shut and chalked the number on the outside before they moved to the next cell.

TIKABOO VALLEY, NEVADA

The President was standing next to the jeep with the communications gear and talking to the sergeant. "Chief Pullman, I understand you're the one who got this built . . . He waved his hand at the

214

odd-shaped structure a mile away that consisted of the front wall, four guard towers that marked the corners of the real compound, a set of stakes that marked the administration building and a facade for the main building. Stairs ran up the left side of the facade to the long balcony that represented each floor. On the left side of each balcony was the guards' office and a string of cells stretched to the right, thirteen to a side.

"I just got the right people involved, sir."

"Like at Ras Assanya when you shanghaied a C-130 for the evacuation?" The President's staff had briefed him early that morning on the people he would be meeting during the day.

"Sir, how did you . . . ?

"Chief, you're a bit of a legend in the Air Force, and I'm your commander-in-chief. I appreciate what you did."

"But . . . but . . ."

"Why all the buts?"

"Sir, I got a confession. I voted for the other guy."

The President's roar of laughter echoed over the worried generals who were standing nearby. "Chief, who should I be listening to during this dog and pony show?"

"Colonel Stansell, sir. He's the only one with a clue."

The President beckoned to his chief of staff, drawing him over, and told him to get Stansell and keep the others away.

"Romeo Team under Captain Bob Trimler and First Lieutenant George Jamison will free the POWs," Stansell told the President. "They were parachuted in last night and if you'll look there"—he pointed to a ditch three hundred yards in front of the prison wall—"you should be able to see them."

The President swept his binoculars over the area. "That's damn close for live bombs."

"If we can't do it here we won't be able to do it in Iran. There . . ." He pointed to the first F-111 streaking up the valley, running past Beasely's in-bound AC-130. "The Rangers will lase the spots where they want the bombs to breach the walls." The President watched the F-111 pull up and toss a five-hundred-pound smart bomb. He could see another F-111 one minute in trail. "The second F-111 is going to ripple off two bombs. One into the wall and the other into the administration building right outside. Romeo Team can only illuminate the wall so they've got to be good to get the second one into the administration building. We use five-hundred-pounders to limit collateral damage. A two-thousand pounder might take out the POWs."

"Who's delivering the mail," the President asked, surprising both Stansell and Pullman with his knowledge of F-111 operations.

"Captain Ramon Contreraz." They watched the attack develop through their binoculars. Von Drexler tossed the first bomb and turned away to the left while Doucette came in behind him. The AC-130 was right behind them. All three bombs exploded. "Three bulls," Stansell said.

·The AC-130 moving over the settling debris of the bombs set up a left-hand-pylon turn over the prison and a torrent of gunfire erupted from its left side. The four towers disappeared in a hail from the gunship's two 40mm Bofors guns. "Captain Beasely, the AC-130 aircraft commander, is only using two 40 millimeter guns on this pass, not the 20 millimeter Gatling guns or the 105 millimeter cannon," Stansell told him.

"I understand they call the pilot the Beezer. Unusual nickname," the President said. By now, Stansell was not surprised by what he knew.

"The AC-130 and other aircraft will orbit clear of the prison," Stansell continued, "while Romeo Team rushes the walls." The President watched the Rangers run for the two holes in the walls. "The gunship is also our airborne command-and-control platform with General Mado and Captain James Bryant on board. They will coordinate the attack and establish communications with the Command Center in the Pentagon. When the airfield is secure they will land and operate from there."

He pointed to a C-130 flying over a drop zone two-and-a-half miles to the east. Parachutes blossomed behind the C-130. "We'll drop a runway-clearing team from Bravo Company to secure the airfield. Two combat controllers will go in with them. Once the airfield is secure they'll clear the C-130s to land. I'll be on board the first C-130 with Lieutenant Colonel Gregory, the ground commander. When we're on the ground, jeep teams will secure the road to the prison. It's Colonel Gregory's job to get Romeo Team and the POWs aboard the C-130s."

They watched while trucks drove toward the prison. Shortly after, three jeeps and a motorcycle came down the road from the airfield. "Two of those jeep teams have to keep moving, they've got to block a key highway intersection—Objective Red—a mile down the road that controls the western approach to the prison," Stansell said.

"Who makes the decision to take off?"

"General Mado."

"Why aren't you there now?"

"If things go right I won't be needed. We've done this six times. Also General Cunningham wanted General Mado to participate this time. "There are trucks moving into position now." The President watched Rangers running out through the wall carrying dummies. "We train under the assumption that we'll have to carry many of the POWs." In the distance they could see the last C-130 landing, and the trucks starting to move out down the road.

"The single F-15E you see orbiting above the AC-130 is Captain Jack Locke. The E model has the fuel to orbit and the ordnance to discourage unwelcome guests like tanks, armored cars, bandits . . . He's our ace in the hole, a Jack of all trades, you might say."

The President generously let that one go and watched the small convoy move down the road. "I suppose the road pattern you've marked out matches the actual route they'll follow."

"Yes, sir," Pullman answered, "and alternate routes if they have to make any detours."

"Now I suppose it's just a matter of calling in the jeep teams, loading the C-130s, and taking off?"

"That's correct, sir."

"Can you delay the takeoff and get all the Rangers back here? I want to meet the men who will have to do it, and take a close look at the mock-up." Both Stansell and Pullman could hear the reservation, at least concern, in the President's voice. Pullman was quickly on the radio relaying the President's request.

"Mr. President," Leachmeyer said, "this is Lieutenant Colonel Gregory, who commands the Rangers."

The President shook Gregory's big hand and talked to some of the Rangers as they piled out of the trucks and formed up by platoons. "Colonel, I'd like to walk through the mock-up with some of Romeo Team." Gregory called out for Trimler, Jamison, Kamigami and the four squad leaders to join them.

The President led the way through the breach in the wall. A target dummy lay crumpled on the ground. Trimler examined it. "Two holes in the head. We reposition the targets every time we practice, and some of them are marked to look like POWs. We train to knock the guards down with the first burst, then to shoot them in the head."

The President took in the small group surrounding him. They were not the normal staff officers he was used to seeing. They were dirty, lean, streaked with sweat, camouflage paint on their faces. But it was their attitude that made the real difference . . . These were warriors, not the uniformed, polished bureaucrats who lined the halls of the Pentagon. A half-formed image of the stir Command Sergeant Major Kamigami would leave in his wake if he walked through E Ring in the Pentagon looking as he did now chased through his mind. He liked it.

The group walked into the main cell block, and the President looked into the guard's office on the first floor. Three dummies lay riddled on the floor, two were standing untouched. "Who cleared this room?" he asked.

"I did, sir." It was Kamigami.

"These two dummies—how do you tell they're POWs?"

"We check hands first," Kamigami answered. "They hold anything, we shoot. Then we look for uniforms and shoes. POWS don't wear shoes." The sergeant major wasn't used to talking so much.

On the next floor the President examined six cell doors that had been blown open. He walked back down the makeshift stairs, back out into the quadrangle and looked around. "Colonel Gregory," he said, "what I've seen is impressive, but I've some questions. Your people ready?"

"Yes, sir."

"Captain Trimler, any misgivings about the mission?"

"None, sir."

"Sergeant Major Kamigami, are the men up for it?" Kamigami jerked his head yes. The President waited, wanting to hear what the sergeant had to say. When the big man said nothing, he asked, "What makes you so sure?"

A flustered look crossed the sergeant's face as he tried to find the words. "Sir, it's like sitting on two hundred Doberman pinschers in your backyard with their pricks all tied to the same tree."

CHAPTER 33

D MINUS 2

THE PENTAGON

"I appreciate your taking time out of your busy schedules to do this every day," the President told the men in the Oval Office. Admiral Scovill and Michael Cagliari relaxed some. "Mr. Camm, good to see you again," he said, puzzled why Director Burke had brought his Deputy for Intelligence to the meeting. "Charlie, we've got to get together for a game of poker." Leachmeyer returned his brief smile and sat down.

"Well, gentlemen, what's the status of the POWs?"

Burke started first. "We're getting some disturbing intelligence out of Iran. Indications are that the POWs are going to be split up soon. There're other developments Mr. Camm and his people have discovered . . ."

Camm stepped in smoothly. "Mr. President, we are convinced the POWs will be split up this week. We don't have the day exact. Also, we are getting reports that dissident elements in the Islamic Republican Party object to giving half the POWs to the IPRP and are causing trouble. Bottom line . . . The POWs are at risk."

"Your sources?"

"Contacts and operatives in Algiers supporting the dissidents inside the Islamic Republican Party," Camm answered. It was going better than he had hoped. He had now established "an Algerian connection." If his Deep Furrow operatives, as planned, got the hijacked airliner to Algiers with half the POWs, all the credit would go to the CIA, and especially his operatives, for surgically exploiting a situation only they—not the military—could analyze and swiftly move to resolve.

The President's fingers drummed on his desk. For reasons he couldn't pinpoint, Camm bothered him. Too smooth? Too *ready* with his answers? Or was it just the contrast between the facade of east coast establishment that Camm presented and the rough asses-on-the-line men he had met yesterday? He thought of Stansell's quiet confidence, found it reassuring. "Yesterday when I was watching Task Force Alpha, Colonel Stansell made reference to that armored regiment forty miles away. Is that going to be a problem? Is that the only threat? Is there something hiding in the bushes here?"

It was Leachmeyer's turn. "Delta Force has taken that into consideration, sir. There's a bridge at the halfway point. We position a blocking force there and blow the bridge. Should that armored regiment move, we will only need to delay them long enough to extract the POWs. Then we fall back and get the hell out of there."

"We have no indications of other threats," Camm said. Not the whole truth, but he rationalized that the reports of activity in the barracks behind the prison were not, after all, substantiated by a second source.

"We've seen photography that indicates the old barracks behind the prison are occupied," Cagliari said.

"My people have looked into that," Burke replied. "They're Kurds—squatters looking for a place to spend the winter."

Camm almost did interrupt to tell about the one report he had to the contrary, that soldiers had been seen occupying the barracks. But he hesitated . . . he did not want to risk American lives unnecessarily, he told himself, but nevertheless he decided not to mention it. After all, it would add confusion; the report *was* unsubstantiated, wasn't it? Camm found strength, and self-justification, in believing that what he was doing was *right*, and that in the long run the best interests of the U.S. would be served if covert operations like his Deep Furrow were restored to a place of preeminence. For the sake of everything else . . .

"Is Delta Force ready?" the President asked.

"Yes, sir," Leachmeyer replied. "As soon as we can position them free of surveillance."

The President believed that Delta Force was the best-trained force he had at his disposal, but the attack needed surprise on its side. Scovill's point about a good plan violently executed now being better than a perfect plan next week came back to him. And he had seen the violence Task Force Alpha was capable of . . .

A replica of Harry Truman's famous "The Buck Stops Here" plaque was on the table underneath the windows of the Oval Office. The President was staring at it now—it was decision-making time.

He punched the intercom button to his chief of staff. "Andy, I need to see the Secretary of Defense. Now." He folded his hands and looked at the men. "Deploy Task Force Alpha."

Leachmeyer was stunned. "May I ask why, Mr. President?"

"Certainly, Charlie." He liked Leachmeyer and had plans for him in the future when he reorganized the DOD. "We've got to get them in place if we decide to use them. Right now they offer us speed and surprise. And I don't think we can wait much longer." He didn't mention his gut feelings were mostly based on impressions—Stansell's confidence, the sight of two F-111s punching holes in the prison's walls, riddled target dummies, *and* Doberman pinschers . . .

NELLIS AFB, NEVADA

The words FLASH SECRET were stamped at the top and bottom of the message that Stansell read to the group.

> THIS IS A DEPLOYMENT ORDER BY AUTHORITY
> OF SECRETARY OF DEFENSE.
> UNIT: TASK FORCE ALPHA
> DEPLOY: IN ACCORDANCE WITH OPORD WARLORD
> LAUNCH: WITHIN TWELVE (12) HOURS OF MSG DTG
> OPTIONS: NONE
> SPECIAL INSTRUCTIONS: NONE

"My God," Pullman said, "we're goin' to do it. I knew it, dammit, I knew it . . ."

Stansell handed the message to Mado, who read it and shook his head. He checked the message's date/time group printed under the list of addresses. "We've got to be out of here in just over eleven hours. Any problems?"

A ragged chorus of "no's" and "none" went around the room. Gregory read the message twice, not believing his luck, before he handed it to Dewa. She read the message without comment. The room rapidly emptied, leaving Stansell, Pullman, and Dewa alone.

"Dewa, Chief, you both know . . . you won't be going with us. I need you to stay behind and sweep up the place."

Pullman went back to his trailer, looked around, made a quick decision, locked the door and headed for his quarters to pack. "Colonel," he muttered under his breath, "I didn't come to this party to be left behind when the music started."

Dewa worked in her office, taking the wall maps down and going through the routine of preparing classified material for destruction. When she had finished she stood in the middle of a large pile of sealed burn bags surveying her handiwork. She crossed her arms and hugged herself. "Damn, damn, *damn.*" She walked over to a bookcase and pulled out an unclassified manual on the law of armed conflict. Sitting on the couch, she drew her feet up and searched through the section on POWs, finding what she wanted.

She stared at the blank wall across the room trying to decide what to do. The manual was very clear on the status of escaped POWs as opposed to a combatant who was trying to evade capture. Once a combatant was captured, he became a POW and could not kill anyone in an escape. That was murder and a POW could actually be tried and executed for it. No, she was no clubhouse lawyer, but Rupert Stansell was an escaped POW, not an evader, and two guards had been killed during his escape. She knew the Iranians too well—she *was* one. If they recaptured Rupe Stansell they would execute him . . .

The choice was hers. All she had to do was tell General Simon Mado and the man she had decided she wanted to marry would be left behind. Except, of course, he would never forgive her. Still . . . she reached for the phone, started to dial, then shook her head and slammed the phone down. She made no attempt to stop the damage to her makeup as she stared at the wall . . .

CHAPTER 34

D MINUS 1

MARAGHEH, IRAN

The Iranian radar operator settled into the still-warm chair as he relieved the sergeant going off duty. "Are the Americans doing anything different?" he asked. The reply was a muffled grunt as the sergeant hurried out the door of the radar shack to catch the truck before it left for the run down the mountain to the comfort of his quarters in the town of Maragheh.

The operator resigned himself to his twelve-hour shift and searched through the drawers for the detailed checklist the Americans had supplied with the radar site. The only one that still followed it, he finally found the thick notebook buried in a stack of newspapers in a corner of the room and thumbed through it until he found the changeover checklist. Carefully he went through each step, checking them off with a grease pencil. He adjusted the receiver-gain, surprised to find it turned to its lowest setting. "How long has it been that way?" he mumbled to himself. When he checked the interrogation circuits he gasped as he counted twelve targets orbiting close to the border. A quick double-check confirmed they were still in Turkey but all were in the buffer zone NATO had established in Turkey next to the Iranian border.

He scanned the log for the previous shift and saw only two entries—the sign-on and sign-off of the departed sergeant. He continued to run the checklist until he reached the communications check section, keyed his mike and called the control center of Maragheh. After several attempts a voice answered his call. "Sir, communications check. Also, I have an unusual number of targets in the tri-border region."

"You have a very short memory," the officer told him, "that is the joint Turkish-American air defense exercise. Perhaps you recall I directed you to report only unusual activity? Only call me with important observations. Or will it take a forty-eight-hour tour-of-duty on the mountain to teach you to follow orders?"

"Sorry to disturb you, sir."

The officer broke the connection, and the operator sighed in relief.

INCIRLIK AIR BASE, TURKEY

Chief Pullman heaved his bulk out of the red canvas parachute seat stretched along the side of the C-141 and peered out one of the small round windows above the seat rail. "Can't see much," he yelled at Kamigami, who was sitting next to him. The loadmaster keyed his mike, acknowledged a call from the pilot and walked back to the two men, telling them to strap in for the approach and landing at Incirlik Air Base in southern Turkey. "Ever been to Turkey?" he asked Kamigami. The Army sergeant shook his head. "Interesting place," Pullman told him.

The passenger-services sergeant meeting the big cargo plane was surprised to learn that it was not the "Turkey Trot," the normal shuttle C-141 that landed every Tuesday. "Chief," he explained, "you haven't got an in-country clearance to be here. That's a biggy, I can't let you off the airplane." Pullman took him aside, spoke a few quiet words. The sergeant jumped into his pickup and sped away.

"We should have transportation and an officer out here in a few minutes," Pullman told Kamigami. While they waited Pullman put the cargo handlers to work and off-loaded the C-141 as he checked off the cargo strapped to six pallets. As predicted a harried-looking lieutenant colonel appeared and demanded to see their orders. Pullman reached into his briefcase and handed him the deployment order from the Secretary of Defense. He pointed out that Incirlik was one of the addresses on the message.

"I've never heard of OPORD WARLORD—"

"And you won't, sir, unless you've got one hell of a need to know. Your wing commander and his plans officer should know about it. I'd suggest you talk to them. Meantime I need your gym and a hangar for a few days. A little transportation would be appreciated. All in accordance with OPORD WARLORD, of course."

The L.C. reread the message, noted the date/time group and drove away, determined to find out why the men were on his base. Two pickup trucks heading for the cargo plane passed the officer before he had driven thirty yards.

"Those are for us," Pullman told Kamigami.

"I didn't know the OPORD said we got trucks," Kamigami said.

"It doesn't. I don't know about you but I'm not about to walk. Hell, we'll be long gone before the motor pool figures it out. Let the officers walk." Kamigami threw his gear into the back of one truck and took the keys from the driver. "If you'll get this squared away in a hangar"—Pullman swept the six pallets with a gesture—"I'll check with munitions. We'll be ready to bed 'em down when the birds arrive."

Six hours later a nervous Pullman paced the ramp in front of the hangar they had been given to use, waiting for the first C-130 to taxi in. Stansell glared at the big sergeant when he climbed down the crew-entry steps. "Chief, I told you to stay—"

Pullman threw him a hasty salute. "Big problems, sir. No GBU-12s on base. All that got shipped were GBU-15s, two-thousand pounders." The chief knew how to switch the colonel's attention away from his insubordination.

Stansell clamped a tight control on his anger. "Somebody screwed up big time. Let's find General Mado and try to sort this out. What else?"

"Under control, sir. We're using the gym to billet most of the Rangers, got the officers in the VOQ, and the mess hall will set up a chow line in the hangar there. We can keep the troops under cover inside."

They found the general at the back of the C-130 talking to Incirlik's wing commander. "General," Stansell began, "we've got a problem. No GBU-12s . . . only GBU-15s were shipped—"

"Someone really screwed up." Mado turned to the wing commander. "We need an emergency shipment of twelve GBU-12s in here ASAP—twelve hours max."

"I can't make that happen, General. The Turks are real touchy about munitions coming in-country, and an emergency shipment like that is too public, too easily monitored—"

"Colonel, we didn't come here to be grounded by some snafu and bullshit regs. Now make it happen and quick."

"Sir," the wing commander persisted, "I know what you're up against but I can't do it that quick without getting us kicked out of Turkey."

Mado glared at him. Angry, yes, but also, it came as something of a shock to him, that he felt a degree of relief. And then he realized why. He wanted the POWs rescued, would do whatever he could to make it happen. Sure, of course . . . But he was, after all, an expert in special operations, and in his firm opinion he had a lot more confidence in Delta Force than in Stansell's less organized, pick-up Task Force Alpha. Besides, there was Leachmeyer breathing down his back. He shunted aside such crass considerations as where his own career was best-served in this Delta-Alpha tug of war . . . Well, whatever, he wasn't going to roll over and play dead because the wrong bombs had been shipped. "Let's go with the GBU-15s—"

"No way," Pullman cut in. "Too much collateral damage. We'd nail at least some of the POWs when we blow the walls if we use those bigger bombs."

"Are you really sure, Chief?" Mado asked.

"I built the damn walls just like the Iranians did. I saw what five-hundred pounders did. I'm sure, General."

"I'll get a message off to the command center in the Pentagon and let them sort it out," Mado said as he turned and walked toward a waiting car, cutting off any further discussion.

"No way, General," Stansell growled. "Chief, you're about to earn your pay this month. Let's talk to Doucette and find out where we can find GBU-12s in Europe. You're going to do some unauthorized requisitioning."

"Now, how in the hell am I going to do that?"

"Let's find Doucette first." They walked into the hangar where most of the aircrews were gathering and found Doucette and Contreraz talking to a maintenance sergeant about their jet. After hearing Stansell, Doucette told them that his unit at RAF Lakenheath had GBU-12s in their ammo dump but that he doubted the 48th's DO, Colonel Billy Joe Barker, would release them since OPORD WARLORD only required the 48th to provide F-111s and aircrews. It would take a special, coordinated authorization from higher headquarters to budge Barker since he had dealt with the Turks before, and that would take days to arrange.

"Would he even know if the bombs were sent to RAF Stonewood

for a practice exercise, like an emergency munitions buildup?" Pullman asked. Doucette conceded that sounded like normal maintenance training that Barker wouldn't be too concerned with. Pullman found a telephone and placed a long distance phone call to a friend at Headquarters United States Air Force Europe in Germany who owed him a favor. Pullman collected favors like a gambler took in markers. "The GBU-12s will be built up and waiting for us at Stonewood. Okay, Colonel," Pullman said, "now how in hell do we get them *here?*" You just don't walk in and shanghai twelve GBUs. Munitions are tightly controlled—"

"Why don't I go get 'em?" Doucette asked.

"You've just ferried your jet in from Nellis," Stansell said. "You're almost out of crew duty, you should go into crew rest—"

"The only people here who know that are you and me, Colonel. Von Drexler hasn't landed yet. Hell, Colonel, flyin' straight and level is no big deal. I'm fine and slept most of the way over here while Ramon flew the jet. Ramon"—he turned to his WSO—"file a flight plan and let's go a'fliegening." Contreraz ran for a pickup truck.

"What?" Pullman said. It was moving too fast even for him.

"A'flyin'," Doucette translated . . . it's supposed to be what the Air Force is all about. Another thought occurred: "Chief, we can one-hop it without refueling going to Stonewood but we're going to need to hit a tanker coming back if we're hauling bombs. Can you arrange a KC-135 for us?" Pullman nodded, pleased to still have something to do, and headed for the telephone to arrange it, muttering about freewheeling jet jockeys. But he was impressed.

"I'll get a message off to Cunningham and have the GBUs released to you by the time you get to Stonewood," Stansell said. "Just get them here ASAP." As he watched Doucette walk out to his F-111 he decided he wasn't going to tell Mado about his midnight requisitioning of GBU-12s until they arrived at Incirlik. He found a pickup truck and headed for the communications shack to send out his own message to Cunningham. We're still players, General, he said to himself.

MARAGHEH, IRAN

A power surge activated the protective circuits of the AN/FPS-8 radar, and the slowly rotating sweep disappeared from the radar scope as the set shut off. The operator caught it immediately and grabbed the checklist, turning to the appropriate page. "Let it cool down first," the maintenance technician grumbled, not caring if the set was working or not. The operator ignored him and worked his way through the checklist, noting all the voltages. The radar was back on line in three minutes.

"Now what are the Americans up to?" the operator sighed as he played the receiver-gain and antenna-tilt for the best return. He could count four skin-paints—returns off a target—that did not correlate with an IFF squawk. When they disappeared off his scope he dropped the antenna tilt and recaptured the returns as they started a westbound penetration run into Turkey at a lower altitude than before. He almost stomped on the pedal under his right foot to call his superior in the control center but thought better of it. Twelve minutes later he picked up four eastbound skin-paints at low altitude inside Turkey heading straight for Iran. Again, there was no IFF squawk from the fast-moving returns. The operator watched as the returns disappeared from his scope, a good indication the aircraft were descending lower. Still, he only monitored the scope, though he was now worried about a border penetration.

Finally, he could no longer endure the waiting and called his control center to explain the developing situation. After acknowledging the call, there was silence from his superior, a sure sign that the officer did not want to hear about it. Then the four returns materialized on the scope as the aircraft turned on their IFFs and climbed to altitude, still inside Turkey. Reluctantly, he reported the latest developments. "You are deaf," the officer finally said, "and cannot learn. Forty-eight hours on duty should teach you something. You will be replaced Thursday at noon." He broke the connection.

The operator swore at his own rashness in calling the control center, turned the receiver-gain to a lower setting, raised the antenna tilt to sweep the far horizon, and walked to a bunk in the far corner to find some warmth and sleep. He glanced at his watch and calculated he had another forty-two hours before he would be relieved.

CHAPTER 35

D-DAY

THE PENTAGON

Colonel Richard Stevens glanced at one of the master clocks above the main situation board in the command center—0012—twelve minutes after midnight local time. He had been on duty since six o'clock the previous morning and was dog-tired. He tried to shrug off his fatigue and finish setting up the Military Command Center for the coming operation. Normally the Joint Special Operations Agency would have handled the drill since JSOA commanded all special operations. But Cunningham had asked him to oversee it and try to make sure nothing fell through the cracks.

Stevens had to admit that General Mado seemed to have thought of everything. The thick briefing books that detailed Operation WARLORD were ready, one for each position in the command center. Every relevant fact, including the names of the raiders, was listed in the books. Mado added a question-and-answer section to the back of each book, trying to anticipate questions the President or another heavy might ask. Mado had even developed the checklist he was using for setting up the command center.

It was going to be a long day.

"When was the master clock last set?" Stevens asked the sergeant trailing around after him.

"I hacked it with WWV at Fort Collins at twenty hundred hours last night. It was right on, Colonel. Keeps damn good time. Almost as accurate as the cesium clock WWV uses."

"What about the mission clock?" Stevens pointed at the digital clock underneath the master clock labeled "H-hour Plus."

"I ran it for an hour when I checked the master. Perfect."

A major interrupted them and handed Stevens a folder. "Two messages from Task Force Alpha," he said.

Stevens signed for the messages and sat down to read them while the sergeant went off to get some coffee. "God," Stevens muttered, "what the hell is going on?" The first message was from Mado explaining that the wrong munitions had been shipped to Incirlik and that an emergency shipment of the GBU-12s needed for the mission would have to be cleared through the Turkish government. Such hasty action would likely draw attention, might compromise the mission and could possibly jeopardize the status of the base with the Turks. Mado was putting the whole problem right in the lap of the command center.

Which, Stevens thought, meant Task Force Alpha was on a hold status as far as the mission was concerned. He turned to the second message from Stansell, which asked twelve GBU-12s at RAF Stonewood be released to Lieutenant Colonel Doucette for immediate upload on an F-111. The bombs would be ferried to Incirlik as part of Task Force Alpha's deployment package. There was no mention of coordination with the Turks.

The colonel glanced at the master clock, then back to the messages. They were running out of time. The weapons had to be ready for immediate upload when the F-111 landed. He didn't have time to go to Cunningham's quarters, wake the general, explain the situation, get an okay and a message sent to Stonewood in time to make it all happen. He decided he would respond to Stansell's request and show the messages to Cunningham when he came in. Maybe the bombs would be in Turkey by then . . .

Stevens drafted a flash message to Stonewood, in Cunningham's name releasing the munitions being built up for immediate upload. "Loose cannons get their peckers smashed for making decisions like this without authorization," he muttered, telling himself that his wife could see him any time she wanted when he was in Leavenworth prison.

MARAGHEH, IRAN

The radar operator kicked off his blanket and stretched, feeling rested after sleeping. He ambled over to his station to check the scope, and was startled to see it was blank. He looked over his shoulder . . . were the other men aware of the problem? No, they were asleep. He sat down, and put on his headset while he checked the voltage. Another power surge had kicked in the automatic protection circuits and had shut the set down.

It was easily fixed and no one was the wiser, he decided as he ran through the restart procedure. Only this time, the circuits would not reset. He was going through his checklist when the control center called. "Radio check," his superior's voice ordered.

"Acknowledged," the operator promptly answered.

"Any questions on reporting procedures?" the officer asked.

"None, sir." The officer broke the connection. So, you're going to disappear for a while, the operator thought, probably to be with your mistress. All the men knew about the ugly woman the officer kept near the control center and often joked about it since he had a beautiful wife. No accounting for taste. He closed his checklist, made sure the antenna was still rotating in case anyone should scan the radar site with binoculars, and turned off the set. "Let it cool down," he grumbled as he picked up a newspaper he had not yet read.

THE PENTAGON

Cunningham's fingers beat a tattoo as he read the two messages from Task Force Alpha. "Current status?" he asked, looking directly at his aide. The inner tension that had been twisting Stevens' stomach eased a bit. He had been fairly certain that Cunningham would approve of his releasing the bombs for movement to Turkey, but like the rest of the staff at the Pentagon, he was never certain about the general, who liked to keep people off balance.

"The GBU-12s are enroute to Incirlik and should arrive there in four hours."

"Good enough. Put these in the message file. Make sure Leachmeyer sees them about the time the GBUs arrive. Overtaken by events." Both men were playing the time-honored games the Pentagon's bureaucracy engaged in. Cunningham was pleased with the way his aide had not hesitated and had done what was necessary. Too many of his officers would have started asking irrelevant questions, trying to fix blame, telling everyone that the snafu was not their fault. He would worry whose fault it was later. "What's on the agenda for today?"

"Battle Staff briefing at 0800 hours. Kicks off with an intelligence update."

"Who's running the show?"

"JOSA. General Leachmeyer has command." The aide regretted adding the last as he said it. Cunningham hated being told the obvious.

"Dick, I'm not senile yet," the general said, going easy on the colonel, who had been on duty for over twenty-four hours. "I've got a problem, though. Leachmeyer is still chomping at the old bit and wants Delta Force to take the mission. He's a good man but suffers from tunnel vision. I've got to convince him we've run out of time and need to act *now*.

A slight smile worked at the corner of Stevens' mouth. "I brought in some ammunition to help 'convince' him." Cunningham's eyebrows went up. His aide may have been tired but he was still cooking. "Task Force Alpha's intelligence officer is waiting outside. I thought you might want to talk to her." The general stared at Stevens. "I had Miss Rahimi flown in from Nellis last night," Stevens said. "Thought she might be helpful."

Try as he could, Cunningham honestly did not approve of women in the military, especially civilian specialists. But that bias did not stop him from using them. "Show her in. Also have the DIA send someone up. I want an independent update from them before the Battle Staff meets. Call Ben Yuriden. I'd like to talk to him."

An hour later Cunningham was still talking to Dewa Rahimi and the brigadier general from the DIA. He was turned around in his swivel chair and they had pulled chairs up next to him. "Excuse me, general," Stevens interrupted. "The Command and Authority Room . . ." He nodded toward the glass enclosed room to the right. The President was standing there with the Secretary of Defense, his National Security Advisor, Bobby Burke of CIA and Admiral Scovill. "They're early," Stevens said.

"I'm not surprised." Everything that Rahimi and the general from DIA were telling Cunningham indicated that the raid had to go within hours or the well would be half-dry at Kermanshah. Obviously the President's advisors were staying on top of the situation.

The President sat down and Scovill bent over a microphone. "General Leachmeyer . . ." His voice quieted the soft buzz in the command center. The tension and expectation could be felt—a physical presence in the room. "Please proceed."

Leachmeyer took the center dais and introduced an Army colonel who reviewed their latest intelligence. It was the standard stuff that

Cunningham had expected—nothing to base a decision on. While the Colonel was talking, Stevens was handed another message. He gave it to Cunningham, who scanned it and passed it on to Dewa. "Why's it so important that the radar site at Maragheh is off the air?" he asked.

Her face tightened as she read the message. "It means the ingress corridor to Kermanshah is wide open," she said, and knew as she did so that Stansell was now closer to the danger waiting for him in Iran.

"Charlie"—it was the President's voice—"this doesn't give me much to go on. I think it's time we stop cutting bait and start fishing."

"Sir"—Leachmeyer's voice was calm, reasoned—"this is the latest we have."

You son of a bitch, Cunningham thought, still stalling for time. You want Delta to take it so bad you're pissing your drawers. It was time to shake the tree. "Our best window is tonight," he said into the mike at his position.

"Nothing we have supports that," Leachmeyer said. The two generals stared at each other from across the room as heads twisted back and forth.

Admiral Scovill bent over his microphone to end it. The President placed his hand over the mike and shook his head. He wanted to hear the two men out. Bureaucrats glossed over. A heated argument often got at the truth.

"I just received a message that says the radar site at Maragheh is off the air," Cunningham said. "That opens a corridor for us."

"*If* you were ready to go," Leachmeyer came back at him. "I understand you do not have the appropriate munitions in place to breach the prison walls." He almost added a dig about piss-poor planning by the Air Force. Round one to the Army.

How in the hell did he know that? Cunningham wondered. Stevens had the only messages. Had someone back-doored a copy to Leachmeyer? Was it Mado? "But the GBU-12s we need will be at Incirlik in less than"—he made a show of checking his watch—"two hours. No problem." Round two to the Air Force, thanks to Stevens.

"You need northerly winds to insert your ground team," Leachmeyer said, still pressing. "And as of twenty minutes ago they weren't there." Leachmeyer had done his homework.

"They will be tonight when we need them. The high-pressure

system we want is building over the eastern Med as predicted." Round three was a draw.

"Gentlemen, time out," the President said. "I want to go over the status of Task Force Alpha and the details of the mission. Run it."

As two Air Force colonels who worked for Mado took the dais and started a detailed briefing on the plan, Stevens handed Cunningham a note saying Yuriden was waiting for him outside. Cunningham walked out of the command center, found the Israeli colonel in a small office. "Thanks for coming over so quickly, Ben. Have you got anything new for me?"

The Israeli colonel's face was impassive. "Trucks and tacan are at Kermanshah. Our agent is with Carroll and knows how to work the set." He paused, trying to decide if he should reveal what else he knew. "General, there's an airliner on the tarmac at Kermanshah's aerodrome. It's for moving half the POWs . . ." He turned and walked out of the room. Cunningham stared at the door, Yuriden had just played a card he wasn't supposed to. Israeli intelligence was the best in the Middle East and like all intelligence organizations, the Mossad was very careful about releasing information that might in any way compromise its sources. Cunningham understood that as well as the significance of what Yuriden had done. The Israeli was trusting him not to reveal where he had learned about the airliner.

Cunningham returned quickly to the command center. The two colonels were finishing their briefing. "Miss Rahimi"—he motioned to her to move her chair closer to his—"I've just received news that the Iranians have an airliner at Kermanshah for moving the POWs. Can't reveal my source. Can you back me up? The President has to order a Go for tonight if we're going to get them out."

Dewa froze. The danger for Stansell was even closer.

LANGLEY, VIRGINIA

Camm paced the floor of his office, ignoring Susan Fisher as he reread the latest reports out of Iran: the airliner for transfer of POWs was in place at Kermanshah with CIA agents aboard as guards, ready to hijack the aircraft once in flight; the transfer of POWs was expected this night or next day; and Iranian soldiers were occupying the barracks behind the prison in company strength.

"Director Burke is with the President right now," Fisher said. "I suspect that the POWs are being discussed. Should we tell him about the airliner and the soldiers? We can always claim we monitored a telephone conversation."

"We've got to rescue the POWs . . . These reports from the prison about troops occupying the barracks . . . did we ever get confirmation from another source?" Fisher shook her head no. "So they might not be there . . . And Defense does know about the armored regiment at Shahabad . . ." Fisher nodded . . . Of course, Camm told himself, he didn't want American lives sacrificed needlessly, and since the attacking force knew about the armored regiment, he reasoned that they were certainly prepared for immediate withdrawal in the face of determined resistance. So . . .

"Considering the source of our information, I think we should say nothing at this time," Fisher said, telling him what he really wanted to hear.

KERMANSHAH, IRAN

Mokhtari's rage filled the hall as he stomped his way toward the basement. His selection of POWs for transfer had been changed, and Mary Hauser was to be turned over to the IPRP. He especially hated this woman who no matter what he had done to her, somehow managed to defy him. Well, he still had Landis . . .

· "Bring them into interrogation," he ordered, then slammed into his chair, grabbed the phone and dialed the main cell block for Mary's special "interrogator." He was beginning to feel better as he planned the last "interview" of Mary Hauser.

"What's that?" Carroll asked, looking into the bed of a truck. He was with Zakia and her contact in one of the numerous warehouse garages that crowded the outskirts of Kermanshah.

"A portable tacan," the man explained, pointing out the antenna and power unit. "You're supposed to set it up north of town and turn in on for the next three nights."

"Why a tacan?"

"For an airdrop," Zakia told him.

"Zakia, who the hell are you?" No answer. She could never tell him that she was a Mossad agent.

THE PENTAGON

"Miss Rahimi, then you have no hard evidence that a movement of POWs is imminent?" This from Director Burke of Central Intelligence. Dewa was standing on the low stage, a microphone in her hand. Whenever the Joint Chiefs or the President were in the National Military Command Center, every word was taped in case a controversy came up about who said what. And that brought out Burke's formal speaking style, intended to enhance him for the record but tending more to make him sound like a rather pompous speaker in the well of the House.

"No, sir." She had to protect Cunningham's source. "But events inside Iran follow a rhythm, and the political beat points to a deal being finalized between the Islamic Republican Party and the IPRP. It may have already happened. The contract will be sealed by the transfer of half the POWs to the IPRP's control. And that will happen very soon, no later than forty-eight hours from now, certainly before their sabbath, which is Friday."

"Pardon me, Mizz Rahimi"—everyone could hear the DCI's patronizing tone—"but my analysts do not agree with you."

Dewa said something in Farsi and left the stage, handing the microphone to General Leachmeyer. "You did good," Cunningham told her.

"Miss Rahimi, we missed your last comment," Admiral Scovill said from behind the glass.

Cunningham handed her his mike, waiting expectantly. "I beg your pardon, I spoke in Farsi. I said, 'That's a shame because events will prove them wrong.'" Cunningham half-smiled.

The President turned to his advisors. "It comes to this. Do we go tonight or not?"

"Wait until Delta gets into place," Scovill said. "Then use them."

Burke stared out through the glass. "Hold. Wait for developments."

"Go with Delta," the Secretary of Defense advised.

"Turn Task Force Alpha loose tonight," Michael Cagliari, his National Security advisor said.

"We know how Leachmeyer and Cunningham would vote," the President said. "But this isn't something that gets voted on." He looked out the window, studying the men and women waiting for his orders. Instinct told him to act now, to go with Task Force Alpha. He liked what he had seen in Nevada . . . but they were still the second team. "How soon can Delta be in place and ready to go?"

"Day after tomorrow," Scovill said.

There were no safe decisions. Again, he looked over the room, coming last to Dewa. She's right, he thought. And said: "We go with Task Force Alpha tonight. Make it happen. I want to be here when the raid starts."

KERMANSHAH, IRAN

Hauser and Landis stood at attention in front of Mokhtari's desk. and for a moment, Landis found himself clinically evaluating the man, like a crazy patient in an emergency ward. Mokhtari ended that.

"Bring him in," he ordered in Farsi. One of the guards opened the door and the Iranian prisoner, the dissipated rapist of Mary Hauser, was shoved into the same corner where he customarily waited for her. At Mokhtari's order the man shed his clothes, sat down, and bowed his head. He did not raise his eyes from the floor.

"No more lies, damn you. Now, why were you assigned to Ras Assanya?"

"Sir," she began, trying again to convince him she was telling the truth, "I was assigned because my superior officers were tired of my complaining, they wanted to punish me . . ."

"So you said. I did not believe you then, I do not now." He pointed at a guard who grabbed hold of Landis' shirt and stripped it off. "Have you ever seen one of these?" He picked up a cattle prod from behind his desk. He walked behind Landis, touched one end of the prod to his bare back and mashed the button in the handle. Landis flinched, moaned. Mokhtari turned a small dial. "It was set on low. Now again, why were you sent to Ras Assanya?"

"I told you the truth, must I lie to you?"

Another order and a guard drew a knife and slashed at Landis' trousers. Mokhtari touched Landis' genitals, mashed the button, and watched Landis collapse to the floor.

Mary had to stop it. ". . . I was to see if the GCI site could be used as a communications listening post . . ."

"I believe you, but you hesitated. Now tell me exactly what you did and what you learned." This time Mary did not hesitate and told everything she knew, pouring it out as fast as she could until Mokhtari held up a hand.

"A pity that you didn't think of all this from the first. A debt must be paid, not, unfortunately, by you." His voice hardened and he spoke in Farsi. A guard grabbed Mary and pushed her out the door. Her last view of the room was of Doc Landis bent over the desk on his stomach, and the Iranian prisoner hunched on top of him.

INCIRLIK, TURKEY

THIS IS AN EXECUTE ORDER BY AUTHORITY
OF SECRETARY OF DEFENSE.

UNIT: TASK FORCE ALFA
EXECUTE: OPORD WARLORD
H-HOUR: NO LATER THAN 2400Z THIS DATE
OPTIONS: NONE
SPECIAL INSTRUCTIONS: JOINT TASK FORCE COMMANDER
WILL INITIATE OPERATIONS WHEN HE JUDGES ALL MISSION
PARAMETERS ARE FULFILLED.

Gregory was the first to break the silence that held the small group clustered in Incirlik's command post. "A Go, a goddamn Go." His voice was little more than a whisper. "Are we going to have the northerly winds we need?"

Mado took the message, his face hard. "The weatherman tells me the winds at altitude are becoming more and more northerly and building. That's what we need, but I'm still worried about the weather. Satellite photography shows a low cloud deck hanging in the Zagros Mountains."

"Right now we've got enough ceiling and forward visibility to fly a low-level route through the mountains," Stansell told him. He turned to the men for their inputs. "The OPORD calls for a two-thousand-foot ceiling and five miles forward visibility. Can you go with anything lower if the weather gets worse?" He watched their faces, suspecting reactions would be the best indication of their confidence. Most of them were entering unknown territory— combat. Experience had taught him that men changed when the fighting started. All bets were off.

"The C-130s can go with a thousand and three," Duck Mallard said, "if I've got Drunkin Dunkin as lead navigator. Otherwise we need the two thousand and five."

No problems there, Stansell decided.

"We can take it a bit lower," Beasely, the aircraft commander of the AC-130 gunship said. "A five-hundred-foot ceiling is okay. Still need three miles forward vis." Thunder had said the young captain was steady as a rock, and Stansell agreed.

"The F-15s need the two-thousand-and-five for escort at low level," Jack said, "otherwise we need to go in at a higher altitude. I can take my E model in at just about zero-zero with the terrain following radar." Jack's evaluation matched Stansell's.

Von Drexler had kept silent, his face a reflection of Mado's. Since Stansell was looking directly at him, he knew he had to commit.

"We need the two-thousand-and five," he said. "The TFR in our jets isn't as good as it should be."

Stansell looked to Jack. What was the matter with Von Drexler? No help from Jack. "Colonel Doucette said he could fly a mission with take-off minimums, three hundred and one," Stansell ventured, trying to discover why Von Drexler was hedging.

"Doucette is irresponsible," Von Drexler snapped.

"We abort if the weather goes below two thousand and five," Mado said, ending it. "We have other things to cover. First, Captain Kowalski and her crew do not go. We cannot send women into combat. Second, decide which four F-15s will escort the C-130s and which four stay on station with the tanker as a backup. Third, select which two F-111s will attack the prison and which one will hold on the tanker."

"General, we're one C-130 short since the crash," Stansell argued. "We need to send six on the raid. I had planned on using Captain Kowalski to insert Romeo Team tonight. That way we'll have six fresh C-130 crews for the raid and we can use her plane as a backup after she returns."

"Why her?"

"She's maybe the best pilot I've got," Mallard said. "She's a hell of a lot better than I am and she's got the second best navigator."

"And she's a good cover if anything goes wrong." This from Thunder. "Dewa says they can claim to be part of the air defense exercise that's going on and that they got lost. Their being women, the Iranians will believe that."

"And they were going to drop the Rangers in Turkey on a night exercise . . ." Even Mado was warming to it. "And that type of mission doesn't quite cross the line into combat. Okay, I'll buy it."

"I plan on sending the F-15s and the F-111s in as we rehearsed," Stansell told him. "We do a systems check just before we depart the tanker and make the final decision then about who goes—"

"I want to change the F-111 lineup," Von Drexler interrupted. "Doucette and Contreraz hold at the tanker."

Stansell could not believe what he was hearing. "Why?"

"Like I said, Doucette is irresponsible. The flight to Stonewood proved it. He was out of crew duty time and should have been in crew rest. Then he flew back here. I don't trust people who play fast and loose with regulations." The way he looked at Stansell insinuated that he was also accusing Stansell along with Doucette.

"Colonel Drexler," Stansell said, "I made those decisions, not

Doucette. It worked out, and Doucette is now in crew rest and will be ready for the mission. I take calculated risks when I have the people who can hack it . . ."

"Doucette flies backup," Mado ruled, making a chopping motion with his hand, ending further argument.

"General, there's some good news," Thunder said, breaking the tension. "The AWACS controlling the air defense exercise is reporting the Iranian's early-warning radar site at Maragheh is off the air. That opens up one hell of a corridor for us."

Mado didn't respond at first. Then: "That's only good if it stays down." He stood there, staring at the status boards on the walls of the command post. Finally: "Colonel Gregory, brief your men on their true objective just before they board the C-130s. Colonel Stansell, monitor the weather and tell me immediately if any problems develop. H-hour will be when I launch Kowalski. Command Post manned, AWACS on station, Kowalski's C-130 and Romeo Team ready to launch at 1700 hours local this evening. Rest of Alpha ready to go at 0100 local. Any questions?" There were none. Mado motioned for Von Drexler to follow him, and they left the command post.

"I can't figure that man out," Jack said, more to himself than Stansell. "You win one with Kowalski and lose one with Doucette. It's like he's trying to keep everyone happy . . . playing it both ways."

Stansell didn't answer him. He'd seen other commanders, especially cautious yet ambitious ones, do the same thing. Press ahead with the mission but try to keep all options. He wondered what Mado would do when they were on the ground at Kermanshah and he had to make a fast decision, never mind the consequences . . .

CHAPTER 36

H-HOUR

INCIRLIK, TURKEY

For a moment Stansell could hardly breathe. He had experienced it all before—the words, the tension, the very atmosphere . . . He was not in Incirlik's command post but in the one at Ras Assanya waiting for a hostile fleet to sortie across the Persian Gulf. He turned, half expecting to see Muddy Waters sitting beside him, waiting to die . . . "Damn," he breathed, relieved to see Thunder Bryant instead.

"Like old times," Bryant said, acknowledging the same feeling. "Colonel, I never said thanks for what you did that Friday night. I was really strung out over my divorce and close to doing something stupid. You kept me on track." Stansell only nodded. "There's something else, sir." Bryant hesitated. "You shouldn't be going on the mission." There, it was out.

Stansell looked at him. "Why? Because I'm an escaped POW, not an evader, and if the Iranians capture me again it's up-against-the-wall time? Come on, it's late in the game for that kind of stuff. And please don't mention it to anyone, especially Mado. He'll cancel me out in a flash . . . Look, Bryant, Waters gave me the job of getting the 45th out of Ras Assanya. I've got to finish it. I watched them shoot four wounded men in the command post when I surrendered the base. I don't know who said that revenge is a dish best served cold, but I damn well want to serve it. Okay?"

241

Thunder nodded. "Okay, let's do it good, Colonel."

The weatherman, a skinny, weasely-looking first lieutenant, was updating the weather map on the front wall. The northerly winds they needed at altitude over Iran were almost there. "How strong, Lieutenant?" Stansell asked.

His answer was reassuring. "Forty to forty-five knots and building."

"Ceilings and visibility in the Zagros Mountains?"

"Our last satellite coverage indicated low clouds in the valleys. I'm forecasting five hundred to a thousand foot ceilings, two to three miles forward visibility. Should start to lift after midnight. Iran doesn't report weather, and our next satellite coverage won't be until tomorrow morning."

That wasn't what Stansell wanted to hear. "It's important, Lieutenant. Keep on top of it."

Mado walked into the command post and studied the weather map. "Not good. Unless we see an improvement, no go."

"General, the lieutenant is calling for the ceilings to lift. He won't have anything to go on until the morning when new coverage comes in. If we're going to insert Romeo Team you're going to have to make the decision now. We've got to catch the airliner and the winds."

"I don't make decisions based on forecasts by lieutenants—"

"Sir, let's find out what the lieutenant's track record is. Why don't we talk to the pilots who've been flying on the air defense exercise here?"

Mado didn't respond, but Thunder was already on the telephone talking to the ops center controlling the air defense exercise. He hung up and looked at Mado. "They say the lieutenant is shit hot."

A hard silence came down over the three men. Stansell kept thinking about the lesson Waters had taught him about listening to his young officers and trusting them to do their job. Now he had to convince Mado. "Sir, can we talk, in private?"

KERMANSHAH, IRAN

Mary heard the guards' footsteps coming down the corridor. "Stop shaking," she told herself. "Don't let Mokhtari use anticipation . . ." The noise of Landis' cell door opening did not break the tension. Was she next? She heard the dull thud of a body being dropped on the floor and the squeak of the door closing.

She curled up on her bunk, her ear pressed against the wall, listening. She tapped out a message and waited for a reply. It never came.

INCIRLIK AIR BASE, TURKEY

"I'm the Joint Task Force Commander, Colonel. Go-No-Go is up to me." Mado was pacing, making a path over the floor of the small briefing room in the rear of the command post.

Stansell had never seen the general like this. Normally he at least seemed cool. "Sir, I know that. But as your mission commander it's my job to run the show for you, to put together the nuts and bolts, spare you the details. Right now some of those details have changed and that means we need to fall back and reevaluate. The reason to go low-level through the mountains is to avoid radar detection, but the radar site at Maragheh is off the air and that does open a corridor for us . . . we don't need to go low-level to avoid it. We can fly above the cloud deck if we have to and still use whatever terrain-masking the mountains offer—"

"Colonel, I don't screw around with a plan that's been carefully worked out in advance and approved by my commander."

Stansell translated it a different way—Mado had never been in combat, he had never experienced the turmoil and chaos that ruined the best of plans, that made constant change S.O.P. Mado had become too much of a staff officer, a bureaucrat playing political games in the halls and offices of the Pentagon. Well, now it was the game *he* would have to play or Task Force Alpha would stay on the ramp at Incirlik.

"Sir, you know there will be a congressional investigation regardless of what we do." Stansell made his voice a matter of fact. "How will it look, sir, to a bunch of congressional Monday-morning quarterbacks when they see we didn't react to the radar gap in the Iranian air defense net?" He had the general's attention. "The harder we press, the better it will look to them. When we tried to rescue the hostages from the American Embassy in Tehran in 1980 the mission fell apart when they landed in Iran on that desert airstrip. Yet most of them came out looking like heroes for at least trying. Carter took the heat . . ."

"Yes, but the situation is different now."

Mado was weakening?

"What *politician* will understand that? Hell, Eisenhower knew the name of the game in 1944 when he made the decision to launch the invasion of Normandy based on a predicted break in the weather.

He knew that failure would hurt him, but sitting on his duff and not trying would kill him. And the invasion. He gutted it out and was proved right. He got to be President of the United States . . .''

The look on Mado's face told Stansell that he had hit the right keys. He pressed his advantage. ''Think how it's going to look when we pull this off and you get up in front of a congressional committee and say a whiz kid of a first lieutenant predicted the weather would improve and I believed him. Ironic, isn't it, General? Because the radar site is down, the weather here isn't a critical factor. But they won't know that, won't understand it.''

Mado turned and walked out onto the main floor of the command post. It was his moment, and he played it for all it was worth. ''We are going to bring the POWs home,'' he announced. ''Status of the AWACS?''

''On station, still reporting Maragheh off the air,'' came the reply.

''Good. When is the Iranian airliner scheduled to land at Rezaiyeh?'' This was the airliner that Kowalski would have to intercept and piggyback on to drop the Rangers.

''In an hour, sir.''

''Weather?''

''No change.''

''Gentlemen, it's a Go. Launch the C-130.'' The general was standing, almost at attention. Stansell noticed his hands were shaking slightly. Well, why shouldn't they be?

The Rangers were already rigged and inspected and formed up in two lines waiting to climb on board the waiting C-130 in front of the hangar. Each of them was loaded with over a hundred pounds of equipment. Gregory drove up in a pickup with Thunder and jumped out, pointing at Trimler. Thunder motioned for Captain Kowalski and her crew to join him on the flight deck.

''Bob,'' Gregory said, returning Trimler's salute. ''It's a Go. But I want to talk to the men first.'' He smiled at the young captain. ''Don't worry, it'll be short.'' The lieutenant colonel walked up the ramp of the C-130 until he could see all the men. ''If you haven't figured it out by now,'' he said, pitching his voice low, ''you're soft in the head. We're the ones going after the POWs being held in Iran. Us—the Third of the Seventy-fifth. It's not going to be a walk through or a piece of cake or exactly like we've trained. Combat never is. Most likely it'll turn into a piece of shit and that's when you'll prove what you are. But I promise you one thing, I'll be there to get you out. We go in like Rangers and we come out like Rangers. Good luck, good hunting." He jumped off the ramp and the Rangers started to shuffle on board.

Thunder was on the flight deck talking to the aircrew. "No changes, do it like we trained. Your call sign is Scamp One-One. The AWACS controlling you is Delray Five-One. Frequencies as briefed." He looked at the four women on the flight deck. "Engine start in fifteen minutes, takeoff on the hour."

"Thunder," Kowalski said, "send Hank up." Staff Sergeant Hank Petrovich was the crew's loadmaster. "Let me tell him."

Thunder climbed down the ladder onto the cargo deck and told Petrovich to see his aircraft commander. His gaze swept over the two lines of Rangers sitting in the jump seats along the side of the fuselage, eleven to a side. The jumpmaster was standing with Trimler on the ramp, talking to the Romeo Team's first lieutenant, George Jamison. A huge lumbering figure walked up the ramp fully rigged with a rucksack slung in front, banging off his knees. It was Kamigami. He nodded his head in the direction of the officers and took the end seat on the right, closest to the flight deck.

Thunder felt better just seeing him.

Stansell was sitting next to Mado in the command post, both enduring the wait. The small loudspeaker mounted in the console in front of them crackled to life. "Ground. Scamp One-One, engine start." It was Kowalski.

"Roger, Scamp One-One," Ground Control answered. "Cleared for engine start. Taxi when ready."

"Roger, Ground."

"Good," Stansell observed, "it sounds routine." Mado's building nervousness played at the edges of his mouth.

"Tower, Scamp One-One. Holding short of the runway."

"Roger, Scamp One-One. Taxi into position and hold."

Mado shook his head. "What's taking so long?"

"They're right on time," Stansell told him.

From the tower: "Scamp One-One. Cleared for takeoff."

"Rolling." Again, Kowalski sounded as if it was business as normal.

"Start the clock," Stansell said. "On the hour at sixteen hundred Zulu."

H-hour.

CHAPTER 37

H PLUS 1

THE PENTAGON

"Your attention please," the loudspeaker in the National Military Command Center silenced the multiple private conversations that were going on. "Operation WARLORD commenced at sixteen hundred hours Zulu."

Cunningham watched the mission clock rapidly scroll through numbers until it caught up. The master clock read 1701 Zulu, Greenwich Mean Time, and the mission clock beneath it read 01:01—H-hour plus one hour and one minute. So, he calculated, command and control system was sixty-one minutes behind real time. And that was without any problems or heavy message traffic. Once Task Force Alpha started using its satellite communications system he'd be in direct contact with Mado and things should speed up. We've still got to rely on the men in the arena to do their job, he thought . . . but have I chosen the right men? Are they up to it? Well, too late for second thoughts now.

The general looked around the room. Heads were bent over the thick mission briefing books Mado had prepared. All were turned to the page for H-hour listing the objectives, actions, and players, reviewing what *should* be happening. Instant Monday-morning quarterbacks, he thought. He twisted further around and checked the glassed-in Command Authority room. The National Security Advisor was alone, sitting in the President's chair, telephone in hand. Probably calling the White House on the secure line with the news.

Well, the President was right, nothing he could do for now. He motioned to his aide. "Dick, I want General Sims to monitor the operation for me." He barreled out of the room, heading for his office. This is going to be a long one, he thought. Mado, we're finally going to find out if you've got what it takes.

Strangely, he never considered Colonel Rupert Stansell.

SOUTHEASTERN TURKEY

"Delray Five-One, Scamp One-One. How copy this frequency?" Kowalski's copilot, First Lieutenant Brenda Iverson, was handling the radios.

"Five-by," Delray, the orbiting AWACS replied. "We should have a target for you in twenty minutes." The radio calls sounded like a routine air defense mission.

"Sue," Kowalski hit her intercom button, "how long to the departure point?" Sue Zack, the navigator, told her seventeen minutes. "It had better be twenty minutes. They ran around in circles too long trying to make a decision and almost blew it." The "they" she was talking about was General Mado. The captain didn't think very much of the general.

The target the AWACS was directing them on was the Iranian airliner they were to intercept as it took off out of Rezaiyeh. The plan called for them to hold just inside Turkish airspace thirty-five nautical miles from Rezaiyeh. The AWACS had been monitoring Rezaiyeh for ten days and had picked up the airport's rhythm of operation. When the airborne controller in the E-3C, the highly modified and specially-built version of the Boeing 707 that had been designed for Airborne Warning And Control, determined the timing was right, he would guide the C-130 into Iran to intercept the Iranian airliner as it climbed out of Rezaiyeh. Since neither had trained together, it was going to be tricky.

"Scamp, your target is moving into position now," the AWACS radioed. "Can you depart holding in eight minutes?" An interpreter aboard the AWACS was monitoring radio transmissions from the airport at Rezaiyeh and had heard the Iranian airliner call for its clearance to Bandar Abbas.

Kowalski over the intercom: "Sue, how far out?"

"Sixty miles. Twelve—twelve and a half minutes."

Kowalski's voice was calm when she answered the AWACS. She could have been an airline pilot acknowledging a routine air traffic call between Kansas City and St. Louis. But she preferred to be where she was. "No problem, Delray. May be a little late. Starting an early descent now." She pushed the yoke forward and nudged the throttles up, accelerating as she started a high speed descent into the tri-border area. "How long, Sue?"

"Ten and a half minutes," the navigator replied, "over two minutes late. Those assholes launched us too late."

"We're not out of it yet." Kowalski said. "How much time can we make up on the leg into Rezaiyeh?"

Sue spun the wheel on her navigation computer, a circular slide rule, "Balls to the wall—little over a minute. Still fifty seconds late. We're going to miss the airliner."

But the pilot had other ideas. She pushed the C-130 for all it was worth, hoping she wouldn't tear the wings off as their true airspeed touched three hundred and forty knots. Kowalski had to time the rate of descent with the distance left to go. She planned to overfly their departure point while still descending and be leveled off just above the mountain tops when they crossed into Iran. She backed the throttles off a bit when the old cargo plane started to shake and buffet. Their Lockheed Hercules had first seen service in 1966 in Vietnam and was older than many of the Rangers it was carrying. During the years it had done great service for the Air Force, hauling cargo and doing endless practice airdrops. Now it was the real thing and Kowalski was demanding that the cargo plane hold itself together once more. "Come on Herky Bird . . ."

In the rear of the aircraft the Rangers looked about, uneasy with the strange sounds the plane was making. "Ain't never heard one sound like it was comin' apart," a sergeant said, loud enough for Baulck to hear.

"Shut your mouth," he told the man. "Kowalski knows what she's doin'. Captain," he yelled across the cargo bay, "time to cammy up?" Trimler gave him a thumbs up and the word was passed. Sticks of camouflage paint appeared and the men started to change their faces into bizarre blends of green and black.

"Man, you look great in living color," a black buck sergeant from the streets of Watts told the white corporal sitting next to him.

"Better than black on white," the corporal shot back.

*   *   *

"Scamp," the AWACs controller radioed, "I hold you at departure now. Turn to a heading of two-seven-two degrees. Target will be on your nose at thirty-five miles."

"Roger," the copilot answered. The last radio transmission was intended to deceive any hostile monitoring of their radio frequency, make it sound like they were turning to the west, back into Turkey. Kowalski reached down onto the center flight-control pedestal and switched the IFF to standby. From here on the Iranians would have to find the C-130 by a skin paint as the Hercules continued on its old heading, straight into Iran.

INCIRLIK, TURKEY

Mado was hovering over the command post's Emergency Actions Controller. The twenty-year-old had sewn on her third stripe a week before and had never seen a general, much less talked to one. And now a man with two stars on the lapels of his fatigues was giving her his undivided attention as she decoded the message from the AWACS orbiting over four hundred miles to the east. Her fingers moved down the page, finding each code group and then reading the correct decode in the column to the right.

"I need that message." Mado's voice was like a threat.

"General, you might want to look at this," Stansell said, drawing the man's attention away. He had rummaged around in his brief case until he had found a map of an alternative ingress route Thunder had drawn up in case of decreased radar coverage by the Iranian air defense net. "This route can save us almost three minutes . . ."

The general studied the route for a moment. "No. Stay with the original plan. That will give us terrain-masking in case Maragheh comes back on line. We won't gain that much by saving three minutes." It was enough time for the command post controller to finish decoding the message and double check it for accuracy. She handed it to Mado, glad to get him off her back.

"Not good," Mado said. "Kowalski hit the departure point two minutes late. Maybe we should send a recall message," he muttered.

Stansell read the message, then checked the clock. "I think it's too late, General. By the time she receives any recall she'll have either linked up with the airliner or be on her way out of Iran, aborting the mission on her own." The general's indecision was almost palpable. "Sir, check the time and look at the numbers. Kowalski left the departure point seven minutes ago. It's thirty-five miles to Rezaiyeh.

She's one or two minutes from intercepting the airliner. We have to relay a recall order through the AWACS. Any order you give now is O.B.E."

Overtaken by events . . . Mado glanced at Stansell, still hesitating.

"Our command-and-control system, doesn't give us the benefit of real time or even near real time in making decisions," Stansell went on, fighting for every second of delay possible. "It's the same old problem, sir, a commander has got to rely on his people to make the right decisions because there's just no way he can control what everybody does." The general only stared at him. "Look, let me query the AWACS for a status report while the Emergency Actions Controller encodes a recall message." And an inspiration hit Stansell. "If you don't like what you hear, then you sign the message for release and we send it."

The general didn't like one bit the thought of his signature on a recall message, proof positive who had sent it for any congressional committee. And for Cunningham. Stansell was already bent over the microphone, calling the AWACS, "Delray Five-One, say status of last mission. . . ."

NORTHWEST IRAN

"Scamp One-One, come right ten degrees, target is at your eleven o'clock position, seven miles." The controller in the AWACS was giving the C-130 a cut-off vector before turning them toward the airliner's stern. Brenda Iverson, Kowalski's copilot, acknowledged the new heading. The crew had practiced intercepting another C-130 at Nellis under the control of an AWACS that was participating in Red Flag. They had repeatedly run against a target aircraft, learning how to follow a controller's directions until they got a visual contact and could complete the intercept on their own. Mostly, they had practiced approaching the target from the rear quarter, a simple matter of using overtake speed and cutoff angles. But this was different. It was going to be a much more difficult intercept as they approached from the front quarter.

Kowalski was pushing the C-130 along at 265 knots, much faster than they had practiced intercepts or ever flown at low level, and the Hercules was protesting.

"Turbine inlet temperatures are high," the flight engineer said, worry etching her voice as she watched the gauges climb past 1,000 degrees. "We're over-temping. Going to have to back off."

"Not yet," Kowalski said. Both pilots scanned the night, straining to catch sight of the Iranian airliner's anti-collision or position lights.

"Negative radar contact," the navigator told them. Sue Zack was trying to find the transport version of the Fokker Friendship with her APN-59 radar set. She was hoping that the props of the twin-engined, high wing turboprop aircraft would help reflect radar energy. No such luck.

"Tallyho," Kowalski called over the intercom. She could see the red anti-collision light flashing in the darkness. "Keep trying to find them, Sue. I need the range. Double-check all lights. Make sure we're dark." Kowalski's commands rippled out as she waited for more information from the AWACS.

"Target at your nine o'clock, five miles," the AWACS told them. "Come left forty degrees."

"What the hell?" the copilot said, worried about the new heading. "We're cutting it close." They waited for the next command from the AWACS.

"Contact," the navigator called out, "Three and a half miles." They had turned enough for the C-130's nose-mounted radar to paint their target.

"Keep feeding me ranges, Sue," Kowalski said. "I think the AWACS is blowing this . . . We're going to shoot by and cross right in front of the airliner." She tried to visualize what was happening from a bird's-eye view.

"I've lost him off the left side of my scope at two and half miles," Sue told her.

"Scamp, turn left twenty degrees." the AWACS commanded. The call was too late and the turn too little. It was going to be a botched intercept.

Kowalski made her decision. She had been judging their closure and watching the Fokker's red flashing anti-collision light. She could still see the airliner at the C-130's left ten o'clock position. They needed room to turn onto the airliner. She wrenched the Hercules further to the left, standing it on its wing in a ninety degree bank, turning away from the Iranian. "Judy," she called over the radio, the command that said she was taking over and maneuvering on her own to complete the intercept.

It was the right decision. Almost immediately, Kowalski wrenched the Hercules back to the right, playing the throttles and sending the turbine inlet temperatures past 1050 degrees. Now they were arcing onto the Iranian's stern and closing rapidly. She wanted to harden up her turn, pull more than two Gs as they turned, but she was worried about her bird standing up to the strain. "Come on, old gal . . ."

The small Fokker transport was still crossing left to right, directly in front of the C-130. Kowalski estimated the Iranian was climbing out at about a hundred and thirty knots and crossing at almost ninety degrees to her heading. Right now it was all seat-of-the-pants flying for the captain. Her instincts had better be good.

"I've got a radar contact," Sue called out. She couldn't quite match Kowalski's cool. "Inside a half mile."

The dark form of the Fokker filled the pilot's windscreen as it surged past them. "Overshoot!" she yelled. Now the C-130 was going to cross directly behind the Iranian. Kowalski rolled wings level and pulled back on the yoke, bringing the nose high into the air. Her heading was ninety degrees off the Iranian's. She rolled a hundred and ten degrees to the right and pushed the nose down, turning after the Fokker. It was as close to a high yo-yo as a C-130 could come.

On the cargo deck only the seatbelts the Rangers were wearing kept them from spilling over the compartment when Kowalski maneuvered, rolling the big cargo plane up onto one wing, then the other. They had never experienced that before. Dirt and dust filled the air and anything loose tumbled onto the men. Only the load-master, Hank Petrovich, had not been strapped in and he had smashed against a bulkhead, gouging a furrow in his forehead. Then they were straight and level, less than a thousand feet behind the Fokker. It had been a near thing.

The two Iranian pilots never saw the dark specter that bore down on them off their right wing because the C-130's camouflage blended into the night and it was running dark. Only the red glow of instrument lights on the flight deck broke its shadow. It was hard to say what their reaction would have been if they had seen the Hercules slice behind them, traveling at 265 knots, slow for a fighter but all too fast and close for a pilot who had last maneuvered like that in pilot training.

Inside the C-130 the jumpmaster unstrapped and ran forward to check on the loadmaster. Blood was pouring down Petrovich's face, and he was groggy from the blow. The jumpmaster ripped a first-aid kit off the side of the fuselage, pulled a compress bandage out and stopped the bleeding. "A Band-Aid would probably do the trick," he reassured the man, binding him up.

The loadmaster sat on a jump seat, put his headset on and checked in with the flight deck. "We're okay back here, captain. Hey, I didn't know a Herky Bird could do that."

"Yeah," Kowalski said, "the old bird is pretty maneuverable. A four-engine fighter. We heard you took a header. Sure you're okay?"

"I'm okay. You didn't get my balls, Captain. Look worse than I am."

The corporal sitting next to Baulck rasped, "I thought you said she knew what she was doing."

"You better count on it," Baulck shot back.

Slowly the tension on the flight deck eased a notch as Kowalski maneuvered the C-130 into position, two hundred feet behind and slightly below the Iranian airliner, as the turbine inlet temperature moved back down into normal operating range. The pilot keyed her intercom. "Everyone on oxygen. Time to start prebreathing and do a little purging." She wanted to get nitrogen out of everybody's blood for when they depressurized at altitude. No point in risking a case of the bends. Then: "Thank you, Mr. Lockheed."

INCIRLIK, TURKEY

Mado was staring at Stansell. The AWACS had not answered the colonel's question about the status of Scamp One-One but had told them to standby. Now the command post Emergency Actions Controller was copying another encoded message from the AWACS. "Send the recall message," Mado growled, his decision finally made. He scribbled his name across the bottom, releasing it for transmission.

"Better wait for her to decode that," Stansell said, still playing for time. Again, Mado hovered over the young woman, willing her to hurry. But she would not rush the decode procedure and risk making a mistake.

Finally it was done and the general snatched it from her. He turned and studied the mission-status board that listed all of Task Force Alpha's aircraft. All were mission-capable and ready for take-off.

"Excuse me, sir," the controller said, "I have to throw that message in the burn bag when you're finished." Mado handed it to her and walked away. She smoothed it out and handed it to Stansell.

Stansell read the one-line transmission from the AWACS:

TARGET AIRCRAFT INTERCEPTED AT 1738 ZULU.

A close one, Stansell thought, handing her back the message along with the recall message that Mado had almost sent.

"Relay the intercept message to the Pentagon's command center," he said, and walked after Mado. He found him by the coffee pot. "Sir, it's a waiting game now. It will be at least four or five hours before we hear anything. I'd suggest trying to get some rest . . . there are bunks set up in a back room . . . I'll notify you the moment anything comes in."

Mado shook his head. "I've got to stay on top of this."

Stansell headed for the bunk room, shaking his head, convinced the general would be a basket case by the time they got on the ground inside Iran. He glanced back over his shoulder. Mado was pacing back and forth, nervously wearing a path in the floor.

CHAPTER 38

H PLUS 2

WESTERN IRAN

Sue Zack was bent over her navigation table, facing the right side of the aircraft. She had pulled the blackout curtain around her and turned up the table lamp, giving her enough light to work by on the darkened flight deck. Her oxygen hose kept getting in the way whenever she moved and she kept pushing it aside. "Pilot, navigator"—she always tried to maintain proper intercom discipline—"problems."

"Go ahead," Kowalski acknowledged. Because they were wearing oxygen masks they could hear each other breathe when they keyed the intercom to talk.

"We haven't got the winds to drop the Rangers as planned. They're out of the north but not strong enough. If we were higher, maybe thirty-four thou instead of twenty-eight . . ."

"Hank," Kowalski said. "You on?" A grunt confirmed that the loadmaster was on headset. "Send Captain Trimler and Sergeant Baulck up to the flight deck."

"Be a few minutes, they have to get out of their gear."

A few minutes later they were bent over Zack's shoulder, listening to her explain how the winds they were counting on to carry the parachutists into the drop zone weren't strong enough. "How close do we have to get for you to make it?"

Trimler studied the map, trying to calculate the wind effect, time and distance. Baulck was much faster. "Fifty miles due north," he told her. "We can stay airborne for about an hour at this altitude, and our chute has a forward speed of twenty-five knots. But we got to clear some high mountains and the wind will drop off as we descend." He looked at the free air-temperature gauge above Zack's head. "Is that the outside temperature?"

She glanced up at the gauge. "Yeah, thirty-five below zero. That's centigrade, Sarge."

The navigator handed Trimler an extra headset and explained the situation to Kowalski. The pilot thought for a few moments, trying to decide what to do. As aircraft commander, the decision was hers. "Bob, we can get you in position for a drop but we would have to drop off this airliner we're piggybacking on. That means the Iranian air defense radar might find us. All bets are off then."

"Right now," Trimler said, "it's no drop. We're just too far away."

Kowalski keyed the radio, calling the AWACS. "Delray, Scamp. Any more trade?" She hoped the controller was smart enough to figure out that she was asking for an update on the Iranian air defense.

"Negative trade at this time." The voice sounded puzzled.

She took in a deep breath and committed them. "Say threat." It was a different radio call and anyone monitoring their frequency would probably catch it, at least a sure clue that something unusual was going on.

The pause from the AWACS seemed an hour long. "Negative threat at this time."

"I hope to hell that means the Iranians are all asleep," the pilot told them. "We'll drop you fifty miles north of Kermanshah. Sue, figure out a point where we can drop off this Fokker and turn west to the release point. After the drop, we'll head due west for the border. We'll drop down onto the deck and fly a low level sneak out through Iraq. Hell, Iraq's air defense is probably no better than the Iranians. And if the Iranians do detect us, they'll think we're Iraqis running for home."

"Roger," Zack said, working over her chart. "Loadmaster, ten minute warning." Then: "Turn point in one minute."

"Hank," Kowalski said, "make sure everyone is on oxygen so I can depressurize the aircraft."

Zack continued to work and they could feel the Rangers shifting around in the rear of the Hercules as they prepared to jump. "Pilot, Loadmaster. Cleared to depressurize."

"Depressurizing now," Kowalski announced. "Hank, watch 'em for any signs of hypoxia." She knew that at twenty-eight thousand feet a person could get groggy or even pass out from oxygen starvation. The flight engineer, Staff Sergeant Marcia MacIntrye, reached up and hit the dump switch on the overhead control panel.

"Turn right to a heading of two-three-zero . . . now," Zack said. Kowalski swung the C-130 onto the new heading and watched the Iranian airliner they had been depending on to cover them disappear into the night. She maintained the same speed and altitude as the airliner, hoping to confuse any radar that might be painting them.

"Loadmaster, navigator. Six minute warning."

"Rog," Petrovich answered, "they're ready. They even look relieved."

"That's the Airborne," Kowalski said. "They teach 'em in jump school to hate landing in an aircraft, too dangerous. Okay, we're depressurized. Cleared to raise the door and lower the ramp." The intercom was silent as they headed for the release point.

"Hank," the pilot said, "tell Sergeant Baulck that we've got a lock on the tacan beacon. It looks good, bearing one hundred-eighty degrees at fifty miles. And wish him good luck." She slowed the aircraft to 130 knots, their drop airspeed.

"Baulck says he's receiving the beacon on his set and thanks," Petrovich told her.

"One minute warning," Zack said. They waited. "Thirty seconds." Then it came. "Ready, ready, ready, Green Light."

At the rear of the aircraft Sergeant Andy Baulck simply walked off the end of the ramp into the night, and twenty-four men shuffled out after him in a long line, one second apart. The last one out was Kamigami, who turned and gave a thumbs up sign as he stepped off the ramp.

EASTERN TURKEY

The return on the green radar scope that marked the progress of Scamp One-One and the Iranian airliner had mesmerized the controllers aboard the AWACS. The tactical director, Lieutenant Colonel Leon Nelson, who commanded the mission crew in the rear of the E-3C, tried to maintain a more detached attitude and attend to other duties. But when the intercom panel at his multiple purpose console shorted out, he bumped a master sergeant out of his seat. He wanted to stay with the action while a technician repaired his panel.

The sergeant stood behind the heavy set black man who was now occupying his seat. He had learned the hard way that Nelson was a no-nonsense type who didn't like long discussions. The sergeant plugged his headset into a long extension cord that led to another intercom station, equally drawn to the radar scope.

"Target separation," a controller reported. "Scamp One-One appears to be moving away from the target aircraft and turning southwest." The men were careful in what they said over the intercom, since all talk was recorded and synchronized with the radar tapes that recorded the mission.

"Scamp One-One must have an emergency of some kind to be diverting from their planned route," Nelson said. "Stay with it." He was an old F-4 driver out of Tactical Air Command and had ended up in AWACS as TAC phased the aging fighters out. His flying experience had proved invaluable as an AWACS controller. He thought about the last radio calls from Scamp and called the navigator who monitored the on-board electronic countermeasures equipment. "Any change in the Iranian air defense posture?"

"Negative. Maragheh is still off the air."

The lieutenant colonel called the radio technicians monitoring the Iranian's air defense radio net. Again, the response was negative.

"Colonel Nelson," the controller said. "Scamp One-One has slowed to one hundred-thirty knots and is now heading due west, directly towards Iraq. Oh, looks like Scamp is descending and picking up speed."

Nelson hit the conference switch on his intercom panel. "All stations, listen up. Scamp will penetrate Iraqi airspace on the heading they're flying. I want complete coverage of both the Iraqi and Iranian air defense net." He toggled the conference switch to "off." "Oh, lord, you are in trouble." He knew the Iraqis were awake.

WESTERN IRAN

The snap and sharp jerk of the parachute canopy opening was reassuring. The oxygen mask Trimler was wearing had twisted slightly in the C-130's wash and he had to straighten it out before he could check his canopy. The heavy gloves he was wearing to protect him from the cold caused him to fumble for a moment. The canopy was good. Then he checked his oxygen connection. Good. He could see the two small position lights on the top of Baulck's canopy, green on the right, red on the left, to his front left and below him. He grabbed the riser extensions that allowed him to maneuver and still keep his hands and arms below his heart. Circulation was going to be critical in the cold air. It looked like he was pulling on puppet strings hanging down from above him as he moved into formation with Baulck, who would lead and navigate the descent. Trimler pulled on his risers, braking and maneuvering until he was lined up above and behind Baulck.

"Radio check," Baulck radioed. Each Ranger had a MX-360 radio strapped to his left shoulder.

Again, Trimler fumbled as he groped for the switch. He wasn't about to risk taking a glove off and dropping it. Trimler checked in with his number in the team. "Romeo One's okay." There was no answer for Romeo Two. "Romeo Three, radio check," Trimler barked. "Have you got Lieutenant Jamison in sight?" The captain reprimanded himself for the breech in radio discipline. He should have never used Jamison's name.

"Romeo Three's okay. Negative sighting on Romeo Two." There was nothing wrong with Romeo Three's radio discipline. The radio checks continued as each man reported in . . .

Since Kamigami was the last man out, he was highest in the stream. He could see a long line of lights stretched out in front and below him, a lighted path descending toward the ground. Baulck curved to the left and the string obediently followed in a synchronized routine. Further below, he could see a broken cloud deck lighted by a quarter-moon lacing the sky. He felt like an eagle soaring through the sky. Off to the right and below he caught a glimpse of two lights. The missing Jamison. He pulled on his risers, braking and slowing his rate of descent. The string snaked away.

"Romeo Two-Five's got Two in sight." Everyone recognized his voice.

"Keep him in sight," Trimler ordered over the radio.

"Probably a bad oxygen connection," Kamigami told them.

The sergeant major had identified the problem. The opening shock of Jamison's parachute had popped the connection between his oxygen hose and the twin green airox bottles he carried. Before he could reconnect the hose he had become hypoxic, starved for oxygen. Jamison was not unconscious but groggy and irrational. He wanted to go to sleep, was drifting.

"He'll come around when we get lower," Kamigami radioed. "I'll bring him back in when he's conscious."

"We'll be goin' through this cloud deck in a few minutes," Baulck told the team. "Maintain a heading of one-six-five degrees until you break out. Fifty percent brakes while you're in the clouds."

"We'll lose Romeo Two in the clouds," Kamigami said. "Bearing and distance to the DZ?" He pulled out his compass but dropped it when he tried to flip its cover open. He fumbled with the cord that tied the compass to his pocket and finally got it open. There was enough moonlight for him to read the luminous dial.

"Bearing one-seven-five degrees, forty-two miles." Baulck's tacan receiver was locked on and giving good readings.

Kamigami made his decision. "I'll stay with Two and rejoin you on the ground. He shouldn't drift too far off course."

"We'll wait as long as we can," Trimler told him. "If we're gone, head for the airfield. Maintain radio contact."

"Entering clouds now," Baulck radioed.

Kamigami headed for Jamison. He could see the string of canopy lights below him disappear one by one into the cloud deck. Some eagle, he thought, if I get lost.

EASTERN TURKEY

"Colonel Nelson," a radio technician called over the AWACS intercom, "the Iraqi air defense net is tracking Scamp One-One and have alerted two SAM sites. No traffic on the fighter loop yet, just surface-to-air missiles."

"I've got search-radar activity inside Iraq," the navigator monitoring the electronic warfare equipment reported.

"Any activity inside Iran?" Nelson asked. All replies were negative. The lieutenant colonel watched the radar blip that was Scamp One-One move toward the Iraqi border. "You ain't gonna live long inside Iraq," he thought. "Sarge," he barked at the man standing behind him, "bring up an overlay of the Iran-Iraq border on the scope." The sergeant leaned around Nelson and pounded a command on the keyboard in front of him. A lighted map of the border etched itself on the screen. Nelson checked the digital readout showing Scamp's groundspeed. "Fourteen miles to go, three minutes to live . . ."

"The heavies are going to have my ass for this if I'm screwing up whatever they've got planned." Nelson keyed the radio. "Scamp One-One, Delray Five-One." He was acting like a controller. "We have trade for you."

"Roger, Delray." It was Kowalski's voice and he could hear the doubt.

"Please trust me," he muttered before transmitting. "Rog, Scamp, come right to a new heading of zero-three-zero. Target is on your nose at thirty miles." He was giving the C-130 vectors to fly northeast along the border just inside Iran. His tension eased a notch when he saw the blip turn toward the northeast less than a mile from the border.

"Delray, Scamp. Authenticate alpha lima."

Good girl, Nelson thought, follow the vectors first, then verify. He checked the current authentication table and found the proper two-letter response to the letters A and L.

"Authentication is poppa tango. Your target is maneuvering, expect a new heading in four minutes." He watched the blip fly along the border. "Figure it out," he muttered, hoping the C-130 crew would see he was keeping them out of Iraq. He hit the conference switch on his intercom. "Everyone listen up. I'm betting the Iraqis will treat Scamp as an Iranian testing their air defense net and won't engage them *unless* there's a border penetration. I plan on keeping Scamp just inside Iran. For God's sake, don't forget to monitor the Iranians for some sort of reaction. With luck we should get Scamp out."

"Colonel Nelson"—it was the radio technician—"the Iraqis are scrambling interceptors."

WESTERN IRAN

The voice was loud and insistent as it penetrated the fog swirling around in Jamison's head. *"Jamison, do you read me?"* Something about the voice keyed a reaction, but the urge to doze was stronger. *"Jamison, you black bastard, talk to me."* Anger at last gusted through the lieutenant and blew his fog away. Fully conscious now, he realized he was hanging in his parachute harness and drifting. And someone was yelling stuff at him.

"Sergeant Major?"

"Welcome to Iran, Lieutenant. You had me worried. Sorry about the name-calling but I had to get your attention."

Jamison had never heard Kamigami apologize for anything. Something had to be very wrong. "I'm sorry, my oxygen hose came loose. My face got all hot and I couldn't think . . . where are you?" He twisted around looking for Kamigami.

"Above and behind you. Hit your brakes and fall in behind me."
Jamison did, and his fear gave way to relief when the sergeant
descended past him on the right and he heard Kamigami check in
with the team on the radio. "I've got Romeo Two, say your position."

"North of target." It was Baulck. "Thirty-three miles out."

"Sergeant Major, are we okay?" Jamison tried to control his
voice.

"Just lost. Keep looking for the team and follow me."

Just lost . . . great.

CHAPTER 39

H PLUS 3

NORTHWESTERN IRAN

"Border in two minutes." The relief in Sue Zack's voice was felt by everyone on the C-130's flight deck. "I don't like this, skimming along just inside Iran."

"When they authenticated," Kowalski told her, "I figured they had a good reason. What the hell, worked out, didn't it?"

The UHF radio crackled, "Scamp, Delray. Turn left to three-zero-zero." Kowalski turned the Hercules onto the new heading to the northwest. "Scamp go gate—*Now.*" The crew could hear the urgency in the controller's voice.

"What the hell is gate?" Brenda Iverson, the copilot grumbled.

"Afterburners." Kowalski shook her head. "Which we ain't got." She shoved the throttles full forward and pushed on the yoke, nosing the plane over and picking up speed as the Hercules headed down. "But we got gravity. How much lower can we go?" she asked.

"Another three hundred feet," Zack replied. "If you come right five degrees, we'll be going down a river valley and you can descend a little lower." Their airspeed was touching 275 knots, and the moonlight was giving them enough light to make out the mountain valley they were in.

"Scamp," the AWACS radioed, "come right five degrees."

"At least we're all playing from the same sheet," Kowalski said. "Border in one minute," from Zack.

EASTERN TURKEY

Sweat was trickling down Leon Nelson's face but his voice was still under control. The master sergeant was standing behind him, impressed with the way he had guided Scamp One-One along the border, changing headings to take advantage of terrain-masking and to keep the C-130 as low as possible in the mountains.

Both men watched the two blips on the radar scope that were Iraqi MiG-23s converging on the C-130. "Damn it, I didn't think they'd go after Scamp as long as there was no border violation," Nelson said over the intercom, not caring if it was recorded. "Well, we've got another card to play. I hope you muthas are listening . . ."

He flipped the toggle switch that allowed him to transmit over Guard, the international frequency reserved for emergencies: "Two fast-moving Iraqi aircraft heading zero-three-five degrees. You are approaching Turkish airspace and will be engaged if you cross the border. Repeat, you will be engaged if you cross the border."

"The bluff's not working, Colonel," the master sergeant said. His eyes did not move from the radar scope. "They're not breaking off the attack."

Nelson slammed his fist down on the console as he watched the two fighters bear down on the C-130 and hit the intercom switch calling the electronic warfare officer. "Jam the shit out of everything those fighters got. Make 'em go blind and deaf."

"Sir," the officer replied, "I'm not allowed to use that capability in peacetime. It's guarded against compromise and if we use it—"

"DO IT."

Every radio frequency Nelson was monitoring exploded in a rasping, screeching clash of sound. With one motion Nelson jerked his headset off and hit the toggle switches that turned his monitoring channels off. His ears hurt. The radar scope in front of him flashed as the AWACS jammed itself as well as every other radar and radio within a hundred miles. Then it stopped.

"My God," Nelson mumbled. The scope in front of him came back to life. The two blips had broken off to the right and were now headed to the southwest, back into Iraq and away from the C-130.

"Well, them fuckers *do* bluff," Nelson said as he leaned back into the seat. "Scamp One-One," he transmitted over the normal frequency, "you are cleared to climb and RTB at this time. We have no more trade for you."

The reply was as cool as his transmission. "Thanks, Delray. I'll be buying the bar."

"Wouldn't miss it." Nelson knew the brass would not like the last transmissions when they reviewed the tapes—very unprofessional—but he didn't give a damn.

WESTERN IRAN

The Rangers had been hanging in their harnesses for over an hour and were numb from the cold. Some were slapping their hands or waving their arms to keep warm as they descended. "Passing over the tacan now," Baulck radioed, still a thousand feet above the ground and headed to the south. When he judged the entire string to have passed over the beacon he would turn back to the north and start a spiraling descent onto the drop zone. "Heads up, we're going in," he warned, and arced gracefully back to the north. He immediately saw three blinks of a flashlight on the ground. "Land on those lights or follow me." It was his last radio transmission.

The string of position lights on the canopies traced a path through the night sky as the Rangers spiraled down. The men started to deploy their rucksacks and weapons containers, letting them fall away on the lowering line to dangle fifteen feet below them. The heavy rucksacks would hit the ground first and the Rangers would touch down a hundred pounds lighter.

Bill Carroll watched the silent shadows spin down out of the sky. He flashed his light again, making sure the Rangers would home on him, away from the two waiting trucks and the portable tacan station. He jumped when he heard a voice directly above him. "It's okay, we don't need the light." A figure dropped down beside him, pulling on the riser extensions and stalling his chute just before he touched down, still standing. It was Trimler, and his cold feet protested when they took the landing shock. Grunts and groans echoed over the DZ as more Rangers landed.

For a moment Carroll did not move. The sight of the parachutists dropping out of the sky and now distinct American accents sent a warm feeling through him. The POWs had not been abandoned—they were not political pawns being cynically exchanged on some geopolitical chess board by old men sitting in comfortable leather chairs, safe in some government office. He pocketed his flashlight and walked over to the American who was busy shaking off his harness and bundling up his parachute. "Sunset Gorge," Trimler challenged, crouching and leveling his pistol at Carroll.

Zakia had passed the challenge and response code to Carroll. "Sweet Water," he responded.

Trimler holstered his weapon. "You Carroll?"

"I'm Carroll."

"I'm Bob Trimler. Jack and Thunder send their greetings. They told me to tell you that they're coming after your sweet young ass and what the hell are you doing here anyway?" It was better confirmation than any code word.

"Form on me," Trimler called out, his voice carrying over the open field. The Rangers quickly broke out their weapons, shouldered their rucksacks, gathered up their parachutes and hurried toward Trimler.

"Have you got everyone?" Carroll asked.

"Negative. We lost two on the drop." He keyed the radio on his shoulder. "Romeo Two-Five, you up?" There was no reply. He explained the situation to Carroll. "How long can we wait here?"

"When do you want to be in position at the prison?"

"We hit it at first light, just before sunrise, at six twenty-five local time."

"We're ten miles northwest of the prison so figure an hour to move into position. It's almost twenty-three hundred now. We can wait six and a half hours at the most. Over there." Carroll pointed to a clump of low farm buildings they could hide in—"It's empty."

Trimler gave his orders and the Rangers headed toward the Kurdish farmstead Carroll had pointed out. Four Rangers ran ahead to scout the building and make sure it was secure while another four stayed behind and swept the field to make sure no equipment was left behind and erase every sign that trucks or people had been in the field. Carroll jumped in the lead truck next to Zakia and told the driver to follow the Rangers.

A Ranger directed the trucks to park next to a shed and was speechless when he saw Zakia get out. He finally found his voice, "Ma'am, why don't you go inside with Captain Trimler." They followed his directions and entered the low mud-brick house, where Carroll introduced Zakia and the man who was her contact.

"We had planned to use the phone here," Zakia said.

"A place like this has a phone?" Trimler asked.

"We installed it to send an arrival message," Zakia told him. She spoke to the man in a language Trimler did not understand. He opened a cabinet where the phone was hidden and dialed. Zakia sent up a torrent of words in a high-pitched, whiny tone while the man spoke. Carroll motioned for Trimler to remain silent until they had finished.

"What the hell . . . ?" The Captain was bewildered.

"He was calling about his father," Carroll said. "Seems the old gent is in failing health but has just taken a turn for the better. He still needs two more days before he's out of bed. Actually, it's a code they set up with their radio operator. You arrived and are two men short. He'll send out the arrival message. They use the phone system to keep in contact. Zakia was making background noises in case anybody was listening."

"Who the hell are they?"

"Don't ask," Carroll said. "I don't know and they won't tell you."

Trimler shook his head and went outside. He checked the security of the compound and ordered half the men to sack out and the other half to stay on alert. "Wade, Baulck, set up a listening post a hundred meters down the road." He pointed to the rut that led to the farmstead, and the two men moved quickly out and disappeared into the night.

The captain checked the disposition of his men again, not surprised to find half of them asleep. He had heard how the strain of actual operations caused men to fall asleep the moment the tension was broken. Good, he thought, I want 'em fresh. He unstrapped the radio from his shoulder and leaned against the low wall that surrounded most of the compound. "Romeo Two-Five, you up?" he radioed. No answer. For a moment he thought maybe he heard a low crackling, but couldn't be sure . . .

"Any idea where we are?" Jamison asked.

Kamigami didn't answer and held the whisper mike to his left ear. He thought he heard something and spoke into the radio. No answer. He set the radio down and pulled out a map and flashlight, hunched down to shield the light and studied the map. The last briefing they had received before mounting the C-130 had pinpointed the drop zone ten miles northwest of Kermanshah. But he didn't know where he and Jamison had landed. He had seen some farm buildings south of them and they had passed over a dirt road before they landed in a field. He stood up and peered into the night, his six feet four inches working to his advantage. When he adjusted his night vision goggles he could make out a low hill the other side of the dirt road.

"We go there." He pointed to the hill, hoping they could get their bearings on top . . . otherwise they would have to wait for first light. When in doubt, he thought, take the high ground.

EASTERN TURKEY

Leon Nelson glanced at his watch, 1948Z, and ran another station check. Each position on the AWACS reported no unusual activity inside Iran or Iraq. The Iraq air defense posture had reverted to normal after the two MiGs that had almost intercepted Scamp had landed. The Iranians had never stirred. They had another hour on station and no aircraft to control. It was going to be an unproductive hour boring holes in the sky.

He relaxed into his seat and tried to rest but his mind would not let it go. He kept thinking about the briefing he and his controllers had received the day before on Operation WARLORD. They had only been briefed on *their* role in the mission and not shown the specific objective. His private theories about WARLORD were confirmed when the C-130 broke off its planned profile and flew within sixty miles of Kermanshah. The cargo plane had slowed to 130 knots before it started its descent to low level. To the lieutenant colonel's way of thinking, there could only be one reason for that— it was an airdrop and it had something to do with the POWs at Kermanshah. But why had the C-130 headed toward Iraq? They should have flown a low-level right back to Turkey. There were too many unanswered questions to let Nelson relax.

"This is what I get paid for," he mumbled before calling the pilot. "Let's head for home plate now," he ordered. Every instinct he had was shouting that he was needed at Incirlik.

CHAPTER 40

H PLUS 4

MARAGHEH, IRAN

The four men in the radar shack were gathered around the TV, engrossed in the program they were watching. Because they were sitting on a mountain top, they had excellent reception and could pick up Turkish and Iraqi channels. Both of those countries offered much better viewing than the Ayatollahs allowed in Iran. It was the only benefit of pulling duty at the radar site.

The radar operator sighed when the channel went off the air. It was almost midnight and he had more than twelve hours to go before he was replaced. He had made a mental promise never to cross the captain in the control center again and returned to the main console. "It's cooled off by now," he muttered, and went through the start-up routine, bringing the radar back on line. His training had been thorough and he wanted to do a good job, but other things kept getting in the way. He didn't even contemplate a communications check that might disturb the captain and felt justified when his sector swept clean. There were no targets over eastern Turkey or Iraq.

Satisfied, he stood up and headed for a bunk at the rear of the room to get some sleep with the other men. He left the radar set on.

INCIRLIK AIR BASE, TURKEY

"Captain Kowalski, let me make this perfectly clear," Mado was pacing the floor in the Intelligence section of the command post, "by deviating from your planned flight path you put this entire mission at risk." Stansell listened to the general work over the captain. He was glad Thunder had awakened him when the debrief started. "If the Iranians detected you," Mado continued, "they are going to start asking questions and all the answers point to Kermanshah—"

"Sir," Stansell cut in, "why don't we let Captain Bryant complete the debrief? Dewa made a checklist of items to go over and it's all in the intelligence appendix of the OPORD." He had said the right words . . . Mado considered the operations order to be etched in stone.

Thunder gave a silent thanks that Stansell was there and that the plan was a good well-thought-out document—thanks to Stansell— and Mado in calmer moments. Mado nodded and continued to pace while Thunder started through the questions. He was interrupted by a knock on the door. Brenda Iverson, Kowalski's copilot, was closest and opened it. A lieutenant colonel in a flight suit was standing there with three other men behind him.

"We're Delray Five-One," he announced and came into the room. "I think you want to look at our mission results."

"It could have waited," Mado said. "You were to remain on-station until twenty-one hundred Zulu."

Nelson, not the least intimidated by Mado, said, "But when Scamp One-One deviated from the briefed mission profile I decided that you needed the results more than us boring holes in the sky turning JP-4 into noise." He looked around the room, picking Kowalski out. "You the aircraft commander?" She nodded. "It was a close one. The Iraqis almost nailed you." Without waiting he went over the mission from their perspective, pointing out how the Iranian air defense net had been totally passive and the Iraqi's alive and well. "One question, Captain," he concluded, "why did you head for Iraq instead of flying a low-level back through Iran to Turkey? Iranian air defense is like a sieve."

"I thought for sure the Iranians would pick us up when we dropped off the airliner and wanted them to think I was an Iraqi heading for home. I figured we could sneak through Iraq and they wouldn't catch us. A calculated risk."

"A bad decision," Mado said. "Now we've got Romeo Team on the ground and—"

"I acted on the best information I had at the time," Kowalski said.

"Excuse me, sir." It was Stansell. "I thought that was the idea . . . Getting Romeo Team on the ground. Maybe it didn't happen exactly like we planned, but we met the objective—"

"Colonel, our plan is coming apart," Mado said. "We've got to advise the Command Center and have them reconsider our situation . . ."

Gregory had been sitting at the back of the room taking it all in. "General, we need to talk. In private." Mado stared at the army lieutenant colonel, surprised by the steel he heard in the man's voice. He nodded and walked out of the room and into a deserted office. "Sir," Gregory began, "I'm your ground commander and I made a promise to my men. I told them I'd get them out. And, sir, *I'm going to do that.* Please don't misunderstand me on this. If you get in the way, or don't do everything you can, I'll tell the world that you're a fucking idiot and then I'll break your neck—personally." The general couldn't take his eyes off Gregory's huge hands. The lieutenant colonel turned and walked away, back to his Rangers.

Mado's breathing was ragged as he struggled to regain his composure. Finally he walked back into Intelligence. "The question before us is"—his voice strained but calm—"has the mission been compromised to the point we cannot continue? Colonel Gregory recommends we launch as planned. Your recommendations."

"Go as planned," Stansell said. Goddamn, he thought, we've been through this before. He's starting to hedge again. What does it take to get the man to make a decision?

"Go," Thunder said.

"As planned," Kowalski said. It was fairly obvious that Mado was big on following *plans.*

"If you're worried about the Iranians," Nelson said, "there's no indication they're awake. But the Iraqis probably know something is going down. No way they'll tell the Iranians, though."

Mado jerked his head and returned to the command post. They all followed him into the big room. The command post's Emergency Action Controller handed him a message. "From the Pentagon's command center," she told him. "The team is on the ground and have established contact."

Again, the general studied the status boards in front of him . . . "Launch as planned . . ."

They could barely hear it.

"What now?" Thunder asked.

Stansell said, "Launch in three hours."

"For sure?" Kowalski asked. They were all studying Mado.

"That's a definite maybe," Stansell told them, face tight.

CHAPTER 41

H PLUS 5

WESTERN IRAN

The hill Kamigami was moving toward was further away than Jamison had estimated. The big sergeant major maintained a steady dogtrot and the young lieutenant was having a hard time keeping up. He wanted to drop some of his equipment and lighten his load but Kamigami had told him to carry it all and keep moving. Jamison was thankful when they moved up a shallow ravine leading to the crest of the hill and their pace eased. Suddenly Kamigami stopped and listened. "Goats." His voice was soft and quiet. Jamison listened but couldn't hear a thing.

The sergeant looked around him and pointed to a shadow on the side of the ravine. It was a little more than a crack or animal burrow. Kamigami dropped his equipment and started to sort it out, pushing what he didn't want into the hole. Jamison did likewise and was about to shove his gas mask in after his parachute when Kamigami grabbed it and handed it back. When they were finished Jamison threw some loose dirt and stones over the equipment while Kamigami carried a big rock up from the dry steam bed and dropped it over the opening.

With their equipment sorted out they made the crest of the hill in a few minutes. It was barren, with little vegetation and no rocks to hide in. The two men flopped down on their stomachs for a break.

"Over there, to the east," Kamigami said. They could see a glow of lights beyond another set of hills that marked a large town. "Got to be Kermanshah." He spread his map and set his compass on it, starting to get his bearings.

"I can hear the goats now," Jamison whispered.

"Goatherder's around somewhere."

Jamison touched the sergeant's shoulder and pointed to the headlights of a car moving in the night. "That must be a highway running east to west. I'd guess we're two to three miles north of it."

"Closer to five. Okay, I've got our position. We're ten miles due west of Kermanshah. On this hill." He pointed it out on the map, carefully shielding his light. "About fifteen miles from the DZ. We head there." He pointed to the next set of hills to the east of them, toward the glow and Kermanshah.

"Should we try to make radio contact?"

"No, the range is too great and the goatherder might hear us." Kamigami shoved his map and compass in a pocket and moved out with a speed that surprised Jamison. The big man disappeared in the dark. Jamison hurried after him, stumbling over the rough terrain. A hand reached out and steadied him. "Tanks make less noise," Kamigami said. "Keep up."

CHAPTER 42

H PLUS 6

KERMANSHAH, IRAN

The key grated in the lock and the guard had to twist it back and forth to slide the bolt back. It gave Mary time to sit at attention and pull the canvas bag over her head. The guard turned the light on and closed the door behind him.

"Please take the bag off." The man was speaking in English and his voice was routine, matter of fact. Mary did. The man was holding a bowl. "Please eat." He handed her the bowl and she took three quick spoonfuls of the stew-like concoction before she slowed.

"Aren't you the one they call Amini?" He nodded. "Can I see Doctor Landis? I'm very worried about him."

"We must talk first." He cracked the door and scanned the corridor, listening for the sound of any activity in the darkened building. It was 1:30 in the morning. "You are being moved this morning with half the men. You're being flown to Tehran, where, I'm sure, your treatment will be better." Mary was astonished by the guard's English. "You'll be turned over to another political party. Should any of your new captors ask you, please do not tell them about me or any better treatment you've received. You must make it sound all bad or I will be compromised. That means a firing squad or a noose." She could hear traces of an American accent.

"You're the friend we've had here," Mary said. She wanted to touch him.

274

He nodded his head and looked out the door again while she finished eating. He turned out the cell light and motioned for her to follow him to Landis' cell. He swung the door back and let her in.

Mary saw the naked man lying on the floor, grabbed his blanket and covered him. "Get the blanket from my cell," she said.

"I can't do that."

"Then help me get him on his bunk." They moved him and Mary was trying to straighten him out.

"Don't," Landis said weakly.

"Get some water," Mary said. The guard took the empty bowl and left.

"No water," Landis told her. She could barely hear his voice.

"Then I'll clean you up. Hold on, doc, we're getting moved today. We'll get you to a hospital."

"Better hurry . . . internal bleeding . . . Mokhtari stomped the hell out of me . . ."

The guard was back with the bowl now, filled with water. "I need a washrag," Mary said. The guard handed her a handkerchief. "Get him some clothes, we can't move him like this."

"He's not going," the guard told her.

"Then neither am I."

CHAPTER 43

H PLUS 7

INCIRLIK AIR BASE, TURKEY

On the ramp at Incirlik the last of the Rangers loaded the C-130s and the wail of a cranking jet engine could be heard above the ear-splitting roar of ground power units that supplied electrical power and bleed air to the planes. Thunder was walking in from the AC-130 gunship when the AWACS taxied out, leading the procession of twenty-two aircraft that made up Task Force Alpha. The captain found Stansell and Mado inside the hangar talking to Gregory. "All systems are go on the gunship," he reported. "They've got an FM radio for contacting the Rangers on the ground and a satellite-communications system on board. They've already established contact with the Pentagon's command center."

Mado nodded and headed for the gunship that was to serve as his command-and-control aircraft. Thunder looked at Stansell and Gregory, snapped a salute and followed the general. Two KC-135 tankers taxied past. They would follow the AWACS into a holding pattern near the border and refuel the F-111s and F-15s. If needed, they could also refuel the AWACS. The number-three prop on the gunship started to turn. "Time to load," Stansell told Gregory. The two men walked out of the hangar and headed for Duck Mallard's C-130. Drunkin Dunkin was waiting for them by the crew-entrance door wearing his battered baseball cap.

Stansell took one last look around and climbed onto the flight deck. Mallard greeted him and the flight engineer handed him a headset. "Starting three." Mallard hit the start button and moved the engine-condition lever for number-three to ground start. The big four-bladed prop started to turn and then spun down. "Looks like a sheared starter-shaft," Mallard said. The flight engineer confirmed the problem.

"Radio Kowalski to start engines while we load her plane," Stansell ordered. The Hercules exploded into furious activity. Stansell could hear Thunder's voice on the UHF radio acknowledging the change in aircraft and hoped he could keep Mado calmed down. The Rangers tore the tie-down chains off the three jeeps and two motorcycles that were on board and drove them down the ramp. Everyone gathered up their equipment and ran for Kowalski's C-130. Stansell took one last look around and hurried after them.

The two F-15 crew chiefs were waiting in the hangar until it was their turn to start engines in thirty minutes. They counted the six C-130s that followed the AC-130 as they taxied out for takeoff. "What the hell's wrong with Mallard's Herky Bird?" Ray Byers asked.

"Line chief says it's a sheared starter shaft," Timmy Wehr answered.

"Shee-it, why don't they fix it?"

"Too busy, I guess, not enough time," Timmy said.

"Keerap, I started out in C-130s. It's no big deal. Let's you and me do it." Byers ran for his toolbox while Wehr pushed a maintenance stand up against the engine. A van drove up and the line chief asked them what they were doing. "Get a starter, Chief," Byers bawled. The sergeant yelled that he'd be back in ten minutes and sped off, heading for supply.

After having her aircraft taken over by Mallard a dejected Kowalski and her crew were walking into the hangar when they saw Byers and Wehr working on the engine. Staff Sergeant Marcia MacIntyre, Kowalski's flight engineer, ran up the steps of the maintenance stand to help them. "Captain," she yelled at Kowalski, "it's just a sheared starter shift. We can fix it in twenty minutes once we get a new starter."

"Sorry," Byers told them as he and Wehr clambered down the stand, "time for us to launch. We'll finish this as soon as we get our jets in the air."

"Thanks a bunch."

CHAPTER 44

H PLUS 8

WESTERN IRAN

The bulky shadow in front of the lieutenant disappeared again. The two men had reached the next set of hills and were moving along the military crest, a line about two-thirds of the way up the hill and parallel to the actual ridge. Jamison hurried, trying to match the constant and relentless pace Kamigami was setting. It had been easier to follow him over the rough terrain when the moon was up, but now the lieutenant found himself stumbling and panting for breath in the darkness. He was seriously wondering if the sergeant major was human.

Jamison panicked and started to run when he didn't see the sergeant. The fear of being separated drove him into the darkness, his foot slipped and he fell against the hillside, slipping and rolling once before he came to a stop. His equipment clattered against the rocks, and he was sure the noise carried at least a mile. He heaved himself onto his feet and tugged at his LBE webbing that held much of his gear, pulling it back in place. Jamison jumped when his K-Pot, the Army Kevlar helmet, appeared in front of his face. Kamigami was holding it for him. He hadn't realized he had dropped it or heard the sergeant pick it up.

"You okay, Lieutenant?" Kamigami could sense the panic building in the young man. He had seen it before. "Got all your equipment? We gotta keep moving." He kept up a reassuring flow of words. "I figure we've come over halfway, got another seven klicks to go."

Seven kilometers, the lieutenant calculated—four and a half miles. They were making good time and still had almost three hours of darkness to reach their objective. "My radio. I dropped my radio." The two men went to their knees and felt around in the darkness. Jamison pulled out his flashlight but before he could use it a vise-like grip was on his arm.

"No lights. Not after all that noise." By now Kamigami was almost certain the lieutenant was a basket case. The young officer must not have secured his radio when he moved it from the shoulder strap of his LBE to his web belt after they landed. "Gotta move. Forget the radio. It's going to get slower the closer we get to the objective." He was going to have to explain everything.

"Should we do a radio check?" Jamison asked, glad they still had Kamigami's radio.

"No. We're still out of range. Just *move.*"

INCIRLIK AIR BASE, TURKEY

"Mornin', Captain. Nice day for a flight." Byers' F-15 was parked on the ramp next to Jack Locke's E model and he actually threw Locke a salute when he saw the captain. The sergeant wasn't big on military courtesy. "You gonna bring that piece of shit back in one piece?" He gestured at the new F-15E, enjoying the chance to rag the pilot.

"Always do, Sarge." Locke had preflighted the jet earlier but he still did another walk around out of habit. The old emotions came back—the empty stomach, the self-doubts, a slight warming of the cheeks. How many times had he been here before? The last few minutes before a mission started he was a man going over Niagara Falls in a barrel.

"Time to do it." It was his WSO, Captain Ambler Furry, who climbed up the crew ladder and settled into the back seat.

Jack followed him up the ladder.

The launch of the fast movers went smoothly with the three F-111s leading the procession out to the runway. Von Drexler led the takeoff and the other two followed at twenty second intervals. Then Snake Houserman led the F-15s onto the active and they took off in pairs with ten second spacing. Jack Locke followed the eight F-15s and took off alone.

The two sergeants stood on the ramp watching Locke's jet reach into the clear night air as an early morning quiet settled over the air base. "Do you think they'll do it?" Wehr asked.

"Get the POWs out?" Byers had heard the rumors and had long ago decided for himself what Task Force Alpha was all about. Some of the POWs were his friends and he badly wanted to help. "They'll do it. Come on, let's get to that Herky Bird."

Sergeant MacIntrye was sitting on the steps of the maintenance stand, the old starter at her feet, talking to Kowalski. She explained how the line chief had not yet returned from supply.

Byers checked his watch. "Over twenty minutes," he grumbled, "Timmy, go see if you can build a fire under some asshole in supply and get us a starter." The younger sergeant disappeared into the hangar to find a phone.

"If you can get it fixed," Kowalski told them, "I'm going to launch. We may only be a backup, but we can be one in the air."

Fifteen minutes later the line chief drove up with Wehr. "Sorry, but you know supply . . ." MacIntyre grabbed the starter and ran up the stairs to the engine.

"Be careful, Mac," Byers called after her, "don't want'a break any fingernails."

"Byers, get your lazy ass up here and do some wrench bending." She gave good as she got.

Byers started to pull himself up the steps of the maintenance stand. "Timmy," he said in a low voice, "I'll help. You go get my scrounge."

"What the hell you need that for?" Wehr asked, puzzled why Byers would want the canvas bag he kept full of small spare parts—nuts, bolts, connectors, gauges, gaskets—parts that he had scrounged up. The bag was highly unauthorized and probably contained over ten thousand dollars worth of parts. It was worth a court-martial for a crew chief or maintenance troop to be caught with a scrounge. But when a crew chief needed to hurry things up and supply was sitting on its dead ass as usual . . .

Twenty-three minutes later they were done and the engine buttoned up. Wehr helped Byers push the stand out of the way as MacIntyre ran aboard the plane for an engine start. "I thought they were a backup and weren't going to launch," Wehr said.

Byers told him, "One thing's for sure, if they go, I go." He picked up his tool box and scrounge bag and ran for the back of the Hercules.

WESTERN IRAN

Trimler roused two men and sent them forward to replace Baulck and Wade at the outpost. "Time for a change out," he told Carroll. Then he went around the compound, replacing the men on alert so they could get some rest and food. When the team settled back down, he propped up his radio on top of the low wall and stared into the night.

"Why don't you do a radio check?" Carroll asked.

"We just listen. They'll call when they're in range. Knowing Kamigami, he's got his position fixed and is moving. I hope the lieutenant is smart enough to listen to him." Trimler sat down at the base of the wall, hoping to get some rest. "Jamison is slightly thick between the ears." Then he reconsidered. "That's not true, he's just green . . . like I was . . ."

"Zakia's been on the phone," Carroll told him. "The town's quiet and the road is open . . . we'll have to move out in two hours. We can't wait any longer."

"I know," Trimler said, accepting the fact that Kamigami would not rejoin them at the DZ. "I can't believe it . . . the way your people use telephones to pass information. That's just asking for a compromise."

"They speak Kirmanji over the phone, not Farsi."

"But what if the phones are tapped?"

Carroll shook his head. "Most Iranians only speak Farsi and wouldn't bother to learn Kirmanji. Too demeaning for them. So the Kurds use it against them."

"Can we trust the Kurds?" Trimler asked.

"Oh yeah, bet on it. Revenge is a lovely thing."

CHAPTER 45

H PLUS 9

EASTERN TURKEY

Spectre 01, of the AC-130 gunship, was turning over the departure point on its second holding orbit. "Hey, Magellan, you ready?" It was Beasely calling his navigator. Mado was not happy with the informality and lack of radio discipline among the AC-130 crew but said nothing.

"Rog, Beezer. We'll hit the departure point right on time if you can fly three-minute legs on this orbit. Ten minutes to departure." The navigator's slight reversion to "professionalism" didn't help offset the anxiety building in the general. He turned and looked at Thunder Bryant, secretly envying his cool and apparent detachment. Thunder was sitting on the edge of the crew-entry well, staying out of the way. He was listening on a headset and making notes on a clipboard. Mado was standing behind the pilot, not able to sit or relax.

As they turned onto the outbound leg Beasely counted the rotating beacons strung out behind him. "General, I count six anti-collision lights in trail. We've got a formation." The six C-130s were stretched out in a line behind Spectre 01.

"Have them check in with their status," Mado said over the intercom.

Before the copilot could comply, Thunder stopped him. "General, we trained to do this maintaining radio silence. If something's wrong, they'll call." Mado did not answer and the copilot did nothing. Beasely rolled out on the outbound leg and started their descent to low level. The six C-130s followed Spectre—chicks in trail.

Now the UHF radio came alive. "Scamp One-One in-bound at this time." It was Kowalski's voice.

"Scamp One-One, this is Delray Five-One," the AWACS answered. "Enter holding at Flight Level two-four-oh"—Nelson had just told Kowalski to orbit at twenty-four thousand feet.

"What the hell is she doing here?" Mado demanded.

"She's backup," Thunder said. "She'll orbit with the AWACS."

"That wasn't what I wanted, order her to RTB."

"She must've misunderstood," Thunder said, trying to soothe the general. "She's not going anywhere. Better we maintain radio silence. We can sort this one out later." The general's right hand clenched and relaxed, clenched and relaxed . . .

The flight deck fell silent as they waited for the next radio transmission from the AWACS that would commit them. The AC-130 turned onto the inbound-leg toward the departure point, still descending. "Sky King, Sky King, this is Delray Five-One with a Romeo Tango message. Do not acknowledge. Repeat, do not acknowledge." It was the transmission from the AWACS they were waiting for. It had been disguised to sound like a normal status report but the Romeo Tango meant the message was for them. The AWACS was reporting the latest status of the Iranian air defense net. "Sierra Hotel Lima. Repeat. Sierra Hotel Lima."

Thunder flipped to his page of code words. "Situation normal, sir."

"Does that mean that the radar at Maragheh is active?"

"Yes, sir."

Mado was silent as he digested this latest information. Had they considered all the factors? Had the threat changed? "It doesn't feel right . . ."

"Why?" This is from the Beezer. "Everything's just like we planned . . ."

"For one, the weather is below mission minimums," Mado shot back.

"Sir, look out the window. It's clear as a bell, well almost." Mado did as the pilot said. Two F-15s flew past on the left and established a racetrack pattern in front of them, easily avoiding the few clouds that were breaking apart. The weather was exactly as the weatherman had forecasted. Mado's whole background and makeup said abort the mission, get back to the safe and predictable routines of the Pentagon. But he knew it wasn't to be, and that for the first time in his career he was actually leading men into combat.

"Departure point in thirty seconds," the navigator broke in. They waited. Then, "Departure point now. Anti-collision light off." The copilot turned the rotating beacon off, the signal to the next C-130 in trail that they were at the departure point. One by one, the C-130s turned off their flashing anti-collision beacons as they overflew the point and turned toward the southeast, heading into Iran.

"Departure point now," Drunkin Dunkin announced over the intercom, business as usual. His head was buried in the radar scope with his mangy yellow baseball cap on backward. "New heading one-two-six degrees." Without looking, his right hand reached up and bounced off the button starting the elapsed time on the clock, and his left hand triggered the stop watch hanging from his neck. For Drunkin Dunkin, if he did his job then Duck Mallard would get him safely home.

"Anti-collision light off," Mallard said. "Loadmaster, double-check all lights out, we're running dark now. How long to penetration, Dunk?"

"Six minutes. I've got a radar contact on Spectre. We're exactly two miles in trail."

"Well, Colonel," Mallard said, "this is it. I wonder how Mado is doing . . ."

"He's carrying a lot of new responsibility," Stansell said. He looked around the flight deck. He could make out the pilots' faces in the muted reflection of the red instrument lights. Sweat glistened on the dark face of the copilot, Don Larson. Mallard seemed calm as he hand-flew the plane, not relying on the auto-pilot at low level. Stansell had heard a slight edge in his voice but didn't worry about it. Duck Mallard had his emotions under control. *I hope everyone else is as cool,* Stansell thought. *Myself included.*

WESTERN IRAN

The engines of the two trucks were idling smoothly as the last of the Rangers loaded. Bill Carroll was sitting on the runningboard of the lead truck waiting for Zakia. The two squad sergeants made another sweep of the compound, a last double-check that no trace of their stay could be detected. Zakia walked out of the house carrying the telephone and an Uzi submachine gun. Trimler was right behind her. He spoke briefly to the two sergeants and they climbed into the back of the trucks. When the Rangers were all out of sight, Carroll, climbed into the cab of the first truck and Zakia into the second.

The trucks rumbled out of the compound and stopped when they reached the outpost a hundred meters down the dirt road. Two Rangers materialized out of the shadows and climbed on board the second truck. Twenty-three of the twenty-five Rangers were accounted for. The small convoy moved down the rut and turned onto a gravel road that would take them to the main highway that led to Kermanshah.

Kamigami made a stay-motion at Jamison and moved toward the back of the building looming in front of them. The lieutenant sank to the ground, thankful for any rest. He was on the verge of exhaustion after following the sergeant major through the hills that offered them a rough path into Kermanshah. He had never credited the stories making the rounds in the battalion about Kamigami and had always chalked them up to the lore the enlisted troops used to scare lieutenants like himself. According to the rumor mill, twenty-mile forced marches were child's play for the sergeant. Now Jamison was wondering how much else that was impossible was true.

The lieutenant caught his breath and tried to fix their position. Judging by the lights and the noises in the distance, he estimated they were on a hillside on the outskirts of Kermanshah, no more than two kilometers away.

A babble of voices erupted from the other side of the building and lights sent a glow over the roofline. Jamison was sure someone had seen or heard the sergeant and drew his pistol, a newly issued 9mm automatic. He tried to find Kamigami but couldn't see a thing. Then a man wearing a ragged suit coat and stocking knit cap pulled down to his ears walked around the corner of the building and looked directly at the spot where the lieutenant had last seen Kamigami. The lieutenant rolled into a prone position and sighted over the barrel. He thumbed the safety to off and then moved back to the hammer, ready to cock the weapon.

Which was when a heavy weight hit him in the back and knocked the breath out of him, and a hand clamped over his mouth and the pistol was twisted out of his grip.

EASTERN TURKEY

Lieutenant Colonel Leon Nelson was pleased with his crew. After the AWACS had launched out of Incirlik, he had briefed them on the coming flight and how they, Delray 51, would be supporting Operation WARLORD. Then something had clicked with every man and woman on-board and a precision he had never seen took hold. The hand-controller at the number three console was hanging up and the operator could not roll the ball full left. Within minutes, the computer technician had it fixed. As the mission developed, Nelson could hear it in their voices. They were committed to WAR-LORD.

Nelson called up the tactical display that reached out 250 nautical miles. The C-130s and the four escorting F-15s were strung out in a line snaking through the mountains. He rolled the hand-controller and the cursor moved over the lead return. He called for identification and information flashed on the screen; call sign Cowboy 31, type F-15, speed 280 knots, altitude 7,250. That's slow and only about four hundred feet above the ground, he thought. He watched two fighters set up a racetrack pattern in front of the C-130s, and for a moment he was jealous and wished he was there . . . anywhere, even in one of the four orbiting F-15s that had to stay behind.

Then he called for a status report on the Iranian air defense. All was quiet. He keyed up the close-in display and watched the two F-111s break out of orbit and move through the mountains. Again he rolled the cursor over the returns and called for identification. They were Mover 21 and 22, F-111F, 480 knots, altitude 7,600 feet. A little high, he calculated, they must have their terrain-following radar set at seven hundred fifty feet. That's going to be a problem if the Iranians are awake.

The crackle of a UHF radio transmission came through Nelson's headset. "Mover Two-Two. Aborting."

"Mover Two-Two," Von Drexler's voice came over the UHF, "this is Mover Two-One. Say emergency."

That's a dumb call from Mover 21, Nelson thought, there's nothing he can do about it. He should simply call for the backup F-111 in orbit to head his way and clear Mover 22 off. What the hell is Mover Two-One hesitating for?

"Yaw Channel light," came the tight reply from Mover 22. "RTB at this time." A telelight was on, warning the crew that one of the triple redundant flight-control channels had failed. But the crew didn't need a light to tell them that. The trim had run full left and they both fought to hold the stick centered and the aircraft under control until the pilot could hit the trim-control switch. They would have their hands full flying the jet at high altitude and the landing was going to be dicey.

Nelson watched the two blips on his screen turn back toward the west. What the hell, they're both aborting . . .

"Ramon, my lad. I think duty calls." Torch Doucette had copied the same radio transmissions. They were hooked up on a tanker and topping off their fuel. Doucette called for a disconnect, and in one graceful maneuver broke out of orbit by rolling the F-111 into a 135 degree bank and pulled the nose over into a 45-degree dive. He reversed and headed for the border. "We got some time to make up if we're going to catch up."

Contreraz's hands flew over his keyboard feeding the backup route into their navigation computer. "We're going to have to take the scenic route, more direct, saves us three minutes over Von Drexler's route. We've still got to go like a stripe-assed ape at five-forty knots to hit the jail house on time."

"Rog, can do." Doucette set the terrain-following altitude at four hundred feet and the ride-control at hard. "I'll squeak it lower in the valleys," he apologized. "Ah, duty is a terrible burden."

"Better tell Delray our intentions," Contreraz said.

Doucette agreed and keyed his radio. "Delray Five-One, Mover Two-Three is inbound at this time."

Von Drexler's voice answered. "Mover Two-Three, this is Mover Two-One, return to orbit, we are aborting."

"You are aborting, asshole," Doucette grumbled over the intercom. He controlled his anger before he hit the radio transmit button. "Roger, Mover Two-One, understand we are to continue single ship." He broke the transmission. "I hope that puckers his asshole, otherwise it's going to be a mess in his cockpit. Ramon, you got a checklist for shit in the cockpit? But maybe I'm being too hard on the boy when all he needs is a little motivation." He keyed the radio. "Ah, Mover Two-One? This is Mover Two-Three." The sarcasm in his voice was clear aboard the listening AWACS. "We're going to be on time. How 'bout *you?*" The sarcasm had turned to steel.

* * *

A ragged cheer broke out among the AWACS controllers when the radar blip that was Mover 21 turned back to the east. Nelson jotted down some notes in his log before he keyed his interphone. "Did we tape those last radio calls from Mover flight?"

The reply was comforting. "Roger, Colonel. We got it all."

CHAPTER 46

H PLUS 10

THE PENTAGON

The President had returned to the Command and Authority Room and was looking out over the National Military Command Center. Cunningham glanced over his shoulder and saw the apprehensive look on his commander's face. "I'm worried too," he said to no one in particular.

"Pardon, sir?" his aide Dick Stevens said.

"Nothing. Dick, if Miss Rahimi is still here, ask her if she'd care to join me."

"I saw her about twenty minutes ago. I'll find her." Stevens left, knowing full well that the general had something in mind and wasn't just being polite asking for her.

"Your attention, please," a woman's voice came over the loudspeaker. The professional-sounding voice demanded attention. "We have established contact with the command-and-control element aboard the AC-130 gunship, call sign Spectre Zero-One, via satellite communications. You may monitor communications or speak with Roundup on channel one." Roundup, they knew, was Mado's personal call sign as the joint task force commander. Every hand in the room toggled the switch for channel one to the on position.

". . . we are encountering scattered clouds, bases five hundred to a thousand feet." Cunningham recognized Thunder Bryant's voice. "Forward visibility is ten miles and improving—"

Leachmeyer interrupted. "Let me speak to Roundup."

"This is Roundup, go ahead." Mado's voice sounded strained.

"Current status?" Leachmeyer asked.

That wasn't very cool, Cunningham thought, for sure no way to impress the President.

"We are on time. However, we have deviated from the mission as planned . . . Mover Two-Two aborted and was replaced by Mover Two-Three, which is ingressing on a different route in order to make up time." Cunningham was more worried about the sound of Mado than any slight change in the plan. "Please standby, we have just established contact with Romeo Team." The command center was absolutely silent. "Romeo Team reports they are in place but two men have become separated and have not reestablished contact."

"Who are the men?" It was the President's voice.

"Lieutenant Jamison and a sergeant."

"Name, damnit."

Well, Cunningham thought, the Pres isn't too cool himself. I hope to hell he doesn't start trying to run the show just because he can talk to someone there.

"A Sergeant Kamigami," Mado answered.

Cunningham heard a gasp behind him. It was Dewa. He looked to the President, who was now on his feet, as though he were standing at attention.

KERMANSHAH, IRAN

"Quiet. Don't move." It was Kamigami's voice next to his ear. Jamison felt the massive weight roll off him and the hand pull away from his mouth. He could breathe again. The two men lay side-by-side and watched the man disappear around the corner of the building in front of them.

"What happened?" Jamison asked, his voice pitched low, not quite a whisper. Kamigami shook his head and the two did not move. The loud wail of a muezzin calling the faithful to prayers came over a loudspeaker in the town below them.

"Morning prayers," Kamigami said. "Move." He pointed to the left, across an open space. The two men came smoothly to their feet and Jamison followed the sergeant, surprised at how soundlessly the big man could move. The cover of darkness they had relied on was giving way to the soft hues of morning twilight, and Jamison could see the town stretched out off to their right. "There." Kamigami dropped down into a dry stream bed that had down-cut a channel around a boulder. "We wait here."

Jamison dropped down beside the boulder and cautiously looked around. They were near the bottom of a low hill and he could see the small city of Kermanshah to the south of their hiding place. On the far side of the city, perhaps two miles away, he could make out the prison. "We're on the wrong side of town," he told Kamigami, and pulled back into the shadows. Kamigami took his place and grunted when he saw the prison.

"Sarge, what in the hell happened back there?"

"Stirred up a rat against the wall . . . it ran into the house . . . I moved on when I heard all the commotion inside . . . Then you tried to shoot the poor bastard. He was just trying to figure out where the rat came from. Couldn't really discuss it at the time so I just took your weapon." The sergeant handed him the Browning. "If we'd made any noise I would've had to kill him and I didn't want to do that."

"It's going to be hard for us to move during daylight. How do we get from here to the prison?"

"People are going to keep their heads down when the bombs start falling and the gunship works the prison over. We move right through the town, maybe borrow a car—something's coming." Kamigami raised his head above the gully, keeping his head in the shadow cast by the rock. It was almost sunrise. "Not good."

A twelve-year-old boy was guiding a small herd of goats across the hillside. He was using a long stick to prod the goats along, humming some tuneless song. Kamigami unsheathed the big black anodized Bowie knife he chose to carry as he watched the boy come straight at them.

WESTERN IRAN

"Turn point in thirty seconds," Von Drexler's WSO announced. "We're five minutes out of the Initial Point." The WSO could hear the lieutenant colonel breathing over the intercom, his breath coming in ragged pants. "We'll be flying down a mountain valley and we've got enough light to squeak it down a couple hundred feet."

Von Drexler didn't answer. He was trying to concentrate on the routine of flying but his restless mind kept jerking him back to one overwhelming fact—they were flying over hostile territory—a land owned by a people who hated Americans and would kill him if he was captured. He berated himself for trying to develop Mado as a sponsor, someone to back him for promotion. Von Drexler remembered all too well the first private conversation with the general at Nellis . . . Mado had promised him that Task Force Alpha was nothing but a cover for the real mission.

"Turning now," the WSO said, the flight computer and autopilot did the work. Von Drexler should have dropped down to four hundred feet and threaded their way down the valley well below the mountain peaks. It would only take a few tweaks on the autopilot, overriding the flight-computer with slight heading changes. And it would have dropped them underneath a hawk that was soaring high above the valley in search of early morning prey.

The hawk sensed the approaching jet before she saw it, folded her wings back and swooped for the ground. She had only dropped twenty feet when they collided. The hawk was a small female and weighed slightly more than a pound, but the impact forces were horrendous. The bird disintegrated when it struck the left-hand glove, the shrouding that streamlined the air flow where the leading edge of the wing pivoted next to the fuselage. Most of the hawk was sucked into the intake of Von Drexler's number-one engine.

Both men felt the impact and saw a slight RPM fluctuation on the left engine, little more than a hiccup. "Bird strike," the WSO said, relieved to see everything normal.

Von Drexler scanned his instruments, took a breath, and made a decision. He keyed the radio and transmitted in the blind. "Mover Two-One aborting, repeat aborting."

Doucette's voice: "Say emergency."

"Bird strike. Left engine." Von Drexler had hit the panic-button.

"Roger," Doucette replied, "run your emergency checklist and if the RPM and oil pressure are within limits, press ahead." He was trying to calm the man, but Von Drexler had already reversed course and was climbing.

"Get back down in the weeds," Von Drexler's WSO shouted, nudging on the stick to get his attention. But the pilot did nothing, and the F-111 continued to climb out well above the mountain peaks. The radar-warning gear started to chirp, telling them they were in the beam of a search radar. Von Drexler sat motionless. "Oh, shitksy," the WSO groaned, and took control of the jet, nosed it over and headed for the deck . . .

"You fucking turkey," Doucette raged in the confines of his cockpit. It was all he could do not to transmit his anger over the UHF for the world to hear.

Some luck, though, was still with them—the radar operator at Maragheh was awake but still in bed, thinking about a certain double-jointed woman he knew in town.

But luck was a fickle lady.

KERMANSHAH, IRAN

"Roundup, this is Romeo One." Trimler was holding the headset of a PRC-77 FM radio against one ear so he could hear what else was going on around him. The Ranger team had moved into position but were still in the trucks parked along a road paralleling the front of the prison. They had stopped so the left sides of the trucks were facing the guard towers and the right sides were shielded from view.

Carroll had reassured him that the Kurds would keep any unwanted traffic off the road and that the other trucks were ready to move in once the prison was secured. The two Rangers with the mules were perched beside him, ready to move. The mules in this case were Laser-Target Designators, short bulky-looking rifles that only shot a laser beam at a target. A laser-guided bomb would catch the reflected energy off the target and home on the spot the Ranger aimed at, hitting within inches of the aim point.

"Come on, answer, damn you," Trimler muttered. He didn't know that Mado was busy talking to the President of the United States on the SatCom. He checked his watch and unable to wait any longer, motioned the Rangers to deploy. The men rolled out of the right side of the trucks into a ditch at the side of the road. Trimler followed the radio-telephone operator with the PRC-77 into the ditch. The trucks drove away, leaving a clear view across the road toward the prison that was three hundred yards directly in front of them. All heads were down . . . with the trucks gone, only the long shadows cast by the rising sun and the ditch offered them cover from the guard's positions in the towers.

Trimler radioed again. This time another voice answered—Thunder Bryant. "Read you five by, Romeo One. Your company is one minute out."

Trimler pointed at his watch and held up one finger. One minute to go. He pointed at his eyes with two forked fingers and then pointed to their objective—the command for spotters. Two men stuck their heads above the ditch, and one trained his binoculars on the guard towers, watching for any sign of detection, while the other searched for the inbound F-111s.

"A guard's looking right at me," the spotter watching the towers said. "Hold on . . . negative. He's watching something on the horizon." The men could now hear the rumble of a distant jet coming their way.

"Spectre Zero-One, Mover Two-Three," Doucette radioed. "IP now." The F-111 was moving at over 560 knots as it streaked over the Initial Point and turned inbound to the target. Doucette had the jet down at two hundred feet as they made the run. They were right on time and the Pave Tack pod was deployed below the weapons bay as Contreraz refined on the target.

"Rog, Mover," Beasely replied, "cleared in hot."

"Spectre, Mover Two-One has aborted for a bird strike," Doucette told the AC-130. "I'm single ship, going for right wall and admin building on first pass." Doucette scanned his weapons panel, double checking the switches. He didn't want to reattack because of a switch error. But he did plan to reattack and punch a hole in the left side of the wall—Von Drexler's target.

Contreraz confirmed that the video tape recorder was on and buried his head in the scope, still working the radar, about ready to transition to the Pave Tack pod. His left hand was by the scope, flicking a switch, changing the scope's picture from radar to the video picture coming from the Pave Tack pod. He kept refining his cursor placement, then switched to infrared, moved the cursors again and activated the system.

On board the AC-130 Bryant and Mado were engaged in a furious argument. "They should hit the left side first," Mado shouted.

"Negative. Too late to change now. Mover Two-Three has got to ripple two bombs off into the admin building to get the guards. Call Jack in. He can punch a hole in the left wall."

But Mado had made his decision. He twisted his intercom wafer switch to UHF and hit the transmit button. "Mover Two-Three, hit the left side of the wall."

"Torch, hit the admin building." It was Stansell. He had been monitoring the UHF radio. "Jack, fall in behind Mover and take out the left side."

"Roger," Doucette answered.

"Rog, copy all," Jack said. It was his first transmission, he had been maintaining radio silence. He broke out of the low orbit he was in and turned toward Kermanshah, now seeing Doucette's F-111 in front of him.

Mado's voice crackled over the UHF. "Use your call signs and authenticate. Repeat, authenticate your last transmissions."

"Fuck that noise," Contreraz grumbled. He had recognized Stansell's voice. He bumped his target cursors a hair to the right—a final refinement. "Ready, Ready . . ." Contreraz watched the range counter on his scope roll down to 23,000 feet as the Time To Go counter ran out. "PULL." Doucette brought the nose of the F-111 up into a forty-five degree climb, smoothly following the command steering from the Weapons-Nav Computer.

The F-111 twitched as two bombs rippled off. "Bombs gone," Doucette called over the UHF. He banked 110 degrees away to the right and began bringing the nose to the horizon. Contreraz continued to track the target through the Pave Tack pod. The bombs would fly for almost thirty seconds before hitting the target . . .

"Romeo One," Bryant's voice came over Trimler's FM radio, "lase the right side first. Repeat, lase the right side of the wall first."

"Romeo One copies," Trimler said, "Right side first." He pointed at the closest Ranger holding a mule. "Laser up, right side," he commanded. The man raised his head above the ditch and leveled the mule at the wall.

"Laser on," came over the radio. Trimler had turned up the audio on the PRC-77 so the Ranger could hear the transmissions. Maintaining silence was not a concern now.

"Gadget's on," the Ranger said, squeezing the trigger to the first detent to place the crosshairs and then to full action to turn the laser on.

"Gadget's on," Trimler relayed.

A spotter yelled, "One of the guards has seen the plane, he's coming down the ladder like his tail's on fire. I can see the bombs . . ."

"Spotters down," Trimler barked, trying to keep them from being hit by flying debris or bomb fragments . . .

Mary Hauser was curled up on her bunk, trying to conserve what body heat she could. For the first time she was thankful for the blanket-like chador. When Amini, the friendly guard, had said it was time to return to her cell and leave Landis, she had covered the doctor with her blanket. Amini had protested but she had insisted and started to raise her voice. Rather than risk discovery, he had given in.

At first the muted rumbling didn't register with her. Then she snapped fully awake as the sound grew louder . . . It was a jet flying by the prison at high speed. She knew what it meant . . . "Come *on*, you beauties, come *on*." Her voice, she realized, echoed down the hall, and she hoped it reached every corridor in the administration building above her head, and especially that Mokhtari heard.

"Doc, hit the deck," she called out as she threw herself on the floor and rolled under the bunk.

The two five-hundred-pound, laser-guided bombs fell in tandem toward the prison. It had been a perfect toss and both seeker heads picked up the reflected laser energy bouncing off the wall. The bombs made little jerking motions, refining their trajectory as they homed. The first bomb impacted two feet left of the spot the Ranger was illuminating with the mule and exploded on impact. The Ranger's reactions were right on. He actually saw the bomb as it struck the wall and threw himself back into the ditch, holding onto his helmet. The explosion blew over the men, pounding their bodies, stunning their senses. But they had been in the same situation before and thanks to their training there was no panic.

The second bomb lost the laser signature it was homing on when the first bomb exploded. It then went into a memory mode and continued on its last trajectory, flying through the crumbling gap the first bomb had knocked in the wall and on into the administration building. It exploded on impact.

The F-15E streaked down the valley, its airspeed riveted on 540 knots. Shadows and early morning mist had degraded their forward visibility but the forward looking infrared sensor in the navigation pod slung under the right intake was creating a perfect picture on Jack Locke's head-up display. They were still ten miles away. "Amb, I'm goin' to lay down a Snakeye," Jack told his backseater.

Furry wished they were carrying a GBU-15 with a 2,000 pound warhead. He wanted to guide something big onto the prison. As he continued to work he did not have to bury his head in a scope like

Contreraz. Instead he sat upright monitoring the four displays in front of him. His fingers played on the switches and buttons of his hand controllers as he readied the system for the delivery. He had his cursors on the same spot Jack was aiming for. And the radar image was a perfect match with the infrared. He activated the system. "You've got steering," he told Jack.

"See if you can get a better picture," Jack said.

Again Furry's fingers played a tune on his hand-controllers as he worked the radar screen. He enlarged the area around the prison and froze the image. He had a high-resolution patch-map of the prison compound that covered two-thirds of a nautical mile.

"Shit hot," Jack called over the intercom, "Doucette did it. Two bulls right on target. Amb, check for BDA." Furry looked over Jack's right shoulder doing a bomb-damage assessment. He could see the smoke and dust still rising from the right side of the prison. They were less than twenty seconds out. The HUD showed Jack that he was dead-on and had the steering wired.

On the videotape that recorded the run it looked easy with all the sophisticated systems working as advertised, but they were working *because* of the men in the cockpit. And there was no better example of that than Jack Locke, a cool pro who had already lived through the pressure-cooker of combat. He had learned through experience how to confront the unbelievable stress that flying a mission generated. Few men juggled the task-saturation, the disorientation, the incredible number of tasks that had to be performed at once and correctly in aerial combat. If he balanced them all, life and success were on the other side of the equals sign. It was a hard formula that most men chose not to solve—Locke was doing it out of choice—and he was a master at it.

As they flashed over the open space in front of the prison, Furry could see the Rangers crouched in the ditch and felt the bomb separate from the left stub pylon. Then they were over the prison, going straight ahead to clear the frag-pattern the bomb would kick up. Jack dipped the right wing so they could get a better view of the compound. Then they were clear, flying over the old barracks behind the prison. Jack pulled up to the right so they could see where their bomb hit.

"A bull," Furry yelled when he saw the hole they had punched in the wall. "Not much left of the admin building. Doucette started a fire down there—nothin' left but hot hair, teeth and eyeballs. Rangers ain't goin' in through there."

"Here comes Spectre," Jack said. The AC-130 gunship was right behind them and setting up a thirty-degree left-hand pylon turn around the prison . . .

Mokhtari was almost dressed when he first heard the deep rumble of Doucette's F-111 running in on the prison. For a moment he stood in his bedroom, the sound not registering as it grew louder. When he realized it was an airplane he dove under his bed. The explosion of the first bomb taking down the outside wall washed over him. He was not prepared for the intensity of the second bomb when it exploded inside the administration building. The power of the noise and shock-wave stunned him but he did not pass out. In a dreamlike state he felt the floor under him collapse, was aware that he was falling through to the floor below . . .

He was semi-conscious as he watched the walls collapse around him. And then he saw the dark gray form of Jack Locke's F-15 flash past, barely clearing the top of the prison. A firebrand of hate burned through him, leaving a raw urge to kill the Americans. Jack's bomb exploded, and again a shock wave pounded at him, this time driving him into unconsciousness.

The two dull booms echoed across the valley of Kermanshah and the young goatherd turned in his tracks, ten feet short of the gully where Kamigami and Jamison were hidden. Like most twelve-year-olds the boy wandered around in a daydream of heroics and fancies. Now he looked puzzled by the sudden intrusion of reality into his perfect world. He stared at the smoke billowing up from the southern edge of the town, fixing its location. And he watched transfixed as Locke's F-15 ran onto the prison and pulled up. For a moment *he* was in the cockpit, guiding the fighter into combat, killing the American enemies he had heard about on TV and the radio.

Then the explosion of the third bomb reverberated through the valley and he knew what it meant. Hated Americans were attacking the prison and bombing the walls. He ran back to his family's compound, away from the death that waited for him ten feet away. He stopped in mid-flight and turned back to gather the goats, then thought better of it, turned again and ran for home . . .

Kamigami waited until he could no longer hear the boy's retreating footsteps, then raised his head over the edge of the shallow ravine, keeping in the shadow of the rock, and made sure they were alone. He returned his knife to its sheath and picked up his M-203, an M-16 rifle with a 40mm grenade-launcher grafted to the underside of its barrel. "Would you actually have . . . ?" Jamison's voice trailed off at the thought.

The sergeant pulled his helmet's chin-strap tight, said nothing. He only pointed down the gully and moved out.

Beasely inched the flaps down as he slowed to 160 knots. The nose came up as he turned the AC-130 into a stabilized gun platform orbiting the prison. "Both IR and TV's got a target," the sensor operator in the booth on the cargo deck told them.

The fire control officer bounced out of his seat and looked over the copilot, gauging the target area's visibility. He squeezed back into his seat next to the navigator. "Take IR guidance," he said, "smoke and dust might cause a problem." He punched at the buttons on his fire-control panel and linked the infrared image with the fire-control computer.

"I count three guard towers," the copilot said. "Tower by the admin building is down. No movement in the compound. Everybody must still be groveling in the dirt."

"Rog," Beasely said, "we'll take out the front tower first, then the two at the rear. Give me the forties." The FOCO worked his fire control panel and linked the pilot's trigger to the two 40mm Bofors Automatic guns that stuck their ugly snouts out of the fuselage behind the left main-gear fairing. The sensor operator in the booth drove the crosshairs on his infrared viewer over the tower, illuminating it with that sensor. When he activated the system a diamond appeared on the IR viewer, bracketing the target. The same diamond appeared on the pilot's HUD.

"Forties are ready," the loader in the rear called.

The copilot maintained their altitude and airspeed while Beasely flew the yoke for bank. It took a carefully synchronized routine in crew coordination to bring the awesome fire power of the gunship to bear. Beasely turned his head and sighted through the HUD mounted beside the left cockpit window. He jockeyed the yoke and rudders to position the lighted circle on the HUD inside the diamond that bracketed the tower. The circle showed where any round he fired would impact. He mashed the trigger and sent a short burst of high explosive 40mm toward the guard tower. The burst lasted less than two seconds as eight rounds smashed into the structure, shredding it.

Beasely now worked his rudder pedals and slipped the gunship into a turn over the next tower. He could see a guard waving something at him. Again, he mashed the trigger and ripped the head of the tower off. "I think maybe he was trying to surrender," he muttered, then moved over the third remaining tower.

The illuminator operator, the fancy term the Air Force chose to give the sergeant in charge of operating the searchlight mounted in the tail section of the cargo deck, was doing his most important job—lying down on the ramp. His parachute was off and a cable snapped onto his harness to hold him in the airplane as he stuck the upper third of his body over the edge of the ramp. He was checking their six o'clock position and he was cold. "Ground fire from the tower," he yelled into his mike.

Beasely stomped on his right rudder pedal to skid the Hercules, then jerked it further to the right. No gunship commander in his right mind ignored a warning from the IO. "Type," he barked.

"Small arms only," the IO told him. "The Rangers are running for the wall."

"Gimme the one-oh-five," Beasely commanded. The fire routine repeated itself as he repositioned the gunship into a new firing orbit. When he hit the trigger button this time the crew felt a dull thump as the C-130 absorbed the recoil from the 105mm cannon mounted in the left paratroop door. The tower flashed into a ball of fire. When the smoke and debris cleared, there was . . . nothing.

The gunship flew an orbit around the prison, letting General Mado and Thunder scan it with binoculars. "The first C-130 is over the airfield," Beasely told them. "Shall I clear the escorting F-15s back to the tanker?" Mado hesitated, and only after Thunder told him that was part of the plan did he give his okay. Beasely turned to the north. "Time to head for the holding pattern and get out of the way." He had decided to start telling the general what he was doing rather than wait for directions.

Thunder watched Duck Mallard's C-130 pass down the airfield two-and-a-half miles to the east. And Mado, that intrepid warrior, was on the SatCom with an update for the command center in the Pentagon.

CHAPTER 47

H PLUS 11

KERMANSHAH, IRAN

The first four-man team of Rangers was against the wall. Smoke and dust were still swirling out of the huge holes the bombs had opened up. The buck sergeant leading them only hesitated long enough to check his back up. Three more teams were behind him, running across the open area in front of the prison. Captain Trimler and his radio operator were coming out of the ditch, running as hard as they could. He could see movement in the ditch—the two M60 heavy machine-gun teams were moving sideways in the ditch—they would offset to each side to hold the flanks of the prison and secure the road.

The sergeant pointed at the wall and went through in a crouched position, holding his 9mm MP5 submachine gun down on its assault sling, ready to sweep the area with gunfire. His high man came through right behind him, looking over the sergeant's shoulder. The third man came through offset to the right, and the fourth came through backward, looking for anything that might spring up behind them. They rushed across the 110 feet of open quadrangle to the main entrance of the cell block. Another four-man team was right behind them. So far no reaction from the guards.

The team paused to reconfigure. The lead sergeant pushed his submachine gun back onto his shoulder and unclipped a stun grenade from his LBE. The high man drew his pistol and the other two waited. The lead pulled the pin while the high man tested the door. It was unlocked. As he twisted the handle and threw the door open the sergeant tossed in the stun grenade, fell back and drew his Beretta. A flash and bang echoed in the building, and the four men went through, exactly as they had come through the wall.

The lead sergeant was the low man and he pounded up the short flight of steel steps leading to the first floor of the cell block. His high man was right behind him, perched over his right shoulder. The door to the first-floor guards' office on the left was open, and the low man went right through it at an oblique angle, his Beretta automatic extended in front in a two-handed shooter's grip. He swept the corner opposite to him and then swung his pistol in an arc to the center, concentrating on anything below the waist. His high man was right behind him, button-hooked to the left and cleared his opposite corner just like the low man, but he concentrated on anything above the waist.

Two guards were in the room, one crouched on the floor holding the telephone in his right hand. The low man pumped two shots into his head. The other man was standing barefoot with his hands above his head. He lived. The second team rushed past the office door heading for the second floor while the third team flushed the basement. The backup man came through the door and slapped plastic flex cuffs on the guard's wrists and ankles while the high man mashed a strip of wide adhesive tape across his mouth. Then they were out the door and up the stairs, following the second team to leap frog them to the third floor.

A burst of rapid shots echoed down the stairwell. The second team had found three guards in the office holding weapons. The first team waited until they were waved past the office before they charged the flight of stairs that led to the next landing. They heard a single shot ring out from the basement followed by four shots from two 9mm pistols. Then silence.

Before they reached the turn landing the sergeant caught a vague movement in the shadows directly above him on the next flight of stairs. It had been little more than a flicker through the open steps, but it was enough. He stopped and pointed with his forefinger to the shadow, his thumb pointed down—hand-sign for the enemy. The backup man leveled his M-16 under his right arm, the forefinger of his left hand extended along the stock in a point-and-shoot position. At the go sign from his lead he moved up the steps to the landing, but his boot caught under the last step and he stumbled, falling out onto the small platform. He rolled and fired up the stairs before a shot ripped into his left leg, just below the knee, shattering the fibula in his lower leg.

Silence.

The lead holstered his 9mm and swung his submachine gun down. He inched up the steps and shoved his weapon around the corner, firing blindly. The high man stepped around him and placed four shots into the shadow above them. A body slid down the stairs.

They regrouped and went up the stairs, and a burst of gunfire came out of the office door, sweeping the area in front of the door but not down the stairs. Whoever was up there obviously did not want to look. The lead unsnapped a frag grenade, pulled the pin, moved soundlessly toward the door, threw in the grenade and moved quickly back. An explosion ripped the room apart and the high man then darted into the room, spraying bullets. Two went into the head of the guard lying on the floor, making sure he was dead before the high man kicked his AK-47 into a corner. The Rangers looked for more guards, and then as quickly as it began, it was over.

"Kamigami would be having your ass right now if he was here," the lead sergeant's high man said.

"What for? It was goddamn perfect except for klutzo here falling on his face." They were watching a Ranger bind up the leg of their wounded comrade.

"Bullshit. You didn't clear the second team past the first-floor office. Next time . . ."

Stansell could see smoke billowing up from the prison as Mallard flew the C-130 across the roofs of Kermanshah at 240 knots. The pilot holding the plane straight and level at 800 feet above the ground, wracked the throttles back, slowing the cargo plane to 130 knots as they approached the airfield and lined up on the runway. "One minute warning." Drunkin Dunkin's voice carried over the intercom.

"We won't come back this way," Mallard said, "but nothing like a little low flyin' to keep a fella's head down and discourage unwanted guests." Stansell silently agreed.

"Runway in sight," Dunkin called. "Thirty-second warning." The loadmaster acknowledged the call. The Rangers were ready to storm the airfield.

The jumpmaster was standing at the left paratroop door, his head stuck out into the slipstream as he checked the field. He had flown enough practice jumps with Drunkin Dunkin to trust him, but this was combat and this particular jumpmaster had gone in with the Rangers in Grenada. He knew what could happen in combat so he did one last double-check himself. Dunkin had it wired. The C-130 slowed to 130 knots.

"Standby," the jumpmaster bellowed at the runway clearing team. The seventeen men were split into two sticks and lined up on the ramp. They would not use the jump doors but go straight off the end of the ramp. The jumpmaster pointed at the first line. They were standing back-to-belly, right hands clenching their static lines, left hands against the man's back in front. Their weapons were strapped to their sides, locked and loaded.

The green light by the jump doors switched from red to green as Dunkin yelled, "Green Light," over the intercom.

"GO!" the jumpmaster shouted when he saw the first flicker of green. It was not the usual static line-jump with the men going out at one second intervals. The first stick of eight men ran off the ramp, pushing each other, the first two out of the plane before Dunkin had finished saying "green light." The Rangers were so close that the deployment bag on the leader's parachute hit the second man in the face. Two swings and they were on the ground.

The jumpmaster pointed at the second stick of nine jumpers and seven seconds later gave the next Go. Again, the men ran off the ramp, the last two out being unhappy Air Force sergeants—the Combat Control Team that would act like a control tower and clear the C-130s to land. "Hate group gropes," one of the Air Force sergeants mumbled, but no one heard him and he landed 1,600 feet down the runway from the first stick.

Most of the Rangers hit the ground with a standard parachute landing-fall and absorbed the shock with a roll that started at the feet and up the leg to the buttocks and then to the upper back muscles. One Ranger did it on the wrong side of his body and came to his feet with a bent M-16. He shrugged off his harness, dropped the useless weapon, and ran for his first objective . . . to help clear and secure the only building on the deserted airstrip.

Other Rangers set up covering positions at each end of the runway while the remainder ran down the runway, throwing debris and rubbish off to the side as they checked its condition. Six men pushed an abandoned car that had its wheels removed off to one side, and the runway was clear. The Combat Control Team ran along the runway, carrying their portable UHF radios and also checking the condition of the runway. "It's in great shape," the controller said, "with a couple of brooms we can even land fighters if we have to." They set up their radios, contacted Spectre 01 and cleared the C-130s to enter the landing pattern.

THE PENTAGON

Harsh static exploded out of the small speaker in front of Cunningham, rasping at his nerves. The telelight confirmed that he was listening to channel one, the SatCom link to Mado aboard Spectre 01. He spun the volume knob down and looked over his console at the Air Force major sitting at the control panel below him in the next row, calmly working the buttons on the panel in front of her, trying to reestablish contact. The SatCom did not rely on the older KY-57 scrambler for security but used a rapidly shifting frequency rotation. Occasionally the receiver and transmitter frequency shifts drifted apart and had to be realigned; otherwise, only a grating noise could be heard, a perfect discouragement for unwanted listeners. The major keyed her mike: "Please standby while the system realigns."

"Damnit," Leachmeyer shouted, "get a clear transmission or we'll get someone in here who can."

"I'm in manual override now. One moment."

Cunningham leaned toward Leachmeyer, who was sitting next to him. "It's a system limitation. She'll sort it out." On cue, Mado's voice came through crisp and clear.

"Roundup, this is Blue Chip," the major transmitted, "please repeat your last transmission." Cunningham liked the way she had handled the situation.

"Blue Chip, this is Roundup," Mado answered. "Romeo Team secured the prison at 0303 Zulu. The airfield was secured at 0311 Zulu." A ragged cheer broke out over the main floor.

"They're ahead of schedule," Dewa told the general. Her eyes were on the master clock as she counted the minutes. She did not need to consult a briefing book to follow the mission's timetable, it was etched into her head. Ninety minutes on the ground . . .

Cunningham noted that they were receiving objective accomplishment times between three and eleven minutes late. Not too bad, he thought.

"I want a head count," Leachmeyer ordered, "and start moving the

POWs in five minutes. Use the jeeps on the C-130s if you have to."

Dewa shook her head. "General Cunningham, the C-130s are still landing and they need those jeeps to secure the road. There's a vital highway intersection—Objective Red—near the prison that we have to control. It seals off the western approach to the prison—"

"Charlie"—Cunningham interrupted her to settle Leachmeyer down—"let them do it as planned. They'll move the POWs when they're ready. We're not running the show." He could see the President over Leachmeyer's shoulder. He was pacing back and forth in the Command and Authority Room, obviously agitated, wanting to control the action.

"Delta Force would be out of there by now," Leachmeyer grumbled.

"They'd be fighting for their lives," Cunningham shot back, "because every swingin' dick in Iran would've known they were coming. Christ, Charlie, why do you think we sent Task Force Alpha in? Now let them do their job."

KERMANSHAH, IRAN

Two-man teams of Rangers were working down the long corridor of each floor, testing the cell doors to see if they were unlocked and throwing open the small shutters set in each door to check on the inmates. Each Ranger had a list of the POWs and methodically checked off names. Outside, the guards who survived the attack were huddled in a corner of the quadrangle. Two were seriously wounded. Trimler had turned the first-floor guards' office into a command post while his RTO established contact with Roundup in the orbiting AC-130.

"Sir," a Ranger checked in. "Head count on first floor complete. We count ninety-seven, including Colonel Leason."

Another Ranger pounded up the stairs from the basement. "Captain, we've got a casualty in the basement. A guard shot a POW before we could secure our area." The man was obviously shaken. "God . . . it's a torture chamber down there . . . the poor bastard was shoved in a box no bigger than a wall locker . . ."

"The POW?" Trimler asked, his anger scarcely under control.

"Dead, sir. We're getting him out now."

"The guard?"

"Four holes in him, sir. He's still alive."

"Bring the body up." Trimler's anger was surging. "Get the first-floor guard in here. Now." A few moments later the guard was shoved into the room, his ankles were unshackled but the adhesive tape was still over his mouth and his wrists were handcuffed behind his back. Bill Carroll skidded around the corner right behind him with a young Iranian in tow.

"Who the hell . . ." Trimler barked.

"This is Mustapha Sindi," Carroll said. "I told you about him. Leads the Kurds. The trucks are outside."

Trimler turned to the guard and pointed to the central control box that unlocked the cell doors on the first floor. "Open it," he said. Fear and confusion ran across the guard's face as he shook his head no. Mustapha let loose a barrage in Farsi and ripped the adhesive off his mouth. The guard paled, spoke a few words.

"Free his hands," Carroll told them. "He'll do it."

"What the hell did he say?" Trimler asked.

"Mustapha told him he had two choices: open the doors and live or meet Mulla Haqui. Of course he would also live if he met Haqui"—there was no humor in Carroll's voice—"for two more days of torture." The guard was freed and rapidly punched the four-digit combination into the control box. A green light flashed on and the guard pulled a lever. They could hear the central-locking bar that ran along the tops of the cell doors slide back. The first floor was free.

"Get Leason in here and load 'em," Trimler ordered. "Do another head count as you load. We'll move them as soon as the road is secured." He turned to his RTO. The man was ready and told him that he had established contact with the AC-130 gunship on the PRC-77. "Relay our status," Trimler told him. "Trucks in place, ninety-seven POWs being loaded, will move them out when the road is secured."

Two more Rangers appeared in the door. "Ninety-five on the second floor," the first one told them.

"Eighty-seven on the third." This from the last Ranger.

"Counting the POW in the basement," Trimler said, "that adds up to two hundred and seventy-nine. We're three short."

Another voice: "They're accounted for." It was Leason, the senior ranking officer. The men gaped at him: dirty and haggard, barefoot, clothes ripped and torn. "Staff Sergeant Macon Jefferson was executed. Lieutenant Colonel Jeffrey Landis and Captain Mary Hauser are being held in the basement of the administration building."

Carroll bolted out of the room, closely followed by Mustapha.

Another Ranger reported in, "Problems, sir. We can't unlock the cell doors on the second and third floors."

Duck Mallard flew his C-130 down final, its nose in the air. He planted the main gear twenty feet beyond the spot the Combat Control Team had told him to use as a touchdown point, drove the nose down and ripped the throttles full aft, lifting them over the gate and throwing the props into reverse. He stomped the brakes and dragged the heavy plane to a halt in less than eighteen hundred feet.

Before the plane had slowed, the rear door under the tail was up and the ramp down. Mallard paused on the runway for a moment as the ramp came full down and two motorcycles and three heavily loaded jeeps drove off. The drivers were careful as they deplaned, but the moment they were clear of the ramp they mashed the accelerators and sped away. They were the first of the Ratsos, the jeep teams who had to secure the road.

Mallard then taxied off the runway onto hard ground, where one of the sergeants on the Combat Control team had marshaled him. The second C-130 was already touching down.

The two modified dirt bikes led the three jeeps off the airfield and turned down the dirt road that led to the prison. The jeep teams took spacing and started to talk to each other on their MX-360 radios. Each Ratso was a mobile firing platform. An M-60 machine gun was mounted on a post in the back seat and another on the hood in front of the passenger seat. Besides carrying four men, the jeeps were stuffed with four light antitank weapons, claymore mines, and four Dragons—medium range antitank missiles that could reach out over a thousand yards and be carried by one man.

At the first intersection the lead motorcycle deliberately took the wrong turn and scouted up the road while the others sped by. He didn't see any traffic so he raced after the jeeps that were following a gravel road that looped around the southeastern edge of town. Another team behind them would guard that intersection. They had to pass the prison and reach Objective Red, the main intersection on the southern edge of town where the road to the prison junctioned with the main highway between Kermanshah and Shahabad. The intersection was in a low pass formed by hills on both sides of the highway, and if the armored regiment garrisoned at Shahabad moved, they would come through the pass to the intersection.

The lead scout slowed his bike as he approached the prison, looking for Romeo Team's road guard, and caught a glimpse of two men in the ditch on the right side of the road in front of him. That should be the M-60 team, he figured. He turned to look at the prison on his left—and died in a hail of gunfire from what he thought were deserted barracks. The dirt bike spun and threw him into the ditch, then crashed down on his lifeless body. The M-60 team returned fire, attempting to suppress the threat coming at them from behind the prison.

The carefully planned raid called WARLORD died with the scout, and a new operation began—the battle for Kermanshah.

"Through here," Carroll yelled at Mustapha as he cleared the broken glass out of a window. The Kurd looked at the prison's administration building and decided he didn't want to go in. Doucette's five-hundred-pound bomb had done its job too well. The top floor had collapsed onto the ground floor, and a fire was burning in the rear half of the building. Mustapha shook his head and followed Carroll through the window. A jagged, gut-wrenching scream stopped them both—a guard trapped in the dying flames. "Let the bastard burn," Carroll said.

Mustapha couldn't let it go. He moved quickly through the wreckage, homing on the shrieking man, saw him through a curtain of flames trapped under fallen masonry. He raised his Uzi and shot the guard.

"MARY!" Carroll's voice carried through the building.

"Down here, in the basement . . ."

Carroll looked at the pile of debris between him and the voice and felt the heat of the fire still pressing on his back. And then a figure came staggering out of the rubble, covered with dust and blood.

"Lifter, this is Ratso Nine. Objective secured." It was the last of the jeep teams checking in on the PRC-77. Lifter was the airfield's call sign. Stansell watched Gregory and his S-3, the battalion's operations officer, mark their maps with Ratso Nine's position at the nearest intersection to the airfield. Stansell hovered just behind them in the temporary command post they had set up in the deserted building. Gregory was commanding the action on the ground while he ran the show in the air. Stansell was making grease marks on a small acetate-covered board he could tuck under his arm and carry with him. A map was taped to one side and a matrix for tracking the status of aircraft to the other.

"Ratso Three and the two M-60 teams all report the barracks are quiet," the S-3 said. "But that fire had to come from somewhere."

"Where are Ratso One and Two?" Gregory asked. "We'll sort that problem out later. Right now we worry about getting past the prison and taking Objective Red." Stansell was impressed by how cool the lieutenant colonel was. The RTO asked Ratso Three where the first and second jeep teams were.

"Making an end run," was the reply. Gregory approved.

"Lifter, this is Ratso Nine." The RTO acknowledged the latest radio call. "I've stopped a big gas truck with two civilians. They say they're making a fuel delivery to the airfield." The men could hear the confusion in the Ranger's voice. "They've got the recognition code."

"Repeat," Gregory ordered. The jeep team confirmed the two civilians had the correct recognition code.

"Ask what type of fuel they're carrying," Stansell said. The question was relayed and the answer came back. The truck was full of JP-4 and was a pumper from the main airport eleven kilometers north of town. "It's welcome," Stansell said. "Bring it in." Gregory ordered an escort team to take one of the extra jeeps and bring the truck in, but to stay well clear of all activity until it and the drivers could be checked out . . .

Ratso One and Two, the lead jeep teams, threw quick U-turns when the motorcycle scout was killed. They told Ratso Three to hold while they doubled back. The Ranger navigating in Ratso One had his map out and pointed to a break in the buildings off to their left. It was not a road but open lots that led into the outskirts of town. The two jeeps bounced across the rough field, past the low buildings and onto a paved street. Both the driver and navigator had memorized the map and knew where they were as they raced for the intersection that was Objective Red. A police car saw the two speeding jeeps and chased them through the almost deserted streets. Ratso Two's rear gunner swung his M-60 around and sent a short burst into the car. It bounced off a parked truck, rolled over and burst into flames.

The two jeeps twisted and turned through the town until they hit the main highway, then turned left, darting through heavier traffic. A short burst from an M-60 determined the right-of-way at an intersection, and six minutes after making the U-turn, Objective Red was secure.

"Up there," Andy Baulck pointed to what was left of the one guard tower at the rear of the prison. "The captain wants to know what's goin' on behind the wall."

"I'll take this one," Wade said. The corporal had been Baulck's best drinking buddy since the fight with the C-130 loadmasters at Texas Lake. Baulck motioned him forward and he worked his way up the tower's ladder. He moved slowly, careful not to make any noise. The ladder had fallen back on itself and Wade had to pull himself up through the last four feet of scaffolding. He poked his head above the wall and pulled it back down, reminding Baulck of a pop-up target on the firing range. Slowly, Wade raised his head again and took a longer look. Then he was back down. "Place is crawling with troops. Maybe fifty of 'em. They've got something inside a shed, the doors are open." And then they could hear a diesel engine on the other side of the wall cough to life.

The first-floor guard kept shaking his head and punched another series of numbers into the control box that unlocked the cell doors on the second floor. The red light stayed on. "He wasn't assigned to this floor and doesn't know the code but is scared shitless," a Ranger said. "We're going to have to start blowing the doors."

"Takes too long," a buck sergeant grumbled, his eyes drawn into a squint. "Damn, I know what I'd do if I was in this cage." He ran out into the corridor and banged against the door of the first cell in his rush. "You know the numbers to the lock box?" he asked the POWs still trapped inside. A voice gave him four numbers and he ran back to the office and shoved the frightened guard aside. He keyed in the numbers and the green light flashed on. The lever was moved down, and the ninety-five POWs on the second floor were free.

"Hey, Bro," another Ranger asked, "how'd you think of that?"

The twenty-year-old Ranger from the streets of Watts mumbled, "My cousin's locked up in San Quentin. He says they got lots of time to do nothing but study the guards and watch everything they do. That's what I'd do . . . that's what they did."

The situation on the third floor was tougher. The frag grenade that had cleared the office had also punched holes in the wiring junction box below the control box. The electronically controlled locking mechanism was dead. "Tell the captain we're going to start blowin' doors up here," the staff sergeant in charge of the third floor said. "Get Baulck up here and see if he can rewire this piece of shit while we do some blastin'." He gestured toward the cells, "Let's get some food and water to those poor bastards."

Downstairs, Trimler was staring at the man Mustapha had delivered to him. The Iranian was still in a state of shock and seemed dazed, but he was standing unaided and trying to brush the dust from his uniform. A Ranger had plastered a bandage to the right side of his forehead, stopping the bleeding.

"He speaks English," Mustapha said, his own English good enough for the job at hand. "Carroll has found the woman and the doctor. He needs help. They're trapped." He pointed across the compound at the burning building.

Trimler sent a team of Rangers to the administration building with Mustapha before he turned to the Iranian. "Your name, rank and identification number."

"Colonel Vahid Mokhtari. I am the commandant of the prison and you are surrounded. I will accept your surrender."

For a frozen moment Trimler said nothing, staring at the man. "I'm supposed to say nuts in situations like this," he said. "But I've seen how you've taken care of these men, so I'll do better. Try fuck off."

Mokhtari smiled at him, sure of his position and how desperate the Americans were. "Keep smiling, asshole," Leason said from the doorway. "I'm taking you with me when I leave."

Stansell could sense that the situation was changing as the reports filtered in from the prison and road teams. It wasn't enough to go on yet, but he knew where to look. He refused, though, to act in haste—a sure way to make bad decisions. He grabbed the mike to the portable UHF radio the Combat Control Team had set up in the command post. "Stormy, this is Lifter. Say position."

Jack's voice answered immediately. "Holding."

Stansell checked his status board. Jack was right where he was supposed to be. "Stormy, I need a visual reccy of the highway. Take it to Point Gold." Point Gold was the code name for the armored regiment's garrison at Shahabad forty-two miles away. Stansell had re-roled Jack as a fast-moving forward air controller—and had tasked him to do a visual reconnaissance.

"Rog," Jack acknowledged, "departing holding now."

The colonel continued to work the radio. "Spectre, this is Lifter." Beasely acknowledged the call and Stansell continued. "We need Roundup here. Please advise him." The wait seemed interminable.

"Lifter, Roundup." It was Mado's voice. "We cannot land at this time. We must maintain contact with Blue Chip."

Stansell swore under his breath. Gregory's RTO had also established contact with Blue Chip in the Pentagon on his URC-101 SatCom set. But they had to use the much more cumbersome KY-57 encoder which slowed transmissions down. Mado knew all that. "Also, say reason for tasking for Stormy," Mado demanded.

"That's why we need you here," Stansell answered. Hell of a time to have to start explaining everything to the man.

"Standby, Lifter," Mado radioed, "Blue Chip is transmitting."

Great, Stansell raged, you're talking to the heavies who haven't got a clue—activity at the door caught his attention.

"Lifter, Roundup." Mado was back on the radio. "Blue Chip wants to know why the delay in moving. We are not on schedule."

"Roundup, I say again, that's why we need you here."

"Unable at this time, explain delay."

"Standby," Stansell snapped. He turned to the newcomers that two Rangers had escorted into the command post. It was Zakia and the man who had become her shadow, her contact.

"Colonel," she began, "I'm Bill Carroll's contact. We"—she nodded to the man beside her—"are your liaison with the Kurds." They exchanged a new set of code words, establishing their bona fides.

"The gas truck?" Stansell asked.

Zakia's face was impassive. "We arranged an impromptu diversion at the main airport and just happened across it. We thought you might be able to use some fuel. And I was directed to establish contact in case you have to escape overland."

It was too much for Gregory. "Damnit, this is no time to get involved with partisans. We've got problems here—"

"Ham, they're not partisans. They're here to help us—"

"Colonel," Zakia interrupted him, "we've got to go and get our people to safety. If you cannot fly out of here, contact us here." She pointed to a road junction eleven miles south of town. Then the two were gone.

Stansell watched them leave, then told Gregory, "I think we've got a two-part problem. First, Mado and Blue Chip are trying to run the show by remote control. We need Mado on the ground, talking to you, making the decisions here. Second, we're in a different ball game. We've been set up. This is a trap . . ."

The UHF radio interrupted him. It was Mado, "Lifter, Blue Chip wants to know why the delay."

Stansell picked up the mike and nodded at Gregory, who was still adjusting to the news. "Tell Blue Chip that we've been bush-whacked. Romeo Team is trapped inside the prison."

"We have no confirmation of that!" Mado was almost screaming on the radio. "Say confirmation!"

Jack's voice came over the UHF. "Lifter, Stormy. Tracked vehicles moving out of Point Gold toward you. Repeat, tracked vehicles moving your way. Number unknown at this time."

"There's your confirmation, Roundup," Stansell said. "We need you on the ground—here."

"Negative, negative," Mado shouted.

"Then standby," Stansell told him. "We will advise you of the situation as it develops."

He had just taken command.

THE PENTAGON

Leachmeyer was standing in front of the computer-generated situation map at the front of the command center. A small microphone was pinned to his lapel and he was flashing an electronic pointer over the screen, explaining the situation to the President. "An enemy force of fifty personnel and an unidentified tracked vehicle are occupying the barracks behind the prison." The pointer circled the buildings behind the prison. "They have not attacked the prison but are in a position to prevent movement in and out. Our two M-60 machine-gun teams here"—the pointer circled the two teams in the ditch next to the road that ran in front of the prison—"are providing fire, suppressing movement to the front of the prison—"

"So it's a Mexican standoff," Cunningham broke in. "They can't get around to the front to go in, and we can't get out."

"I assume they are a holding force until that armored column arrives from Shahabad," the President said. "When is it expected to reach Kermanshah?"

"We're querying Roundup, that's General Mado, sir, for an ETA," Leachmeyer told him. The major sitting at the console keyed on

314   FORCE OF EAGLES

Leachmeyer and started talking on the SatCom, asking for the position and ETA of the armored column.

"General Mado should be at the airfield," Dewa said from behind Cunningham's shoulder. "He needs to be with his ground commander to coordinate a breakout, not on Spectre." The general turned and looked at her. "And if Romeo Team can get out of the prison in thirty to forty minutes, Task Force Alpha will be gone before those tanks get to Kermanshah."

Cunningham grunted and keyed his mike. "Charlie, I think we had better start talking to the people on the ground. At this point Roundup is a relay point and we need to cut out the middle man. They've got thirty minutes to make a break and get the hell out of Dodge."

The President's voice boomed over the loudspeakers. "I want them out ... now. Make it happen." A new worry for Cunningham—the President was butting in at the wrong time.

KERMANSHAH, IRAN

"Lifter, this is Roundup." The urgency in Mado's voice filled the room Stansell and Gregory were using as a command post. "Say number of POWs ready to move at this time."

"Keep him off my back," Gregory said. "We'll be ready to break out in five minutes." He turned back to his operations officer and made their last-minute arrangements with Romeo Team.

"Roundup, standby on the POW count," Stansell transmitted over the UHF radio.

"Lifter, you don't tell me to standby. I'm landing at this time—"

"Like hell, you are," Stansell grunted. He keyed his mike, still on the same frequency. "Spectre Zero-One, Mover Two-Three, and Stormy Zero-Two, I have tasking for you." Beasely, Doucette and Locke acknowledged in order. "Spectre your target is the barracks behind the prison. Laydown fire-suppression on command in approximately four minutes. Continue to engage until the trucks transporting the POWs are well clear of the prison." Beasely acknowledged.

"Mover Two-Three, take out Objective Yellow and RTB." Objective Yellow was the highway bridge at Mahidashi, halfway between Shahabad and Kermanshah. Doucette acknowledged and broke out of his holding orbit.

"Stormy Zero-Two, run another visual reccy on the highway. We need the position of Gold." Gold was the Iranian armored regiment moving on Kermanshah. Jack acknowledged and headed after Doucette.

"Well, well, Ramon," Doucette said to his WSO, "good old Rupe had our fuel figured down to a gnat's ass. Looks like you get to do your own lasing this time." Contreraz buried his head in the scope, driving his cursors out to the highway bridge. Doucette deployed the Pave Tack pod below the weapons bay.

On board the AC-130 Beasely had to quell a mutiny by one of his crew. As aircraft commander he had total control of his plane, regardless of rank. The fact that Mado was a two-star general and he was a captain didn't matter. "General, we land after we hose down the barracks. End of discussion or you get off my flight deck." He headed for the prison.

"That's tellin 'em, Beezer," came over the intercom from some unknown voice in the rear.

"Okay, ready to blow the door," the Ranger told the three men inside the cell on the third floor. "Get against a side wall and under your mattress, put your fingers in your ears, close your eyes and open your mouth." The three men told him they were ready. The Ranger yelled, "Fire in the hole," pulled the ring on the fuse-igniter that started the timing cord burning and took cover.

The C4 plastic charge exploded, and they ran for the cell with two more Rangers, kicked at the door . . . but nothing happened.

"You need a bigger charge, numb nuts," another Ranger growled.

"Yeah, well this is going to take a little experimenting to get it right. These damn doors are tougher than I thought. Don't want to kill the poor bastards inside." He carved another piece of explosive off the brick and stuck it next to the hinge, ready to try again. It was going to take a long time to blow all the doors on the third floor. He called for help and worked faster.

Outside, the last of the freed POWs were rushed across the quadrangle and helped through the gap in the wall. "That's a hundred ninety-one," a sergeant yelled at Trimler. "Six trucks loaded and ready to roll."

"Colonel Leason"—Trimler turned to the gaunt man standing beside him, amazed at the strength he still had after what he'd been through—"I think you should go with this group."

"No, I go with the last man."

Trimler understood. "We need to take cover. All hell's going to break loose in a minute." They could hear the AC-130 bearing down on them.

THE MAHIDASHI HIGHWAY BRIDGE

"We're going to be skoshi on fuel," Contreraz grumbled, taking his final cursor placement on the highway bridge.

"We gots enough my lad, we gots enough." Doucette was breathing hard. They were down on the deck, screaming across the valley floor, leaving a visible shock wave behind them. Doucette could see the small village of Mahidashi less than a kilometer from the bridge. "No short rounds on this one, Ramon. Please." He was thinking about his own children when they were little.

"Ready, ready . . . pull," Contreraz called. Doucette pulled the F-111's nose up and two bombs rippled off. "Was that a switch error?" Ramon shouted, his head still in the scope. He had been expecting a single bomb to come off. Doucette owned up to the error but claimed two were always better than one.

Contreraz watched the time-to-impact counter on his scope run down. "Laser on," he told Doucette, illuminating the bridge for the last few seconds of the bombs' flight as the F-111 arced away.

On the ground the guidance-control operator of a Soviet-built SA-8 Gecko, a surface to air missile, tracked the F-111 as it pulled away from the target. The operator assumed the F-111 for some reason had aborted its run and was not going to bomb the bridge. He was thankful that his superiors had positioned him well clear of the bridge and he was in a position to engage the American. After over a week of waiting he was ready. He decided to launch, using the electro-optical tracker and not the radar. Why send an electronic warning? He mashed his fire-control button and sent two missiles on their way, then watched in satisfaction as the rear of the F-111 flashed and exploded.

Doucette fought for control of his dying jet. "Eject! Eject!" Contreraz did as commanded and grabbed the ejection handle beside his left knee. With a press-squeeze-pull movement he started the sequence of events that fired explosive bolts and guillotines that freed their ejection capsule from the airframe. A rocket motor with a 40,000 pound thrust kicked them skyward.

The SA-8's guidance-control operator watched the crew module separate from the F-111 and make its parachute-controlled descent. He switched to radar guidance and tracked the module before he launched two more missiles. His men cheered when the module and parachute disappeared in a fireball. They were too busy congratulating themselves to reload, or notice the F-15 that had its nose on them.

CHAPTER 48

H PLUS 12

THE MAHIDASHI HIGHWAY BRIDGE

"I've got the reticle on him," Jack told his backseater. Furry checked the video screen in front of him that repeated whatever Jack saw through the HUD. It matched the video image he was getting from the seeker head of the Maverick Jack had called up. He drove the crosshairs on his scope over the six-wheeled vehicle that was starting to move down the road and pulled the trigger on his right-hand controller to half-detent. He liked what he saw and went full action. The Maverick's sensitive, cooled infrared seeker-head was locked on to the SA-8.

"Locked on, cleared to pickle," Furry called.

Jack waited as they bore down on the vehicle. A cold anger drove him on and he started to jink his jet back and forth in small random heading and altitude changes.

Meanwhile Furry was busy at monitoring their position for hostile radar activity and glancing back at their six o'clock position. "Lots of radar activity in front of us," he said. "But no threats. They haven't had a chance to reload—"

"Hold on . . ." Jack mashed his pickle button, sending a rocket-powered Maverick with its 125-pound warhead shrieking at the SA-8.

The crew of the SA-8 finally saw the F-15 before the Maverick leaped off its launcher and had slewed their vehicle to a stop. They were scattering when the missile hit, destroying the village. Jack circled and watched three men running for the nearby vehicle. "Not fast enough . . ." He thumbed back the auto-acquisition switch on the stick, changing his HUD display to guns. Since the cannon in the F-15 was canted up two degrees for air-to-air, it was going to be a low-angle strafe-run with a real low altitude pull-out. He triggered a short burst into the enemy . . . the cannon gave off a soft burring sound . . . and watched them crumble. He came in for a second pass and fired again.

He pulled off and checked the bridge. It was destroyed, as ordered. Then he turned over the smoking wreckage of the crew-module before heading down the road . . .

KERMANSHAH, IRAN

"On three . . ." The four men threw their weight against the heavy beam they were using as a lever. Slowly, they inched a heavy chunk of reinforced concrete out of the way before it fell and kicked up a cloud of dust. "Mary? Mary? You still okay?" Carroll called out.

"I'm okay . . ."

One of the Rangers looked up when he heard the approaching AC-130. "Take cover," he yelled. Four other Rangers were in position next to the back wall with M-203s. A command barked over their MX-360 radios and they started to pump 40mm grenades out of the launcher slung under the barrel of their rifles. They reloaded and kept firing rapidly as they could, lobbing the grenades high over the wall into the barracks area, providing indirect fire, driving the defenders for cover . . .

Beasely could see puffs from the grenades mushrooming up in the barracks compound as he set up his firing orbit. This time he selected the two 20mm cannons mounted in front of the left wheel-well. Again the crew went through the synchronized routine of bringing the gunship's firepower to bear. The Beezer wasn't concerned with hitting a specific target and walked the lighted circle on his HUD that showed the point of impact around the barracks. If he saw a likely target he pressed his trigger button and sent a hail of high-explosive bullets raining down. One of the Iranians caught in the open panicked and bolted around the side wall of the prison—to meet a burst of fire from the M-60 machine gun team holding the right side of the ditch in front of the prison.

The six trucks carrying the POWs gunned their engines and roared out of the protective shadow of the prison's front wall and raced for the airfield. Two jeep teams, Ratso Three in the front and Ratso Four in the rear, joined up and escorted them down the road, their M-60s swinging onto the barracks, raking them with gunfire.

When the first radio call reached the airfield that the trucks were moving, Stansell keyed his UHF radio. "Scamp One-Six and Scamp One-Seven, engine start. Repeat, start your engines. Scamp One-Four and Scamp One-Five, standby for engine start." The dull roar of two turboprop engines coming to life swept the airfield.

The illuminator operator in the back of the AC-130, studied the barracks compound as Beasely took one last orbit. This time the guns were silent as the crew did their own damage assessment. The IO didn't see the movement at first, then he saw the tracked, four-barreled anti-aircraft ZSU-23-4, the Shilka, break into the open from its protective shed. The four barrels of its turret-mounted twenty-three-millimeter guns were swinging on to the gunship as the tanklike, extremely dangerous anti-aircraft package clanked through the compound. "Break left! Poppin' flares and chaff!" the IO shouted, mashing buttons on the remote control in his left hand, sending flares and chaff cascading out behind the AC-130.

The Beezer wrenched the gunship to the left as commanded and jerked back on the yoke. Immediately he pushed it forward, driving the nose up and down as he pumped the rudder pedals, skidding and jerking the big Hercules—anything to break a tracking solution.

But it was too late. The ZSU-23-4 had Spectre dead to rights and sent a stream of 23mm bullets into the belly of the gunship. The bullets ripped the underside, tearing it apart. But the ceramic armor plating under the flight deck and cargo compartment held and the gunship was still flying. Two 23mm bullets hit the right wing, behind the number three inboard engine. Flames flickered behind the trailing edge of the wing and pieces of the center-section flap tore off in the windstream. Beasely slammed the big plane down onto the deck and managed to escape over the town's roof tops, but trailing smoke behind him . . .

The enemy ZSU-23-4 spun on its track and headed for the right side of the prison wall, into the same spot where the M-60 team had gunned down the Iranian moments before. The ZSU depressed its four guns as low as they would go. Because each gun had an automatic feed and was liquid cooled, it could sustain a rate of fire of a thousand rounds a minute. The commander inside the PT-76 tank chassis fired as he turned the corner, but the barrels were depressed too low and the bullets struck the ground in front, kicking up a cloud of dirt and gravel. The M-60 team returned fire and some of their 7.62mm rounds punctured the thin skin of the turret. But it was no contest. The ZSU's 23mm, high-explosive bullets dug a trench leading to the ditch as the ZSU commander lifted his sight and kept firing.

The ZSU-23-4 then backed around the corner and rumbled through the destroyed barracks compound, abandoning their wounded in the burning barracks.

THE PENTAGON

The announcement that Scamp 15 and 16 were airborne out of Kermanshah with 191 POWs aboard sent a round of clapping and an occasional whistle through the command center. Even the President was standing, a smile on his face, his right fist clenched in front of him. Only Cunningham did not respond. He sat quietly scanning the status boards.

Leachmeyer was on the stage holding his microphone, also smiling. When order settled over the crowd, he directed: "Send four of the F-15s orbiting on the tanker to intercept and escort the C-130s to safety."

"Sir"—it was Dewa—"that's a bad move. The radar at Maragheh is up and it might follow the F-15s into Iran. The C-130s have good terrain-masking and should be able to sneak out undetected. The Iranians must know we are on the ground at Kermanshah, but thanks to the Ayatollahs their command-and-control net is a shambles. They won't have their act together for another thirty, forty minutes."

"Charlie"—Cunningham hit his mike button, he wanted the President to hear what he had to say—"let the tactical director in the AWACS make that decision. He's in a much better position to evaluate the threat. That's what he's there for." He glanced at the President. There was no sign of disagreement so he went on. "Relay what you just said as an option for him to consider. But don't get in the way. Our troops seem to have their act together so far." Leachmeyer grumbled something he couldn't hear and the major relayed Leachmeyer's "suggestion" to Nelson aboard the AWACS.

The President sat down and turned to Bobby Burke, his CIA director. "Bobby, we walked right into an ambush . . ." He reached into his shirt pocket and pulled out a cigar. Andy Wollard, the President's chief of staff, recognized the signs and motioned the others in the Command and Authority Room to leave. He closed the door on the two men, leaving them alone. "We're not out of this yet, but after the dust settles I want to know why Intelligence missed it and I want the problem fixed."

Burke nodded. He knew better than to argue with the truth. He made a mental promise that he would, indeed, "fix" the problem. And if heads had to roll . . .

"Sir, let me get Camm over here for an update on the situation."

"Do that."

KERMANSHAH, IRAN

The flight engineer and the copilot went through the drill of shutting down number-three engine. Beasely pulled the engine condition lever for three to the feather position and the copilot continued with the checklist. The right scanner in the rear reported flames were still coming from the engine and the prop had feathered. The engineer double-checked the fuel-shunt valves and pulled the tee-handle that activated the fire bottle. The scanner reported the fire had gone out. Beasely established an orbit ten miles north of town and ran a crew check. Other than flying on three engines and the flaps being sticky, the AC-130 seemed to be in pretty fair shape.

"Captain Beasely," Mado said, "when you have it under control, land at the airfield and drop me off." It was the general's first time being shot at and hit. His stomach was around his eyeballs.

"General, no way I can land this beast and get it airborne with only three engines on that short of a runway. These puppies are heavy. If you want on the ground, you're going to have to make a nylon approach and landing. Got lots of extra chutes." There was no answer. A few moments later Mado was back on the SatCom, talking to the command center in the Pentagon.

* * *

"Sergeant Major," Jamison called from under the boxes in the rear of the dilapidated Japanese mini truck, "what's happening? Where are we?"

"Quiet," Kamigami commanded. They were parked on a side street leading to the back of the prison. It had taken them almost two hours to work their way unobserved down the hill and into the edge of town. There, Kamigami had hot-wired an old pickup truck that was parked next to a building. He was working under the dash when the owner found them. The Iranian still had a look of confusion on his face when Jamison shot him in the head. It was the first time the lieutenant had ever seen a dead man, much less one that he had made that way.

Kamigami had bundled the stunned Jamison into the rear of the truck and buried him under a pile of boxes. He sat behind the steering wheel and had wrapped himself in a blanket, his pistol and helmet on the seat beside him, and driven through town. He had decided that his oriental face would draw less attention than, say, a black one. As he suspected, in the confusion following the attack on the prison, no one seemed to notice. Ten minutes later he had found the spot on the side street near the prison, and was in time to watch the AC-130 lay a cloud of fire-suppression on the barracks and the six loaded trucks escape.

"Someone's coming," he told the lieutenant as he gunned the engine and threw a U-turn.

The ZSU-23-4 was moving down the street toward them and he did not want the enemy troops he could see running behind it to commandeer their truck. He turned down a dirt alley as the Iranians ran by. When the last of the men had passed, he followed them. This time he explained what he was doing. "Lieutenant, we're following some unfriendlies that came out of the barracks behind the prison. They look pissed and dangerous. I want to check 'em out."

"Shouldn't we rejoin Romeo Team or check in on the radio?"

"Not yet. Want to maintain radio silence. I've got my whisper mike plugged in and have been listening to the chatter on the MX-360. Romeo Team is still blowing doors down on the third floor. They'll be at that for at least another thirty minutes before all the POWs are free. We got time to join up." He didn't tell the lieutenant that the ZSU-23-4 was headed north. But then, that was in the general direction of the airfield where they wanted to go anyway . . .

NEAR SHAHABAD, IRAN

The F-15's TEWS painted overlapping hostile radar threats on the road leading from Shahabad to Kermanshah, and Jack's wizzo was worried. "There's at least one SA-8 and ZSU-23-4 moving down the road," Furry told him. "There's got to be more."

"About what you'd expect with an armored battalion," Jack said. "But we're going to take a look anyhow. Let's circle to the south and sneak up behind them." He dropped his F-15 down onto the deck and headed south away from the highway and paralleled the mountains on the west side of the valley. He rolled into a 135-degree bank and turned up a shallow canyon that crossed the mountains and led into the next valley. When they crested the ridge, Furry hit the EMIS LIMIT switch and activated their radar. Then they were back to silent running as Jack headed north toward the highway.

Suddenly Furry called out. "Someone's got us with a ZSU-23-4. Jamming now." Furry hit the buttons that brought the electronic-counter-measures part of the TEWS alive. He watched his video monitor to be sure it was working. "Got 'em. They won't have the foggiest where we are."

"Yeah, but they know we're out here." Jack dropped lower and pushed the throttles up, touching six hundred knots. He was doing easy jinks two hundred feet above the ground. "Look at that!" Furry, looking over Jack's right shoulder, saw a convoy stretched out on the road in front of them. "Amb, check the left, I'll check right. We're going to cross right over and get the hell out of Dodge. None of this parallel-road reccy shit." He dropped the jet even lower and flew around a low knoll, taking what terrain-masking he could. They flashed out from behind the knoll and bore down on the highway and crossed it at ninety degrees. Then they were clear and Jack was twisting and turning up another mountain valley.

"I counted eight T-72 tanks and at least six armored personnel carriers," Furry said. "Maybe a dozen trucks."

"Yeah. I got six tanks, four BTR-60s, Two SA-8s, and a ZSU-23-4 in the lead." Jack's eyes were better than his backseater's. "They're moving at about thirty miles an hour. Should reach the bridge in twenty to twenty-five minutes. Good thing Doucette and Ramon got it . . ." But he wasn't thinking about the bridge. In his mind was the smoking wreckage that was their ejection module.

"It's a shallow stream bed and the water's low," Furry told him. "It should be an easy crossing."

"We better tell Lifter. Time they got out of there. Us too, almost bingo." Bingo—the low fuel level that would force them to return to the KC-135 for an inflight refueling . . .

KERMANSHAH, IRAN

Carroll and Mustapha pulled the last of the rubble away and crawled through the low opening, wiggled under a reinforced concrete beam that had fallen into the basement and were at the door to Mary's cell. "Mary," he called, testing the door. It was locked.

"In here."

He jerked at the handle. Nothing. Mustapha pushed him aside and slapped a chunk of C4 explosive on the lock. He quickly wired the blast cap to the timing fuse and attached the fuse igniter. "Take cover," Carroll warned her, "we're blowing the lock." She told them she was under the bunk. Mustapha pulled the ring and they stepped back. The small charge blew the lock out of the heavy wooden door.

Carroll helped Mary out from under the bunk and to her feet. For a moment, they stood there, not touching, just looking at each other.

"Why did I know you'd come?"

"Because you were here. Where's doc?"

She motioned at the wall. "Next cell, he's in bad shape."

They rushed out of her cell and found Mustapha testing the door to Landis' cell. "The wall has shifted here." Mustapha pointed to the left side of the door. "I think the door is supporting the roof."

"We're going to need help," Carroll said. "Come on, let's get you out of here."

"Bill, I'm not leaving without doc. You go get help. Oh, there's a prison guard here named Amini. I think he's a CIA agent and I want to make sure he's okay. See if you can find him." Carroll didn't argue, he knew Mary Hauser too well.

"Lifter, Stormy," Jack radioed, still twenty miles away from the airfield. Stansell acknowledged. "Roger, Lifter," Jack continued, "the armored column moving up the highway is approximately ten miles short of the highway bridge at Mahidashi. At current rate of travel will reach the bridge in twenty minutes. We count fourteen

T-72 tanks, ten BTR-60s, twelve trucks, two SA-8s and a single ZSU-23-4. I am bingo minus one."

Stansell understood that Jack was getting dangerously short on recovery fuel and was already a thousand pounds low. "Say status of bridge," he radioed, "and Mover Two-Three."

"Bridge destroyed, Mover Two-Three splashed. No survivors." Jack's voice was dead flat.

The command post was silent as Stansell drew a line through Mover 23 on his board. So easy, he raged at himself, just draw a line and they cease to exist. I ordered them against that goddamn bridge and now . . . He fought to contain what he felt and returned to business. "Roger, Stormy, copy all. Understand you are bingo at this time. You are cleared off to the tanker. Be advised we have three thousand feet of runway and a fuel truck available here."

Jack did not hesitate. "Rog, Lifter. Landing now." Thanks to the deposed Shah and the massive economic buildup under his regime, the airports used American equipment and the fuel truck was fitted with a standard single point fuel nozzle. And thanks to Zakia, it was at the airfield.

Gregory was talking to his operations officer. "Colonel," he called to Stansell, "here, please." Stansell turned his attention away from his small board and the black line through Doucette's name. "Trimler reports that it's slow going blowing all the cell doors and expects it will take another forty minutes before he has cleared the prison. That makes that armor coming at us a threat. I plan to deploy Ratso One and Two down the road toward the highway bridge. I'm going to position a blocking force there." He pointed to the east side of the bridge. "They hold as long as they can and then withdraw back to Objective Red." He pointed to the intersection near the prison.

"Two Jeep teams against an armored column . . ."

"And reinforce them with Second Platoon, Bravo Company. I want to airdrop them, Colonel. They're ready to load. Hell, sir, I'll get 'em out, that's why I'm sending Ratso One and Two ahead. They're to pick a DZ and commandeer vehicles. We only drop Second Platoon when we've got something to move them in and I can't think of a faster way to get them there. Besides, quite a few of those unfriendlies got away from the barracks and are running around loose in the town. We leap frog 'em."

Stansell nodded. "Okay, load 'em on Mallard's plane." The S-3 ran out of the room, calling for Bravo Company's captain and Mallard to join him. Gregory studied the map. He was in his element, meeting the challenge he had trained so long for. There was nothing political to interpret, no deep analysis required. It was a tactical field problem that required an answer he was prepared to give. Gregory would never make a good colonel, but he was one hell of a good battalion commander. Stansell let him go, not getting in his way.

"We're going to need to use Spectre for a radio relay," Gregory said, "Mahidashi is beyond the range of the PRC-77."

"Spectre can still provide fire suppression," Stansell said.

"On three engines?"

A pained look crossed Stansell's face. "It's what they get paid for." The demon was back on him. He was ordering another crew into harm's way and his stomach was twisting itself into knots. Oh Christ, Muddy, he thought, is this what you went through? But he wasn't looking for approval from the shadowy figure from his past. Still, for the first time, he understood the agony of command, of what Muddy Waters must have known.

For the next five minutes Stansell and Gregory went over the ground situation while the RTO relayed the latest developments over the SatCom to the Pentagon's command center. Jack Locke came into the room, then, his refueling completed. "A hell of a mess you have here, Colonel." The two men shook hands while the sound of Mallard's C-130 taking off filled the room.

The MX-360 radio the RTO had set up next to his PRC-77 crackled to life. "Lifter, this is Romeo Two-Five with Romeo Two."

"About time," Gregory yelled. "That's Kamigami and Jamison!"

"Lifter," Kamigami radioed, "you've got company coming your way. Expect incoming mortar fire in the next few minutes."

"Say position of mortar teams," Gregory answered. He jotted down the coordinates while he called for a sergeant to spread the word and for the men to take cover. Stansell was on the UHF ordering the three remaining C-130s to start engines and launch before the attack started. Jack sprinted for his Eagle, intending to do the same. "Colonel," Gregory shouted, "have Spectre hose the shit out of these coordinates. We got problems."

CHAPTER 49

H PLUS 13

KERMANSHAH, IRAN

Scamp 14 was the first C-130 to bring all four engines on line and was turning onto the runway when the first mortar round hit the airfield. Because of the short runway, Scamp 14 paused while the pilot ran the engines up to max power before starting his takeoff roll. The nose of the C-130 tried to dig into the concrete as the props wound up. Then the big cargo plane was rolling, but before its nose gear could come unglued from the ground, Scamp 14 disappeared in a fiery cloud. A mortar round had scored a direct hit.

The pilot in Scamp 13 now taxied across the runway and onto the open flat area next to the runway. After landing with the Rangers he and another C-130 pilot had driven around the field in a jeep and staked out a long stretch of dirt that could be used as a makeshift runway. He lined up and ran up his engines, sending a cloud of dirt and dust out behind him, then he started his takeoff roll. But before he reached lift-off speed a barrage of mortars walked across in front of him, he tried to dodge a crater but it was too late. The left main gear of the Hercules sank into the mortar's crater. The crater was a minor obstacle for the gear to handle, but the left wing tip dipped too low and the number-one prop hit the ground. The plane wrenched to the left as the prop broke off the engine and smashed into number-two prop. Propeller fragments ripped into the fuselage as the pilot fought to bring the plane to a halt. The engineer pulled the emergency tee-handles on the fire emergency control panel for one and two, shooting the fire extinguishers in each engine and cutting off all fuel flow, which saved the crew.

The two props on the right were still spinning down when the five men jumped out of the plane and ran for cover . . .

Furry scrambled out of a ditch when he thought the attack was over and jogged for his F-15. Another mortar round exploded behind him, knocking him down.

"Lifter, tell Spectre to come right ten degrees and the target will be on his nose." Kamigami was talking on his MX-360 and having Stansell relay vectors that would guide the gunship to the soldiers they had followed and who were now mortaring the field. "Also, friendlies are two hundred meters north of target on road in a dark pickup truck."

"Roger," Stansell replied after he had relayed the messages to the gunship. "Spectre has target in sight and are aware of your position."

Kamigami watched the gunship set up a firing orbit around the cluster of buildings the mortar teams were firing from. "Those muthas are in some kind of trouble, Lieutenant." Jamison wasn't sure who the sergeant was talking about, the mortar teams or the gunship. The ZSU-23-4 was hidden not far from them and he had seen what it could do.

"We go," Kamigami grunted, and drove slowly past a walled compound. "Now," he ordered. Jamison sat up in the back of the pickup and raised the sergeant's M-203, pointed the barrel skyward and fired the grenade launcher, sending a 40mm cartridge over the wall. They were sending indirect fire onto the ZSU-23-4 that had run to earth inside the walls. Jamison reloaded and fired again and again as Kamigami turned down a side street and moved down the other side of the compound. Their plan was to keep the crew of the ZSU-23-4 occupied while the gunship was in range.

In the distance they could hear the gunship work the mortar teams over, destroying the low buildings where they were hiding, then they heard the distinctive whomp of the 105mm cannon as Beasely leveled his target.

The attack on the airfield was over.

Inside the compound the ZSU commander ordered his driver to

break out of the compound. The Iranian gunned the engine and smashed through the rear gate. Kamigami's eyes were drawn into narrow squints as he watched the ZSU-23-4 clank away from him. Only this time there were no supporting troops or trucks following it. The sergeant grunted in satisfaction and followed. He had a score to settle with the ZSU commander, preferably alive. Besides, as he told the lieutenant, the ZSU was a threat to any aircraft taking off from the airfield and they had plenty of time to rejoin . . .

MAHIDASHI, IRAN

"Spectre, Scamp One-Two." Mallard was calling Beasely, who had joined him orbiting near the highway bridge. "Glad you could make it. Are you in contact with Ratso and what the hell is taking so damn long? We've been holding for over ten minutes."

"Rog, Scamp. Sorry for the delay. Had to see a man about a mortar. Ratso is up and heading for the bridge now." The two Hercules continued to orbit, with Beasely stacked above Mallard. Now they could see a small convoy move out of Mahidashi village toward the destroyed bridge. Three trucks, two vans and a small bus were sandwiched between the two jeeps. "Scamp," Beasely called, "check the highway to the west. I've got the lead tanks in sight. Time to do some discouragin'." Beasely broke out of orbit and started to climb, straining his three remaining engines.

"Scamp," Beasely called, "Ratso is in position and says to drop on him." The jeeps with their commandeered vehicles had pulled up near the bridge. Mallard could see civilians, the former owners or drivers, running back to the village. A Ranger in one of the jeeps popped green smoke, the signal to drop.

Drunkin Dunkin watched the smoke drift lazily upward. Satisfied that winds would not be a problem, he keyed his intercom. "Three minute warning."

In the rear of the C-130 the jumpmaster stood by the left paratroop door. "Get Ready," he bellowed. "Stand Up!" The forty-five jumpers were on their feet. "Hook Up!" Forty-five hands snapped the hook on their static line to the anchor line above their heads. "Check Static Line!" Forty-five sets of eyes took one last look at their static line and took the slack out of it by forming a bight and clenching it tightly. "Check Equipment!" Each Ranger used his free hand to jerk and tug at his equipment one last time, making sure everything was secure. "Sound Off For Equipment Check!" The last man in each stick tapped the Ranger in front and yelled, "Okay!" The signal was passed until the stick leader got it and yelled, "All Okay!"

The jumpmaster rooted himself in the door, holding on to the stanchions on each side. "One minute warning," came over his headset. He stuck his head out and checked the approaching DZ. He could see the green smoke. Dunkin was right on. He stood back and pointed at the door with two fingers. "Stand In The Door!" The Rangers shuffled forward, two lines on each side of the aircraft.

The red jump light by each door snapped off and the green light flickered to on. "GO!" The Rangers took little hops as they went out the door one second apart. Ten men on each side had gone out when the jump light flicked back to red and Dunkin yelled over the intercom. "Red Light! Red Light! Stop Jump! Stop Jump!"

The jumpmaster stepped into the door and pushed the next jumper back with both hands. The Hercules rolled into a ninety degree left bank, pulled down and away . . . and the jumpmaster fell out the door as a smoke trail and tracers passed behind the C-130.

"What the hell happened?" the loadmaster yelled over the intercom. "The jumpmaster fell out and I got bodies all over the deck . . ." They were flying straight and level now, less than two hundred feet above the ground.

"The fuckers hosed us down with a SAM and Triple A," Dunkin told him. "We were lucky they were too far away . . . We got the jumpmaster in sight, he's waving he's okay." The Rangers on the ground had a different view. The jumpmaster was coming down in his chute, swearing, and giving the C-130 the finger.

"Yeah," the loadmaster shouted, "Well, I've got about twenty pissed-off Rangers that want to get on the ground."

Mallard turned to his navigator. "Okay, Dunk, if we go in low enough, we can stay under all that crap they threw at us." Dunkin reached for "the gadget" in his navigation bag.

KERMANSHAH, IRAN

"Scamp One-Four destroyed on runway, five crew members KIA," the RTO was transmitting on the SatCom, giving the Pentagon command center a status report after the mortar attack on the airfield. "Scamp One-Three damaged and out of commission. Aircrew, okay. Scamp One-Five is undamaged and mission capable. Stormy Zero-Two is slightly damaged, status unknown at this time, the WSO, Captain Furry, is wounded. One Ranger KIA, two wounded."

"Say status of runway," the woman's voice came through the scrambler loud and clear.

"Runway is closed," the RTO answered.

"Say current threat."

"Negative threat to airfield at this time. Armored column reported at Mahidashi highway bridge . . ."

Gregory turned to Stansell, "We're in big trouble unless we can get a runway open. And we could sure use another C-130 to help Scamp One-Two and One-Five get us out of here."

Stansell thought a moment. "That hulk will have to turn itself out on the runway before we can push it off."

"How we going to do that?"

"Jeeps and winches. But right now we're going to see if the crew for Scamp One-Three can get their two good engines started and move about a hundred feet out of the way. We fill in the craters on the dirt strip and we've got a runway."

"What about the F-15?" Gregory asked.

"Have to wait and see if Jack can get it started, it took some battle damage from that mortar round that got Furry, and if we can clear the main runway."

"We still need another C-130," Gregory reminded him.

"Right." Stansell asked the RTO to let him talk to the command center. "Blue Chip, this is Lifter. We need airlift. Scamp One-One is in orbit with Delray Five-One. Send Scamp One-One our way now. Repeat, send Scamp One-One our way now."

The wait for Blue Chip to make a decision seemed forever. Jack Locke walked into the silent room. "Furry's in pretty bad shape," he told the colonel. "Shrapnel in the back. Frag also punched two small holes in my jet. Doesn't look bad but the nitrogen bottle for the jet fuel starter won't hold a charge. Can't start engines."

The silence grew heavier.

"Lifter," the SatCom came alive. "This is Blue Chip. Be advised Scamp One-One is departing orbit at this time."

Lydia Kowalski and her crew were finally going to war.

"Now we got to get that C-130 moved," Stansell said.

A voice came over the PRC-77. "Lifter, this is Romeo. We're ready to load. All POWs released and accounted for but one. Working to free him now."

Gregory looked at Stansell, waiting for a decision. "They'd be safer in the prison than here . . . until we get the field open."

"Move them now," Stansell ordered. "Jack, get out to the dirt strip and get it opened. We load the POWs on Scamp One-Five. It launches the minute we get a runway."

MAHIDASHI, IRAN

"Captain, this is all you're gonna get," Beasely's flight engineer told him. The AC-130 had managed to climb to eleven thousand feet on its three engines and it wasn't going any higher. Beasely wanted more altitude to increase his stand-off distance from the tanks approaching the bridge. Because the terrain elevation was 4,000 feet, he was only 7,000 above the ground. That meant a thirty-degree bank in his firing orbit would give them a stand-off distance of 12,000 feet—enough to stay clear of the ZSU-23-4 that was moving with the tanks, but it also put them inside the range of the two SA-8s Jack had seen.

Beasely told his electronic warfare officer and the illuminator operator to stay alert for SA-8s and entered a firing orbit to engage the lead tank that was almost at the bridge.

Mado wanted to order this AC-130 to stand clear but sensed that it would develop into a contest of wills and he wasn't sure who would win—him, or Beasely and Thunder. So instead he continued to relay information to the Pentagon over the SatCom.

"Flaps aren't coming down evenly," Beasely said. "Scanner, check the flaps on the right side."

A sergeant from the rear reported back. "Center section looks like its hanging up because of battle damage. The flap-drive motor is screaming its head off." He was talking about the hydraulic-driven flap-drive motor nestled between the wings in the overhead above the cargo deck. Beasely eased the flaps back up and raised the nose with the yoke, playing the trim for all it was worth. When he was satisfied with the orbit, he sighted on the lead tank and sent a 105mm round on its way, the AC-130 shuddering as it absorbed the 105's recoil.

"Direct hit!" the sensor operator in the rear called out. Then silence. "Beezer, that didn't stop it. He's still moving."

"We do it again," Beasely said. He could see the muzzle of the tank point at him as he sent three rounds toward the tank, until he blew a tread off. Then he turned to the second tank and fired.

"SAM lock on!" the EWO yelled over the intercom.

"Break right!" from the IO. Hanging out the rear of the aircraft, the illuminator operator could see two smoke trails coming at them.

Again, he sent a stream of chaff and flares behind them. Beasely rolled into a 110-degree bank and pushed the nose down while turning to the right, pulling two Gs. As he did, a loader feeding the 105mm was thrown across the aircraft into the ammo rack and knocked unconscious. The first missile streaked harmlessly overhead, but the second passed close enough that its proximity fuse activated, and the missile's fireball sent a burst of metal fragments into the right side of the fuselage.

Again, the AC-130 retreated, trailing smoke from the right main gear well . . .

While the gunship was engaging the tanks, Mallard ran in for the second drop. Drunkin Dunkin was holding onto the back of the copilot's seat, sighting the depression angle through the "gadget." He was going to give the green light exactly six hundred feet short of where he wanted the first Ranger to land, which meant a depression angle of sixty degrees. "I need a hard altitude of three hundred and fifty feet, Duck." Mallard checked his radar altimeter and squeaked it lower. The smoke trail of an SA-8 passed over them.

"What happens if they have a chute malfunction?" Don Larson, the copilot said.

"They won't have time to think about it," Dunkin said. "Ready, ready . . ." He sighted the depression angle, waiting to hit sixty degrees . . .

Actually, Dunkin was good enough to have eyeballed it, but this way he was deadly accurate. "Green Light!" The Rangers streamed out the back, their chutes popping open at the end of the twenty-foot static lines. Most were on the ground before they had made one swing, then were running for their rally point . . .

KERMANSHAH, IRAN

The two Rangers were pushing against the wood brace, trying to lever it into place and shore up the ceiling. "Hernia time," one grunted as they tried again. This time they wedged it next to the cell door. "Might be able to blow the door now," the Ranger said. "That beam should take the weight." Mary and Carroll looked apprehensively at the ceiling above them.

Mary put her ear to the cell door. "Doc, can you hear me?"
No reply.

Another Ranger called down into the basement. "Captain Trimler says it's time to go. We got all the POWs loaded we're moving out—"

"I don't go without doc," Mary said.

Carroll decided it. "Tell Trimler to leave us a truck. We'll stay here with Mustapha. Tell the road team holding the intersection—"

"That's Objective Red," the Ranger told him.

"—Objective Red," Carroll continued, "that we're here and to pick us up when they withdraw. We'll stay in contact over the MX-360."

"We'll stay," the Ranger standing next to Mary said. The other Ranger nodded agreement.

THE PENTAGON

"Sir, the President wants to see you." It was Cunningham's aide, Stevens. He pointed to the Command and Authority Room. Cunningham grunted and pushed his chair back. When he stood up he could see Admiral Scovill, Leachmeyer and Camm from the CIA in the room. He had been expecting this.

The President was leaning back in his chair, pointing an unlit cigar at Burke, the CIA Director, when Cunningham entered the room. "The DIA tells me that a partisan force of Kurds attacked the main airport at Kermanshah in conjunction with our raid. Further, that they destroyed an airliner on the field that was waiting to move the POWs. Now what the hell is going on?"

Burke was fighting for his job and knew it. "I wish I knew the DIA's sources so I could confirm that information—"

"They're talking to the Mossad," the President said, his voice tight. "Our allies—damn good ones too when it comes to intelligence. Don't you talk to them?"

"Of course, we do . . ."

Allan Camm stepped in. "Excuse me, sir, but we carefully evaluate everything we get from the Israelis. We have found that the quality of their intelligence has degraded in the last few years . . ."

"Well, there's nothing wrong with the *quality* now." The President swung back onto Burke. "Bobby, you're a pro . . . I need better intelligence." He pointed at the situation boards with his cigar. "Now how do we get the rest of our people out of there?"

"Mr. President, it's still salvageable," Cunningham said. All eyes in the room were on him. "First, two-thirds of the POWs are out of

Iran and should be landing at Incirlik within thirty minutes. Second, the last third are moving to the airfield right now and we've got a C-130 waiting for them."

"And no runway," Leachmeyer jabbed.

"They will have shortly, Charlie. You underestimate what a C-130 can do and how motivated those people are."

"That still leaves my Rangers trapped."

So now they're "yours," Cunningham thought. "We've got two C-130s airborne that can land, and if the Rangers can disengage from that armored column we'll get 'em out."

The door opened and Andy Wollard, the President's chief of staff, came in. "Sir, latest transmission from General Mado: the Rangers are holding at the bridge and his aircraft has taken another hit engaging a tank. But he's going to stay airborne. Also, all of the POWs but two are at the airfield."

"Mado's a goddamn hero," Leachmeyer said.

Not if I have anything to say about it, Cunningham thought. He damn well should have been on the ground at the first opportunity . . .

The President dismissed them and huddled with his National Security Advisor.

Outside, Burke drew Camm aside and grabbed his right elbow. "We had better be clean on this . . ."

Camm felt sick. He knew he had badly misjudged the whole deal. What he said was, "We are, sir. We are."

MAHIDASHI, IRAN

"They're disengaging. Repeat disengaging," a Ranger on the left flank transmitted. They had been deployed on both sides of the destroyed bridge when the tanks came at them. In front of him the hulks of two tanks were burning, one less than thirty meters away. It had taken their last Dragon shoulder-launched anti-tank missile to knock out the T-72. The rattle of heavy machine-gun fire echoed down from the right and the tank that the gunship had disabled kept firing round after round at the east bank. The tank on the right that the Rangers had finally nailed with the third Dragon was erupting with internal explosions. The smell of burning flesh drifted over them.

The captain in command tallied his losses: three dead, eight wounded. He knew what was coming next—a mortar barrage.

"Time to beat feet," he mumbled, and passed the word to withdraw. On his order a hail of smoke grenades rained down from the Rangers onto the river bank, and the dull thumps of two 60mm mortars throwing smoke added to the confusion.

The Rangers ran for the waiting trucks while the two jeep teams sprayed the smoke with short bursts from their M-60s. They had held the bridge for twenty-four minutes, destroyed three tanks (not counting the one disabled by the AC-130 but still firing), knocked out two BTR-60s, killed two dozen of the enemy and wounded another forty-three. More than a fair exchange.

KERMANSHAH, IRAN

The four trucks carrying the eighty-six POWs and most of the Romeo Team drove directly up to the rear of the waiting C-130—Scamp 15. Before they could unload, Stansell directed the trucks to disperse around the airfield and to keep their motors running, ready to move if the airfield came under attack again or if it was time to load the C-130. Scamp 14 was still burning on the runway, sending a dense pillar of black smoke into the air.

Across the runway on the makeshift dirt strip the crew of Scamp 13 was having trouble starting number-four engine, the pilot and flight mechanic trying not to burn out the starter. Finally, the engine did come on line and wound up, and a noisy sigh of relief escaped from Stansell. He watched as the pilot jockeyed the throttles back and forth on the two good engines and slowly inched the damaged plane off the strip. When he judged the Hercules was going to move clear, he waved for the trucks to return and twirled his right forefinger above his head, motioning for the crew to start engines on Scamp 15.

Trimler bounced out of the cab of the first truck, the Rangers threw the tail-gates of the trucks open and helped the POWs unload and move up the ramp of the C-130. Trimler had to help a tall, gaunt man out of the truck—his clothes in rags, he was barefoot and very weak. The man spoke a few words to the young captain. Trimler pointed to Stansell, and the POW slowly crossed the thirty feet that separated them, Trimler walking beside him. When they reached Stansell, the man somehow pulled himself to attention and slowly saluted.

"Colonel Clayton Leason, 45th Tactical Fighter Wing, reporting for duty."

It was all Stansell could do to return the salute.

Kamigami wheeled the pickup truck down a deserted street, still dogging the ZSU-23-4. The sound of gunfire and mortars had driven most of the people of Kermanshah to cover, and the few who were outside and moving were too preoccupied to notice a pickup. He turned into an alley and stopped when he saw the ZSU clank to a halt. A hatch popped open and a man climbed out carrying what looked like a RPG, the standard Soviet shoulder-held anti-tank missile and an assault rifle. Kamigami watched the man hurry into a house, leaving the door open behind him.

"They're putting out a road guard to cover their flank," Kamigami said. "Means they're near their next position. Lieutenant, cover me and keep your eye on the ZSU. Don't want to lose it now. I'm going in." The sergeant grabbed the lieutenant's rifle and moved toward the empty doorway. Jamison covered him with the M-203, figuring a well-placed grenade would discourage anyone from moving down the street. He marked where the ZSU turned into a grove of trees . . .

Kamigami got to the doorway and paused, listening. The ugly sounds from inside indicated the Iranian soldier he had seen was engaged in a rape. He moved the rifle back onto his shoulder, drew his Bowie knife and darted soundlessly through the door. A moment later he was out, carrying the RPG, not saying a word.

The lieutenant pointed to the grove of trees where he had last seen the ZSU. Kamigami nodded and sprinted down the alley, leaving the pickup truck behind. Jamison ran after him.

The last of the POWs, minus two, were aboard the C-130. Trimler and a sergeant were comparing lists, making sure all the POWs were accounted for. Two men were carrying on a body bag—the POW who had been killed in the basement before the Rangers could save him. Four wounded were helped on board, including Ambler Furry, Jack's WSO. "All accounted for except Carroll, Hauser, and Landis," Trimler told Stansell and Leason.

"Launch without them," Clayton said. "I'll stay until they're here."

"You should go," Stansell told him, not wanting to tell him the obvious . . . that there was nothing he could do to help.

"I'll stay. Load Mokhtari on board. I want that son of a bitch to stand trial. And there's an Iranian guard, Amini, who should go with us."

"Why the guard?" Stansell asked.

"He helped the POWs, says he's a friendly agent working for someone called Deep Furrow," Trimler put in. He turned to a sergeant. "Get the Iranian colonel and the guard on board." The sergeant headed for the last truck.

Heading toward them, a jeep bounced across the field on the other side of the runway, skirted the still burning hulk of the C-130 and skidded to a halt beside them. It was Jack Locke. "Trouble, sir," he gestured toward Scamp 13. "The bird's stuck and its tail is still in the way."

The sergeant who had gone to put Mokhtari and the guard on board came running back. "The Iranian colonel—he's gone—escaped . . ."

Mokhtari had not escaped. In the confusion of loading the trucks at the prison, he had simply walked into the ruins of his prison and been left behind.

MARAGHEH, IRAN

The radar operator was aching and his eyes were tired as he monitored the radar scope. He wanted to get outside and walk around, anything to break the long monotony of sitting in the radar shack. He made a mental promise never to again antagonize his superior, the captain in the control center. A flicker on the scope at forty-five nautical miles, bearing 215 degrees, caught his attention. He played the antenna tilt and receiver-gain and caught it again. He hit the IFF interrogator. No response. Again, he got the skin paint on what was now definitely an unidentified aircraft. His spirits rose. He had an intruder. The radar return disappeared off his scope.

He jerked a drawer open, pulled out an acetate overlay and slapped it over the scope. The overlay outlined the mountains that masked his radar from detecting low-flying aircraft. He proceeded to calculate where the return would next appear on the scope when the intruder lost its terrain-masking.

Suddenly the door of the radar shack was kicked open and the operator spun around. His captain stomped into the room followed by four armed men and a black-robed, turbaned old man—an Ayatollah. "Stand to attention," the captain ordered. He glanced at the scope. "The Americans have attacked Kermanshah, obviously to rescue the filth being kept there. *You* should have detected their aircraft—"

"But, sir, I have—"

"You have been asleep," the young officer told him, very worried about his own immediate chances of survival. The armed guards were not his men but the Ayatollah's. "Take him out and shoot him—now." When the Ayatollah nodded, two guards grabbed the operator and took him outside. The captain glanced back at the scope but jerked his head away when he heard two gunshots. Well, someone had to pay . . .

"Get another operator in here," he ordered, missing the return that flickered on the screen and then disappeared.

WESTERN IRAN

"Thirty more seconds," the navigator Sue Zack said, "then we'll be back in behind some mountains." The tension on the flight deck of Scamp 11 eased when they flew behind a mountain, away from the open valley that led to Maragheh. "ETA to Kermanshah, thirty-three minutes."

"Roger," Kowalski acknowledged, "let's see if we can get this old girl to go a bit faster." She shoved the throttles up.

Sergeant Ray Byers climbed onto the flight deck and stood behind Kowalski. "What in the hell are you doing here?" she asked, amazed to see the crew chief aboard.

"Is this the Marrakech express?"

"You asshole," she said, suppressing a smile.

CHAPTER 50

H PLUS 14

OBJECTIVE RED, KERMANSHAH

The three teen-aged boys crouched behind the plaster-covered rock wall and watched the cloud of dust coming from the airfield move toward them. The wall was set back thirty yards and paralleled the road that led from the prison to the main intersection where the Americans were. By the time the dust cloud reached the prison, they could make out the lead jeep and the two trucks that followed. The oldest of the three told the other two to keep down. Being sixteen gave him the leadership of his small band and he told them to check their weapons. He moved the safety to off on the Heckler-and-Koch assault rifle his cousin had brought home from the Iraq war. The fifteen-year-old clutched his family's double-barreled shotgun and wished he had the Heckler-and-Koch. The thirteen-year-old had to be satisfied with an old revolver with five rounds.

The boys had listened to the mullah at their school and understood how the cowardly Americans always ran when confronted with the just anger of the faithful. And they were among the faithful. The sixteen-year-old listened, and when he thought the small convoy was almost to their position shouted "now!" and the three boys jumped up and started to fire from behind the protective cover of the wall.

The lead jeep returned fire with the M-60 machine gun mounted on the hood. The gunner in the rear swung his M-60 and raked the wall. A Ranger in the bed of the first truck cut loose with his SAW while another fired an M-203, sending a grenade over the wall. No one had ever told the boys what firepower meant, and they were stunned when the first burst of fire from the M-60 tore the wall apart in front of them.

The thirteen-year-old found himself lying on the ground, covered with pieces of the wall. He tried to crawl over to the other two boys, who were still. But he could not—his right leg would not move. The boy looked down. There was nothing below the knee. He stared at it, not understanding why he didn't feel a thing, then tried to crawl away. But a pain stopped him. He had never hurt like that before. He slipped into unconsciousness as he bled to death.

The mullah was safe at home.

"Knock it off," the lead Ranger yelled. "We got 'em." The Rangers scanned the wall, looking for movement. Then they were at the main intersection—Objective Red.

Trimler got out of the lead truck and found Bravo Company's commander while Romeo Team unloaded. They conferred with the squad sergeants and the leader of the jeep teams, then parceled out their remaining Dragons and moved into position. "How long until they get the airfield open?" Bravo Company's C.O. asked.

"Anybody's guess," Trimler said. "But we've got to hold here."

Thunder was working the FM radio aboard the AC-130 and was talking to the RTO at Objective Red. "The Rangers are in position," he told Beasely. The pilot orbited over the intersection, marking the position of the Rangers. He could see the first of the tank column approaching the low pass that led to the intersection.

"Okay, troops," Beasely announced over the intercom, "time to rock and roll again." Each station checked in.

"Captain," Mado demanded, "what the hell are you doing? We've got battle damage."

"What we get paid for, general. The last hit only got the right main gear. Just a little rubber burning. It's out now." Beasely wasn't paying much attention to the general as he concentrated on setting up his first orbit and sighting on the lead tank. He mashed the trigger, and the plane shook as he sent the first 105 round on its way. In the back a loader had already reloaded and Beasely fired again. "Goddamn," he yelled in frustration, "those are tough sons a bitches." He fired again . . .

KERMANSHAH, IRAN

"Stand back," the Ranger commanded as he pulled the ring on the fuse igniter and stepped clear of the cell door. It was the third attempt to blow down the door and he had made each charge progressively bigger, risking blowing down the ceiling on top of them. The sharp explosion filled the corridor with dust and smoke. Their ears were still ringing when they saw the door. It was, finally, off its hinges. Mary quickly pushed it out of the way and went into the cell.

"Doc, oh God." She was beside Landis. Doucette's bomb had blown down part of the ceiling onto him. The lower half of his body was crushed under a massive concrete beam that pinned him to the floor. At least he was still alive. She lifted his head. "Doc . . ."

"Mary, go, get out . . . I'm not going to make it."

"No, not without you."

"Tell my wife—"

"*You'll* tell her."

Landis looked at her. He knew what had happened to him and that his body would fight death for hours. But he also knew without a surgeon and an operating room he was not going to make it. In the distance he could hear cannon fire. "Mary, I'm ordering you to go, goddamn it . . ."

Carroll reached down and pulled her to her feet. At first she fought him but Mustapha helped and the two men dragged her out of the cell. One of the Rangers came back in and gave Doc Landis a double shot of morphine. Doc understood the Ranger was trying to administer a fatal dose, but it wasn't enough. He watched the man go before he closed his eyes. And waited.

"I'm slow," Gregory muttered under his breath. He was watching Scamp 13 run up its two engines, trying to break out of the rut it was stuck in and move clear of the dirt runway. "You"—he pointed to a sergeant—"get the fuel truck and use it like a bulldozer. Get behind the C-130 and push like hell." He went over to Stansell. "Help's on the way." He pointed to the big fuel truck that was nosing in under the tail of the Hercules. The sergeant driving the truck gunned the engine and pushed. The thin skin of the C-130 crushed and buckled but the raised ramp held against the fuel truck's bumper. The big cargo plane jerked, then at last broke free and moved clear of the dirt strip.

Scamp 15 with its load of POWs and wounded was already moving into position at the end of the makeshift runway. The men on the airfield watched as the pilot set the brakes and ran the engines up to max power. It seemed forever before he released the brakes and started to move. The takeoff roll seemed even longer until the nose gear lifted and the Hercules was airborne, climbing steeply into clear air. Then the plane dropped down onto the deck and arced around the north side of town, heading for freedom. No one at the airfield saw the stream of 23mm high-explosive bullets that reached out to the Hercules, falling short because of the range.

"We just may do this yet," Stansell said, pointing to Mallard's C-130 that was coming in to land, and in the distance they could see Kowalski's Herky Bird approaching. Stansell studied the still burning hulk on the runway. "We can use that fuel truck again—when that baby stops burning."

Gregory was running back inside the makeshift command post. "Colonel, we got work to do. Time to dry this place up." Stansell agreed and followed him. In the distance, he could see a truck approaching the field . . .

Gregory and his S-3 were on the radios organizing a withdrawal, working out how to pull in the Rangers from Objective Red and bring in the road teams. While they worked Stansell located one of the incendiary explosive devices they had brought along. He planned to shove it into a gear-well of Locke's F-15, pull the pin and leave another burning hulk at the airfield. The sooner the better, he calculated, too many things were against getting it airborne. Besides not being able to crank the engines, the F-15 needed the hard surfaced runway to take off. And the burning C-130 had that blocked.

Jack appeared in the doorway of the command post. "Colonel," and he stepped aside. Stansell looked up and saw Bill Carroll and Mary Hauser standing there.

Stansell tried to find the right words, couldn't. "You had us worried . . ." was all he could come up with, but they didn't need words. Carroll told Stansell and Leason about Doc Landis while Mary stared into a corner. "That's a rough one," Stansell said. "We'll go back and get him if—" Lydia Kowalski came into the room then with Duck Mallard.

"Sorry to take so long getting here," she said.

The MX-360 radio above the RTO's head crackled and a strange voice started talking. "You are surrounded. Your position is hopeless. I will accept your surrender."

"*Mokhtari*," Mary said. Leason went rigid . . . Just the sound of that voice . . .

"Why waste lives needlessly?" Mokhtari went on. "We have, of course, taken prisoners."

"The bastard," Leason said. "He's got someone, he'll torture—"

"It's Doc Landis . . ." Mary said.

"Ah, you don't believe me," the voice went on. "Here, perhaps I can encourage him to talk to you . . ."

Mary was crying. "I knew I shouldn't have left him . . ."

The sound that came over the radio was unintelligible, pathetic.

"What the hell?" This from Jack.

"Mokhtari, the prison commandant," Leason said. "A sadistic, vicious"—he fought for control—"he tortures . . ."

"Please don't make me encourage him again. Perhaps you would like to talk to the doctor. He is conscious now."

The voice was faint, but more intelligible. "Cleared in hot, nail the bastard—"

They heard the sharp report of a small caliber weapon, then nothing.

"What?" Kowalski said, then understood.

"Doc was telling us to bomb his position," Jack said bitterly. "I wish to hell my jet would crank . . ."

Kowalski looked at him. "I've got a crew chief named Byers on my bird who might be able to—" Jack was already out of the room and running for Byers.

Stansell looked out the window. Again words couldn't express his feelings. Get on with it. "The C-130 . . . it's stopped burning . . . let's see if that fuel truck can play bulldozer again."

OBJECTIVE RED, KERMANSHAH

Trimler on the ground was listening on the PRC-77. "We knocked out the lead tank," Thunder reported from the gunship. "They're laying a lot of smoke ... hold on ... there's five tanks in a V formation coming at you."

Trimler passed the word that another attack was starting.

The two army captains bent over a map and planned their withdrawal to the airfield. "We stop 'em here and make them regroup," Trimler said. "When that happens we lay down smoke and have Spectre move in for another pass—make it look like we're counterattacking. But the forward fire teams pull back and we leapfrog backwards to the prison—fast. We lay smoke all the way and shoot at anything that comes through it." He glanced at the low hills that framed both sides of the road and intersection. They should help hold the smoke in the area.

"It will get tough past the prison," Bravo Company's C.O. said. "The terrain opens up ... hard to hold ... the tanks will spread out and flank us."

"Yeah, you're right, we need to fall back to a holding position at the prison, get Spectre to slow 'em down while we disengage and run like hell for the airfield." Trimler keyed the PRC-77 and relayed their plan to Gregory.

"My mother didn't raise me to be a hero," Andy Baulck said to his buddy Wade. They were holding the point furthest away from the intersection and closest to the advancing tanks. A jeep team was backing them up 150 meters down the road, around the comparative safety of a bend. "You ever fire one of these suckers before?"

"Yeah, me and the Dragon are old friends," Wade told him. He wiggled along a shallow depression, searching for a good spot to fire the missile. "Those got to be the new T-72s with laminated armor. They're tough, takes lots to knock 'em out." He could see the tanks, still over 1,000 meters away, advancing up the road, almost to the pass that led to Objective Red. "I'm going for the tracks ..." He fired the Dragon at 800 meters and kept the crosshair on his tracker riveted on the front left track of the T-72. Wade never actually saw the missile as it followed the commands coming from his tracker and fed through a thin wire spinning out from behind the missile, but the Dragon hit within inches of where Wade had placed the crosshairs, blowing the tank's track off a sprocket. The tank jerked to the left and stopped. The other four tanks turned and headed back, laying smoke. "Son of a bitch," Baulck yelled, "I don't believe it. MOVE." The two men ran for the rear as a mortar team sent round after round toward the retreating tanks, adding to the confusion. They piled into the waiting jeep and raced for the intersection.

Behind the smoke, the tanks headed away. Until a radio command stopped them and they pivoted on their tracks and headed back up the road, toward Objective Red.

KERMANSHAH, IRAN

Byers was under the left wing of the F-15 poking into an open access panel on the underside of the fuselage. "Cap'n, you ever hear of the golden BB?"

Jack Locke did not answer.

"What's that?" Staff Sergeant Marcia MacIntyre, Kowalski's flight engineer, asked.

"A goddamn lucky shot," Byers answered. "Two bits of frag hit, one knicks a wiring bundle in a fire-control junction-box and one fractures the coupling for the nitrogen bottle." Byers didn't take time to explain how the jet fuel starter used compressed nitrogen to start and how the JFS, in turn, started the engines. "Mac," Byers called, "go get my scrounge bag. I think I got a coupling." MacIntyre ran for the C-130 and Byers dove into his tool box. He pulled out a set of wrenches and reached inside the access panel, working furiously. "Cap'n you may just be in luck."

MacIntyre was back in moments with the canvas bag full of spare parts Byers had misappropriated from supply. "Got to go," she told them. "We got the word to start engines. The Rangers are pulling in."

Jamison watched Kamigami drift through the trees. He was a ghost, floating soundlessly toward the hidden ZSU-23-4. The lieutenant could not credit it—that such a large man could move with so much skill and grace. Then the sergeant stood up and ran back toward him, not caring about the racket he made. Now Kamigami was a very noisy and visible tank. "It's moving," Kamigami said, hardly slowing.

The ZSU had already passed when the two men piled into the pickup they had abandoned in the alley. "It's outta range here," Kamigami explained. "It's going to get closer to the airfield and hose down the planes when they take off."

Jamison was on the radio, relaying the information to Lifter. "Gregory wants us to come in," he told the sergeant.

"Tell him right after we nail this bastard . . . tell him not to wait for us." Lt. Jamison did as he was told . . .

The ZSU was weaving its way through town. It turned onto the road that led to the airfield and the modified tank had just turned a bend when it ran into Ratso Nine. The jeep team had been making a last sweep of the road, making sure no unwelcomed visitors would appear on the Rangers' flank as they drew back from the prison. Ratso Nine reacted first, but only the rear gunner could bring his M-60 to bear on the ZSU. His loader grabbed a LAW and fired. He missed. The driver wrenched the steering wheel back and forth, zigzagging down the road as he raced for the protective cover of a large concrete structure, a wheat granary, less than a hundred meters away.

The ZSU leveled its quad-mounted barrels and fired a long burst down the road. The jeep careened and rolled over, skidding off to the right. The ZSU kept firing as it advanced, turning the jeep into a flaming pyre.

Kamigami pulled off to the side and waited. He watched the ZSU pull in behind the four concrete towers of the granary and stop. They were well within range of the airfield. A side hatch flopped open and two men crawled out. They were looking toward the airfield.

"Not good," Jamison breathed, "all they have to do is pull around the far end of the towers and they've got a clear field of fire."

"We do it now, before they get their act together," the sergeant said, got out of the pickup and grabbed the RPG. "You cover me, Lieutenant, he belongs to me." Kamigami checked the RPG and satisfied that it was ready to fire, he ran toward the ZSU.

Jamison watched him go, then followed. He had taken four steps when the two men saw them. The lieutenant yelled and drew their fire. The pickup behind him burst into flames and he flopped down on his stomach to return fire, but low bushes and a slight rise blocked his field of view. He stood up and fired. It wasn't very smart but it did give Kamigami the time he needed. The sergeant dropped down into a shallow rut and took his time sighting the RPG. A bullet tore off his helmet. He shook his head and sighted again, then squeezed the trigger. The ZSU's guns were swinging toward him when the rocket hit, blowing open the thin skin of the turret. A flash of flame was followed by billowing smoke.

When Kamigami swung the rifle off his shoulder and stood up he could not see Jamison or the two men who had been shooting at him. He ran toward the burning vehicle. A man dove out of the forward hatch and rolled away, the commander of the ZSU. Another figure followed, clothes on fire. Kamigami mercifully shot him.

The Iranian commander was scrambling for cover when Kamigami fired a short burst in front of him. The man changed direction and reached for an assault rifle pinned under one of the men Jamison had cut down. Again, Kamigami squeezed off a short burst, driving the man back. The ZSU commander backed against the wall of the granary yelling at the huge figure bearing down on him.

Kamigami had seen this man kill six of his Rangers. He wanted him. The Iranian dropped to his knees, scrambling for something in the dirt, then jumped up with a short length of pipe left over from when the granary was built, held it ready to swing. Kamigami dropped the lieutenant's rifle and drew his Bowie knife. He did not slow down. The man started a swing but the sergeant snatched the pipe away from him and knocked the man's arm away. He grabbed the Iranian's hair, jerked his head back and let go as the Bowie knife flashed across his throat.

Kamigami then drew his Beretta and put a bullet in each of the other three ZSU crewmen, then trotted back to where he had last seen Jamison, trying to make his radio work and report the ZSU out of action. The radio had a dent in it, either from a bullet or him falling on it . . . He found the lieutenant lying in a bloody heap. He was still alive . . . "Lieutenant," the sergeant's voice was soft. "I was supposed to do the Rambo, you were just supposed to give me cover." He shook out his first-aid kit and bound up Jamison's chest and left thigh. "They do give medals for titanium testicles," he said as he picked up Jamison in a fireman's carry and jogged for the airfield, tossing the dead radio into the burning pickup truck.

Get off my goddamn runway, the Air Force sergeant who led the combat-control-team said to himself as he revved the engine and nosed the big bumper of the fuel truck against the nose of the burnt-out hulk of the C-130 that had closed "his" runway. He pushed hard at the wreckage, clearing the runway while Rangers came behind him, throwing debris to the side.

The runway was, finally, clear.

The flight engineer on Scamp 13, the disabled C-130 next to the dirt strip, ignited an incendiary bomb on the cargo deck of his aircraft, and flames shot from the back of the Hercules as the man ran for the two remaining C-130s that were starting engines. The number three prop on Kowalski's Hercules started to wind up for an engine start. Then it spun down.

Inside the shack, Stansell heard Kowalski over the UHF. "Sheared starter shaft," she said unhappily.

Mallard's voice was calm when he answered. "Start your other engines and follow me on the runway for takeoff. I'll taxi in front of you. When you're in position I'll back up and give you a buddy start. I'll take off first . . ."

Stansell looked out the window. Mallard was turning onto the runway and Kowalski was taxiing on two engines as the third came on line. She followed and stopped at the very end of the runway while Mallard threw the props of his engines into reverse and backed up, stopping just in front of Kowalski. He ran his engines up, sending a sixty-mile-an-hour wind over Kowalski's wings. Her number three prop started to turn, faster and faster, finally roaring to life. Mallard taxied clear and his loadmaster lowered the ramp, waiting for the first Rangers to board.

"Colonel Leason," Stansell said, "please take Captains Hauser and Carroll aboard the first C-130." Leason led the two outside. A Ranger drove them out to the waiting aircraft. "Ham"—Stansell turned to Gregory—"time for us to go." Gregory nodded and issued orders for destroying the shack. The RTO slung the PRC-77 onto his left shoulder, picked up the SatCom radio and ran outside. Stansell grabbed the UHF radio and followed. Last man out was Gregory's operations officer, who threw an incendiary grenade into the room and ran after his C.O. for the C-130s.

Stansell got into the jeep driven by one of the combat-control-team sergeants and drove out to the F-15. "Jack, leave it." He picked up the incendiary block and headed for the nose-gear wheel-wall.

"Hold on," Byers yelled. "I almost got this mother." He was buttoning up the access panel. "Cap'n, get in the cockpit. I got to pump up the nitrogen bottle."

"You got five minutes to get it cranked," Stansell told Jack. "You're moving by then or you burn it." He dropped the incendiary by the nosewheel and got back into the jeep, heading for the C-130s.

* * *

"What the hell we doin' this for?" Wade complained to Baulck. They were lying in the ditch outside the prison in the same spot where the first M-60 team had died. The wreckage of the dirt bike and machine gun was still there. Ratso One, the jeep team they had ridden with out of Objective Red, was parked three hundred yards away alongside the prison wall. They were both looking down the road toward the intersection.

Three trucks and a jeep sped by, heading for the airfield. The jeep slammed to a halt. It was Trimler. "One more jeep and that's it," he told them. "Fall in behind it and get your ass to the airfield." The jeep spun its wheels and took off. Down the road they could see the last jeep approaching followed by a cloud of smoke and dust.

"Bet you anything that's a tank breathing down their ass," Baulck said.

THE PENTAGON

The sour mood that had hung over the command center broke when Stansell and Mado reported the airfield was open. Now it was turning into jubilation as the AWACS reported that Scamp 15 with the last of the POWs was only thirty minutes away from the Turkish border and safety.

The smiles and good words disappeared when the AWACS reported that Iranian fighters were being scrambled and would be airborne within minutes.

Leachmeyer was on the stage, pointing at the last position of Scamp 15 with an electronic pointer. ". . . and have the AWACS relay an order to Scamp One-Five to turn to the west and escape through Iraq."

Cunningham spun around in his chair, looking at the President, who was standing, apparently thinking about Leachmeyer's proposal. We've been down this road before, Cunningham thought, and was on his feet. "General Leachmeyer, a good suggestion, but I say let the tactical director on board the AWACS make that decision."

Leachmeyer's tone was patronizing. "Those men are tired and not thinking, we've got the big picture here. It's time we started acting like a command center." A murmur of agreement went around the room.

Cunningham leaned forward over the console, fighting to control his anger. These people were a bunch of bureaucrats playing a war game with high-tech toys and *real* people. "Charlie, we've sunk billions of dollars and who knows how many hours of training into the AWACS concept. Right now those men are in the arena, doing what they've trained for. As a command center it's our job to support them, keep the strategic picture in view"—he forced the next words—"and to let *them* make the tactical decisions." He paused to let it sink in. "What you're proposing falls under tactics . . . Sounds like a good idea, so tell them about it—as an option to consider. But let them do what they were trained for."

"Gentlemen"—it was the President—"I agree with General Leachmeyer. Order Scamp One-Five to escape through Iraq."

The major working the communications panel looked at Cunningham for confirmation. He clenched his jaw, not trusting himself to speak, jerked his head yes and sat down.

CHAPTER 51

H PLUS 15

EASTERN TURKEY

Aboard the AWACS Lieutenant Colonel Leon Nelson heard the transmission from the command center directing him to order Scamp 15 into Iraqi airspace. "Acknowledge that," he ordered. "Status of Iraqi air defense net?" he asked.

He got an immediate answer. "All stations on alert and reporting. It's hotter than hell." A pause. "Colonel, they'll engage anything coming their way."

Nelson studied the tactical display in front of him. He ran the numbers through his head for the time-distance, rates of closure, intercept geometry when the Iranian interceptors actually become airborne. He made his decision and keyed his intercom. "Disregard that last transmission from Fort Fumble." He knew everything he said was being recorded and could be used against him in a court-martial. Then to his Fighter Allocator: "Start talking to Cowboy and Rustler flights. You've got trade for them." Cowboy and Rustler were the eight F-15s orbiting with the KC-135 tanker.

KERMANSHAH, IRAN

Thunder was standing behind Spectre's copilot as he watched the three tanks move past the abandoned intersection that had been

Objective Red and toward the prison. "Those tanks are moving with a ZSU-23-4 and two SA-8s."

"Just trying to discourage us," Beasely said.

"Captain," Mado interrupted, "the Rangers are reaching the airfield and loading now. I want you to fly a protective cover over the field."

"In a moment, General, in a moment," Beasely answered. "We got troops in contact down there. Let's give them some cover first so they can withdraw." They could see the jeep team behind the prison wall and Baulck and Wade in the ditch.

"Damn it, Captain. That's an order."

"Right, sir. And I'll comply. In a minute." He started to orbit. "Okay troops, we're in again. Rock and roll time."

Mallard's C-130 was rolling down the runway and lifting into the air, loaded with half the Rangers. All the jeep teams except Ratso One and Nine had pulled in and established a perimeter defense on the airfield while Gregory and his S-3 double-checked with Stansell, Trimler and Bravo Company's captain on where everyone was. "Ratso One with Baulck and Wade are still at the prison, in contact with the tanks," the S-3 confirmed. "No word on Ratso Nine or Kamigami and Jamison."

"I think that's Ratso Nine," Gregory said, pointing at the smoke coming from the granary. "Lots of activity going on there. Have Spectre check it out." Stansell nodded. "Okay, draw in the perimeter defense and load." Trimler and the captain went to work. Gregory stared at the smoke billowing above the granary. "Ratso One needs to disengage and come this way," he told Stansell. Neither man wanted to mention that they would leave them behind if they had to.

"Spectre's engaging the tanks now," Stansell said. "I'll get Locke and Byers." He motioned to his driver, and the jeep headed for the F-15 still sitting on the ramp.

"Byers, I've got to crank," Locke said when he saw the jeep racing toward them. The crew chief was standing in the left maingear well just behind the landing-gear strut, pumping. He had a breaker bar inserted in the manual pump for the jet fuel starter and his arms went back and forth as he tried to pump up the nitrogen bottle's pressure. Normally it took 250 strokes to recharge the bottle but his quick fix was leaking.

"Do it," Byers called out. Jack pulled the tee-handle that manually activated the jet fuel starter. Nothing happened. Byers tried to pump the bottle up again but his arms gave out and he fell to the ground exhausted, then dragged himself upright and grabbed the handle.

"Leave it," Stansell ordered from the jeep.

Byers ducked out from under the gear well. He could hardly move his arms. "Colonel, one more time."

"No time . . ."

"Help me, goddamn it," Byers blasted. "One more time . . . Christ-a-mighty, Colonel, these are my jets . . ."

And Stansell remembered another time . . . He darted under the wing and pumped at the breaker bar. Slowly the pressure built, then stabilized. "*Now,*" Byers shouted, and Jack pulled the tee-handle again while Stansell kept pumping. This time the the JFS wound up, hesitated, and caught, coming to life.

"You *got* it," Byers said. Stansell dropped the breaker bar and ran back to the jeep.

The left engine successfully engaged the JFS and was soon on-line and idling. The right engine started with no problem and JFS shut down. Jack hit the parking-brake toggle and jumped out of the front cockpit and bent over the backseat. "Furry, do I ever need you now . . ." His hands went to the switches, setting the F-15 up for a solo flight. "Hey, Byers, want to go for a ride?" The sergeant was still waiting and could not hear him over the engine's noise. Jack pointed to the empty backseat, then to him. Byers gave a thumbs-up.

Jack was back in the front seat, and Byers scrambled up over the left wing onto the top of the variable inlet ramp and into the cockpit. When he was in the seat, Jack taxied for the runway . . .

The AC-130 shuddered as Beasely fired the 105 at the SA-8 that was behind the tanks. He had to open a corridor onto the tanks if he was going to survive. The thin-skinned SA-8 disappeared in a ball of fire.

Before he could sight on the second SA-8 a hail of 23mm cannon fire cut into the cockpit. The C-130 had come in range of the ZSU. The armor plating under the floor boards and along the sides absorbed most of the damage, but the three rounds that penetrated the flight deck hit the crew. Thunder was standing at the top of the ladder coming up from the crew entry well. He was talking to Mado and had his back to Beasely. Metal fragments and splinters pounded into his back, throwing him against Mado, blowing the two men into the crew entry well and against the television camera mounted in the crew-entry door.

Thunder pulled himself back up onto the flight deck. The carnage sickened him. Only the decapitated trunk of the flight engineer remained. The copilot was dead, most of his head blown off. The navigator and fire-control officer were slumped forward. The navigator had a left-shoulder wound, and blood was gushing from the fire-control officer's head.

Beasely was still conscious, face gashed and bleeding, right arm hanging down. He was flying the Hercules with only his left hand. He looked at Thunder, sending a wordless plea for help.

Thunder unbuckled the copilot's lifeless body and dragged it back onto the flight deck. He got into the seat and grabbed the yoke, taking control of the plane. "General," he said, "for God's sake . . ." The wind blast from the holes in the right side of the cockpit drowned his words.

Mado was back on the flight deck, still dazed from the fall. He shook his head, not knowing what to do. "Beasely," Thunder called out, "tourniquet on right arm . . . help me."

Mado reacted slowly, then more quickly as his head cleared. The Sensor Operator from the booth was on the flight deck helping with Beasely as Mado crawled into the pilot's seat. "I've never flown a C-130," he told Thunder.

Neither have I, Thunder wanted to say.

Mado headed for the airfield, gaining some confidence. The tee-handle for number-four engine on the fire-emergency control panel was lit up. Thunder looked out his shattered side window to check on the engine, which was a mass of flames. "Fire on number four."

Mado feathered number four, he would only be flying on the left two engines. Could he do it? Could he gain enough altitude for them to bail out? Trying to land had not crossed his mind. "It's getting worse," Thunder told him.

"Feather number four," Mado said. Thunder reached out and pulled the tee-handle, shutting the engine down and shooting the fire-extinguisher bottle. Mado looked at the center console, then moved the number-four throttle aft and the flight-condition lever to the feather position, matching number three. The plane started to descend. They could not maintain altitude on two engines. Mado pushed the two good throttles up and lowered the flaps, trying to gain altitude.

A gunner from the rear came onto the flight deck to help the wounded. "Stop lowering the flaps," he said. "The hydraulic drive motor can't hack it." Mado looked at the sergeant and disregarded his warning as they headed for the airfield. He decided they were going to land on the runway. By the numbers . . .

"The Herky Bird's had it," Baulck told his partner Wade, "and do we need him now." The lead tank was less than four hundred meters in front of them.

"I really hate this," Wade said as he sighted the Dragon and sent the missile on its way. At the same time the jeep team from behind the wall sent another Dragon into the tank. The two missiles hit the tank on opposite sides, and a mass of flames and smoke broke over the tank. When the smoke cleared the tank had stopped its forward motion but its turret was swinging onto the prison and the barrel of the 122mm cannon was lowering, aiming at the prison wall where Ratso One was hidden.

"Those muthas just don't want to get the message," Wade mumbled, jamming his last missile-launcher onto the tracker. He aimed, squeezed the trigger, and this time, the tank exploded.

Stansell was holding the mike to the UHF radio he had thrown in the jeep as he watched the F-15 takeoff. Jack had to use his afterburners to get airborne on the short strip and now was rapidly gaining altitude. Abruptly the nose came down and the plane arced away.

Thunder's voice came over the radio, demanding his attention. "Lifter, this is Spectre. In-bound at this time for emergency landing."

"Say emergency," Stansell responded. In a few short words Thunder recounted their situation and how Mado was flying the plane. "Land on dirt strip north of main runway," Stansell ordered.

"Roger," Thunder acknowledged. Stansell watched as the disabled C-130 came into view, trailing smoke. It lined up on the main runway, pointing directly at the waiting Kowalski.

"For Christ's sake . . ." Stansell growled and keyed the radio. "Scamp One-One, taxi clear of the runway."

"Roger," came the reply. Kowalski's bird was moving, and she taxied off the main runway and onto the dirt strip.

* * *

"Right main isn't coming down," Thunder said. "Retract and do a gear up landing." Mado said nothing. Thunder pulled up the gear handle.

"What the hell!" Mado exploded. The flight controls had just become very heavy.

"There's hydraulic fluid all over us from the flap-drive motor," a voice from the rear shouted over the intercom. "It blew a seal. Hit the emergency hydraulic switch. You gotta isolate the utility system." The flap-drive motor had ruptured and was spewing flammable hydraulic fluid over the crew in the rear. Thunder scanned the instrument panel in front of him until he found the switch and toggled it down, and Mado could feel the controls again respond.

The AC-130 gunship came down final, much too fast for a normal landing. Mado pulled the nose up as it touched down on its belly. A shower of sparks and smoke trailed behind the big plane as it skidded along the concrete. Mado worked his rudder pedals, using the big vertical stabilizer, trademark of the C-130 for maintaining steering authority. At the very last the plane ground-looped to the left and came to a halt half off the runway. Smoke belched from the right gear well as the left two props spun down.

A man jumped off the rear ramp and ran for safety, then stopped and ran back, helping to carry Beasely off the plane. Four more jumped down and carried off two wounded. Beasely's men were leaving as a crew. Rangers ran from Kowalski's C-130 to help them. Stansell counted thirteen off the plane, two obviously dead. A tall figure jumped off the ramp. It was Mado. Stansell ran to the general. "Is this it? Everybody off?" Mado nodded dumbly. "Where's Thunder?" Mado stared at him, then pointed to the flight deck. Flames were shooting out the rear of the plane as the hydraulic fluid ignited.

Stansell ran to the front of the Hercules, to where the low-light-level TV and laser-target ranger were bolted into the open crew-entrance door. His small size worked to his advantage as he squeezed around it and up onto the flight deck. Thunder was still strapped into the copilot's seat, unconscious. Stansell ripped at his lap and shoulder harness, freeing the big man. A groan urged him on. His hands, wet from Thunder's blood, slipped. He grabbed Thunder's flight suit and dragged him to the crew-entry well. The rear of the aircraft was a wall of flame.

Now Stansell had to fight down his own panic. A 40mm-round in the ammo storage racks cooked off and he glanced at the cockpit windows—no help there. He looked up and saw the emergency escape hatch in the ceiling but doubted he could manhandle Thunder's 235 pounds through it. He managed to drag him down to the crew-entrance door, the way he had come in, and shoved his head through the gap below the TV camera. Blood was running over Stansell's hands as he pushed, but Thunder was wedged between the door and the camera. Then someone was pulling at Thunder from outside. Gregory and a Ranger. The two men pulled Thunder free, and Stansell squeezed through. Together they half-dragged, half-carried Thunder to Kowalski's C-130 as the gunship flared into an inferno.

The F-15 started a curvilinear approach, running in on the tank that was maneuvering past its burning leader, and headed for the Rangers blocking the road at the prison. Jack ran through the procedure he had practiced in the weapons simulator trainer for calling up a Maverick and launching it from the front cockpit: air-to-ground master mode selected; master arm on; move the Castle switch on the stick to the right; nose gear steering-button depress and release; move the crosshair with the target designation control switch on the left throttle. By the book—except the crosshair wouldn't move—battle damage from the mortar attack and the frag that had nicked the wiring bundle.

"Byers," Jack said, "you got to do some work back there." A skeptical grunt answered him. "On one of your scopes, you've got a TV picture with crosshairs down at the bottom. Grab the hand controller on the right side, move the crosshairs with the left button top. Yeah, that's it. Now position the crosshairs over the tank you see." The crosshairs moved over the image of the tank that was coming through the seeker-head of the Maverick Jack had called up. "You got it. Now pull the trigger. Right. You just locked that sucker up."

Jack was jinking back and forth, dodging the 23mm rounds that he knew were coming at him from the ZSU moving with the tanks. His TEWS was chirping, warning him of an SA-8 lock-on. He saw the two missiles launch and jerked the Eagle's nose up, waited for the missiles to commit on him, then turned hard into them and dove. The TEWS did the rest and the missiles flashed by. "Wait your turn," he said, and sent his Maverick on its way. He pulled off to the left, still jinking hard, and repositioned for another run.

"Okay, Byers, you got the hang of it now. We're going after the SA-8 that just shot at us. It looks like an armored car with six wheels. Get it locked up as soon as you can." Again, he rolled in and could see the burning hulk of his last target. A T-72 tank could shake off round after round from 105mm cannons and Dragon anti-tank missiles, but it was no match for the warhead of a Maverick. This time Buyers got an early lock-on, and Locke mashed the pickle button at max range, broke off and turned away.

"ZSU is next," he said. "Hold on. We got other things to do." Jack had just seen another threat on his TEWS . . .

"He got him!" Baulck cheered as the first Maverick killed the tank two hundred meters in front of them. The two sergeants were very much surprised to find themselves still alive as the last tank broke off and retreated into the smoke it had been laying down. Ratso One was accelerating from behind the prison wall, coming straight at them, its two M-60s blasting at the tank. Soldiers on foot were moving out from the smoke and running toward them. The jeep skidded to a stop and they piled in. The gunner in the front seat held on to the straps of Wade's LBE as the loaded jeep raced for the airfield. All the while the gunner in the rear was spraying the area behind them.

Stansell was on the flight deck behind Lydia Kowalski, who waited for the order to take off. The jeep teams had all come in except Ratso One and Nine, and the Rangers had set up three firing teams as a close-in perimeter defense. The jeeps had all been driven together and Gregory had ordered them stripped of weapons and destroyed.

The Air Force sergeant leading the combat control team had crawled into the emergency escape hatch on top of the flight deck and was scanning the area with binoculars. Now he dropped down to the deck and pointed to the north. "There's some big guy coming in. He's carrying someone. I mean that guy is *big!*"

Stansell grabbed the binoculars and climbed into the hatch. It was Kamigami. He waved at Gregory, who was still on the ground, pointed at the slowly jogging sergeant and gave a thumbs-up. Gregory spoke into his radio, and two Rangers from a firing team sprinted out to help their sergeant major. In the distance Stansell saw two smoke trails etching the sky and followed them to their source—two Iranian F-4s. He dropped down to the deck and grabbed a headset, transmitting over the UHF radio. "Stormy! Two bandits to the northeast, coming our way."

"I got 'em," came Jack's flat reply. "There's two more behind 'em fifty miles out." He did not have to tell Stansell that the airfield would soon be under attack.

Stansell ordered the sergeant back into the hatch and told him to fire a red flare, the signal to board immediately for takeoff. The Rangers came running for the C-130. Gregory climbed up onto the flight deck and pointed at the road leading to the prison. A jeep was kicking up a cloud of dust. "That's Ratso One," Gregory said. "Kamigami and Jamison are on board. Ratso Nine bought it." He looked at Stansell, waiting for the decision.

"We can't wait for Ratso One," Stansell said, hating the words.

Jack's F-15 slashed by, two hundred feet off the deck. "Let's see if he can discourage those assholes first," Kowalski told them, waving at the first two F-4s. "The other two are still five, six minutes out." She was the aircraft commander and the silence on the flight deck indicated that she had made the decision. She ran the engines up, ready to release the brakes and roll if the F-4s got through.

Byers hands were braced against the instrumental panel as the F-15 jerked and bounced two hundred feet above the ground. He knew enough about the digital readouts on the screens in front of him to realize they were traveling at 500 knots and he was scared . . . the ground rush . . . the noise . . .

"Come on, baby . . ." Jack was breathing hard and talking to himself. Byers wished Furry's helmet fit tighter. Even a little slop became a major rub when Jack pulled two Gs. At four Gs it was pain and at six . . . Jack punched the air-to-air master mode, called up one of his AIM-9 Sidewinder missiles, locked onto the lead F-4 and mashed the trigger. The missile leaped off its rail on the left wing and traced the path of a sidewinder rattlesnake through the sky. Jack then pulled into the vertical and rolled, ready to bring the nose of the F-15 back into the fight. The Sidewinder hit the left intake of the lead F-4 and the Iranian fireballed. His wingman broke hard to the left and ran to the east.

Now Jack dove for the ground and headed for the next two F-4s. He could hear Byers puking in the back seat.

Ratso One slammed to a halt under the tail of the C-130 and the six men scrambled up the ramp. Kowalski promptly released the brakes and the cargo plane started to move, slowly at first, then with greater speed. The ramp was up and the door coming down when the nose gear lifted into the air, then the main gear came unglued, and the Hercules leaped into sky.

EASTERN TURKEY

"Cowboy, this is Delray Five-One." The AWACS fighter controller's voice was precise and measured. Snake Houserman acknowledged the call for his flight of four F-15s still in trail with a KC-135 tanker orbiting thirty-five miles from the Turkish-Iranian border. "Six bandits are being scrambled from Tabriz onto Scamp One-Five. Scamp One-Five is one-two-zero degrees at one-one-five nautical miles from your position. Standby ..." The controller in the AWACS paused, evaluating the lastest information that he had received. "The bandits are now airborne and being vectored into Scamp One-Five. Fly heading one-one-zero degrees. KILL. Repeat. KILL."

Snake again acknowledged for his flight, and the four F-15s split into flights of two, crossing the border into Iran ...

KERMANSHAH, IRAN

The closure rate for the three planes was over a thousand miles per hour. Jack's air-to-air radar display had the second pair of Iranian F-4s at twenty miles and 5,000 feet above him. He did not have a tallyho yet. Even though he had no qualms taking on two F-4s with his Eagle, he had to remain on the offensive and use everything he had that gave him an advantage. And speed was his number-one advantage. He rotated the selective-jettison knob to the first detent to shed the five bombs and three Mavericks he had left to reduce the drag that slowed him down. But before he hit the red button in the center of the knob he reconsidered and turned the knob back to off. He had a use for them.

A tactic used by Willie Driscoll, a famous Navy jock, came back— "Turn to kill, not to engage." Now he had the F-4s visually in his HUD. They were still flying straight and level, in echelon, not maneuvering, coming straight at him, still high, holding their altitude. "Hold on, Byers." He turned forty-five degrees to the left and dropped still lower. Just before the two F-4s came by him on his right he reefed the F-15 into a hard right turn and pulled up and into them. It was a stern-conversion and the bandits had not yet seen him. With his thumb he toggled the weapons-select switch on his throttles to the rear and selected his 20mm cannon. He surged into the bandits' right rear quarter, still below them, and sent a short burst of high-explosive shells into the lead F-4 on the right. Two puffs of smoke trailed from the Iranian F-4 and a tongue of flame licked out from under its belly. Then it pitched nose down, tumbled, and exploded.

Jack pulled back to the left and up, again using the vertical to reposition for a reattack or to disengage, whichever looked better when he was on top with energy to maneuver and choose his options. The other F-4 had buried its nose and was reversing course, running away. Jack let him live and headed for the prison, and mentally went through the switchology that would allow him to call up a Maverick missile . . .

NORTHWESTERN IRAN

"Cowboy," the fighter controller's voice was more rapid and high pitched now. He had never directed fighters into an actual engagement before. "Bandits at zero-niner-zero degrees, seventy nautical miles."

"Burners, now," Snake ordered. His three flight members shoved their throttles forward into the fourth-, then fifth-stage afterburner, and the F-15s accelerated straight ahead. He had worked out a mental map of the C-130's position and the converging bandits. He had to hurry to get between them.

"Multiple hits, zero-eight-zero, sixty-five miles," his wingman sang out. He had a radar contact on the bandits. The F-15s started to sort them out, deciding who would engage who. But above all, Snake was determined to keep the bandits off the C-130. He had learned his lesson.

KERMANSHAH, IRAN

Jack flew past the prison, monitoring his TEWS. It was quiet. The Iranian tanks had reached the airfield. "Byers, put the crosshairs for the Maverick smack in the middle of the admin building. Got it?" Byers asked if the admin building was the one with the smouldering fire that had been hit by a bomb. "That's it, we're in. "Jack rolled the F-15 up onto its left wing and rolled out into a shallow dive. Byers had the knack now and drove the crosshairs onto the admin building and locked on. Jack hit the pickle button and launched the first Maverick. He called up another Maverick. "Lock on again." Byers did, and it was sent on its way . . .

Mokhtari was in the first-floor office of the main cell block trying to reconnect the telephone a Ranger had ripped out of its connection when he heard the F-15. Instinctively he dived for cover under the desk and threw his arms over his head. The blast from the two Mavericks momentarily deafened him. Then a hard look of satisfaction spread over his face when he realized the attacking plane had hit the wrong building . . .

Jack came off the target and repositioned. He selected bombs, ripple and started his second run, placing his target reticle on the edge of the prison. He would walk his five remaining bombs across the main cell block and into the admin building . . .

The sound of the returning F-15 pounded at Mokhtari. Fear was numbing. At first he had an overpowering urge to urinate, then panic drove him from the office. He ran down the short flight of stairs and out the main door heading for the reinforced concrete tunnel that served as the prison's entrance . . .

Jack saw the lone figure running across the exercise yard. "I hope to hell that's you," he said aloud, designating with the pickle button. His right foot feathered the rudder pedal, skidding the F-15 onto a new path . . .

Terror had replaced hate as Mokhtari realized the F-15 was pointed directly at him, freezing him in his tracks. He lost control of his bladder when he saw the five bombs separate cleanly from the aircraft. He raised his head and watched the F-15 pull off. And watched as the first bomb exploded only fifteen feet in front of him . . .

NORTHWESTERN IRAN

"Cowboy, Delray," the AWACS transmitted. "Bandits are now at zero-two-zero degrees, twenty miles."

"Rog, Delray," Snake replied, "Judy." With the Judy-call he told the AWACS they were taking over the intercept. As flight lead,

Snake was still working on how best to engage the six bandits they were closing on. He and his wingman were going to attack the lead aircraft while his other F-15s, the second element of F-15s, were going to attack the rear aircraft. He had to keep the bandits off the C-130, but his weapons could only be fired forward. So he had to have his nose pointed at the enemy to be a fighter. Otherwise he could easily become a target. Even the most advanced fighter was at a disadvantage against an old, obsolete jet that had maneuvered to the six o'clock position and was firing.

Snake updated his three-dimensional image of the relative position of the bandits. The F-15s were closing from the bandits' front-left quarter and the C-130 was behind him. He was in time.

Now he entered the attack phase of the engagement. Snake understood the psychological advantage an aggressive attack gave him—no matter the odds, put your opponent on the defensive and keep him there—otherwise, get the hell out of there. But since he couldn't disengage and leave the C-130 unprotected, he was going to make the bandits turn away from the Hercules. At the same time he wasn't going to be sucked into a turning dogfight—like Jack, he would only turn to kill, not to engage.

"Cowboy flight, deploy now," he ordered. It was a simple command but one they had worked out in repeated training flights. Houserman and his wingman pulled up into the sun, gaining altitude, while the second element dove for the ground. They would attack in a pincers movement, Snake from above and in front, his second element from the rear and below. The contract they had worked out between themselves was to launch AIM-7M radar missiles when they were inside fifteen miles, then to blow on through the formation and reposition for another attack. Only this time, Snake and his wingman would go low and the other element would go high.

"Bandits are Floggers," the leader of the low element whooped over the UHF. The MiG-23 the Iranians were flying was a good jet but it couldn't turn with an F-15 and the pilot couldn't check his six-o'clock position.

The MiGs first realized they were under attack when their radar-warning gear started screaming that a hostile radar was locked on them. That was immediately followed by the sight of two smoke trails coming at them from out of the sun. Hard to ignore a brace of AIM-7s when pointed at you, and the MiGs broke formation as they turned—scattering across the sky.

Snake's AIM-7 missed, but his wingman's came within a few feet of its target and the proximity fuse did as designed and detonated, sending a shower of expanding rod-core into the underside of the MiG, ripping into the lower half of the pilot. The Iranian saw his fire light come on and felt the flight controls go dead, but all he could do was watch the ground rush up at him . . .

The two trailing MiG's never saw the low element of two F-15s but reacted to their radar-warning gear and broke hard for the ground, evading the missiles shot at them. The AIM-7 was well-named the Great White Hope.

Cowboy flight blew on through the turning MiGs as they had planned and repositioned for another attack.

Now Snake and his wingman came back into the fight from below. Although Snake was going almost straight up it looked like he was porpoising as he maneuvered on his next target. The MiG buried its nose toward Snake and turned under while Snake did a loop over the top and fell in behind the MiG. Now they were going straight down with the AIM-9 seeker-head tracking the Flogger's afterburner. Snake fired a Sidewinder and broke away, leaving the fight. The Sidewinder flew up the MiG's tail pipe and exploded.

That was it. The MiGs disengaged and headed east into Iran. The F-15s had shot down two MiG-23 Floggers in less than seventy-two seconds. Snake called for a fuel check and joined up on the C-130, escorting the POWs across the border into Turkey, and safety, ignoring two other bandits who were looking for them.

THE PENTAGON

The main floor of the command center was pandemonium. People pounded each other on their backs and shook hands. The noise wouldn't die down. But the major who was handling the communications panel sat quietly, not joining in the celebration over Scamp 15's safe deliverance. She folded her hands in her lap and looked at Cunningham, waiting. The general nodded at her. His Air Force, it was a-changing.

Stevens told him the President wanted to see him, and Cunningham heaved himself out of his chair and hurried to the Command and Authority Room.

The President came directly to the point. "I gave a direct order for Scamp One-Five to escape through Iraq. That order was disobeyed."

"That's true, sir," Cunningham had to bite his lip, not trusting himself to say what he was thinking—that the President had made a dumb decision.

"I want to know why. And I want some balls crunched."

"May I smoke?" Cunningham asked, pulling out his favorite cigar. "I've got to cut back . . ." He lit it up and puffed, and it became a waiting game to see who would speak first.

The President made the move. "Lawrence, today has been a new experience for me . . ."

Cunningham knew that was as close to bending as his commander in chief would come. "Sir, I need to check it out about why your orders were not followed. It will take some time. But look at the results." He motioned at the center situation board. "As of now, sir, it looks like the tactical director in the AWACS had a more current, more accurate grasp of the situation than we did. He did what he judged to be correct. It may not have been the best decision, but it *worked.*"

Cunningham looked uneasily at the President, saw no special reaction and went on . . . "We train them, give them multi-million-dollar toys to play with, then we've got to trust them when the heat's on. Just the way it is, sir." The President stared for a moment, then slowly nodded. "We look at the results," Cunningham continued, encouraged, "try to learn from what happened, pick up the pieces, give 'atta boys to the ones who did good and try to do it better next time." He didn't mention that some balls would still need to be crunched.

"Thanks, Lawrence." The President stared out over the room that was now quieting down. "Is it always this hard?"

"Yes, sir. It is. And we're not out of it yet. Two more C-130s to go."

CHAPTER 52

H PLUS 16

WESTERN IRAN

"How's it goin'?" Kowalski asked her loadmaster over the intercom. Hank Petrovich looked around the cargo deck. Almost every Ranger was asleep. Gregory and his S-3 were huddled with a medic going over the casualty list while another medic crouched on the deck working on Thunder. Stansell was there trying to help. Petrovich was relieved to see that they had stopped the captain's bleeding. "Most everyone is asleep," he told her. "But one of them wants to come up and talk to you."

"Send him up." Petrovich motioned at Andy Baulck, who worked his way through the sleeping men and up onto the flight deck.

Kowalski turned and looked at him. "How ya doin', Sarge?"

"Playing in the major leagues, Captain, swingin' one hell of a big bat." Kowalski smiled at him. It was the truth. "Captain, I wanted to say thanks. They told me how you held the takeoff waiting for us to pull in . . ."

"My job, Baulck. Besides, you didn't think I'd turn an asshole like you loose on a bunch of unsuspecting civilians?" Baulck grinned and crawled back down the stairs onto the cargo deck and fell into a deep sleep.

"Well, now," her copilot Brenda Iverson said, "we got a visitor." Jack Locke had joined up on the C-130's right wing, giving them a thumbs-up.

EASTERN TURKEY

Nelson sank back into his seat on the AWACS, aching with fatigue. He had been airborne too long and needed rest. When the AWACS had landed at Incirlik after their first sortie and the insertion of Romeo Team aboard Scamp 11, the flight crew had changed out. But the mission crew in the rear had stayed aboard. Should have told more people about Operation WARLORD, he thought, so the mission crew could also have swapped out. Mustn't suffer from "get homeitis," we're not headed for the barn yet. He studied the tactical display in front of him and called his fighter allocator for an update.

"The situation is fluid," the fighter allocator told him. "I have six bandits airborne, two F-4s and four Floggers. They just seem to be roaming around. Someone over there must have figured out by now we're egressing through the tri-border region and should try to position them as a blocking force." Another voice interrupted to announce that four more bandits were now airborne out of Tabriz and two more were being scrambled.

"Any idea who they'll commit on?" Nelson asked. "Scamp One-Two or Scamp One-One?"

"Whichever one they can find. I've got four F-15s, Rustler flight, still with the tankers and gassed, ready to go. Why don't we send them in to escort Scamp One-Two since its the closest to the border, put Cowboy flight on the tankers for gas and then send them in to escort the last C-130 out?"

"Sounds good. Do it."

MARAGHEH, IRAN

The new controller sitting at the radar-control console was sweating. He had seen the body of the last controller still lying on the ground when he had driven up the mountain. At least he had the undivided attention of the captain in the control center and didn't have to make any critical decisions. The captain had a vengeful Ayatollah looking over his shoulder and would have to answer for any mistakes. Still, there was guilt by association . . .

"Do you have the C-130s on your scope?" the captain barked over the command line from the control center.

"Not at this time. But I do know their approximate position. The first is halfway between Kermanshah and the tri-border area. The other has only taken off from Kermanshah and is headed north.

Please standby, I have activity." The controller studied his scope for a few moments. "Four fast moving targets have departed the tanker and are descending. I will lose them for a period of time when they are in the mountains. But I will paint them later. They are most likely fighters ingressing to escort the C-130s. I have four more targets now joining on the tankers."

There was a long pause on the other end. "The last time," the captain said, "they directed four F-15s to escort one C-130. It is a pattern. Monitor the four fighters that are penetrating our airspace. We will send four of our fighters against them when they rendezvous with a C-130. We use our remaining fighters to attack and destroy the C-130 they leave unprotected." The Iranian command-and-control net had finally gotten its act together.

WESTERN IRAN

"Shee-it, Cap'n," Byers grumbled from the back seat, "what's all that bleepin'?" The F-15's sensitive Tactical Electronic Warfare System was sending loud warning signals through Byers' earphones.

"That's the TEWS," Jack Locke told him. "The chirp means airborne search radars are looking for us. There's a knob on your left console that can turn down the volume." The pilot glanced at his TEWS, not liking what he saw. "Lots of Gomers up and about."

The UHF radio came alive as Rustler flight joined up on Duck Mallard's C-130. Then the transmissions crackled with commands as Rustler flight reported bandits in the area. The frequency became a torrent of words as Rustler flight capped the C-130 and sorted out the bandits. Jack listened to the radio traffic, building a mental picture of the developing engagement, then rechecked his own radar and TEWS and it all fell into place . . . Four bandits were bouncing Mallard's C-130 and the four F-15s of Rustler flight while he and Kowalski headed straight for a hornet's nest of at least eight orbiting fighters that were obviously looking for them.

He called Kowalski over to another frequency, leaving the channel clear for Rustler flight. He keyed his radio. "Delray Five-One, this is Stormy Zero-Two. How copy on this frequency?" The answer came through scratchy but readable. "We have multiple threats in the area," Jack told the AWACS, "and need to divert to the west."

"Negative, Stormy," the AWACS answered. "Hostile reception to the west." The Iraqi air defense system was still up and active.

"Then send some damned help," Jack demanded.

"Stormy, be advised Rustler flight is engaged. Cowboy flight is refueling. Will send Cowboy in flights of two as they come off the tankers."

"Tell 'em to hurry. Scamp, you copy all?"

"Roger," Kowalski answered.

"We got to get down in the rocks and weeds. We're going right under a cloud of Gomers looking for us. They don't have a very good lookdown capability so they got to find us with their eyeballs. Help's on the way."

"Roger on the help," the C-130 pilot answered, skepticism lacing her words.

"Cap'n"—it was Byers—"look behind you." Jack twisted his head around, glad for the excellent visibility in the F-15. Two distinctive sets of smoke trails were coming right at them. Iranian F-4s.

He reversed course with a hard slashing pitch-back to the left. "Two bandits six o'clock, seven miles, I'm engaged," he transmitted for both the C-130 and the AWACS to hear. At the top of the vertical he studied the oncoming bandits and continued to zoom, delaying the completion of the pitch-back and letting the F-4s close. Then he pulled down into the fight.

"Hank!" Kowalski shouted over the intercom to her loadmaster, "get everybody strapped in and tie everything down. It's about to get rough."

The two F-4s had a late tallyho on Jack and barely had time to split, one going high and to the left, the other diving to the right. Jack chose the high man and went for a head-on pass. He selected guns, snap-rolled to the right, squeezed the trigger for a long burst of cannon fire and brought the F-4 aboard, passing almost canopy to canopy. He saw smoke puff from behind the F-4 as he turned his attention to the other bandit. "Watch him," he told Byers, "don't lose sight."

Byers turned to look at the rapidly disappearing F-4 behind them just as Jack wrenched the fighter after the other jet. The sergeant's head snapped to the left and his helmet banged off the canopy, but he did keep his eyes on the first Iranian . . .

The second Iranian, for his part, was concentrating on the C-130, trying to get behind the slow-moving cargo plane. Actually Kowalski's low altitude and slow speed were causing problems for the Iranian pilot . . .

Jack selected a Sidewinder and sweetened the shot, taking his time to get well inside the launch parameters of the missile. The reassuring growl of a lock-on grew louder and louder. He pressed the pickle button and watched the missile streak home. The rear of the Iranian jet flared into a long plume of flame as the plane spun into the ground.

"My guy ran away," Byers told him. "What happened?"

"We got one," Jack said as he flew past Kowalski. "You did good, Byers. Rule number one is always check six. You did that. That guy died because he forgot rule number two."

"What's that?"

"Never forget rule number one—"

"Bandits," Kowalski called over the UHF, "ten o'clock high."

A welcome voice came over the radio. "Snake and Jake on the way." Snake Houserman and his wingman were now off the refueling tanker and headed into Iran.

"Hurry, Snake," Jack answered. "Multi-bogies on us." He checked his armament-control set. Two AIM-9 missiles and 450 rounds of 20mm showing on the rounds-counter were left. In a hurry, Jack missed that he still had one Maverick left hanging under the right wing and creating drag. He turned toward the four Floggers that had their noses on him . . .

EASTERN TURKEY

"Rustler Four-Two," the fighter controller on the AWACS radioed, "four miles to the fence."

"Roger," Rustler Four-Two answered, his voice strained. "I can hold it until then."

The situation on the tactical displays aboard the AWACS told its story: Rustler flight had shot down one of the four MiGs that were attacking Duck Mallard's C-130. The other three had been driven off, and one of the F-15s, Rustler Four-Two, had taken a hit by an Aphid, the Soviet-made dogfight missile hung under a Flogger. The F-15 was still flying, leaving a trail of smoke and hydraulic fluid behind it, trying to make it across the border before the pilot ejected. Two F-15s of Rustler flight were still escorting Mallard, ten minutes away from the border, and one was escorting Rustler Four-Two.

"Crossing the fence now," the AWACS transmitted.

"I'll hold it for another minute to clear the border," Rustler Four-Two said. It was a matter of waiting now. Then: "Ejecting now."

"He's got a good chute," the pilot escorting Rustler Four-Two transmitted, hoping for but not counting on a happy landing . . .

WESTERN IRAN

Jack stroked his afterburners, going for another head-on pass. If he and Byers were going to survive he had to hit-and-split, but he couldn't split too far or the MiGs would be onto Kowalski. He planned a series of rapid reattacks, using the F-15's ability to turn rapidly and maintain its airspeed at the same time. Jack did not warn Byers he was about to pass out . . .

He selected a Sidewinder and waited for the growl to come through his headset that told him the missile's seeker-head was locked on and tracking. The Lock-Shoot Lights on the top of the canopy bow flashed, showing him that a shoot cue was generated. The MiGs saw him and started to split just as he fired the missile. He headed straight into the pack, chasing his own missile, taking a snap-shot with his cannon when another MiG passed in front of him. Then he was clear, pulled back on the stick and pushed the right rudder. He could hear the double-rate beeper of the overload warning system as he loaded the F-15 with nine Gs and pitched-back to the right, reentering the fight. He could see a MiG spiralling into the ground and a parachute blossoming above it.

The F-15 slashed through the area where the MiGs had been, but they were disengaging. A reprieve.

"What the . . ." came from the back seat.

"You passed out when we pulled six Gs," Jack told the sergeant. "You need a G-suit."

He rejoined on Kowalski and checked his radar-display and TEWS. "Snake, say position."

"Six minutes out, coming in from the north."

"I'm still getting a lot of attention. I now count five bandits in the area." Jack checked his fuel. Getting low, but still okay. He thanked the fast-pack tanks strapped onto the side of his E model as well as that fuel truck on the ground at Kermanshah. He called up the systems-display on his left video for another weapons check. One AIM-9 and 250 rounds of 20mm. Damn, go easy on the trigger, he told himself, shorter bursts. Then he finally noticed he had one Maverick left. He reached for the jettison knob so he could clear that station. What the hell, he rationalized, anything when your ass is all hung out . . .

"Cap'n, behind us," Byers warned. He had not forgotten rule number two. A stream of four aircraft were coming at them. "Four bandits, six o'clock, on us," Jack radioed. Kowalski started jinking the C-130. She's getting the hang of it, Jack noted. Actually, Stansell was standing behind her on the flight deck, giving the pilot a crash course in defensive maneuvers. The colonel had ordered Hank Petrovich to raise the cargo door under the tail and to call out anytime he saw a MiG come to their six o'clock.

Jack turned hard now into the oncoming fighters, wondering how much longer his luck would hold. "Your tactics may suck," he grumbled, "but you are persistent suckers . . ." Now it became a wild scrap. Jack would twist and turn, always bringing the nose of his F-15 onto a MiG, taking a snapshot, then disengaging. Once he had a good self-track during a head-on pass and fired a Sidewinder. It streaked past two Floggers and caused them to break off and momentarily run from the fight. But it missed, probably from being too close. Byers kept checking their six; it was the only thing he knew to do. And when he would warn Jack of a bandit at their six, Jack would wrack the F-15 around, dropping a flare every two seconds by mashing the trim button on his stick. In every one of these break turns Jack was loading the F-15 with anywhere from six to nine Gs and Byers would pass out. When Jack unloaded, Byers would start to regain consciousness, checking six as soon as his head cleared.

At one point Jack had let his airspeed decay to 250 knots as a MiG closed on him. He pulled into the vertical, doing a slow loop, and the MiG shot by below him. He then snapped the throttles into afterburner and taxied into a guns-firing position behind the Flogger, whose wings were starting to sweep forward as it slowed down. He fired the last of his 20mm rounds into the MiG, tearing it apart. And now he was dry. Again he pointed at a MiG in a head-on pass, wondering how long before they cottoned to the fact he was defenseless.

"Tallyho the fox," came over the UHF, and Snake hooked into the fight from below, his wingman in an offensive fighting-wing position. Jack turned back to the C-130. It was gone. He had lost sight of it in the fight . . .

* * *

"A MiG's behind us!" Petrovich yelled over the intercom. Kowalski sawed back and forth on the rudder pedals and yoke, skidding and jerking the Hercules, trying to break any tracking solution the Flogger might work out. Stansell was holding on to the back of her seat with both hands.

"Oh Christ!" from Petrovich. "Break left!" The MiG was firing its 23mm Gatling gun. Kowalski stood the C-130 on its left wing and tried to pull back into the fighter, as Stansell had told her. But it wasn't enough. A string of shells tore into the right wing, ripping, tearing it. The prop on the number four engine on the right outboard flew off, separating from the aircraft. One of the fuel tanks in the wing was punctured and sent a stream of fuel into the slipstream. The number-three engine's turbine froze when two high-explosive shells tore into it. Pieces of skin and paneling shredded away and part of the anti-icing boot on the forward edge of the wing peeled back, still flapping over the wing.

Kowalski fought for control while the MiG repositioned.

"Did you *see* that fucker," Wade yelled at Baulck. Baulck had twisted around in his seat and was staring at the right wing. "Wish we had a tail gunner like a B-52," Wade shouted. The two buck sergeants looked at each other, unstrapped, grabbed two SAW light-machine guns and ran for the rear of the plane. They threw themselves onto the ramp, which was in the up-position, and stuck their weapons out under the door that Petrovich had raised so he could look out behind the Hercules.

They could see the MiG start another run and both fired into the blue, sending bullets toward the MiG. The MiG pilot saw the flashes coming from behind the C-130 and broke off his attack to reposition. This time he would attack from above and behind, avoiding any gunfire from under the tail of the C-130.

But he forgot rule number two.

Jack climbed and used his radar to find the Hercules C-130. He accelerated after it in time to see the MiG break off its second attack and zoom for altitude. "What the hell do I do now?" he muttered. "Ram him?" He headed for the MiG as it repositioned. "Byers, the Maverick . . . the crosshairs . . . put 'em over the MiG and lock on." Jack had called up his one remaining weapon.

Jack had never thought about using the Maverick as an air-to-air weapon and he sweetened the shot as best he could by closing to inside three miles. "Not too close," he warned himself. He checked the ready-light on the armament-control set and mashed the pickle button. The anti-tank missile leaped off its rail and streaked toward the MiG that was almost in position to gun Kowalski's C-130 out of the sky. The Maverick's 125-pound shaped-charge warhead that was designed to penetrate heavy armor and kill fifty-ton tanks speared the MiG. The plane disappeared in its own fiery cloud.

Jack checked his fuel, joined on Kowalski, and the Eagle and its Hercules headed for home.

CHAPTER 53

H PLUS 17

INCIRLIK, TURKEY

Chief Pullman was waiting with a crew van when Jack taxied into the chocks and shut the engines down. The chief waited impatiently while the pilot and then Byers climbed down the boarding ladder. "What the hell . . ." he muttered. Byers was a mess. The front of his shirt was streaked and it seemed he may have wet himself. The crew chief lay down on the ground and moaned. His neck hurt and his body ached.

Jack got down beside him. "You gonna be okay?"

"Fuckin' A . . . heroes never die . . . oh, God . . ."

"Captain," the chief said, "they want you in Intel for a debrief."

"It can wait," Jack told him. "Kowalski's twenty minutes out."

Pullman nodded, reached into the van and handed Jack a plastic water bottle. He drained about half and poured the rest over his head, splashing his face.

"Captain Bryant's hurt bad," Pullman said, looking at the four ambulances that were waiting.

"Yeah. I know." And now they had to endure the agony of waiting for the C-130 to land.

"Turbine inlet temps against the peg," MacIntyre said.

Kowalski acknowledged the flight engineer. "Sue, how we doing on fuel?" she asked the navigator.

"Going to be close . . ." The C-130 was flying on its left two engines, and because of the drag created by the damaged right wing, the turbine inlet temperatures were in the red and fuel consumption was high. Kowalski had to keep pushing the throttles up to maintain altitude and control. Every time she backed the throttles off, the right wing came down—it was all but dead.

"Pilot, this is the loadmaster." The formality in Petrovich's voice struck at the flight crew. Something was up.

"Roger, loadmaster, go ahead."

"Be advised that Captain Bryant has died."

Silence. Then . . . "Please have everyone strap in. We're starting our approach into Incirlik."

"There," Jack half-pointed, half-nodded at the approaching C-130. The ramp was unusually silent as activity came to a halt. A huge crash truck rumbled down the taxiway followed by an ambulance, finally stopping near the approach end of the runway. Another crash truck was off to the side, halfway down the runway. Jack could hear the motors of the ambulances idling in the background as he watched the right wing of the approaching Hercules drop while the plane descended. "Up, get it *up*," he muttered to himself. The wing dropped lower.

"*Come on* . . . ." Now he was shouting. He glanced at Pullman. The big sergeant's left arm was bent at the elbow and his palm was up, making a slight upward pushing motion. Further down the ramp a sergeant was standing beside a small tug, leaning to the right. Jack realized both he and Pullman were also leaning, trying to will the right wing of the C-130 to lift.

Slowly, slowly, the wing came up as Kowalski increased her airspeed. Then, finally, she touched down and rolled to a halt. And Jack could feel the tension drain.

The pain would come later.

THE PENTAGON

"Your attention please." The major was making her last announcement to the command center. "Scamp One-One has safely recovered. Operation WARLORD is now terminated." The reaction on the floor was more subdued this time as people congratulated each other on what "they" had done.

Cunningham was certain that most of them had been more than willing to write off Task Force Alpha once the POWs were safe. He stood up and looked at the major. She was still sitting, gathering her code books and getting ready to leave. She nodded at him and turned back to her work. Cunningham glanced at the Command and Authority room. The President was standing, accepting congratulations from his staff. The two men stared at each other for a moment.

Cunningham turned away. "Miss Rahimi, thank you." He jammed a fresh cigar into his mouth. "Dick," he snapped to his aide, "what the hell's on the agenda?" And then he was out of there.

EPILOGUE

HOLLOMAN AFB, NEW MEXICO

Colonel Rafe Thompson, Holloman's wing commander, sat behind his desk glaring at the staff sergeant standing at attention in front of him. The colonel was, for perhaps the first time in his career, at a loss for words. The sergeant's eyes kept darting from the colonel to the canvas bag sitting on the desk. It looked like his scrounge bag, but it couldn't be. He had left it behind at Kermanshah.

"Goddamn it, Byers . . ." The colonel stood up and started to pace. "I don't know what to do with you." He was building momentum now. Byers braced for the rush. "Captain Jack Locke has been credited with five confirmed kills and one probable . . . Which makes him an ace. A certified card-carrying aerial assassin."

"Sir, that's great."

"No, it's not great. According to Air Force regulations the back-seater is usually given equal credit for those kills." The colonel's face was turning beet red. "It's unofficial, but that means . . . I have on my base . . . under my command . . . the only staff sergeant ace in the entire goddamn *world*." He flopped back into his chair, driving it against the back wall.

"But, sir, I didn't do nothin'. Hell, I was knocked out—"

"Locke claims different."

"There's something else . . ." The colonel stood back up, leaned across his desk and shoved the canvas bag toward the sergeant. "This is your scrounge. I ought to court-martial you . . ."

"Sir, that ain't mine. I left it behind at—"

"Byers, the Air Force Chief of Staff, one General Lawrence Get-the-hell-out-of-here-by-sundown Cunningham, says it *is*. My chief of supply says there are over twenty thousand dollars worth of parts . . ." The colonel fought for control. "Take it and get the hell out of here." Byers grabbed the bag, saluted, and spun around.

The colonel's voice stopped him. "Sergeant Byers, General Cunningham sends his thanks. Also . . . there's a letter and a medal in the mail."

THE PENTAGON

"Congratulations on your third star," Cunningham said, scarcely able to maintain his civility. He motioned for his aide to leave and close his office door.

Simon Mado decided to play gracious and not push the general. Anyone could *feel* the hostility below Cunningham's surface, ready to break out. "Thank you, sir, it was totally unexpected . . ."

Cunningham chomped his cigar, bit the end off without intending to. He decided to indulge himself. Just a little. "Yes, it *was*, you pigfucker." His voice was nicely calm.

"Sir?"

"How about shit . . . you got promoted because the President and a clutch of generals thought you did a great job in Iran. Everything I've seen tells me you were the highest-paid radio operator in the Air Force. I had a major in the command center doing the same thing you were doing. You *look* like a hero because a gutsy AC-130 crew wasn't afraid to press the real fight, Thunder Bryant never blew his cool, and Rupe Stansell was able to function as the task force commander—which was your job. You bought your promotion on their backs." Cunningham leaned across his desk. "Why don't you think about retiring, General?"

Mado squelched a slight smile building across his mouth. Time for you to get the message, you old bastard . . . "I don't think that's necessary at this time."

It wasn't over. Cunningham pointed at the door. "You're going to need a hell of a lot of help to survive in my Air Force," he promised.

Mado saluted deadpan and left.

Outside, Mado allowed a smile at Cunningham's aide, even whistled a tuneless song as he went back to his office. The old S.O.B. is right about one thing, he thought. I am going to need help.

He went off to place calls to his divorce lawyer, and then to Barbara Lyon.

FORT BENNING, GEORGIA

The two buck sergeants marched into the command sergeant major's office and reported in. The sergeant major kept them standing at attention. "Lieutenant Jamison tells me you two were fighting at the Service Club last night after the awards parade." The CSM's voice was quiet. "He's asked me to handle it. Why the fight?"

"Sergeant Major," Wade answered, "there were four pukes out of the First Battalion telling everyone how rough it was at Grenada—"

"It was," Kamigami interrupted. "I was there."

"We know that," Baulck said, "but those four assholes were still in junior high school when Grenada went down . . ."

"You two only fight when I tell you to," Kamigami said, ending the discussion. "Be here at 0500 tomorrow morning. We're going for a little run. Dismissed." The two men retreated out of the office. Kamigami watched them go and made a mental note to find out who won the fight. Everything would be okay if Baulck and Wade had cleaned up on the other four . . .

CLEVELAND, OHIO

The small church in the inner city slowly filled as the relatives and friends attending the memorial service found places in the wooden pews. The patina on the altar and pulpit, the well-worn pews, the carefully polished candlestick holders all reflected the loving care of the church's congregation. Most were surprised to see the Air Force colonel sitting in the front pew next to the family. His immaculately tailored uniform could not hide the gaunt frame beneath it. His was the only white face in the church.

When the time for the eulogy came the colonel stood up before the congregation and clasped his hands in front of him.

"I'm Colonel Clayton Leason and I was Macon Jefferson's commander while we were in captivity at Kermanshah. You have all heard of Macon's sacrifice and how he volunteered to pass a message to a fellow POW in an effort to save that man's life. Macon was successful, but at the price of his own life. I'm not here to praise him, his actions have done that far better than anything I could say, but to ask for your help. When it happened I made a promise no one could hear—that I would make it right. But I don't know how to make it right, and that's why I'm here—to ask your help . . ."

WASHINGTON, D.C.

Susan Fisher was worried. She had not seen Allen Camm for two days, and now she had received a telephone message to meet him in the basement of the warehouse where the CIA's isolation chamber, primary, was housed. The elevator doors opened and she stepped into the antiseptic hallway, walking briskly to primary. A technician was waiting at the door and ushered her in. She tried to mask her surprise when she saw not Camm but Burke, Camm's boss, the head of the CIA. "Please sit down, Miss Fisher." He was watching the TV monitor. Someone was in primary.

She almost lost control when she realized the bound figure in the darkened isolation chamber was Camm. He was lying naked on the floor, bound with wide straps, a mouthpiece taped into place. The mane of graying, carefully styled hair was unmistakably Allen Camm.

"How long has he been in?" Burke asked a technician.

"Thirty-four hours," came the answer. "He's tough. I don't think you're going to get the answers you want soon enough, Mr. Burke."

"There are other people," Burke said, and turned his attention to Fisher. "Well, Miss Fisher, do you care to tell us about Deep Furrow?" A glance at the screen and she started talking.

"Please, not here," Burke said. "Another office . . . we have a stenographer waiting." A technician escorted her out.

Immediately, the other technician threw the door to the isolation chamber open and turned on the lights, unstrapping the man and helping him out. He put on a robe and removed the wig he was wearing. "Don't want to do that again," he said.

"I appreciate your help," Burke told the agent, "and I doubt such services will be required again." Of course, the man would be rewarded for playing the role of Camm in the isolation chamber. Burke added that Miss Fisher realized an error had been made and that he expected Mr. Camm to be more than forthcoming upon his return. "If not, I *will* throw that son of a bitch into primary."

ARLINGTON NATIONAL CEMETERY, VIRGINIA

A high cloud deck scudded across the cold December sky, creating a bounded universe. For Stansell, it was a perfect domain, setting limits while holding the promise of things above, just out of sight, there for the reaching. He found the formal, predictable routine of the funeral comforting as the mourners gathered at the grave site . . . the flag-draped coffin, the honor guard, the ordered rows of crosses.

Dewa stood beside him as they waited for Thunder's family to take their seats by the grave, aware that the man beside her had changed and would never be the same again. He radiated a quiet confidence, a sense of sureness about who and what he was that reached out to her. She searched the crowd, looking for familiar faces and was not surprised to see General Cunningham walking toward them. The general stood beside Stansell, another one of the many who had come to pay their last respects to James "Thunder" Bryant.

"He did good," Cunningham said.

"They all did good, sir."

The general turned to face him. "And you." The look on Stansell's face told Cunningham that the colonel had not accepted or realized the truth yet. "You proved an old belief of mine. With good leadership, training and for the right reasons, every one of them"—he swept the crowd with a broad gesture—"is an eagle. Task Force Alpha was a force of eagles. You made them that way." He waited for it to sink in. "Come see me tomorrow. I've got work for you." He fell silent as the interment started.

As the flag was being folded, the smoke trails marking the approach of four F-4 Phantoms from the west etched the sky. "Thunder loved that old jet," Stansell whispered. As they approached in finger-tip formation, number three pulled up and away, leaving the others to continue in a missing-man formation, a final tribute to their fallen comrade. The lone Phantom climbed into the sky. "Jack," was all Stansell said as the warbird disappeared through the clouds.

And then it was over and the mourners broke apart, going their separate ways. Stansell walked alongside Dewa back to her car. They stopped, not touching. "Dewa . . . is there anything for us?"

She reached out and caressed his cheek. "I hope so, Rupe . . ." It was enough for now.

Two solitary figures remained by the open grave. Mary Hauser did not move, waiting for Carroll. "It's over," she told him.

But it was not. The memory of Doc Landis, of all the others, of what they had been through would never be over. Both understood that as they walked off together from the gravesite.

TERMS

ACM: Air Combat Maneuvering. The training that leads to ACT.

ACT: Air Combat Tactics. Dogfighting.

ACTIVE, THE: Main runway in use.

AGL: Above ground level; i.e., the height of an aircraft directly above the surface over which it is flying.

AIM: The designation for a U.S. air-to-air missile, i.e., AIM-9.

AIRCRAFT COMMANDER: The pilot in command of an aircraft regardless of the rank of other officers on board.

AWACS: Airborne Warning And Control System. A highly modified Boeing 707 that is an airborne radar sentry.

BACKSEATER: A Weapon Systems Officer.

BANDIT: A hostile aircraft.

BDA: Bomb Damage Assessment. A post-attack evaluation of results.

BOGIE: An unidentified aircraft.

BOQ: Bachelor Officers' Quarters.

BTR-60: An eight-wheeled, Soviet-built armored personnel carrier. Can carry 14 to 16 troops. There are special versions for commanders and communications.

CAP: Combat Air Patrol. A protective umbrella of fighters.

DCI: Director of Central Intelligence. The head of all intelligence agencies in the U.S. government and the head of the CIA.

D-DAY: In military planning the day an operation or hostilities starts.

DIA: Defense Intelligence Agency. Coordinates intelligence for the Department of Defense.

DRAGON: A man-portable, shoulder-fired, medium range anti-tank rocket.

EMIS LIMIT: Emission Limit. A switch in the F-15E that turns off electronic emissions such as the radar that hostile defenses could detect.

FLOGGER: NATO code name for the swing-wing, Soviet-built Mikoyan MiG-23 fighter.

FORT FUMBLE: A polite name for the Pentagon.

FOX ONE: Brevity code for a radar guided air-to-air missile.

FOX TWO: Brevity code for an infrared guided air-to-air missile.

GATE: Brevity code meaning fly at maximum possible speed.

GBU: Guided Bomb Unit, i.e., a "smart bomb." A GBU-12 is a five hundred pound laser guided smart bomb, a GBU-15 is a two thousand pound smart bomb with a laser/TV/imaging IR seeker head.

GCI: Ground-Controlled Intercept. The interception of another aircraft that is controlled by a ground or airborne radar station.

H-HOUR: The specific hour on which an operation or hostilities starts.

HUD: Head Up Display. A transparent glass screen in front of the pilot that displays tactical and flight information. Consequently, the pilot does not need to look down into his cockpit.

IFF: Identification-Friend or Foe. A radar transponder used for aircraft identification by ground-based radars.

INS: Inertial Navigation System.

IO: Illuminator Operator. Crewmember aboard an AC-130 gunship who controls the searchlight system in the aft cargo section of the airplane. He is also responsible for maintaining a visual lookout behind the aircraft for SAMs and Triple A.

IP: Initial Point. A small, easily identifiable, easily found point on the ground close to a target. It serves as the last check point and points the way to the target.

IR: Infrared.

JFS: Jet Fuel Starter. A self-contained, nonelectrical unit for starting a jet engine independently of outside power sources.

JINK: Continuous random changes in altitude and heading to defeat tracking by an enemy.

JSOA: Joint Special Operations Agency. The multi-service organization responsible for managing the elite units of the U.S. armed forces that carry out special operations.

JUDY: Brevity code for the aircrew taking over an air-to-air intercept from a GCI controller.

LANTIRN: Low Altitude Navigation and Targeting InfraRed for Night. This system uses two pods that contain a forward looking infrared sensor, terrain following radar, a missile boresight correlator, and a laser designator.

LAW: Light Antitank Weapon. A shoulder-fired, tube launched rocket with a shaped charged warhead. Good against light armor and vehicles.

M-203: A single-shot 40mm grenade launcher attached to an assault rifle.

MARK-82: Designation for five hundred pound bombs.

MAVERICK: An electro-optical guided, aircraft launched, anti-tank rocket with a shaped charged warhead. Extremely effective against tanks.

MPCD: Multi-Purpose Color Display. A color video screen in the cockpit of an F-15E. One in the front cockpit and two in the rear cockpit.

MPD: Multi-Purpose Display. A video screen in the cockpit of an F-15E that lacks color. Two in each cockpit.

MT-1X: A rectangular, nonrigid airfoil, parachute that has excellent glide and steering capability.

OB: Order of Battle.

OFFICE OF SPECIAL INVESTIGATIONS: The criminal and counterintelligence investigative office of the Air Force.

ORDER OF BATTLE: A listing of hostile armed forces by type, strength, and location.

OSI: Office of Special Investigations.

PAVE TACK: A target designator sensor pod that swings down out of the weapons bay of an F-111F. The pod contains a tracking head, a forward looking infrared sensor, a laser, a wealth of electronics, and a digital computer.

PSI: Fictional. Abbreviation for the Peoples' Soldiers of Islam. The military arm of the Iranian Communist Tudeh Party. Later integrated into the Iranian armed forces.

PUZZLE PALACE: A polite name for the Pentagon.

RADAR CONTROL POST: A Ground Control Intercept (GCI) site that controls and reports on aircraft.

RAMP: The concrete or asphalt apron used for parking aircraft. The sloping entrance way for loading an aircraft. On a C-130, located under the tail.

RECCY: Slang for reconnaissance.

RED FLAG: A recurring exercise at Nellis AFB, outside Las Vegas, Nevada, that tries to create a battlefield environment, simulating combat. Used for training aircrews in the disorientation and sensory overload of combat.

RHAW: Radar Homing and Warning. Equipment that warns aircrews about radar threats.

ROE: The rules of engagement.

RPG: The standard, shoulder-held, Soviet anti-armor weapon.

RTB: Return to Base.

RTO: U.S. Army term for a radio/telephone operator.

SA: Designation for a Soviet-built surface-to-air missile, i.e., SA-8.

SAM: Any surface-to-air missile.

SAW: Squad Automatic Weapon. A Belgian-designed 5.56mm light machine gun.

SCROUNGE: A highly unauthorized stash of spare parts by crew chiefs and maintenance technicians keep handy to rapidly repair aircraft. Without a scrounge, hours or days can be spent waiting for parts that Supply is slow in delivering or may not have due to budget limitations.

SNAKEYE: 500 pound high explosive bomb that can be selected in flight for either "slick" or "retarded" (high drag) delivery.

SRO: Senior Ranking Officer. In a prisoner of war camp, the SRO is the highest ranking prisoner and is in command of the POWs.

TAC: Tactical Air Command. The Air Force command that controls fighters.

TACAN: Tactical Air And Navigation. A radio beacon that transmits a bearing and distance to its location.

TALLYHO: The radio call for a visual sighting.

TDC: Target Designation Control. A switch on the throttle quadrant of an F-15 that controls the radar.

TEWS: Tactical Electronic Warfare System. An integrated countermeasures system that can detect and defeat an electronic threat.

TF/TFING: Terrain Following. Flying very low to the ground.

TFR: Terrain Following Radar. Allows an airplane to avoid obstacles and fly low and fast near the ground.

TSD: Tactical Situation Display. An electronic moving map that integrates navigation and tactical information.

TOT: Time Over Target.

TRIPLE A: AntiAircraft Artillery; same as AAA.

UFC: Up Front Controller. A computer keyboard that controls the systems in an F-15E. The UFC in the front cockpit is directly underneath the HUD.

UHF: Ultra High Frequency radio. Transmissions limited to line-of-sight (approximately 180 miles at altitude).

UTM: Universal Transverse Mercator grid. A system of map coordinates.

VEE: Air Force slang for "versus."

VOQ: Visiting Officers' Quarters.

VSD: Vertical Situation Display. The radar display in an F-15 that gives a pilot information on an airborne target such as speed, altitude, and range. The E model of the F-15 has a radar display, but not a VSD.

WEAPON SYSTEMS OFFICER: Flies in back seat of a fighter. Combination radar operator, bombardier, electronic countermeasures operator, radio operator, observer, and copilot. By nature a very trusting soul.

WIZZO: Slang for WSO.

ZSU-23: Soviet-built 23mm antiaircraft artillery. An excellent air defense weapon. The ZSU-23-4 is a mobile, radar laid, four barrel version called the "Shilka." It is extremely dangerous and to be avoided.

ZULU: The International Civil Aeronautics Organization phonetic alphabet for the letter Z. Also refers to Greenwich Mean Time.